GAME *of*
SHADOWS

GAME *of* SHADOWS

ERIKA LEWIS

TOR

A Tom Doherty Associates Book

NEW YORK

GAME OF SHADOWS

Copyright © 2017 by Erika Lewis

All rights reserved.

Map by Eric Gravel

A Tor Book
Published by Tom Doherty Associates
175 Fifth Avenue
New York, NY 10010

www.tor-forge.com

Tor® is a registered trademark of Macmillan Publishing Group, LLC.

The Library of Congress Cataloging-in-Publication Data
is available upon request.

ISBN 978-0-7653-8138-5 (hardcover)
ISBN 978-1-4668-8152-5 (e-book)

Our books may be purchased in bulk for promotional, educational, or business use.
Please contact your local bookseller or the Macmillan Corporate and
Premium Sales Department at 1-800-221-7945, extension 5442,
or by e-mail at MacmillanSpecialMarkets@macmillan.com.

First Edition: February 2017

Printed in the United States of America

0 9 8 7 6 5 4 3 2 1

For Timberlake, Riley, and Jack.
*Without whose unending support
this book could never have been written.
You are my happily ever after. . . .*

Acknowledgments

To Robert Gleason and Elayne Becker, my incredible editorial team at Tor Books. I cannot thank you both enough. Your insights into the story have been invaluable, and have helped make it what it is today. Even more, your constant support has meant everything. Thank you, truly. To my wonderful agent, Sally Wofford-Girand at Union Literary, from all the brainstorming calls to the pestering e-mails from me along the road to publication, thank you for your patience and never losing faith.

To my feedback team, Beau DeMayo, Emily Freedman, Eva Katz, Tawadi Kecken, and John Mott, thank you for all the time and superb feedback. You're the best. To my Celtic Studies experts, Dara Hellman and Daniel Melia. A big thanks, or should I say, *go raibh maith agaibh* for all the help, and for not laughing at my many random questions and bizarre translation requests.

And finally to my mentors, Stan Lee, R. A. Salvatore, D. J. MacHale, Lorin Oberweger, and Sherrilyn Kenyon. Thank you for your inspiration, enthusiasm, and invaluable lessons.

Armes Tara

And in the end the war against the *Milesians,* against
    humanity, was lost,
Because we could no longer find humanity within
    ourselves.

As we depart for the *Otherworld,*
It is with heavy hearts we must leave behind our people,
Hidden in a place named for our Tara,
For the name marks our home in both the beginning, and
    in the end.

Once gone our clans will again divide,
Repeating mistakes of the past,
Dooming this new Tara to the same terrible fate,
And yet there is one hope.

Only one.
He will possess the sacred gift, *radharc.*
He will not be of Tara,
But will come to understand the heart and soul of *Tarisians*
    like no other.

However, an understanding alone will not be enough.
Only if he can find an inner strength,
Unattained by any mortal before,
Can he lead our sons and daughters out of the darkness.

For in darkness there is always light,
And in the face of death a reason to fight.

—BRAN THE BLESSED, B.C. 1699

GAME of
SHADOWS

❖ ONE ❖

"E than Makkai, freedom is a state of mind."

Ethan shook his head at his mother's canned response. It was the same thing she said every time he told her it was time to cut the parental leash.

He dropped his backpack next to the kitchen table and sat down with a loud huff. "Wrong. Freedom is the state of *not* being imprisoned."

"Will you please stop saying that?" Keeping an eye on the toaster oven, she poured herself another cup of coffee. "You're not in prison."

But Ethan was in prison. Incarcerated for life if she had her way. She wouldn't let him go anywhere without her. *Ever.*

The only time she let him out of her sight was during school. He'd contemplated sneaking out. Skipping class. But every time he made a move for the exit, one of his teachers was there. They were always watching.

A few seconds after the timer dinged, Caitríona padded over and playfully pushed his shoulder. "Can't a mom want to spend time with her son?"

"Not when she makes him look like more of a total reject than he already is."

The woman had no idea what it was like to walk the halls of Venice High School after the bell rang. A freshman, Ethan was already considered a bottom-feeder. As it was, most of his class was forced to walk invisibly through the halls to avoid persecution. The smart ones paid off the bullies for a modicum of protection. Ethan didn't have the money for that. He barely had enough to buy lunch most days.

"You're not a reject. I see your friends. Brock and the other boys always say hi to you."

Ethan choked on the sip of orange juice he'd just taken. Every morning his mother would stand out front of the school, refusing to leave until he was inside. Stayed until the late bell rang and doors ceremoniously slammed shut. Seriously. And Brock Martin made sure everyone knew about it. Without a stitch of imagination, the idiot's infuriating diatribe never changed. "Where's your mommy, Ethan? Did she forget to change your diaper before you left for school? Did you have nightmares again last night?"

The guy lived to make others feel worthless and instill fear. Not that Ethan was afraid of him. Compared to the things that stalked him day and night, Martin was nothing. The thought sent an unforeseen chill down his spine.

"Of all people to bring up . . . you do know Brock's an unmitigated asshole, right?"

"Ethan—"

"Don't!" He held his hand up, cutting her off. "Why do you always defend him? If you saw how he tortured everyone, including me, you'd stop. Trust me."

"He's going through a hard time." Caitríona Makkai never liked to say anything bad about anyone, not even when they deserved it, and it drove Ethan nuts. "Show a little compassion."

For him? Ethan snorted. "Whatever."

"You know I hate that word. It's dismissive."

She was right. It was dismissive. He was dismissing this entire conversation because she had no idea what she was talking about.

His mother set a plate of strawberry toaster waffles smothered in maple syrup and powdered sugar in front of him. She waved her hand over the dish, beaming. "Happy birthday. And look, the kitchen is still in one piece."

Ethan shoveled a huge bite in his mouth and forced a smile. "Mom, you have officially mastered the art of cooking from the frozen food aisle."

That earned him another punch in the shoulder. "Stop hitting me."

"Then stop giving me such a hard time this morning. I got up early to make that for you."

"I'm serious. It's good," Ethan insisted. "Thank you."

"Oh, then you're welcome." Caitríona slid into the seat across from his and began sketching on a small piece of paper. Ethan poured her a glass of orange juice, and watched as her pencil swept the page. She was an incredible artist. He never understood why she wasted her time cleaning houses when she could have sold her art, but she said her drawings captured memories, and they were just for them.

The sketches that covered an entire wall in their tiny studio apartment were mostly of Ethan, chronicling his life. Meticulous drawings that she slaved over anytime she wasn't at work or out somewhere with him. His baby pictures lined the top, and depicted him growing older as they descended halfway down the wall. There was only one of the two of them together. He was two, sitting in her lap, holding up a flower. That was his favorite.

By nineteen, his mom had lost both her parents. After her father died, she had come to the U.S. on a boat, illegally and with nothing. Alone and pregnant. She had no family, no friends. No one but Ethan.

His father, Runyun Cooper, died before he was born. His mother flatly refused to talk about him. There were no pictures, no old clothes, nothing. Ethan Googled his name once a month, but the search never turned up anything. It was like Runyun Cooper had never existed. And judging by the way his mom reacted when Ethan brought him up, the guy must have done something horrible to her, so horrible that it turned her off men forever.

Because of that, Ethan had spent his entire life trying to please her. He didn't want her to lose faith in him too. But what had it gotten him? She still didn't trust him.

Caitríona set her pencil down, lifted the paper, and stared at it, wide-eyed.

"What's the matter?" As Ethan leaned over to see what she had drawn, she tore the picture to shreds.

"Why did you—"

"It was terrible," she said definitively. Even though the paper was ripped, Ethan could make out the narrowed glaring eye of a bird that looked like it belonged to one of the black crows that had started nesting under the eaves of the building, right above their only window. Since the day the birds moved in, she wouldn't let him open it. She said they were dangerous. Birds.

She'd even moved her bed next to the window to keep an eye on them. Yet another symptom of the perpetual paranoid state she lived in, constantly worrying about his safety. And she worried about *him* being called crazy.

Ethan checked the clock above the refrigerator and panicked when he saw it was almost eight. He had only a few minutes to get downstairs or he'd miss Sky. He shoveled in the last bite of breakfast and dropped his plate in the sink with a clank. When he lifted the rusted knob on the faucet it popped off in his hand.

"Not again," Ethan said, disgusted.

"Why are you in such a hurry? I'm not even dressed yet."

No. She wasn't. She was still in her yellow bathrobe, her long brown hair clipped to the top of her head like a Japanese anime character. And that was all part of his plan. But he had to time this perfectly. "No reason."

Caitríona reached into the cabinet under the sink, pulled out a small wrench, and passed it to him.

The loose knob was nothing. If one of them flushed the toilet with the shower running, water erupted like a geyser from the bowl and sprayed the ceiling. But it wasn't like they were ever moving. No one left a rent-controlled apartment on the west side of Los Angeles, even if it was a dump. It was the only way they could afford the neighborhood.

"Hey, um . . ." Ethan set the wrench on the counter and turned to face her. "I know what I want for my birthday."

Caitríona winced. "Sweet, I lost two houses this month. We'll barely make rent. Can it . . . you know . . . ?"

"Wait? No." He put his hands on her shoulders. "But good news! It won't cost you a cent," Ethan said in his best game-show-host voice, then sobered. "Let me go to school alone."

Groaning, she twisted out of his grasp. "Ethan, we can't keep having this conversation," she scolded, unleashing her Irish accent.

"I'm fourteen. In most religions I've been considered an adult for more than a year. I don't understand why this is such a big deal!"

"Rúini na chroí." Caitríona rubbed her hand over the braided Celtic-knot tattoo that wrapped around her wrist like a bracelet. On the underside, below her palm, was a symbol, three connected spirals stacked like a triangle. She made that move whenever she said those words to him.

"I know the *rule*. I promise I'll be careful." Ethan stared at her with pleading eyes. "Come on. It's my birthday. I'm begging you, if you love me, let me go."

When she didn't answer, Ethan threw on his backpack and started for the door, but she was too fast. She slid past, coming between him and his only escape route.

"Ethan, give me a moment to think."

Shocked, he didn't move. He didn't even breathe. She'd never even contemplated saying yes before. Ever. This was finally going to happen. He could feel it. Inside his head, he'd already started a victory dance as he hurried to the window and looked down. Sky was still there, waiting for him on the sidewalk.

"Mom?" He rushed back, but she still didn't answer. Every second that ticked by felt like an eternity. *How long does it take to say the word "yes"?* Finally, he couldn't take it anymore. He reached for the doorknob, but she leaned her back against the door, making it impossible for him to open it.

Frowning, Caitríona fingered her silver unicorn necklace with one hand and pointed to his unmade bed, which doubled as the living room couch. "Make your bed."

Ethan rushed over, and in one move lifted the metal frame and glided it into the sofa. As soon as he'd tossed on the pillows, he started for the door, but she still hadn't moved.

"I'm going to be late," he insisted.

"Ethan." She placed her hand firmly against the door.

"Mom!" He pulled her hand down.

"Ethan!" She put it back. "I can't let you do this."

"You've got your first day cleaning the new place in Beverly Hills, right? That's a long bus ride."

"Yes. And I know you're old enough, and you can take care of yourself. Most days you take care of me. But the answer is still no."

Unlike in the past, Ethan wasn't giving up. He'd had enough. He reached for the doorknob again. This time, Caitríona placed her hands firmly against his shoulders, holding him back. Unfortunately, at five foot eight, she had a good four inches on him and could still wrestle him to the ground if he tried to escape.

She looked down at him with a sympathetic frown. "I know what it's like to want something so much it hurts." Her eyes closed on the word "hurts." "But we can't always get what we want in life, Ethan." As she opened her eyes, she cupped his cheek with the palm of her hand. "We have to look to the future, never the past. I truly wish I could give you your freedom, but I *can't*."

"Can't or won't?" He knew he was pushing it. But what kind of future was he going to have if he couldn't even set one foot out the door without constant supervision? Teachers called him distracted. They even hovered during lunch and free period like he was some kind of a delinquent. Kids had other choice names like *mental case mama's boy*.

"Clíodhna give me strength," Caitríona whispered under her breath, and met Ethan's scowl with a stern glare. "I know you think you know everything, but you don't. Your ability is a gift, but there are dangers in this world because of it."

Barely able to contain his temper, Ethan stepped away from her. "It's not a gift. It's a curse." He knew what she was afraid of. If anyone ever found out, they'd lock him up and do experiments on him, but was that worse than hiding behind a bunch of lies that made everyone think he was crazy?

"Don't you trust me?"

"Of course!" she shouted, exasperated. "I trust you more than anyone in this entire world. But the answer is still no."

"This isn't fair."

"Life isn't fair." She paused between each word for emphasis. "Wait here. I'll get changed." She stormed into the bathroom and slammed the door shut.

What would she do when he left for college? Go with him? Perish the thought. He'd never get a girlfriend. Never have a life at all. He loved his mother more than anything, but it was time for her to let go. There was only one thing left to do.

Ethan swung the door open.

There it was, the empty hallway, and his shot at freedom. He tiptoed across the threshold and quietly closed the door behind him.

Sprinting, he raced down the hallway and into the stairwell that perpetually smelled of stale urine. Taking three steps at a time, Ethan found himself repeating the same Irish phrase his mother spoke. *Rúini na chroí. Secrets of the heart.* A reminder to never tell anyone he saw ghosts.

◧ TWO ◧

Ethan spotted her the second he hit the street. Skylar Petrakis. The most beautiful girl in the ninth grade, maybe even the whole school. She stood on the sidewalk, pacing tightrope-style along the cracks.

Ethan had known Sky his whole life. They lived in the same building. Sky's parents worked late. In the afternoons she used to come over to Ethan's apartment and hang out until they got home. Sky hated to be alone.

She'd bring her console down from her place, and he'd help get her homework done quickly so they could play video games. Competitive to a fault, the girl had some serious skill when it came to first-person shooters and seemed to relish holding it over his head every time she offed him in the game, which was pretty much every time they played. But Ethan didn't mind. He just liked hanging out with her.

Whenever Sky was over, ghosts would always show up. That was a given. The dead radiated a painful, bone-chilling cold that only Ethan felt. But if he got goose bumps and shivered on a hot day, or mumbled bizarre non sequiturs trying to get rid of apparitions, Sky would smile and laugh. Unlike everyone else, nothing Ethan did ever seemed to faze her. She thought he was being funny. And her laughing made the ghosts bearable.

As soon as school let out in June, Sky had gone away to camp. It had been the longest summer of Ethan's life. Not a single hour of a single day spent without his mother. From home to her jobs and back again. That was it.

And when Sky returned the day before the new school year started, everything had changed. Sky had changed. He was suddenly persona non grata. If Ethan said hi to her in the hallways between classes, Sky would look away, or hide behind her friends, pretending she hadn't heard him. She probably thought he didn't notice, but he did, and it hurt.

The only time he did see her was in the mornings, but he could never really talk to her because his mother was always with him. But not today.

Sky's shiny black hair was pulled back into a tight braid. She had a perfect face and big, almond-shaped brown eyes that now focused on him, causing his heartbeat to shift into high gear.

"Hey, E," she said, gifting him with a shy smile.

Dressed in her usual black boots, leggings, and long T-shirt, Sky also had on a black leather jacket that looked three sizes too big, and oddly familiar. The jacket seemed like overkill. Even in early November, temperatures in Los Angeles rarely if ever fell below seventy during the day, and today was no exception. In fact, it was unseasonably hot and had been all week.

"Thanks for waiting for me. Nice jacket. Aren't you hot?"

Sky shuffled her feet from side to side. "Oh, this, I borrowed it from a friend yesterday. Just bringing it back."

Ethan shifted his backpack and glanced over his shoulder. He only had three minutes tops before his mother noticed he was gone. "Let's go."

As they made their way down the block, Ethan couldn't take his eyes off Sky's face. There was something different about her. "You've got makeup on."

"Um, yeah." She looked over at him. "You don't like it?"

Ethan shrugged. "Never seen you wear any before."

Sky rolled her eyes at him. "I wear it all the time. You just haven't noticed."

Ethan noticed everything about her, but didn't see the point of arguing. "Did you study for Miguez's test?"

"Tried. I really hate Spanish. Next year, I'm switching to French."

"Oh, right, study a totally useless language in LA."

"True." Sky laughed and brushed his hair off his face. "Your hair is getting so long." She sounded as if she approved. The unexpected contact caught Ethan completely by surprise. Perhaps she wasn't blowing him off at school. Maybe he'd been misinterpreting her signals all along.

"Happy birthday," she sang. She pulled him to a stop, lifted a brown paper bag out of her pocket, and held it out to him.

His mouth went completely dry. Wearing a stupid smile, he took the bag from her. "Wow. Thanks." She'd remembered.

As much as he wanted to enjoy the moment, he knew that if his mother caught up to him, she would chew him out right in front of her. An unbearable thought, he started walking again, fast.

As they neared the end of the block, a shadow darted out from behind the Mexican restaurant they'd just passed. Ethan kept walking. If a ghost was following him, he didn't want to know.

Rounding the corner, Sky yanked on his arm, slowing him down. "Wait! Where's your mom?"

"It's cool. She's at home."

Sky tossed him an approving grin. "Wow. Happy birthday to you. Look at you, you're positively beaming."

"You would be too if you were finally free. You have no idea how annoying it is to have your parents follow you everywhere."

"Yeah, but at least your mom's around. Neither of my parents has been home before nine the past three days."

"Why didn't you come down?" Ethan asked, concerned. He picked up the pace again.

"Why are you in such a rush?" Sky countered, ignoring his question.

There was still no sign of his mother, so he slowed, a little. "Didn't realize I was going so fast."

"Well, then . . ." Sky elbowed him gently in the ribs. "Open your present."

"I will. When we get to school."

"I'd rather you open it now," she insisted with an impatient smile.

She got him with the smile. If it made her happy, he was more than willing to oblige. Ethan reached into the bag. His fingers tangled in thin tightly wound strings as he pulled out a small, blue circular hoop with white thread woven into the shape of a spiderweb. Seven yellow feathers dangled off the bottom.

"It's a dreamcatcher," Sky explained. "It's supposed to filter out bad dreams. My grandmother swears by them. I got it when I visited her last month on the reservation in Los Coyotes."

He held it up by the top string and watched it spin as a slow grin spread across his face. "You've been thinking about my birthday for a month?"

Sky rolled her eyes at him again and pulled on his arm. "Come on, now we are going to be late."

As they neared the streetlight, Ethan's chest tightened and he slowed. Standing at the end of the block was none other than Brock Martin and a few members of his ass-kissing fan club.

Always in his signature vintage Air Jordans, jeans, and a Diesel T-shirt, Brock had attained celebrity status years ago when he'd starred in a Coke commercial. He didn't even speak in the commercial. All he had to do was drain the bottle and smile at the camera. A chimpanzee could have done that, and the chimp wouldn't have let it go to his head.

Adding to his overinflated ego was the fact that Brock was the only freshman to make the varsity football team. Considering he towered over Ethan, outweighed him by at least thirty pounds, and had serious anger management issues, his making the team wasn't much of a surprise. Besides, Ethan had heard that, for liability reasons, the school needed to find an outlet for him that *legally* allowed him to hurt people.

The worst part, until a few months ago Ethan's mother had worked for the Martins, cleaning their house. Something Brock never let him forget.

As usual, standing by his side was the extremely popular Sharon Pulp. With bleached blond hair, she mocked the school dress code by wearing shirts she tied to show off her finely toned midsection. Most days, she stood against the lockers between classes, laughing like a hyena with her clones, desperate for people to notice her. But she didn't need to try so hard. Even if she was as mean as a snake, she'd filled out in all the right places over the summer. *Everybody* noticed her.

Ethan held his breath, hoping they could slip by unnoticed.

"Hey, Sky!" Sharon called.

Ethan froze. So much for not noticing.

"Um, yeah, I'll see you later, okay?" Ethan didn't wait for Sky's response. He started in the other direction, but she hooked his arm and yanked him back around.

"No. It's not okay. They're really not that bad."

Not that bad? Was she insane? When did they become friends?

"Come on," Sky said as she pulled him toward them.

Ethan sucked in a deep breath, shoved his hands in his pockets, and started a silent countdown in his head. He had only ticked off two seconds before Brock began his initial assault.

"Oh, look who's here. Makkai." Never one for originality, Brock pronounced Ethan's name *Mak-kay*.

"Actually, it's *Ma-k-eye*," Sky corrected him.

Instead of tossing out one of his usual condescending retorts, Brock came next to her and eyed her arm still hanging on Ethan's. "You with *him*, Petrakis?" It sounded like an accusation.

Sharon screwed up her face like she smelled something unpleasant. "Um, yeah, Sky, what exactly is this? You and Looney Tunes?"

Sky met Brock's concerned gaze, and lowered her eyes to the ground. Ethan suddenly felt like an outsider, intruding on an unspoken conversation between them. She unhooked her arm from Ethan's and let out a nervous laugh. "What? No. You know Ethan and I live in the same building, that's all."

Ethan's mouth dropped open. *No. That's not all!* He gripped the bag holding her birthday present to him, contemplating giving it back to her.

Sharon whispered in Brock's ear, and he looked at Ethan with a thin-lipped smirk.

"Oh right. Makkay. Where's your mommy?" Brock circled him. "She finally let you out of your cage?" He placed his hands next to his mouth, and megaphoned, "Watch out! Nutter on the loose." His fans all laughed.

"Someone, call the institution for a padded ambulance!" one of them yelled.

"Brock, what are you doing?" Sky scolded.

"What?" Brock gave her an innocent shrug.

Shaking her head, Sky slid out of the leather jacket and threw it at him. He caught it, put it on, and tossed Ethan a cocky smirk.

That's why it had looked so familiar. Ethan's stomach twisted. Was she hooking up with him? *Happy birthday to me.* The frozen toaster waffles his mother worked so hard on this morning were about to make another appearance.

Sharon stepped back, looking as ill as Ethan felt. She must not have known about Sky and Brock either.

Brock leaned over his shoulder, so he was right next to Ethan's ear. "Nice shirt."

Reluctantly, Ethan looked down. He wore a dingy white tee that had a picture of a green food truck being eaten by an enormous pig with the words JURASSIC PORK hanging over it. Idiot. He was in such a hurry this morning he'd thrown on the first shirt he'd pulled from his drawer. Most of his clothes came from his mother's clients' giveaway bags, and until recently that had included several of Brock's castoffs. He thought he'd tossed all of Brock's, but his mom must have snuck this one back into his drawer for god knows what reason. He was really going to let her have it after she finished yelling at him for taking off without her.

Right on cue, Ethan's phone started ringing. He stepped away from Brock and yanked it out of his pocket. The letter "M" flashed on the screen. He sent her to voicemail and flicked the switch to silent.

"Still wearing my old hand-me-downs, huh?" Brock asked.

Ethan clenched his jaw. He'd been dealing with Brock long enough to know that the moron was trying to get a rise out of him. Stay silent and Brock moved on. He had the attention span of a gnat.

"It's so nice of you to give him your old clothes," one of his fans said.

"Well, sadly, his mom got fired, so I guess he won't be getting any more," Brock replied.

"What? Why?" Sky asked.

Ethan had to hand it to Brock. The guy was a better actor than he gave him credit for. And he might have pulled it off except for the fact that Ethan wasn't about to let him get away with it. "You're so full of it, Martin."

"I'm full of it?"

"My mom didn't get fired. Yours did."

"Oh really?" Brock sniffed at his friends, then tossed a stiff arm around Ethan's shoulders. He brought his forearm up against his neck. "My mom didn't want *you* around anymore, nutbag. She said she caught you in the kitchen one too many times talking to yourself, making weird faces at the refrigerator. Who were you talking to, Ethan? Your imaginary friends?"

Your dead grandmother. But Ethan couldn't say that out loud. She talked Ethan's ear off every time he was forced to go to Brock's. She'd let Ethan in on the fact that Brock's mother had lost her job, and that his father had split. Mrs. Martin couldn't afford to have Ethan's mother clean anymore.

Damn! Ethan wished he'd been smart enough to set his phone to record as soon as he saw Brock. Then he could prove to his mother once and for all that Martin didn't have a decent bone in his body.

"Answer me!" Brock tightened his arm, pressing on Ethan's larynx, stifling his breath.

"God! Your pits stink!" Ethan twisted, forcing Brock's grip to loosen, but Brock still didn't let go. Their faces inches apart, Ethan leaned away from him. "You know I love you, man, but please, don't kiss me. You are so not my type."

A couple of Brock's gang laughed.

"What did you say? Oh, you want to play, squib?" Brock shoved Ethan into the front window of the vacant building behind them. Ethan bounced off and fell forward, landing on his hands, crushing the dream-catcher.

Rolling up to his feet, he dropped his backpack and checked the damage to Sky's gift. The webbed threads were mangled and a few were broken, but it was still in one piece.

Catching sight of Sky's frightened expression, Ethan knew it was time to go. Slipping his arm through the loop of his backpack, he tried to maneuver around Brock, but Brock lowered his shoulder and plowed into Ethan's chest.

Ethan hit the window again. Every bit of air in his longs burst out. He dropped to his knees, gasping for breath.

"Leave him alone!" Sky yelled, and tried to grab Brock, but two of his goons held her back.

Flustered, Sharon pulled Sky away from them. "Come on. Let's get to school."

Sky nodded and looked back at Ethan. "I'll get help!"

"Oh, you do that . . . ," one of the dipshits called after her.

Despondent, Ethan watched as they raced across the street. Help was not going to come soon enough. He was about to take a pounding, one that he might actually deserve. He should never have left the way he did this morning. His mother was probably worried sick at this point. And once she caught up to him . . .

He didn't have time to finish that thought. Wispy cold fingers ran down the back of his neck. *Not now! Please not now!* To his dismay, two guys, maybe twenty, covered with tattoos, floated through the window, stopping directly in front of Ethan.

Their skin an inhuman pale gray, they were wrapped in an electric aura. Their yellow T-shirts were peppered with large bullet holes ringed with blood. The yellow and white bandanas tied as belts for their jeans, combined with the similar color of their shirts, marked them as part of a gang who walked the neighborhood, recruiting members.

Caspers. Poltergeists. Phantasms. Spirits. Shades. Wraiths. And then there was Ethan's mother's name for ghosts, taibhsí. Different name, but always the same game. Restless souls who spent their afterlife tormenting and torturing Ethan.

The sickening chill expanded. It rolled over Ethan's shoulders, stiffening his entire body. His hands ached from what felt like nails being hammered into the pads of his fingers. Clenching his fists, the pain traveled up his arms and down his spine.

Breathe. Just breathe.

He couldn't give away that he could see them or they'd never go.

I can feel it, Manuel. This one can see *us, can't you?* The smaller one leaned in and pinned Ethan with a heated glare. *What the hell is happening to us? Why are we still here?*

Shivering, Ethan looked away. Even if he wanted to, there was nothing he could do for them. He didn't know why any of them were trapped here.

Talk to us! the bigger taibhsí fumed.

Ethan made the stupid mistake of looking at him.

You can *see us.* He grabbed Ethan's shoulder, but his hand passed right through. The contact was so painful, Ethan fell to his knees and wrapped his arms, grabbing his shoulders. He leaned against the building to keep from falling over.

"Look at him, he's terrified!" Brock said to his goons. He stared at Ethan as if he had the plague. "If you think this crazy act of yours is going to save you this time, you're wrong!"

Only one thing could save him now. Tunes. Ethan's main line of defense. He'd figured out a long time ago that ghosts were incredibly vulnerable to music. Sound waves traveled on a frequency that pounded ethereal eardrums, and only the most tenacious souls could stand more than a few seconds of Led Zeppelin's "Kashmir." With shaky hands, he whipped his phone out.

"Trying to call for help?" Brock sneered. "I don't think so." He grabbed Ethan's phone and tossed it on the ground.

Brock fisted Ethan's shirt and pulled him toward him. "Before I beat you to an inch of your life, I thought you should know that I hooked up with your friend Sky last night, and the night before that, and the night before that . . . she tastes oh-so-sweet. . . ."

Devastated, Ethan's chest heaved with rage. As soon as the ghosts were gone, Brock was dead.

Brock threw a punch but Ethan ducked. His fist plowed into the window. Webbed cracks splintered through the glass on impact. It shattered into a million pieces.

The alarm blared and Brock's pals scattered, but not the ghosts.

"Mother f—" Brock shook his hand, splattering blood all over his expensive sneakers.

With seething determination, Ethan scooped up his phone and hit play. He cranked the volume to max. The effect was immediate. The ghosts' eyes pulsed to the beat, and their faces contorted in pain. A second later, they vanished.

Relief was followed by intense pain. Ethan never saw Brock's right hook coming, but felt it when it struck its target: his nose. Pain exploded inside Ethan's cranium. Blood poured down his face, and pooled in the sidewalk crack underneath him.

Shaking his head, Ethan leveled his eyes on Brock's. The ghosts gone, he was ready to pound the shit out of this asshole. He rolled his shoulders before he took a step toward him. "I'm going to kill you."

Brock picked up a wedge of broken glass and held it like a knife. "Make my day!"

"Did you really just say that? Make my day?" Ethan wiped his bloody nose with his arm. "You really are an unimaginative Neanderthal."

"A Neanderthal who is about to take you out. Kiss your ass goodbye, Makkai!" Brock thrust the shard at Ethan's gut.

Ethan stepped back and kicked Brock's arm so hard, the glass flew out of his hand and into the street. Ethan lunged, but Brock ducked and shot a hand out, grasping the back of Ethan's neck. Then he latched on to Ethan's throat with his free hand and squeezed, cutting off Ethan's windpipe. Ethan pounded his arm, but Brock held firm.

"Release him!"

A man with a black eye patch flew out of the alley, panting like he'd just run a marathon. The rest of his face was lost in his scraggly gray hair and long white beard that had a yellow tint running along the bottom whiskers. His black coat, pants, and boots were all covered in dry mud.

"Release him," the man repeated.

Brock glared at him. "Or what, old man?"

Ethan lifted his bent leg like he was going to knee Brock in the privates. That did it. Brock dropped his hands, letting go of Ethan's throat. With everything he had, Ethan punched Brock's neck.

Brock clutched his throat and backed away, gasping for breath.

"Get out of here!" the old guy barked.

With a last look that promised revenge, Brock took off. Ethan started to run after him, but the old man caught his wrist.

"Let go!" Ethan yanked, but the man held firm.

"Ethan Makkai, what do you think you're doing?" His Irish accent was even thicker than his mothers.

"How do you know my name?"

"Caitríona is worried sick! Now get your scrawny arse home!"

"What? Who the hell are you?"

"Captain Cornelius Bartlett." The man said it like it was supposed to mean something.

"So?"

"What do you mean, so? Do—" Bartlett was cut off by the battle caws of a pack of crows. They leaped from the cable wires above their heads and swooped down, heading straight for Ethan.

Bartlett jumped on top of him as the black birds swarmed.

"Get off!"

But Bartlett didn't move. The frantic flapping of wings and ear-piercing screeches came from every direction. It was one thing to watch an Alfred Hitchcock film, and another thing entirely to live it. Ethan pushed up, but the man crushed him back to the ground.

"Stay down," Bartlett ordered.

"I can't breathe."

Ignoring him, Bartlett pulled an inch-long thin wooden cylinder out of his pocket and held it to his mouth.

A loud whistle blasted Ethan's right eardrum, leaving him momentarily deaf in that ear. Immediately, the birds flew away. Most darted high into the sky, vanishing, but a few of the abnormally larger ones headed back to the wires above them.

Something on Bartlett vibrated. With the whistle perched on his lips, he kept his eye on the birds and slid out the ringing cell phone. Still under the captain, Ethan flipped his head just in time to catch a glimpse of the screen. It said COISEAINT.

As Bartlett raised the phone to his ear, his sleeve dipped, revealing a braided Celtic-knot tattoo that wrapped around his wrist with three-connected spirals on the underside. Ethan's mouth fell open. It was the same tattoo as his mother's. Was it possible he actually knew her? She had never mentioned the name Bartlett before. She never mentioned anyone at all. His mother was a loner. Avoided interacting at all cost except when she had to for work.

Bartlett stood abruptly. No sooner had Ethan popped up than he heard his mother's shrill cry blast out of Bartlett's phone.

"Give me that!" Ethan reached for it, but Bartlett pushed his arm away.

"Dear gods! Follow me now!" The old man took off, heading in the direction of their apartment. "Hurry!"

Unsure if this was such a good idea, Ethan raced after him. Had that really been his mother? It sure sounded like her. But what if it was all some elaborate ruse this guy used to kidnap people? He could be a vicious murderer, and like an idiot, Ethan was sprinting right into his trap.

Stunted caws from behind them grew louder and louder. Ethan made the mistake of glancing back. A huge murder of crows flew up the street. Cars honked and tires screeched as panicked drivers tried unsuccessfully to avoid hitting them. His heart racing, Ethan pressed on, running faster than he'd ever run in his life. But it wasn't fast enough. The sky blackened from the sheer number of frenetic birds now flapping directly above his head.

"Bartlett!" Ethan yelled, leaping over a homeless man spread across the sidewalk.

Bartlett didn't stop. He turned the corner first, disappearing as the pack overtook Ethan. He fell to the ground and threw his hands over his head as pointy beaks and razor-sharp claws dug painfully into his arms and back. Thrashing, Ethan tried to get to his knees, but couldn't. He was trapped and never going to get to his mother.

❧ THREE ❧

Bartlett's whistle broke through the sonic cries of the crows. They flitted in all directions, desperate to get away. Bartlett helped him to his feet, and they started running again. Ethan was dazed, every inch of his visible skin marked with long, blood-soaked, stinging scratches. He looked like he'd been in a fight with a lawnmower and lost. He was a disaster. His mother was going to freak out when she saw him.

Once inside the hallway to Ethan's apartment, he could see the door was ajar.

"Mom," Ethan called, panting heavily. He rammed the door with his shoulder, stepped into the apartment, and immediately tripped over a piece of torn-up pillow from his couch-bed. The place had been trashed. Slashed sofa stuffing was everywhere, the only window, shattered. Broken dishes littered the countertops. The kitchen cabinet doors lay on the floor, ripped from their hinges. The worst part was that someone had shredded his mother's wall of sketches. They were completely destroyed.

"Mom!" Ethan called again. But there was no answer. No sign of her anywhere.

"Caitríona?" Bartlett bellowed, then rushed to the busted window, his shoes crunching on the broken glass.

Ethan stared at the few torn pieces of her beautiful drawings that still hung on the wall, and realized his favorite was missing. When his eyes shifted to the closed bathroom door, her furious tone ordering him to wait for her echoed in his ears. The bathroom. His heart skipped a beat as he ran to the door and threw it open.

"Mom?" he said, the word sounding like a prayer.

It was empty. Distraught, his eyes fell to the blue tile floor. There it was, the missing picture, still in one piece and weighted down by his mother's necklace. Ethan's hands trembled as he reached for them. There was blood on the top of the unicorn's horn and the chain was broken in the middle, as if it had been dug into her skin and ripped off her neck.

A lump grew in his throat, making it impossible to breathe. He folded up the picture and grasped the necklace in his hand, then slipped both into his pocket for safekeeping. If he'd only been here . . . or she with him . . .

Ethan had barely taken a step into the living room when Bartlett turned on him. "This is your bloody fault. You two were not supposed to separate! I can't be in two places at once!"

"What are you talking about?"

"You left without her this morning. When I showed up she sent me after you, to protect *you*. And that's exactly what I'm going to do. Let's go. We've got to get you out of here."

Bartlett moved toward him and tried to grab his arm, but Ethan spun out of reach and held his hands out. "Don't touch me. I'm not going anywhere with you." Ethan pulled his phone out of his pocket to call the police, and saw his mother had left a message.

His hands shaking, Ethan kept his eyes on the old man as he listened. "Ethan, they've found us. Go with Captain Bartlett. You have to get away! Please," she pleaded. "Whatever you do—" The message abruptly cut off.

Ethan hung up and immediately called her back, praying she would pick up, only to have the call go straight to voicemail. He tried again, but it was useless. Her phone was either off or dead.

Without hesitation, Ethan started for the door. Bartlett blocked his exit.

"Move!" Ethan shoved him, but it had no effect.

"Where do you think you're going?"

"After my mom."

The old man stared down at him. "Can't do that. At the speed Ravens travel, we won't catch them, not here. And the longer we sit, the more likely it is that others will come for you."

Unsure of what to do, Ethan looked back at their destroyed home. *Keep it together.* His mother needed him. He sucked in a deep breath to steady his nerves then took a large step backward, away from Bartlett. "Who exactly are you?"

"I told you. Bartlett." He paused and then added, "Your grandfather, your legal guardian now, so you have to go with me."

Ethan shook his head. "Bullshit."

Bartlett closed the distance between them, backing Ethan up against the wall. "Don't curse at me, or I'll give you the beating your mother should be giving you right now." The tone in the old guy's voice was clear. It wasn't a threat. It was a promise.

"If you really know my mother, then you would know that that's something she would never do."

Bartlett leaned over Ethan in an obvious attempt to intimidate him. "I said should, not would."

Unnerved, Ethan gripped his phone. It was the only lifeline he had. "I don't have a grandfather."

Bartlett stood tall and groaned. "Your mother never told you about having a grandfather who was going to show up in case of an emergency?"

Ethan folded his arms over his chest. "Nope. Never mentioned it."

"Of course, she didn't." Bartlett rolled his eye. "This just isn't my day." He ran his fingers through his hair, causing his sleeve to slip, once again revealing the familiar markings.

"My mother has a tattoo like that. What is it?"

"It's not a what, it's a where. Tara. Which is where those bloody birds have taken her." Bartlett picked up a long black feather from the carpet under the window and thrust it at him.

Ethan let out a stunted laugh. "You honestly believe crows trashed our apartment and kidnapped my mom?" And they called Ethan a nutbag. He started to call the police when Bartlett ripped the phone out of his hand.

"Give me that," Ethan hissed. He reached for it, but Bartlett raised it over his head, out of his grasp.

Ethan swung at Bartlett's gut. Somehow, the old guy slid the phone in his jacket pocket with one hand and pinned Ethan's wrists together above his head with the other in a move so fast, Ethan hadn't even seen it coming.

"Get off!" He kicked and flailed, but Bartlett held fast.

"Hear me out. If you don't believe me, then I'll give you the phone back, and you can call whoever you think it is that can come and save you."

What choice did he have? With a calm Ethan didn't feel, he slowly nodded. "Fine."

Bartlett released Ethan's hands and took a step back. "They aren't crows, they're Ravens."

"Ravens. Crows. Same difference. Ravens are just bigger crows. And they're not dangerous. They just don't seem to like you."

Bartlett chuckled. "I'm not talking about the birds on the street. They were clearly sent to stall us."

"Clearly," Ethan said, his tone dripping with sarcasm.

"I'm talking about a very *different* kind of Raven. You don't know what a Raven is?" The way he intonated the word "Raven" triggered a long-forgotten memory of an Irish fable his mother had told him. Something about enchanted women trapped on a lonely island.

"Are you talking about mythical creatures? Shape-shifters that transform into women?"

Bartlett walked over to the window and peered out. "Very good. But there is nothing mythical about them. And I wouldn't call them women. They're purveyors of evil, and by the age of five have the strength of three men combined."

As much as Ethan hated to believe it, the guy could be telling the truth. It certainly would explain his mother's irrational fear of the crows nesting above their window.

Ethan joined the captain, who was gaping out the casement, and looked up. The birds had gone. Their nest lay in pieces on the ground below. As much as Ethan hated to admit it, he was starting to believe what Bartlett was saying. He stared at the broken, empty nest and his heart sank. With their mission accomplished, they weren't coming back.

"You two were *never* supposed to separate. Of all mornings for you to pull the stunt you did . . ." Bartlett's words trailed off and hung like an albatross around Ethan's neck.

"You were watching us." It came out as an accusation.

"Guarding you both. Since the day your mother came to Los Angeles almost fifteen long years ago."

So this was the reason for his mother's insane overprotective, overbearing behavior? "That was why we always had to be together? But when I was at school, and she was at work—"

"Once you were in school, I could follow her. We paid the teachers to watch you at *all* times." Bartlett pulled his sleeve back and held up his tattooed wrist. "By the cuff alone, you know I'm a Shadowwalker. This band is how you can tell a Tarisian living here. It carries a death sentence. Expose our world and you die, instantly. So long as you were never alone, no Shadowwalker would have dared try anything. Least of all Ravens, who would have had to partially morph to carry you off." Bartlett turned his arm over and touched the connected spirals. "By this symbol you can tell what part of Tara I'm from. This is the mark of Landover. Your mother's home."

"My mother's from Ireland."

"No. She's not."

"What?" Caitríona Makkai wasn't from Ireland. *What else has she lied to me about?* But then his mind stuck on something else Bartlett had said. "My teachers were paid to watch me? Are you serious?"

Bartlett gritted his teeth. "It was a necessary part of your security, which I guess means nothing to you. But it meant everything to me, and your mother!"

Brimming with guilt, Ethan fought to keep it together. All this time she had been trying to protect him. But from what? Ravens? "Mom was here alone because I left without her this morning."

"Inside your apartment was the perfect place to attack. The Ravens could morph and no one would see. Especially not me. They saw me go after you and had a wide-open shot at her." Bartlett growled and punched the wall, breaking the plaster.

Ethan sat on the floor and pulled his knees into his chest. Blood dripped from his nose again, but he didn't care. "I don't understand. Why would anyone want to hurt us?"

Calming slightly, Bartlett looked down at Ethan. "Because of who you and your mother are."

"Who are we?"

"She didn't tell you anything?"

"About what?" Ethan stood up and sniffed, trying to stop his nose from bleeding.

Bartlett closed his visible eye and pressed his thumb and forefinger to the top of his nose like he had a headache. When he opened his eye, he pinned Ethan with a gimlet stare. "We don't have time for this."

Moving lightning fast, Bartlett flicked up his eye patch, fisted Ethan's shirt, and yanked him so that their faces were an inch apart.

"Hey!" Ethan's protests were cut off by a bright light pulsating from Bartlett's unpatched eye. His limbs grew weak and the room spun.

"What did you do to me?"

Then everything went black.

◈ FOUR ◈

Ethan's eyes fluttered open. His head ached as if he'd been hit in the temple with a sledgehammer. The unfamiliar room was dimly lit by moonlight streaming in through a small round window.

Moonlight. He'd lost an entire day.

Moaning, Ethan slowly lifted his head and threw his legs over the side of the bed he'd been sleeping on. He tried to stand up but the floor rocked, dropping him back on the bed, disoriented.

The stale air was thick with salt water, and the walls creaked from strain every time the bottom rocked. A ship, and judging from the size of the room, a big one.

The place was an unbelievable mess. Clothes lay scattered everywhere. Old bread and dried-up cheese that looked like a science experiment sat on a table next to the bed. The mattress was bare except for a tattered blanket balled up near the footboard.

Ethan checked his pockets for his phone, but it was gone. The only things he had on him were his mother's drawing and her necklace.

Standing up, he noticed a door on the wall opposite the bed. He cautiously padded over, then grabbed the knob and twisted. Locked. Ethan tried again, turning it back and forth, yanking and kicking, but the door wouldn't budge.

"Bartlett!" No response. He kicked the door again. Still nothing. He wasn't going anywhere.

Ethan trudged over to a large desk in the center of the room before the ship could rock again. On it was an old-fashioned feather quill and inkwell. His English teacher, Mr. Burrows, used one of those pens. He thought it made him look cool, but his fingers were always covered in sticky black goo. It wasn't a good look.

To the right of the inkwell was a wooden model-map with the word TARA carved into the top.

At three feet long, the map took up most of the desk. It had raised mountain ranges peaked in white, and rivers running through deep valleys. Detailed green fields had actual grass that waved as if blown by a breeze, but the air in the room was perfectly still.

Ethan touched a blue spot labeled DRYDEN LAKE. It felt wet. When he lifted his fingers up, water dripped from the tips. It *was* wet.

Ethan counted eight territories—five in one large landmass and three islands. The islands were called Talia, Cantolin, and Isle of Mord.

Waving grass fields spread from Landover, the far eastern territory on the continent, into its western neighbor Gransmore.

As Ethan ran his fingers through Landover's warm fields, a wave of emotions sprang from the map into his fingertips, up his arms, and then throughout his entire body. Adrenaline coursed through his veins. Filled with pure, unbridled courage, he felt strong, like he could rip someone apart with his bare hands.

Next, Ethan glided his index finger through the breezy rolling hills of Gransmore. His spirits instantly lifted, and he burst out laughing.

On the other side of Gransmore were Kilkerry and then Algidare. In Kilkerry, a small forest led to rocky surfaces. The entire place was filled with a frenetic energy.

Algidare was covered with snowcapped mountains that numbed Ethan's fingertips. He couldn't feel anything.

Then Ethan came to the last territory, Primland. The most northern, it bordered each of the other territories on the continent. As soon as his hand touched it, an inviting, gentle heat warmed his fingertips, but within seconds Ethan's whole hand sizzled like it had been shoved into the middle of a pile of hot coals.

Crying out, he tried to pull his hand off the map but couldn't. It was stuck. He set his foot on the desk and pushed, but that didn't work either.

A few seconds later, the heat slowly dissipated. But Ethan's momentary relief vanished as it came with a hollowness he'd never felt before, as if his soul had been burned out of him.

Then the map let go. His fingers skated off easily. The odd sensation faded, but his hand didn't come away unscathed. His fingertips were red and stung like he'd touched a hot stove.

"Bartlett!" Ethan called again.

The ship rocked hard to port. Ethan's feet slipped out from underneath him, but he managed to grab hold of the edge of the desk, which appeared to be nailed in place, to keep from falling over.

An old green-glass bottle tumbled across the floor. Ethan threw his foot out, stopping it. Inside was a rolled-up piece of paper. He picked it up and held it in the moonlight, illuminating the paper's edge that was caught in the neck.

The only thing he could make out was his name written in cursive.

After failed attempts to poke his fingers inside, Ethan smacked the bottle on the corner of the desk. When that didn't work, he set it on the floor, picked up a heavy, rock paperweight, and dropped it on the bottle. The rock bounced off and rolled under the bed.

"Unbelievable." Ethan picked up the bottle. It didn't have a scratch on it.

With an exasperated bellow, Ethan was about to hurl it across the room when the door creaked open. "That bottle won't break. The message wasn't meant for you," a female voice scolded.

Startled, Ethan spun around. The room was completely empty.

"Hello?" Ethan came around the desk, clutching the nose of the bottle, holding it like a club, prepared to strike.

"The captain wanted me to check on you. He won't be pleased when I report you've been snooping around his room, maliciously attempting to read his personal messages." A low rumbling growl reverberated around the room, but the voice seemed to be emanating from the darkness beyond the door.

"First of all, there was no malicious intent. Simply intent. That message has my name on it so it seems it was meant for me."

A pair of piercing blue eyes appeared in the moonlight only a few feet away and stared intently at him. Ethan moved closer, then froze.

A large black panther skulked toward him. Trying not to make any sudden moves, he slowly backed up until he bumped into the desk.

The panther paused, tilted her head, and then continued toward him with a slow methodical prowess as if stalking her next meal. "If it was meant for you, then it would allow you to read it. It didn't, so be a good boy and put it down before I permanently maim important body parts."

Ethan cringed as the feline stopped only a few inches from him. At waist height, it would be some very important body parts. He was preparing to jump up on the desk when she did the most unexpected thing: she rubbed her ear against the side of his jeans and began to purr. "Oh, that feels good—"

Ethan cautiously set the bottle down on the desk, and stood perfectly still. "Please don't eat me."

"You don't need to be afraid, Ríegre. I won't bite."

"Said the predator to his prey." Ethan scooted to the other side of the desk to put some distance between them. "I'd rather not take any chances." An unexpected laugh escaped as the absurdity of the situation dawned on him. It was bad enough he talked to ghosts. "I've seriously lost my mind. I'm talking to a panther."

"I'm not a panther." One minute the panther was at waist height, and the next, she'd morphed into a stunning woman with chocolate-brown skin and long wavy dark hair, wearing a solid black unitard. Close to the same height as Ethan, she looked like she was in her mid-twenties.

Ethan's mouth dropped open and he slid even farther away from her. "Oh yeah, I've lost it. Completely."

Ignoring his comments, the woman leaned over the map on the desk and smiled. "I'm a Cat Sidhe. My name is Mysty." Her pale eyes glistening in the moonlight, there was a playful wickedness about her. And the way she smiled at him made him very, very uncomfortable.

"Where is Bartlett?"

"*Captain* Bartlett. On deck, of course. The storm is getting worse. We're so close to the doorway, I can already taste the sugarloaf." Mysty turned her longing eyes to the map.

"Where is Tara, exactly?" Ethan asked, following her gaze.

"When our homelands were no longer safe, our ancestors were granted their own continent on Earth. The god of the sea, Manannán mac Lir, hid it from mankind. But he left doorways for us to travel between our lands and the rest of Earth, and this one will take us to the very heart of Brodik Bay."

The boat swung hard. Staring down at the map, Ethan grabbed the desk. Brodik Bay was on the northeast side of Tara, next to Landover. His thumb skimmed the calm waters. It felt peaceful.

"That's it." Mysty waved her hand. "Up on the cliffs sits Weymiss, your family's home."

"My home is in Los Angeles."

"Trying my patience, aren't you?" Mysty morphed. The panther leaped up on the desk, baring her long, sharp canines, and gave a roar so ferocious that Ethan's heart skipped several beats.

Holding his hands out, Ethan slowly backed out of the room.

"Where do you think you're going? You're to remain in this room for the duration of the journey. Captain's orders." Mysty jumped off the desk, bared her sharp teeth again, and headed straight for him.

Before she could ruin his chances at procreation, Ethan bolted out the open door and raced up a short flight of steps that led to the deck. Freezing rain poured down. The ship rocked. He slipped and skidded into one of the masts.

The skies were black, the wind whipped the sails, and the ship continued to rock furiously from side to side. It looked like they had sailed straight into a hurricane.

"Keep a lookout!" Bartlett bellowed from the helm at men who hustled from stern to bow along the railings, scanning the dark sea.

"Nothing. I don't see anything, Captain!" a man yelled from a tiny platform on top of the tallest mast.

Waves crashed against the ship from both sides, tossing it back and forth, taking Ethan's stomach with it. He crawled toward Bartlett, latching on to the masts to keep from slipping again. As he grabbed hold of the last pillar before the helm, a tall, burly guy in a dingy white shirt, black pants, and boots came around from the other side and glared down at him. His long black hair clung to the side of his face where a large jagged scar ran from his right eyebrow to his chin. "What're you doing up here?"

Noticing Ethan, Bartlett leered over the wheel at him. "Ethan Makkai, get yourself back down those stairs!"

Ethan glanced into the darkness of the hull below, and heard Mysty growl. "Think I'm safer up here, Captain."

Bartlett shook his head and tossed a rope at Ethan's feet. "Fine. Tie yourself to the mizzen then!" he shouted over the gusting wind and pounding rain.

"The mizzen?" Ethan wondered aloud.

The scarred man slapped him on the back and laughed. "Doesn't even know what the mizzen is?"

Ethan wanted to punch the smirk off the guy's face.

"The mast on the end there." Bartlett gestured to the far post on the very front of the ship. It was cloaked in darkness and pointed into the unknown ahead. It looked like the perfect spot to get killed.

"No thanks." Ethan tossed the rope back at Bartlett.

"Donnagan, drag him there! Tie him up! Hur—" Bartlett was cut off by a rogue wave barreling in to the starboard side, spraying freezing seawater over the railing.

Before Donnagan could reach Ethan, the ship leaned hard to port. Ethan flew into the railing, whacking his shoulder, and then started sliding over the edge. He grabbed on to the rail to keep from falling overboard. The ship righted and Ethan tried to stand up, but his stomach heaved. Still on his hands and knees, he swallowed over and over again, but it didn't work, and he was forced to lean over the side and puke.

When Ethan finally lifted his head, raucous, high-pitched squawks cut through the thunderous echoes of the storm, growing louder and louder with each passing second.

"Ravens. Hold on!" Captain Bartlett yelled.

The whoosh of flapping wings and forceful caws of the Ravens were so loud, they drowned out Bartlett, who spouted off something unintelligible, waving a fist at Ethan.

A shadow flew over. Ethan looked up as a half-woman, half–black bird moved to hover over the water, next to the railing. With long, dark hair, her body was covered in black feathers that blended seamlessly with her large, strong wings. She tilted her neck and locked her eerie yellow eyes on Ethan.

Mesmerized, Ethan watched her as she moved so close to him, he could make out every facet of her severe face. With a wicked grin, she lunged with her clawed feet, latching on to his arm.

"No!" Bartlett yelled.

Ethan braced his feet against the railing to keep from falling overboard. He was strong, but the Raven was stronger. She yanked, and Ethan rolled over the top of the railing, which gave him a terrifying look at the freezing, violent ocean below.

Donnagan reached over and wrapped an arm around Ethan's waist. Another man latched on to his arm clutching to the ship, and then another and another, until one of them could reach the center mast.

"Pull!" Donnagan bellowed.

With a combined heave, they yanked Ethan over the railing. The Raven's claws slipped off, leaving a painful trail of scratches down Ethan's forearm.

Ethan grasped his arm, which was now bleeding all over the deck, when Donnagan let out a horrifying cry. Ethan spun and his stomach ceased. The Raven had stabbed Donnagan in the back, the tips of her claws visible through his right shoulder.

Ethan grabbed hold of Donnagan's arms, yanking him forward, forcing the Raven's claws out of his body and him to curse loudly in a language Ethan didn't understand.

Hissing, the Raven flew toward the dark skies, vanishing.

Donnagan sank to his knees. Ethan placed his hands over Donnagan's wound, trying to stop the bleeding, but there was no time.

More Ravens bombarded.

Ethan frantically scanned the deck for something to fight them off with when a deep-throated rumble came from behind the ship.

Bartlett hurried back to his perch. He swung the wheel hard, and the ship reacted, turning sharply as a huge creature rose out of the dark water, fire blazing from its nostrils.

"Ethan, grab hold of that mast and don't let go!" Bartlett shouted.

Ethan crawled as fast as he could toward the pole, but between the swaying ship and the wet deck, his knees kept slipping. With the next tilt of the ship, Ethan skidded into the mast, hard. He grabbed on, but his arms couldn't reach all the way around.

One of the men slid down the shaft, landing next to him.

"What is that thing?" Ethan asked.

"The Nuckelavee," the man said in a reverential tone. They both watched it circle the ship completely in seconds. With a body measuring at least fifty feet long, it looked like a dragon with long, leathery wings, but also had whale-sized fins. It could both fly and swim, making the odds of the ship losing it slim to none.

A loud whoosh shook the ship as fire cascaded down from above, skimming the wet deck. Men scattered, trying to take cover.

Bartlett flipped the wheel again. The ship responded, turning hard to starboard as the Nuckelavee rocketed down. It missed and dived headfirst into the ocean.

Seconds ticked by as the men waited for the beast to come out of the water and make another pass from above. But it didn't. Instead, a loud crunch reverberated from below. The Nuckelavee must have latched on to the bottom of the ship. The hull sounded like it was being crushed from both sides.

"Fire the cannons!" Captain Bartlett ordered. He flipped the wheel again, but this time he didn't stop. He spun it in circles, around and around, and the ship responded, making wide turns that grew tighter and tighter with each passing second.

Ethan tried to hold on, but the centrifugal force was too much. His hands slipped off the mast, and he barreled toward the starboard side, slamming into the railing, bringing him much closer to the monster than he wanted to be.

The Nuckelavee had crawled up the side, its spearlike claws sinking farther into the belly of the ship. With cannon barrels pointed down, the men lit the fuses.

One after another, the cannons exploded. With each blow, the creature lifted its claws off the hull, only to put them right back. Meanwhile, the ocean churned, creating a whirlpool that threatened to take the ship down.

Flames spewed over the side of the deck, and Ethan was forced to let go or be barbecued. He rolled away from the railing as walls of spinning water rose up, forming a tube hundreds of feet above the ship.

"Hold on! We're going through!" Bartlett cried.

With a stilted whine, the Nuckelavee was ripped off. It spiraled up the flume as the ship headed in the other direction, straight for the bottom of the ocean.

Seconds later the ship smacked into the seafloor. The impact lifted Ethan off the deck and dropped him down hard on the same shoulder that had twice slammed into the railing. Crying out from the pain, he crawled toward the mizzen, hoping to reach it before the ship did something else unexpected.

But he didn't move fast enough. The ship jerked. Then it jerked again, sinking into the ocean floor. With each tremor, the bottom sank farther and farther into the sand, with huge chunks of its hull disappearing.

The spinning started again, sending Ethan flying into the starboard side, his legs lifting out from underneath him. He held on with everything he had left, but it wasn't enough. He slipped off.

An arm caught him around the waist and dragged Ethan back to the mast, reaching it as the water walls crashed down. The next thing he knew, they were submerged.

Ethan's lungs ached, desperate for air. He had to get to the surface. Pinned and suffocating, he pushed against the body holding him, but whoever it was wouldn't move.

Just as his lungs were ready to burst, the ship shot straight up, like an arrow from a bow, then burst through the surface and splashed down.

"Breathe." Bartlett smacked him on the back, hard.

Ethan spit out about a gallon of salt water and gasped.

"Welcome to Tara."

▣ FIVE ▣

The sun beat down and the air was crisp and cool. There was no more rain, no more wind. Ethan clung to the mast, his eyes burning from the salt water, his soaked clothes heavy and chaffing. Bartlett stood there too, still crushing him to the pole. At least the water had washed away the old guy's stench—most of it anyway.

"Thanks, but you can get off me now."

"That I can." Bartlett peeled himself off. He glanced over to Donnagan, who sat propped against the mizzen, holding a hand over the puncture wound in his shoulder. "Donny, you gonna live, lad?"

"Oh, I'll live, Captain. Nothing more than a souvenir from the ruckus," he said, wincing.

"Good." Tossing a proud grin at his men, Bartlett launched his fist above his head. "Better luck next time, Nucky!"

"We're home!" one of the men cried.

"And you said we'd never make it back alive," another added.

"Who doubted his captain?" Bartlett demanded. His eye darted from one man to another. "Who was it? There'll be no ale for him."

The men all laughed.

Ethan didn't feel much like laughing. He was sore, soaking wet, worried about his mother, and for the first time in his normally carefully planned life, he had no clue what was going to happen next. He glanced over at the sea captain, who had apparently doubled as his and his mother's secret service protection, wondering if there was a possibility they were truly related.

He scanned Bartlett's face for a trace of similarity, but there wasn't any. "You're not my grandfather, are you?" The hint of disappointment in Ethan's voice surprised even him.

Bartlett smirked. "No. I'm not."

Be happy. Would you really want this guy for a grandfather? But Ethan had so little information about his mother's family, or his father's, for that matter, it might've been nice to have a connection to someone or something, especially now.

The ship drifted smoothly through calm blue waters. To starboard, open ocean. To port, a wall of gray cliffs at least fifty feet high. Small pristine white birds with purple beaks circled overhead while a gentle breeze tickled the back of Ethan's neck. He sucked in a mountain of air and let it out slowly. It tasted sweet.

"Brodik Bay is as peaceful as it felt on the map," Ethan said.

Bartlett raised an eyebrow. "Touched my map, did you? Now look here." He patted Ethan's back and gestured to port. "These cliffs are the boundaries of your mother's home, Landover. These waters hold the strongest fleet of ships in all of Tara, of which I am captain."

Ethan was glad to know Bartlett was an actual captain of something, and grateful they'd made it to Landover alive, but he had only one thing on his mind. "Do you know where my mother is?"

"I don't. But we'll find her," Bartlett said, his voice tinged with regret or uncertainty, Ethan wasn't sure which. "General Niles will be waiting for us on the dock. He'll have more information, don't fret."

Don't fret. With each passing second, whoever took his mother was getting farther and farther away.

The ship docked at a long wooden pier. Above it, a large solitary tree grew straight out of the cliff, reaching so far over the dock that its green, feather-shaped leaves skimmed the surface of the water.

A crewman slid a short plank between the ship and the dock, and Bartlett prodded Ethan. "Off we go."

Once across, they swiftly strode to the bottom of a long flight of stairs. It was a straight shot up the face of the cliff, with more than a hundred steps. Ethan jogged, taking two at a time, in a hurry to find this General Niles.

At the top, a man with shoulder-length blond hair smiled warmly as they approached. He wore a dark green cloak with the mark of Landover stitched into the left shoulder, tan pants, black boots that reached his knees, and a sword on both hips.

"General," Bartlett called.

"Captain Bartlett. Fifteen long years. Nice to see you've arrived home and without loss of limb." "General" was the right title for him. He had to be at least six foot five, and the deep resonance of his voice commanded attention.

The two men grabbed each other's arms at the elbows.

Bartlett held up the note from the unbreakable bottle. "Tearlach?"

General Niles shook his head.

The captain paled and gave a heartfelt nod. "Please give my condolences to Clothilde. I'll be up to pay my respects shortly." Bartlett paused and added, "I'm afraid your warning was late, Julius. Caitríona was taken, by Ravens."

"I know," General Niles replied, glancing sideways at Ethan.

"You know?" Ethan stepped around Bartlett so he could talk to the general. "Do you know where they've taken her?"

"You must be Ethan." Niles extended his hand.

Weighted down by exhaustion and worry from the devastating events of the last twenty-four hours, Ethan had no patience for niceties. "That's not an answer. General, where is my mom?"

The general folded his arms over his chest, and grimaced. "There's much to fill you in on. The Ravens have taken your mother, but they haven't hurt her, not yet."

Ethan sighed, relieved, but the infuriating general still hadn't answered the question. "Where have they taken her?"

Niles set a hand on the pommel of one of his swords. "I'm afraid to say any more until we get you home. And there's the matter of your family, who is waiting for you."

"What family? I don't have any family."

Niles tossed a curious look at Bartlett before answering. "Your aunt and cousin are there."

"I can't believe this." His mother did have family. Ethan fisted his hands and shook his head. Another lie.

"It seems Caitríona hasn't told him anything about . . . well, anything," Bartlett explained, sounding as dismal as Ethan felt.

"Wonderful," Niles groaned.

"I'll leave you two to it then. . . ." With a sympathetic pat on the general's shoulder, Bartlett gave a nod to Ethan then turned to leave.

"Cornelius, once the ship is settled, I need to speak with you."

"Of course you do. No rest for the weary," Bartlett grunted over his shoulder, disappearing down the long staircase.

"This way." General Niles walked toward two horses, one black and the other chocolate brown, grazing under a tree. Ethan followed slowly, his heart pounding harder against his chest with each step closer to them. There was only one thing in the world he was deathly afraid of—horses.

For the past two summers, his mother forced him to take horseback-riding lessons at a ranch about an hour outside of LA. The lessons ended up being more like stunt training. Every horse he got on invariably ended up tossing him off. One got stung by a bee and took off at a gallop so fast Ethan fell into the pricker bushes that lined the trail. It took him over an hour to get them out of his legs. Not to mention his back was sore for weeks. He swore he'd never get on another horse, and he wasn't about to change his mind.

When Ethan and the general came within a few feet of the brown horse, he looked up and snorted as if he could smell Ethan's fear.

"Devlin is one of our fastest horses," Niles told Ethan. "A present from my family to you." The general pointed to a dirt road on the other side of the horses. "It's a short ride along this path to Weymiss." He walked over, untied Devlin's reins from the tree, and held them out to Ethan.

He put up his hands. "General, I can't accept such a . . . large present."

"Nonsense," he dismissed him. "Shall I give you a leg up? Or can you manage it?"

"You know, I think I'll walk. Legs are stiff. All that sitting on the ship." Ethan started down the dirt path.

A few seconds later General Niles trotted up next to him on the black horse, leading Devlin behind him. "It's a long way on foot. Please, let me help you on. If you're scared, I can lead the horse. I did it for my children when they were learning to ride."

"Do I look like I can't ride?" Ethan lied. "I just need to stretch my legs, that's all."

After a few more steps, the smirking general asked, "Are they limber enough yet?"

Ethan glared up at Niles and let out an aggravated sigh. "Fine." He spun around and walked over to Devlin's side. His heart clamoring, Ethan stared at the saddle for a beat, and then lifted his left foot to the height of the stirrup. It was so high, he managed to get only the tip of his shoe into it. He pushed off with his right leg, but Devlin moved. His left foot slipped out of the stirrup and he fell, landing on his butt.

Ethan cursed and dusted himself off.

The general bit his lip to keep from laughing. "Sure I can't help?"

Ethan ignored Niles and walked back to Devlin. He pulled the bridle down so the horse was forced to turn his head and Ethan could look him in the eye.

"Hold still," he hissed.

Devlin lifted his nose, yanking the bridle out of his hand. Determined, Ethan walked to the horse's side again, lifted his left leg, and this time, managed to slide his shoe in the stirrup securely only to realize his leg was so high he couldn't push off with his right leg at all. He was stuck in a ridiculously embarrassing position.

Without saying a word, General Niles dismounted. He came behind Ethan, grabbed his right leg, and tossed it up and over the saddle.

"Thanks."

"You're most welcome," the general said, handing Ethan the reins. Then he climbed back on his horse.

Devlin whinnied as Ethan shifted nervously in the hard leather saddle, praying he wouldn't throw him off.

"Sit tall, grip with your knees, lean back on the run, and you'll be an expert soon enough," Niles instructed, making it sound so easy. He made a clicking sound and nudged his horse.

Sit tall . . . grip with my knees . . . okay, just breathe. I can do this. The horse ambled down the path. "Good boy. That's it. Nice and slow."

Niles kicked his horse again, bringing him to a trot. Devlin mimicked and suddenly every part of Ethan bounced, his butt pounding repeatedly into the saddle.

"Oh no . . ." Yanking the reins, he said, "Walk boy. Slow down."

But Devlin didn't slow down. Instead, he jerked his head, turned off the path, and took off at a full gallop, heading into a wide-open field.

"Stop!" Ethan grabbed hold of the horse's mane and tugged, but that only seemed to piss off Devlin more. The horse tossed his head from side to side, trying to throw Ethan off.

Green splotches mixed with yellow specks whizzed by. The reins slipped from Ethan's grasp. He latched his arms around Devlin's neck, hoping the tempermental beast would take the hint and slow down, but he didn't. Devlin moved even faster.

Ethan's knees strained, gripping the saddle, trying to stay on. Devlin pivoted right, trying to avoid a white horse that suddenly appeared in front of him. Ethan slid down in his saddle. He didn't know how much longer he could hold on. Panicked, he looked for help from the rider on the white horse a second before she catapulted onto him, sending him crashing to the ground.

Ethan hit, hard, landing on his chest. The attacker fell on his back, knocking the wind out of him. Showing no mercy, she sat up, pinning him to the ground, and making it impossible for him to catch his breath.

Ethan rolled, taking his attacker with him, until he was on top of her, and staring into the most beautiful, livid green eyes he'd ever seen. Their faces inches apart, a subtle, spicy lavender scent dusted his nostrils as he sucked precious oxygen back into his lungs.

"Sorry . . ." Captivated, he leaned up and started to climb off her. Before he could wipe the stupid grin off his face, she kneed him in the stomach, winding him again.

Ethan fell on his back, clutching his gut, and glowered up at the sky, wondering what he could have done so wrong in his life to deserve a day like today. He'd abandoned his mother to kidnappers. He deserved exactly what he was getting, and worse.

He started to stand when he felt sharp, cold steel slide against his neck.

"I wouldn't do that!" There she was again. Standing just out of arm's reach, ready to cut his head off with a long sword. In formfitting brown pants, ankle-high black boots, and a white short-sleeve shirt, she had a long blond braid that reached all the way down her back.

Ethan raised his hands, surrendering. He had been miserably wrong. "Beautiful" wasn't the right word. More like . . . *Fatally attractive.*

"Be glad I didn't aim lower, thief." She glanced at his groin then lowered the sword, pressing the tip against his chest, right over his heart. "The penalty for stealing a horse isn't usually death, but then again, Devlin is my brother Adam's horse!" She fisted the grip with both hands, raised it a few inches, preparing to do what? Kill him? Over a stupid horse?

"Lily! Stop!" General Niles yelled.

Annoyed, she rolled her eyes and lowered the blade, resting it on his chest again.

"What do you think you're doing?" The general pulled his horse to a stop a few feet from them and dismounted.

"I was patrolling when I saw you chasing after this diminutive who'd stolen Devlin," Lily explained.

"First I'm a thief and now I'm a diminutive?" Ethan snapped.

"One's not exclusive of the other," Lily tossed back. She circled her sword over his gut, taunting.

"Put your weapon away, now." General Niles pushed her shoulder, forcing her to move, then reached a hand down and helped Ethan up. "Lily, Ethan didn't steal Devlin. He was a gift."

"It's all good. Keep the horse. I don't want it or need it. I'm much happier on foot," Ethan said, dusting off his clothes.

General Niles grabbed Devlin's reins and slapped them in Ethan's hand. "Ethan, this horse is yours. Trust me when I tell you, you will need him in Tara." Before Ethan could argue with him, Niles turned to Lily. "What are you doing here? I told your aunt to make sure you stayed close to home today."

"I'm fourteen and don't need permission to leave."

"You most certainly do."

Lily glanced right and left, then looked up at her father. "With the arrival of the Ríegre, I thought you could use some assistance."

General Niles paled. "How do you know about that?"

She glanced around again. "So he is here!"

"Answer me!" Niles roared. The general stood over her, wide-eyed and fuming.She seemed completely unfazed by his anger, but Ethan took a cautious step back.

"I overheard you telling Aunt Morgan this morning." She held her arm across her body, gripping the hilt of her sword, still scanning the field, searching for something or someone.

"So you were eavesdropping? We were behind closed doors."

"Not exactly eavesdropping. I'd gone into the cellar to get some mugwort for brewing. How was I supposed to know you and Aunt Morgan use the cellar as a secret meeting room?"

The general took a long, deep breath and let it out slowly. "Lily, you can tell no one."

"Of course, Da. I swear. But where *is* the Ríegre?"

The general's eyes darted to Ethan.

Lily's mouth fell open. "Him?"

"Me?" Ethan imitated Lily's confused tone.

General Niles started to respond, but stopped as a tall, thin woman with equally blond hair hustled up the road. Her blue dress swung with each stiff step. "Lily Prudence Niles, you get back to the cottage now. The medicinals are nearly done brewing and must be bottled and delivered, all by sundown."

"Prudence?" Ethan couldn't help himself.

Lily pulled her sword.

"Lily!" Her father snatched the weapon from her and greeted the woman with a kiss on the cheek. "Perfect timing, Morgan. Ethan, this is Lily's aunt, Morgan McKenna. And this, Morgan, is Caitríona's son, Ethan."

"It's a sincere pleasure, sire. Welcome home," she said.

Sire? "Thanks. Nice meeting you too, but it's just Ethan, Ethan Makkai."

Confused, Morgan's eyes slid to General Niles, who was too busy gaping at Ethan to notice.

"Dear gods, Bartlett wasn't kidding. Your mother didn't tell you anything about anything." He took a step toward Ethan.

Ethan instinctively took a step back and held his hands palms up. "About what?"

"He doesn't know?" Lily arched an eyebrow and smirked. "Are you sure he's the right one, Da?"

What the hell? There were a lot of people in Ethan's life who disliked him, but it usually took at least a couple of days to generate this kind of animosity. What could he have possibly done in the last sixty seconds to tick her off so much?

Morgan clapped her hands together. "Lily, don't be rude."

"One what, exactly?" Ethan asked.

Ignoring him, General Niles pushed Lily toward her aunt. "Right, then. Ladies, off you go. And, Lily, if I find you on the grounds again without permission, you'll be confined to the house for a fortnight."

"What?" Lily exclaimed.

"You heard your father. Let's go," Morgan replied for him.

With a fleeting scowl at Ethan, Lily stormed off, leading her horse through the flower-filled meadow, muttering, with Morgan following.

The girl was a serious pain, and yet Ethan couldn't take his eyes off her. After a few seconds Lily glanced back, catching him staring. Mortified, he quickly looked away.

Once they were out of sight, Ethan let Devlin's reins fall to the ground. "What is it I don't know, General?"

A crease formed between General Niles's eyebrows as he stared down at the reins, then met Ethan's wary gaze. "Your name may be Ethan Makkai, but there's nothing 'just' about it or you. Your mother is a princess."

Ethan burst out laughing. "Yeah, right. Good one."

Niles pursed his lips together and gave him a gimlet stare.

"Oh my god! You're not kidding?"

The general slowly shook his head.

"He's not kidding . . . ," Ethan groaned, his temper flaring. This had been the absolute worse day of his life and he had only one person to thank for that. "So let me do a count of all the lies my mother told me so far. One, she isn't from Ireland. Two, she does have a family. And three, she's a princess?" That one was impossible to believe. "In the past twenty-four hours I've been attacked by birds, kidnapped by Bartlett, had a shape-shifting panther *and* your daughter threaten my manhood, and was forced to ride a horse. I hate *horses!*" Ethan elongated the word "hate" to make sure Niles heard him.

"I see."

"Do you? I don't think you do. I swear to god I'm about thirty seconds away from losing it."

Unfazed, General Niles placed his hands on his hips and gave Ethan a fatherly grimace that only infuriated Ethan more. "I'll enlighten you as much as I can. We'd hoped to keep you hidden until at least your eighteenth birthday, but your uncle, your mother's brother, Tearlach, the king, died a week ago, and an emergency meeting of the Council of Kings has been called. They gather shortly in Coventry, and you must be there."

"Why me? If my mother is the princess, shouldn't she be there?"

"Radharc did not pass to your mother. You were chosen as the Ríegre." He said that as if Ethan should know what he was talking about.

"What does that mean?"

"The heir. You possess the sacred gift, radharc. You see spirits."

Ethan took a large step away from him. "How do you know that?"

Niles smirked. "It's my job to know."

"That word, 'gift,' that was my mother's word for it. It's definitely not mine."

The general moved next to him and placed a hand on Ethan's shoulder. "It's what sets you apart."

Ethan stepped back again, forcing the hand off. "I never asked to be set apart. I can't believe I'm even talking about it. I'm never supposed to talk about . . . it."

"Radharc."

"Radharc" sounded way too bold a word for something that made Ethan feel like a freak.

"Radharc chooses the heir, Ethan. Once confirmed by the Council, you will be the next king of Landover."

SIX

King? Oh no no no. I'm no king. You've definitely got the wrong guy. Someone should tell this radharc to choose another heir. I just want to find my mom and go home."

Niles settled his hands on the pommels of his swords. "Ethan, it is your destiny. As you will learn to ride, you will learn to be a strong king. All of this must be very confusing. A new place, new people, a different future than you'd ever imagined. It must be very hard to believe."

This wasn't just hard to believe. It was utter insanity. Ethan stormed down the path, determined to stay off that horse. General Niles caught up to him and grabbed hold of Ethan's arm.

Ethan yanked, but the general held tight and then kneeled on one knee. "Ethan, I am the one person in all of Tara who will never, ever lie to you. I am your humble servant, leader of your armies during times of war, and your strategist when we are at peace. The Niles family has been in the service of the Makkais for centuries. We are your most loyal subjects."

Great. A man he'd never met before was telling Ethan he was his humble servant. And that Ethan should trust him. But at the moment, what choice did he have? He had no idea where to start looking for his mother.

"That all sounds very nice, but loyalty is proven with actions, not words."

"Truer words were never spoken." General Niles stood up and strode toward the horses. "Now, please, allow me to give you a leg up." Stopping next to Devlin, he laced his fingers together and then spread them flat.

Ethan came over and looked at the general's open hands. He had no idea where he was or where this path would lead him, but the one thing he did know was that if he didn't get up on that horse by himself, he would never have the courage to see this through and find his mother.

"I got this." He pushed the general's hands away. Niles nodded and went to his horse.

Sliding his left foot into the stirrup, Ethan boosted up with his right leg and landed in the saddle. It wasn't graceful, but he'd done it.

Back on the path, Ethan's horse trailed the general's as he wound along the cliff's edge. To one side was a sheer drop all the way down to the bay, and on the other side, more overgrown fields of grasses and flowers.

In the distance was a behemoth of a castle that sat on top of a short hill behind a tall, circular stone wall. It had four square towers, one on each corner, and stretched as long as a football field. A green flag with the mark of Landover waved from the top of each turret.

The general slowed his horse until he and Ethan rode side by side. "Weymiss Castle. This is your mother's home."

Ethan's jaw dropped. "Not possible." There was no way Caitríona Makkai ever lived in a castle.

Niles smiled knowingly. "Come. See for yourself."

Ethan and his mother had subsisted in one tiny room with bad plumbing and cockroaches for roommates when they could've lived in a castle? If this was true, Ethan was really going to let her have it.

They rode past a row of thick bushes toward a wide gap in the castle's monumental wall. A steady stream of people paced in and out, and crowd noises could be heard. With a pensive glare, Niles scanned the area, then took the lead again.

Fixated on the approaching opening, Ethan had the eerie feeling that once he crossed the threshold, for good or for bad his life was never going to be the same.

▨ SEVEN ▨

General Niles and Ethan dismounted and led the horses into a bustling market in the gigantic courtyard of Weymiss Castle. The place looked medieval. Wooden carts lined the fence, selling everything from clothes and dishware to swords and knives. The food carts immediately caught Ethan's attention. The smell of cooking meat made his mouth water. He hadn't eaten since breakfast.

The general probably had money, but not even Ethan's growling stomach could get him to ask him for some. *Never owe anybody anything.* A lesson he'd learned a long time ago.

The farther into the market, the more subdued the crowd became. Long faces and hushed conversations replaced good-natured bantering. Guarded apprehension blanketed the people's greeting smiles. Something was very wrong.

When they neared where a large throng had gathered, Ethan stopped to listen to an angry voice that rose from the center of the group.

"I'm telling you, with the death of the king—" an extremely fat man started. Unlike the simple clothes of those around him, he wore a red cloak with white stitching on the collar and down the back.

"What? They'll invade?" A nervous woman in the back dropped a basket, and waited anxiously for the man's response.

"That's exactly what I am saying."

A moment of shocked silence was broken by panicked murmurs until another man who looked like a clone of General Niles—uniformed, with the same blond hair and height—came behind him and set an authoritative hand on his back. "Stop scaring everyone, Linus Flinch! No one is going to invade Landover and steal your ale out of your cellars."

Laughter broke out as Niles pulled Ethan toward a dark-haired boy, maybe ten, who stood eagerly waiting with his hands out. With a nod to the general, the boy took the horses' reins. Ethan tried to say hello, but the general shooed the boy off.

"As I explained to Lily, you are a secret," General Niles said, keeping his voice low. "And I need you to remain that way for a bit longer."

"Why?"

"Because your uncle was murdered." The word hung in the air long after Niles said it.

"Murdered?" Ethan said a little too loud. Several people turned and stared.

Niles faked a laugh, wrapped an arm over Ethan's shoulders, and started walking, dragging him reluctantly along.

"And I'm a secret because . . . ?"

"I don't want you to share your uncle's fate."

The man certainly didn't sugarcoat anything.

As Ethan followed the general, he couldn't help gaping at two figures standing over a nearby cart. Their bodies were covered in black fur and they stood upright like humans but walked on curved legs. With white fur circling their piercing green eyes, set off against their furry black faces, they looked like they were wearing masks. Dual swords mounted on their muscular bare backs, they wore tight-fitting maroon pants.

The stand appeared to be selling fish, but not like any fish he'd seen before. With red scales, six eyes, and two tail fins, they looked like a radioactive science experiment gone wrong. The wolf-men tossed the merchant some gold coins, snatched two fish each, and scarfed them down. A yellow substance coated the soft fur around their mouths, which they lapped up with their exceedingly long tongues.

Ethan was too curious not to stop. "Um. What are they?" he whispered, hoping they couldn't hear him.

"Faoladhs, hailing from Kilkerry. Weymiss has the biggest market in Tara. All are welcome to trade here."

The Faoladhs rounded the cart. With their ears perked at attention, they tilted their heads in a very canine manner, and eyed Ethan. The general stepped between them, obstructing Ethan from their view. He turned, removed his cloak, and wrapped it around Ethan's shoulders.

"Let's keep moving," Niles said.

The cloak hung below Ethan's knees and it weighed a ton. He started to shrug it off when the general put a stiff hand on his shoulder.

"Your clothes are a bit different," he said. "Best not to take any chances."

As they came to the end of the carts, a heavyset woman rushed the general, carrying several bottles of colored liquids.

"General Niles, these are for Morgan. Lily was here this morning and said you would take care of the charge for them?"

"Of course she did. Very well . . ."

As the general dealt with the woman, a man about Ethan's height, dressed in a sleek brown vest and matching pants, slipped behind the woman's stand. He had caramel-colored skin, wildly curly brown hair, and thimble-sized horns on his forehead. As he snuck a bottle with yellow liquid from the cart, his twinkling hazel eyes caught Ethan's. He flashed a mischievous smile, and then ran off so fast no one seemed to notice.

Ethan started after him, but General Niles snatched his arm. "Hey! Where do you think you're going?"

"There was . . ." Ethan searched the crowd, but the thief had vanished into the masses.

"There was what?" Niles laid a hand on the pommel of his sword, scanning the crowd. "What did you see?"

Unsure what to say, Ethan shrugged. The thief was long gone. "Nothing, I guess."

Niles eyed him with a suspicious brow. "Then let's keep moving."

The rest of the way the general stayed beside him, keeping the crowds on his left, Ethan on his right, and a firm hand on Ethan's sore shoulder.

As they climbed the hill to the castle, teams of soldiers rolled cannonballs up raised planks to other men who stacked them in pyramids next to large black cannons. In fact, as Ethan looked back over Weymiss, both above and below the castle wall, men readied cannons, heavy metal spears, bows, arrows, swords, and shields.

"Landover *is* going to be invaded," Ethan said, repeating what he'd heard.

"Since the death of your uncle, tension with one of the territories has been high. We must always be prepared."

As they came to a drawbridge that spanned the moat surrounding the castle, Ethan stopped again. Annoyed, Niles groaned as he stopped beside him.

"So let me get this straight: my mom was kidnapped, my uncle murdered, and Landover is about to go to war."

After a long sigh, Niles shook his head. "I didn't say we were about to go to war. I said we must always be prepared."

On the other side of the bridge were large thick metal doors that stood open. Two people waited in the doorway to greet them. First up, a woman with dark hair yanked into a tight bun. Her long maroon dress did nothing to soften her pinched nose and deep scowl. Ethan assumed this was his aunt.

On her left was a brawny guy at least seventeen and more than a foot taller than Ethan. He had short, spiky black hair, and wore a white long-sleeved shirt and dark pants.

As Ethan and the general reached them, a squat, stout man with light brown skin hurried out of the door. Similar to the thief in the market, only older, he had thick brown hair neatly slicked back. "Forgive me. There was a mishap in the kitchen," he said, wiping his hands on his stained white apron. Underneath he wore all-black clothes that looked like they belonged to an undertaker.

"Julius, you'd better have a very good explanation for urgently summoning us outside," the woman snapped. "There is danger all around."

"I can assure you, Madam Clothilde, my guards will keep you quite secure. As you are aware, it's customary to introduce anyone new coming into the castle on the landing." General Niles stepped behind Ethan and pulled the cloak off his shoulders. "This is your nephew and the king's heir, Ethan."

Ethan felt like a rabbit that had been pulled out of a hat.

Clothilde gasped. "I don't understand." She tipped her head, pointing her nose down at Ethan.

"Ethan . . ." The general paused to toss him a reassuring smile. ". . . is Caitríona's son."

Clothilde scrunched up her face. "Th-this is preposterous," she stammered. "If Tearlach were here—"

"The king was well aware of his nephew, and that he possessed the sacred gift," General Niles interrupted.

"Any day radharc will come to Christian." She set her hand on her son's shoulder.

"No. It won't. It is Ethan who bears the gift. *He* is the heir to the throne. I tell you this because he will need his family, especially now. But his existence must be kept secret until he can be presented to the Council."

"I don't believe any of this," Clothilde whined.

"Mother," Christian said with disgust, "let it go." He took a giant step forward, forcing her hand to drop. "We have an heir. This is what we've been waiting for."

"And where is Caitríona?" the horned man asked, concerned.

"Missing," Ethan answered.

"What do you mean, 'missing'?" Clothilde scoffed. "That impetuous girl ran out on her responsibilities when she vanished more than a decade ago."

Ethan glared at Clothilde. "My mom is not impetuous, and she doesn't run out on responsibilities."

"Ignore her. She can't help herself," Christian said.

"Christian Makkai, how dare you speak of me that way? I am your mother and your queen."

Christian turned to face her. "You're no longer queen, are you, Mother?"

Perhaps life alone with his mother hadn't been so bad after all. These folks defined the term "dysfunctional family."

"Scully, sire, in charge of the manor. Welcome to your new home." The horned man gave a slight bow.

"Thanks," Ethan said, drawing out the word, his eyes fixated on the horns.

Seeing Ethan's confusion, General Niles came to his rescue. "Scully is a Brownie, one of many who serve the monarchies of Tara. He is a dedicated servant to the Makkai family and has been for more than two centuries."

"Two hundred years? But that would make you . . ."

"I'm three hundred and fifty-two years young, sire," Scully boasted.

"His new home, indeed. This is ridiculous," Clothilde mumbled.

"Let's get inside, shall we?" General Niles motioned toward the archway that led into the castle.

Guards folded in behind them, blocking the only escape route, leaving Ethan with no real choice. Reluctant, he crossed the threshold, wondering if this wasn't some elaborate plan to take him prisoner. Everything his mother told him had been a lie, but was General Niles, for all his words of loyalty, telling him the truth? Were these people really Ethan's family?

◀ EIGHT ▶

O nce everyone was across the threshold, soldiers on both sides pushed the tall metal doors closed, and bolted them, trapping Ethan inside.

On the right side of the entrance hall a spiral staircase climbed into one of the four towers. Ethan peeked in. Well-armed men stood at watch next to strategically spaced openings in the stone—arrow slits. The place felt more like a prison than a home.

Clothilde led everyone through a narrow hallway where large tapestries covered the cold walls. Threadbare, the first several appeared very old. They depicted massive battle scenes in which some soldiers wore leather armor, while others had on mail or went bare-chested. As they reached the end of the passageway, the tapestries looked newer. The soldiers were dressed in dark green cloaks, like General Niles's. These battles were much more recent.

The group continued into another drafty corridor, passing one portrait after another. Ethan didn't recognize anyone until he came to the last.

In a yellow dress, the young woman's long brown hair was braided and draped over her shoulder. A necklace with a silver charm, a unicorn, hung from her neck. Her vibrant blue eyes stared at the empty space above Ethan's head.

"Mom." He slid his hand into his pocket and fingered the very same necklace she wore in the portrait. This really had been her home.

Until this moment, none of this had felt real. But now, as he stared up at her image, Ethan's mind filled with the things his mother had said that, looking back, were all well-guarded clues. Like the time Sky's parents kept inviting them over for dinner, wanting to thank Caitríona for watching Sky in the afternoons. The answer had always been no. Caitríona insisted that they would ask too many questions. Ethan had always figured she was worried they'd learn about his curse, or her illegal residency in the country.

Now he fully understood how important it had been for those secrets to remain secret. According to Bartlett, his mother had lived under a death sentence if she breathed a word about this place. Even to him. It dawned on him just how lonely the last fifteen years must have been for her.

Everyone had continued on ahead, except General Niles, who remained next to Ethan. The room was so quiet, he could hear the general breathing.

"Your mother was my wife's best friend," the general said, looking up at Caitríona's portrait. There was a hint of sadness in his voice.

"Really?" Ethan looked at him.

Niles cleared his throat. "We should continue."

Ethan turned back to the painting. The image was so lifelike. It was hard to leave.

"Ethan . . . ," General Niles pressed.

Ethan swallowed the lump in his throat. "Yeah. Coming."

The others were waiting at the end of the passageway, in a drafty, dark room as large as Ethan's school gym. Pillow-covered sofas and large wooden chairs circled a fireplace that was so tall, Ethan could have walked into it without hitting his head on the mantel. The wooden shutters were closed, blocking out the daylight. The only light came from candelabras that sat on every available flat surface.

Ethan flopped onto a large chair, sinking into the cushions. It felt so good to sit down. He was exhausted. "I'm guessing no TV."

They stared at him blankly.

"Never mind." There was only one thing Ethan needed to know. It was time for the general to start talking. "How about we all sit and you—"

"I'm sure you'd like to see your chambers and get settled," Niles said, cutting him off.

"Honestly, I've got nothing to unpack." Ethan stood and went to General Niles. "Let's say we skip the room tour and you tell me where they've taken my mother."

Niles opened his mouth to speak but Clothilde cut him off.

"Julius, how are we supposed to believe that this is truly Caitríona's son, and that he possesses radharc? My husband never mentioned a thing—"

"I know this is a shock," the general interrupted sharply, "but King Tearlach knew Ethan had the gift before he was even born. Caitríona didn't run off. She was sent into hiding to keep him safe. I was asked to keep it in confidence for the protection of the realm, and so I did."

"What?" Ethan's breath caught at the revelation. Suddenly, the pieces of the puzzle fell into place. It all made sense now. His mother had to leave Landover because of him, because he had this gift.

"General, where is my mother?" Ethan demanded.

"After I speak with your aunt," he replied.

"That's not acceptable." Ethan wasn't going anywhere until he got some answers. "Captain Bartlett fed me the same infuriating crap and then knocked me out." The scowl the general gave him should have been warning enough to back down, but Ethan didn't. "Now unless you plan on doing the same thing, I want to know where she is and I want to know *now.*"

Seething, Niles eyed him, his lips pressed into a thin line, but Ethan wasn't backing down.

Scully touched Ethan's arm softly. "In times of trouble we must all have patience, Master Ethan. Supper will be ready shortly. General Niles will be able to speak to you then." Scully shot a weary glance to Niles, who nodded. With that, the Brownie turned back to Ethan. "I'd like for you to see your chambers and make sure they meet with your approval."

"Scully, I'll take him," Christian volunteered. "Which one is to be his?"

"Your father's childhood room seems appropriate."

"Christian," Clothilde barked. "You're not a servant. You'll do nothing of the sort."

Christian pulled the back of Ethan's shirt, yanking him from the room. "Come on. Let's go before she starts up again."

Christian was in such a hurry to get away from his mother that Ethan had to jog to keep up. They climbed two short flights of steps and then continued down a seemingly endless hallway. "This place come with a map?" Ethan joked. He was never going to be able to find his way back.

"You're smart. I'm sure you'll figure it out," his cousin retorted, and kept going.

Finally, Christian stopped at a set of double doors and grandly swung them open. "Your chambers."

Sun cascaded through three small windows as they stepped inside the biggest bedroom Ethan had ever seen. His whole apartment could have fit inside, twice. On one side stood a four-poster bed that could sleep a family of five, easily. Directly across was a wall lined with cabinet doors. There was also a sitting area with a couch, two chairs, and a small table in front of a fireplace.

"This whole room is just for me?"

"Of course. Were you expecting someone to sleep with you?" Christian teased. "Do you get scared at night?"

"Sometimes," Ethan admitted. "You would too if you saw . . ." The word "ghosts" stuck in Ethan's throat, his mother's warning never to talk about his gift echoing in his ears.

Christian's smug grin fell into a grimace. Ethan hadn't realized what he'd said until that moment.

"Sorry. Didn't mean that the way it came out." Christian leaned over him. "Look, if you want the gift, it's all yours. Seriously, you be king. I just want my mom back."

"Do you now?" Christian fisted his shirt.

What the hell? Ethan's entire life had been turned upside down. His mother was missing. Their apartment had been trashed. He'd been knocked out and kidnapped from the only place he'd ever lived. After practically drowning on the trip here, he had been thrown off a horse and threatened with disembowelment. And now his cousin was going to pommel him for what? A slip of the tongue? He had been tortured enough for one day.

He shoved Christian, hard. "Get out of my face. I said I was sorry."

Instead of pounding him, Christian smiled, causing Ethan to wonder what kind of psychosis his cousin suffered from. "Well done. You didn't cower or run." He swatted Ethan's back. "Those instincts will serve you well."

Ethan slid around him and walked toward the window, keeping Christian at a safe distance.

"Now, we must do something about those clothes." Christian opened one of the built-in closets and glanced back at Ethan. "It seems as if Scully knew of your existence. Try these." He tossed him a pair of pants with wide thighs that grew tiny at the ankles, and a long-sleeved white shirt with frills around the collar.

Ethan would rather be forced to wear Brock Martin's hand-me-downs every day for the rest of his life than parade around in clown pants and a shirt straight off the cover of a romance novel. He quickly tossed them back. "What's wrong with these?" He motioned to the jeans he had on. They were slightly damp, but otherwise in perfect condition, especially considering the fire-breathing beast attack. Hell, his new family should be happy. The spin cycle through the saltwater whirlpool probably made them the cleanest they'd ever been.

Christian tossed the pants back at Ethan and folded his arms across his chest. "They hang so low, I can see the tops of your undergarments."

"Oh, and these are stylish?" Ethan held the clown pants by the thighs to show their obvious hideousness.

"They're a little ornate. But they're practical. You don't want your trousers catching in the stirrups."

Since Ethan had no intention of getting back on a horse anytime soon, that didn't seem like an issue.

"What's with the holes?" Ethan held up the sleeve of the white shirt that had a thumb-sized hole on each cuff.

"The opening allows you to make use of a bow without interference from your sleeves," Christian explained.

Ethan held up an arm. "See, short sleeves. The perfect bow-pulling clothing." Ethan threw the clothes back to Christian. "I'll stay in mine."

"Suit yourself, but the general will likely have something to say about it." Christian tossed the clothes back in the closet and shut the doors.

Ethan walked to the fireplace and marveled at the sword mounted above the mantel. With a black grip, it had a silver half-moon-shaped guard and pommel. A thin fuller ran almost the entire length of the three-foot-long steel blade.

"My father's first sword," Christian said. "How are you with a blade?"

"Never even touched one."

"Oh. I'll speak to the general. He and I will start training you immediately."

Ethan cocked his head at the sword and wondered what one would feel like in his hand. Was it heavy? Was the blade sharp? His mother hated weapons of any kind. She said nothing good ever came from them, and the world would be a much better place if they were all destroyed. She had a point, but he still wanted to touch it.

Without a word, Christian pulled the sword off the wall and held the pommel out to him. Ethan hesitated.

"It won't bite."

Ethan wrapped his hand around the cold grip. Christian let go of the blade, and Ethan felt the full weight of the steel. It was very heavy, and the grip was too thick for Ethan to comfortably hold it, but it was still the coolest thing he'd ever touched.

"Your father really fought with this?"

"He did. Many times. Even when he was young, Landover was at war."

Ethan stabbed the blade downward then lunged into the empty space in the fireplace. "The general said that one of the other territories may attack because of your father's death."

Christian walked to a bookshelf next to the bed. When he returned, he took the sword from Ethan and handed him an old book opened to a map of Tara. Setting the sword carefully on the mount, Christian stood over him and set his finger on Landover. "We are here. And this"—he moved his finger over one territory—"is Primland. The two realms have been fighting for centuries."

Ethan stared down at the map, nerves tightening his chest. He rubbed his thumb across the pads of his fingers, which were still tender from touching Primland on Bartlett's map. He'd felt something unnaturally dangerous there.

Ethan set the book down. "Why?"

After pouring himself a glass of water from a nearby pitcher, Christian sat down. Ethan followed suit. He picked up a bread roll from a tray in the center of the table. His stomach rumbled in anticipation as he broke off a hunk and stuffed it into his mouth.

"Best to start at the beginning, I suppose. It all began in Ireland, shortly before our kind fled to Tara. Our ancestor Padraig Makkai served as Aire-echta, general for the armies of King Innes Traynor. It was well known that the king loved Clíona Ratigan. The daughter of Clíodhna, the queen of the Banshees and the goddess of love and beauty, Clíona was the most beautiful woman in the land. But unfortunately for Innes, Clíona loved another."

"Padraig Makkai," Ethan surmised.

"Yes. With the hasty departure of the gods and goddesses to the Otherworld, our ancestors arrived in Tara. It was then Clíona declared her love for Padraig, and he for her.

"As a favor to her mother, Manannán mac Lir, the god of the sea and the protector of Tara, gave Clíona Landover to rule, making her the first queen of the new realm. She possessed radharc; it was deemed Landover's monarch's essential trait. After marrying, Padraig ruled by her side, serving as general for Landover."

"Innes Traynor got Primland," Ethan guessed.

Christian nodded. "And he never forgave Padraig for stealing his love and no longer serving him. He swore Clíona would one day be very sorry. And since that day, Landover and Primland have been, shall we say, at odds."

"Over a woman?" Ethan shook his head as he ate another piece of bread. He held the tray out for Christian, who took a piece.

Christian fingered the bread and continued without taking a bite, "For centuries, after brief periods of war, things would settle down. They even tried an arranged marriage—Fenit Traynor's sister, Jana, was married to our grandfather Maximus. Fenit was a staunch ally, loyal to his sister, and kept the peace, until his sorcerer died mysteriously, and Sawney Bean became the sorcerer of Primland."

"Sorcerer? As in magic?"

Christian eyed Ethan with a concerned frown. "Your mother told you little of Tara?"

Ethan took a long swig of water. "She told me nothing."

"I see. Well, in each territory, there is a monarch, a sorcerer, and a scáthán—"

"A what?"

"A book of magic. Now—"

"Hold up," Ethan interrupted again. "So your dad had a sorcerer to, like, do magic spells for him?"

"A sorceress to be exact," Christian said, sounding annoyed.

That was a definite plus to the job. "Where is she?"

"Dead. By Bean's hand. At present, Landover is without magic."

"Oh." That didn't sound good.

"As Bean's power grew, a mysterious cloak of darkness draped over Primland. The borders became dangerous. Visitors unwelcome. They say the color of Fenit Traynor's eyes turned from green to black, Bean's mist consuming his body and soul. And then Fenit Traynor demanded your mother's hand in marriage to Bean."

"Why?"

Christian arched a knowing eyebrow at him. "Bean must have sensed something inside her connected to radharc."

"Is that why the Ravens might have taken her? They still believe she has something to do with it?" Ethan rubbed his palms on his pants nervously.

Christian nodded. "My guess is they believe radharc passed to her when my father died. I expected her to return any day, as well. What else was there to think? No one knows you exist." Christian paused, and then continued, "Now, when Grandfather refused to give your mother to Bean, war was declared, and they attacked Landover. Primland's armies went on a murderous rampage. Much of our biggest city, Coventry, burned."

"Since the Makkais still rule Landover, Maximus must have won, right?"

Christian took a sip of water. "Maximus was slain in battle, his head cut off, his heart ripped from his chest and sent in a box to our grandmother Jana."

"Are you serious?"

Christian gave a slow nod. "Afraid for my father's and your mother's lives, Jana secretly went to her brother and begged him to end the war. No one knows the outcome of that conversation because she died on the return journey."

Ethan dropped the piece of bread he had been about to eat. No wonder his mother was so paranoid. Her entire childhood was even more twisted than a Shakespearean tragedy, one in which the final act hadn't been written yet, and Ethan had a sinking feeling that this one was going to end disastrously.

"Guilt-ridden over the death of his sister, Fenit had a moment of weakness and left Bean without support. Although my father lost his sorceress in the final battle with Bean, his forces managed to overcome him. Bean was imprisoned in a cave high in the mountains of Gransmore. After that, Traynor surrendered." Christian finally popped the piece of bread he'd been holding into his mouth.

"What happened to Traynor?"

"Banished to the Isle of Mord for the rest of his life. His own son, Lachlan, took his place on the Council of Kings and cast the deciding vote."

As Ethan reached for his water glass, an overpowering rose-scented perfume filled the air, and a wave of bone-chilling cold rolled over him and settled in his chest.

When Ethan started to tremble, Christian sat up straight. "Are you all right?"

Ethan couldn't respond. His jaw felt like it was frozen shut. He scanned the room, trying to find the ghost, but it wasn't until he sensed frigid fingers tickle the back of his neck that he realized it was right behind him.

He jumped out of his chair and spun around to find an ethereal woman glaring at him. She had skin the color of porcelain, rather than dull gray like most ghosts. Her wild red hair hung lose to her waist. Her long green dress swayed as she hovered closer to Ethan. *Do I have your attention?*

Ethan nodded.

Oh good. You see, this—she swept her hand, gesturing—*is my room, and I'd like you both to leave.*

"What's the matter?" Christian pressed.

"Um . . . is there another room available?" Ethan asked, his teeth chattering.

"This one isn't good enough for you?"

"It appears to be taken."

"Taken by who?" Christian glanced around the room.

And I suppose this is to be your room? It's not bad enough that the only man I ever loved murdered me, and left me eternally cursed to a miserable existence, trapped, forever waiting for him to return and release me. Bastard that he is.

In Ethan's experience, a bad love life seemed to be the most common complaint from ghosts. He shot off his canned response. "Yeah. That's too bad."

"What's too bad?" Christian asked.

You men are all alike! the lady hissed, and flew out the window.

Christian grabbed a pillow from the couch and whacked Ethan upside the head. "Answer me."

Ethan swiped the pillow and hurled it back at him. "There was a ghost whining about some guy who cursed her and how she's stuck here. Apparently this is her room."

"You were speaking to a spirit then," Christian said with a note of finality in his voice.

Ethan walked over to the open window to warm his hands in the sun. "One with a serious bad attitude. Doesn't seem too happy with men at the moment. Think Scully would be offen—"

Ethan abruptly stopped as General Niles appeared under the window with the same soldier who had addressed the fat guy sounding off in the market.

Ethan crouched low so they couldn't see him.

Christian took a heavy step toward him. "What are you loo—"

Ethan held his finger to his lips, silencing him. His cousin kneeled beside him, listening intently.

"Seamus, I need you to watch over Ethan while I'm gone," he heard Niles say.

"Where are you going?" Seamus asked.

"To find Runyun Cooper."

Ethan had to cover his mouth with his hand to keep the exclamation rising in his throat from being heard. His father was alive? How could his mother have lied to him like that? All the times he asked her about him, for just a tiny bit of information. Ethan could hear her now: *It doesn't matter, Ethan. He doesn't matter.* But he did matter to him.

"They say the mist on the borders of Primland has turned Cooper. That he's gone mad and become a dangerous vigilante," Seamus warned.

"Vigilante or not, we need him to get to Bean's cave. The Ravens who took Caitríona are on their way there. We need to get there first if we are to have any hope of saving her. And Runyun Cooper is the only one who knows where it is," Niles responded.

"And what do we do if he kills you? I've seen him best twenty men, and that was before he was sent to the border."

"Are you questioning your father's skills?"

"Never, General. But a full legion should go with you. *I* should go with you," Seamus pressed.

"I can handle Cooper. I need you here, with Ethan."

Seamus nodded solemnly. "And what of Ethan's safety at Weymiss? Do we know who killed King Tearlach?"

"The poison in his system came from Ó Duinnín's brew. He's still insisting he's innocent."

"And the poison was?" Seamus asked.

General Niles paused before answering. "Bás bán."

"Not again," Seamus growled.

Christian's face blanched.

"What?" Ethan mouthed to him.

"Primland," Christian mouthed back. He ground his teeth together and fisted the grip of his sword.

"Ethan will be safe in Weymiss, so long as you keep a close eye on him," General Niles continued.

"When do you leave?" Seamus asked.

"At dawn."

"Why not sooner?"

"The Ravens are moving through Primland. By tomorrow night, they'll enter Gransmore and have to travel only at night. By my calculations, it'll take them at best three days before they reach the road to the cave. I need tonight to prepare. With Cooper leading the way, I'll get there in plenty of time." General Niles chucked Seamus's arm. "Now, let's get back inside before we're missed."

Once Niles and Seamus were gone, Ethan started for the door, only to have Christian pull him to a stop. "Where are you going?"

"To talk to General Niles. I'm going with him."

"That'd be futile. He'll never let you go. Landover needs an heir. Our people are frightened, Ethan. You must remain at Weymiss."

Ethan shoved Christian off and grabbed the doorknob. "I'm going whether he likes it or not."

Wearing a knowing smirk, Christian shrugged. "For sure. Go on then. Yell at General Niles again. He'll simply lock you in this room and won't let you out until the Council meeting."

Damnit. He's right. Ethan turned back. "Older and much wiser cousin, what would you suggest?"

Christian turned his head toward the fireplace, his eyes glazing over, then he turned back to Ethan. "We leave as soon as night falls, before the general."

"We?"

"If you're determined to go, which it seems you are, I can't let you go alone. Besides"—a slow tic worked Christian's jaw—"whoever took your mother had a part in my father's death, and I want revenge."

The door to Ethan's room opened, startling them. Scully entered, carrying a large tray of food, and set it down on the table in front of the fireplace.

As Ethan moved to close the door, he noticed two guards looking back at him from across the hall, and two more guards had taken up positions on either side of the door. Seamus had been busy. Sneaking out was not going to be easy.

"Scully, I thought we were all having dinner together?" Ethan asked, shutting the door.

"The general needed to leave on urgent business. I thought you and Christian might like to continue your conversation over supper here. Your aunt has taken to her room and does not wish to be disturbed."

"Of course she doesn't," Christian commented.

"And when did the general say he would be returning?" Ethan couldn't help asking, even though he already knew the answer.

"He didn't, sire." Scully walked to the door. "Do you require anything else?"

Christian came up behind Scully. "We do. Ethan and I are leaving shortly, and we need your help."

Ethan whacked Christian on the shoulder. "What are you doing? He'll tell General Niles."

The Brownie locked eyes with Ethan. "I am at *your* service, and yours alone, sire."

"Really?" Ethan couldn't believe it.

Scully nodded. Ethan breathed a sigh of relief that was short-lived for Scully placed a hand on his arm, and told him the one thing he really didn't need to hear.

"But I must warn you. The journey you're about to take will be long and arduous, and I fear one you may not return from alive."

◙ NINE ◙

An hour later, Ethan and Christian were ready. With guards watching the door, the best way out was through the window. Ethan secured one end of the rope they'd cobbled together from sheets and an old white satin dress he'd found in the closet to the bedpost. He nodded to Christian, and his cousin dropped the other end out the window.

"I'll go first." Christian peered out, making sure the coast was clear. He fisted the sheet with both hands, climbed out, then gripped the dangling rope with his knees, and slid down in one smooth move.

Imitating Christian, Ethan wrapped his hands around the rope and came out the window. With each drop, the rope spun and he had to stop to regain composure. Giving up, he let go and fell the last few feet to the ground.

"Graceful," Christian chided.

"Give it a rest. This is my first castle break."

Christian turned and started walking fast. Ethan tried to follow but tripped over the rope on the ground. Mortified, he jumped up, hoping Christian hadn't seen, when two arms wrapped him, pinning his arms to his sides, and hoisted him into the air.

"Hey!"

"You can't be out. General's orders." Ethan recognized Seamus's voice. The Niles family was really starting to tick him off. Ethan kicked Seamus hard in the knee but it had no effect.

"Stop fighting. You'll only get hur—"

Ethan heard a loud clunk and Seamus instantly released him. He turned to find Christian with a smug grin and Seamus lying between them, face-down.

"Thanks for the assist."

Christian nodded and sheathed his sword.

"He's not dead, is he?" Ethan asked.

"He's not, but we should hide him. Don't want anyone to wake him up too soon."

They each took an arm and dragged Seamus behind a row of bushes. After they set him down, Christian pulled out a small vial of yellow liquid.

"What are you doing?"

Christian grinned as he lifted out the cork top. "This will ensure he sleeps like a baby until morning." He carefully dripped three drops into Seamus's mouth.

"You think of everything, don't you?"

"I try. Let's go. Dawn will come quickly." Christian took off, sprinting along the wall.

Ethan trailed after him.

Don't be a fool, someone railed on him from above. *Get back in—* The voice cut off abruptly.

Ethan froze midstep and scanned the darkness, but there was no one there, dead or alive. He shrugged and hustled after Christian, who had vanished into the thick greenery along the wall.

Ethan heard a click and a creak. Christian leaned out from the bushes and held back the stiff branches for Ethan. He stepped into the thicket and saw a small wooden door that was ajar. Once through, Ethan found himself in the hedges outside the castle walls. Emerging from the trees, Scully walked toward them, leading Devlin and another saddled horse.

"Well done," Christian said to Scully as he handed him his horse's reins.

Scully turned to Ethan and passed him Devlin's. "I'll be sure to keep the guards happy for the next few hours with food and ale. You be careful, sire."

"I will. Thanks, for everything."

With a grateful nod, Scully hustled back to Weymiss.

Ethan checked the saddlebags hanging from Devlin's sides and found them filled with food, water, and a blanket. He slid his left foot in the stirrup and pushed off with his right, but he didn't jump high enough and landed right back down on the ground.

"Not a lot of horses where you come from?" Christian commented.

"Not everyone grew up in a castle." Slipping into the stirrup again, Ethan propelled himself up, grabbed hold of the pommel, and managed to throw his leg over the other side. He was up, but for how long?

Devlin whinnied and stepped side to side.

"Whoa, boy. Steady now."

"He's simply saying hello," Christian explained.

"Felt more like he was saying, 'Get off.'"

Christian laughed. "Come. Let's go find Runyun Cooper."

The night air was cool, and the moon cast an eerie, gray halo as the horses walked down a dusty path. The only sound came from the clomping of their hooves. Otherwise it was quiet.

Too quiet.

LA was a spiraling metropolis that never shut down. Nights were noisy and bright. Between the overhead lights, loud people partying on the streets, and blaring police sirens that screamed by every five minutes, Ethan had grown used to the disruptive chaos. In fact, the noise was comforting.

Here, there were no streetlights, only the moon. Fortunately it was almost full, but even so, it was hard to see more than ten feet ahead. Unsettled, Ethan was glad when Christian finally spoke.

"You must miss your mother."

"Yeah," Ethan said, keeping his eyes on the road ahead. "It's always been just the two of us."

"She left when I was very young. I don't have many memories of her, but I remember being quite sad when I was told she'd gone."

"I'm sure you miss your father."

"Well, there are things I miss." Christian stared off into the night, making it clear he didn't like the guy much.

"What was he like?"

"Strict. Never satisfied, always pushing. But then, aren't all fathers?"

Ethan hadn't actually thought about that. He'd never had a father before. "I don't know."

"What did your mother tell you about yours?" Christian asked.

Nothing. No, less than nothing. "That he was dead."

"I see."

Ethan's mind raced as he tried to wrap his head around the fact that all these years his father had been alive. He gripped the reins so tightly, his fingernails left marks in his palms. Nerves twisted his stomach at the idea of actually finding Runyun Cooper. What was he going to say to the man? Did he even know Ethan existed?

For that matter, Ethan had no idea what the guy looked like. His own appearance gave a few clues. Ethan and his mother had matching blue eyes, but the rest of him looked nothing like her. She had very dark hair; Ethan, dirty blond. And unlike his mother, Ethan had deep-set dimples in both cheeks. Those could have come from him. Maybe.

Then there was the one possibility he didn't want to consider. What if what Seamus said was true, and Runyun Cooper had turned into a sociopath? Ethan quickly pushed that thought out of his mind because no matter what, they needed his help to get to Bean's cave and find his mother.

"I've met him only once. Cooper came to see my father a few years ago. I'll never forget when he stormed into the main hall. It was the only time I'd ever seen my father look scared. Cooper was pissed. Apparently the guards were less than welcoming, and he took exception to their attitudes. He made sure my father was well aware which guards caused his ire too."

"What did he do to them?"

"Left them tied up to the bridge, without a stitch of clothing." Christian's smiling eyes darted to Ethan. "And it was winter."

"Nice."

"The guards were less than amused."

"Why was he there?"

"He'd heard rumblings of a possible assassination attempt. My father said the rumors were bollocks. He told him to leave and never come back."

"Why?"

"I don't know. They didn't seem to like each other much."

As the path wound to the left, the wind picked up. Ethan reached in his sack and pulled out a blanket, then wrapped it around his shoulders.

"Clíona, the first queen of Landover, you said she could see ghosts."

Christian nodded.

"So it's a biological thing? Passed from generation to generation like a genetic disorder?"

"It's not a family trait, if that's what you're asking. The grantor of that particular power is her mother, Clíodhna. She chooses the heir of Landover, even to this day."

"You seriously believe a Celtic goddess plays with our lives? That she can manipulate our destiny?"

"She did with you, didn't she?"

He had a point. "And why is seeing ghosts so important? It's a completely useless power. Zapping people with lightning like Zeus or Thor, now that would be particularly choice."

"Zeus and Thor are not a part of the Celtic pantheon."

"I know that."

"Then what is your point, cousin?"

"My point is there is no *power* in seeing ghosts."

Christian shook his head. "Not true. You can see the ancients."

"Who?"

"The past kings and queens of Landover. There are those who believe it is vital for a king to have their guidance so that mistakes of the past are not repeated in the future." Christian eyed him suspiciously. "Have you not seen them?"

"Nope. No old kings or queens have ever stopped by to chat."

Christian pursed his lips and fell silent.

Ethan took that as a bad sign. Maybe he wasn't what he was supposed to be. Maybe they had the wrong heir. Maybe the real radharc was given to someone else or would come to Christian like Clothilde believed.

"Look, it's not like ghosts are everywhere," Ethan explained. "The ones I see are usually here for a reason. They didn't like how they died, or they want to get a message to someone, or like the taibhsí in my room, they had a bad breakup."

Confused, Christian stared into the darkness ahead.

That only served to worry Ethan more, so he changed the subject. "Do all the kings or queens in the other territories have to see ghosts?"

"Only in Landover is that the requirement. In Kilkerry, upon the death of their leader, the Faoladhs hold pasáiste, a fight to the death for anyone who wants to claim the throne. Gransmore, it's based on popular vote.

Algidare, whoever has the most children takes control, and in Primland, bloodline."

"So in Primland, you would be king."

Christian nodded.

"What about Cantolin and Talia?"

"The Ravens inhabited the island of Talia on their own. They're considered unwelcome guests by most. They have a mistress who rules, but no line of sorcery. And Cantolin is a mystery to us all. The Cat Sidhe allow no one to travel there, and to leave means permanent exile."

After a few hours conversation had long since died. Ethan struggled to keep his eyes open as the horses maintained a steady rhythmic pace. When they reached the entrance to a dense forest, Christian came to an abrupt halt. Ethan brought Devlin beside Christian's horse.

"What's wrong?"

"Bramblewood Forest. Keep your eyes open, and follow me closely."

With an uneasy feeling, Ethan prodded Devlin to fall in behind Christian's horse, and the two slowly entered the forest. Bramblewood had the thickest trees Ethan had ever seen. High branches braided together over the path, creating a makeshift roof. Moonlight streamed through small openings, leaving a spotted trail to follow. It was beautiful in a terrifying and unnerving kind of a way.

Ethan hunched over as it dawned on him that this was exactly how victims in horror movies met their demises. With his luck, a masked, hatchet-wielding serial killer was going to drop from a tree and slice his head off. That last thought kept him looking up until he got dizzy.

A twig loudly snapped nearby. Ethan yanked on the reins, and Devlin halted. "It sounds like someone is following us."

Christian grimaced and glanced back. "I didn't hear anything, but I'll search the perimeter. Keep on the path."

Ethan scanned the dark trail ahead. "I'm not sure that's such a good idea." But Christian had already vanished into the gloomy woods.

Taking a deep breath for courage, Ethan continued, keeping Devlin on a very slow walk. After only a few paces, a subtle breeze lifted the back of his hair, sending chills up and down his spine. Expecting something lethal to leap out at him, he was pleasantly surprised when a woman's melodious voice sweetly sang, *"Techt baeg amhin. Techt baeg amhin. Techt baeg amhin. Techt baeg amhin."*

She continued to repeat the words, filling Ethan's heart with a kind of joy he had never experienced before.

"Techt baeg amhin. Techt baeg amhin. Techt baeg amhin." Her beautiful voice warmed his soul. An unfamiliar longing tugged at his chest. She was singing for him. Her overwhelming allure smothered every rational thought, and her message became crystal clear. She had been searching for him for a long time, and he had to find her.

"Where are you?"

The woman answered, repeating her gentle, hypnotic aria, *"Techt baeg amhin. Techt baeg amhin. Techt baeg amhin."*

"I can't come if I don't know where you are."

"Techt lom. Techt lom."

Ethan turned Devlin off the path, and headed into the trees as the music filled him with an unnatural courage.

"Ethan, stop!" he heard Christian yell, but he couldn't. *She* was calling for him. A woman more beautiful than he could ever imagine, she was his everything. He prodded Devlin until he was moving faster than Ethan had ever voluntarily gone on a horse.

The enrapturing song grew louder. A mysterious shimmering light on horseback came out of nowhere. And he knew he'd found her, until she smashed into Devlin, knocking Ethan to the ground.

▣ TEN ▣

Confused and dizzy, Ethan heard a familiar voice say, "Hold still!"
"Jesus, Lily! Are you trying to kill me?" Ethan snapped. The
ballad whispered in his ear, calling to him again. His head still
fuzzy, everything spun. He tried to stand, but she leaped on his back,
pinning him to the ground.

Two metallic objects slipped over the tops of his ears and clamped
down. Instantly, the sound stopped, and he popped out of the trance, completely baffled. Why was he off the path, and in the middle of the forest?
He reached for the things clasped to his ears.

"Keep those on!" Lily Niles's muffled voice ordered as she drew her
sword. "Glatisant calls for you." She kept her blade at the ready while moving in a circle around him, scanning the dark forest.

Ethan rolled his head, trying to clear the remnants of the hypnotic
song. "Who is Glatisant and why would she call for me?"

Before Lily could answer, a huge tree uprooted and crashed to the ground,
forcing them to jump out of the way or be crushed. His heart pounding
against his chest, Ethan got to his feet. His mouth fell open as an enormous
beast emerged from the forest into the moonlight. It had the body of a leop-
ard, the head of a giant sea snake, and was coming straight for them.

"Glatisant," Lily whispered in awe.

That was not a beautiful woman. Talk about a bait and switch. Ethan
backed up, bumping into Lily. "What is that?"

"She's a Questing Beast. Stay behind me and keep those winsa over your ears unless you wish to become her next victim."

As Ethan and Lily moved behind a tree, the horses snorted and took off. Glatisant rushed after them; as fast as Devlin was, the beast was faster.

Without his horse, Ethan would never be able to find his father. Besides, he couldn't just let the monster eat Devlin, even if he hated horses.

"Yo, baby! I'm over here!" Ethan called.

Glatisant stopped at the sound of Ethan's voice and immediately turned around.

"What are you doing?" Lily scolded.

"I have no idea. Run!"

As they sprinted into the thick woods, the beast tossed its head from side to side, knocking down trees, heading straight for them. Ethan made the mistake of looking back to see how close Glatisant was and tripped over a tree root. He crashed down on his stomach, the impact knocking the winsa off. Flustered, he ran his hands along the ground, trying to find them, but came up empty.

A low guttural growl emanated from Glatisant's throat. Panicked, Ethan got to his feet. He'd only taken a step when the beast's growl rolled to a moan that rose in tone and pitch, until it felt like a thousand needles stabbing his eardrums. He clapped his hands over his ears, but it didn't do any good. The pain pounded his head as though he were being hit repeatedly with a hammer. It was too much. His trembling legs gave out, and Ethan fell to his knees.

Unable to move, he watched in horror as Glatisant stalked toward him, crouched and preparing to strike.

Lily snuck out from the tree beside Ethan. With a gymnast's precision, she flipped forward, landing on her feet directly behind him, and slipped the metal pieces over his ears again.

Glatisant came up on her hind legs and swung her snake head like a battering ram. Lily saw and ducked, but Ethan didn't. Glatisant's neck barreled into his gut, knocking him ten feet, into a tree.

Ethan's breath exploded from his chest on impact.

Lily reached down and yanked him up by his elbows. "Move!" she said, and took off.

He raced after her as she darted behind a tree, then another and another. Glatisant matched every move and then shot out in front of them, blocking their path.

Lily raised her sword. "Stay behind me!"

Under normal circumstances, Ethan would *never* let a girl get hurt, especially for him. His mother raised him better than that, but these were *not* normal circumstances. A, he had no sword, or spear, or anything to defend them. And B, he'd seen Lily's moves and almost felt sorry for Glatisant.

"Christian!" Ethan yelled. "We need help!" There was no response. They had to keep moving. "This way." Ethan yanked a reluctant Lily to the right, heading back toward the path, but old venom-breath caught up easily.

She threw her head in their direction again. Together, Ethan and Lily jumped. Lily easily cleared Glatisant's neck, but Ethan didn't get high enough and tripped. He fell facedown. When he rolled over, the beast was standing above him, her mouth open wide, her fangs oozing milky phlegm.

"Get back!" Lily stabbed the creature in the back, ripped the blade out, and struck again.

Unfazed, Glatisant's long, thin forked tongue shot out. It wrapped around Ethan's waist, cinched, and jerked, causing him to do a face plant into the dirt.

Lily raised her sword, and brought the blade down on Glatisant's tongue, slicing it clean off. Glatisant stumbled back and screeched in pain. The part of the tongue still wrapped around Ethan's waist fell to the ground, and instantly liquefied, melting the dead leaves beneath it.

A bush next to Ethan rustled, and the thief from the market poked his horned head out.

"Ethan!" Lily cried.

Distracted by the Brownie, Ethan hadn't see Glatisant thrust her head. She was aiming for his leg. Thanks to Lily's warning, he scooted back just in time. Glatisant missed, slamming her upper fangs into the ground. With a wicked hiss, the beast pulled up and threw out her front legs, kicking Ethan in the stomach, knocking him flat on his back.

"Enough!" Lily roared as she thrust the blade so far into Glatisant's neck that the tip came out the other side, but still the beast didn't fall.

Ethan started to roll right when he felt something sharp scrape across his left leg, slicing through his jeans.

"Shit!" Ethan looked back and saw his blood dripping from one of Glatisant's fangs. Ignoring the throbbing pain in his leg, he got on all fours and tried to crawl away, but felt the beast's hot, fishy breath inches from his neck.

"Get away from him," Lily said, charging.

She slashed the side of the monster's mouth as Christian sprang out of the woods with a sword in each hand. He struck Glatisant in the back but, like when Lily stabbed her, it had no effect.

Glatisant turned on Christian. He took three steps back and tripped over a tree root. The beast whipped her head back and forth, knocking the blades out of his hands in opposite directions and beyond reach.

With her arms out, Lily slid in front of Ethan and Christian. Glatisant lassoed the three of them together with her long tail and then lifted her head high and unhinged her jaw.

Pinned together, they couldn't move. They could barely breathe. They were going to die if they didn't think of something fast.

Ethan looked back at where he'd seen the Brownie and yelled, *"Help!"*

As soon as the word came out of his mouth, a blur of dark shadows sped out of the forest. Glatisant's tail tensed and her body trembled as the distortion passed between her and them. She was thrown back with such force that she had no choice but to release them.

The blur slowed and came into focus. Three midnight-black steeds, almost twice the size of Devlin, each with a spiraled silver horn on the top of its head, continued circling.

Unicorns.

Just like the one on his mother's necklace.

The three steeds formed a protective ring around Ethan, Lily, and Christian that radiated an unbridled power. The unicorn directly in front of Glatisant let out a deep scream in warning and rose up on its hind legs, kicking. Glatisant hissed and backed away, then turned and hustled off into the darkness, vanishing, hopefully forever.

Dropping back down, the unicorn stomped and snorted, then the steed gracefully spun to face them.

Neigh hhmmm, the largest one whinnied and lowered its head. Ethan tentatively reached out and ran his hand along its twisting horn.

When the unicorn looked up, his gaze met Ethan's. He had no idea what to say to a mythical creature that had just saved his life. "Thanks."

Christian and Lily stared in disbelief.

"How—" Christian began, but stopped as one by one the unicorns took off, vanishing as swiftly as they came.

As soon as they were gone, Lily noticed Ethan's injured leg. "Are you all right?" She kneeled down and reached out to examine the wound when the Brownie peered out from behind the tree.

"Hey, you!" Ethan limped toward the Brownie with Lily and Christian in tow.

"Ethan, where are you going? I need to examine that leg," Lily ordered.

As Ethan reached the tree, the Brownie's skin faded to a camouflaging black and he too vanished.

"There was a Brownie. I saw him at Weymiss. He must be following us."

Christian paced the circumference of the tree, and then shrugged at Ethan. "I didn't see anyone."

"Me either," Lily added.

Ethan didn't see the point in arguing with them even though he knew what he saw. That Brownie was up to something, and he had a feeling it wasn't something good.

"Unicorns in Landover," Christian mumbled, wide-eyed.

"My aunt told me they died off long ago," Lily said.

"I guess she was wrong," Ethan said.

"I guess she was." She took a long step, coming next to Ethan. "Let me have a look at that leg."

As she bent down, she placed a hand on his forearm for balance and winced. Ethan's breath caught at the contact. From the top of his head to the bottom of his feet, every cell in his body felt like it was exploding, but strangely, it didn't hurt, rather the opposite. It felt like a light switch had been flipped, allowing something deep inside him to be released. His eyes locked on Lily's and saw hers seared with the same frightening intensity that he felt.

A sizzling energy ignited where her hand sat on his arm, then spread until it circled her entire body. All the while Ethan couldn't speak. Or move. Or breathe. His body was frozen in time and space.

The light emanating off Lily grew so bright, Ethan was forced to close his eyes. The heat in his limbs traveled through his veins, electrifying his entire body. And then it slowly subsided.

When he felt seminormal again, he opened his eyes and gasped.

"Ethan, what's wrong?" Christian asked.

Standing with her eyes tightly shut, Lily's golden aura now surrounded both of them. She too opened her eyes, and instantly the glow faded, then dissolved completely. Lily's frightened eyes locked on Ethan's, and she ripped her hand off him.

"You both are acting very odd," Christian commented. "What's going on?"

"I don't know," Ethan answered then turned to Lily. "What was that? Did you see that? Feel that?"

Lily shook her head, but her expression gave away the truth. Whatever had happened terrified her. She took two steps away from him and frowned. "I don't know what you're talking about. I didn't see or feel anything." She smirked at Christian. "Glatisant is still rattling around in his head, that's all."

There was nothing rattling around in Ethan's head. Something had happened between them, something preternatural, but she obviously didn't want to talk about it.

"Best check that leg, Lily," Christian said.

Lily bent but hesitated before taking hold of Ethan's calf. Both flinched, waiting for something weird to happen again, but thankfully it didn't. She examined the wound under the tear, pressing her index finger into the sore skin around the cut, hard.

"Ow! What are you doing?" Ethan tried to release his leg, but Lily refused to let go.

"You're lucky. None of Glatisant's venom made it into the open wound."

"Venom?"

"To paralyze its prey," Christian answered.

She dropped his leg. "It doesn't need sewing, but come. I have something for the pain and to prevent infection."

After Lily and Christian retrieved their swords, the three walked out of the dense forest and back to the path, where they found their horses huddled together.

Lily went to her saddlebag and returned with a jar of tiny pale yellow flowers. She poured a few in her hand, popped them in her mouth, chewed, then spit them back out. Disgusted, Ethan stepped away from her.

"Don't be such a baby," she said, grabbing his leg again. She smeared the soggy flower paste over the cut, and the pain subsided.

Ethan screwed up his face. "Thanks. I think."

"Lily, what are you doing out this time of night, in Bramblewood no less?" Christian demanded.

Lily glared at him. "Don't take that tone with me, Christian Makkai. You two shouldn't be out here either. If you must know, I followed you when you left the castle, and it was a good thing I did or this one would have been taken by Glatisant." She poked Ethan in the chest. Annoyed, Ethan rubbed the spot, wanting to argue with her, but as much as he hated to admit it, she was right.

Christian scanned the dark forest. "What was the Questing Beast doing in Landover? She never leaves her cave on the shore of Kilkerry."

"Mating season. Every ten years Glatisant claims another mate." Lily shifted her gaze to Ethan.

"Excuse me?"

"She wanted to marry you, Ethan," Lily added.

"I know what a mate is." Ethan was never going to get that decidedly unpleasant image out of his mind. "I probably shouldn't ask, but what happens to her mates?"

"She eats them, when she's through with them," Lily blurted out.

Ethan nodded. "Very romantic."

Christian pointed to one of the winsa, which were now hanging off the bottoms of Ethan's ears. "Do you have more of these?"

Lily walked to her horse. "Plenty. My brothers had a run-in with her the last time she was out, so Aunt Morgan always keeps four pair in each of our saddlebags." She lifted another pair out of her satchel.

"I'll take them. You should go home." Christian tried to grab them from Lily's hand when she snatched them back.

"You get these, and I get to go with you."

"Don't be ridiculous. You don't even know where we're going," Christian said.

"Oh, but I do. You're going to find Runyun Cooper and I'm going to help." She swatted Christian on the shoulder.

"No." Christian adamantly shook his head. "General Niles would kill me. It's too dangerous." He started for his horse, but Lily wasn't letting him get away that easily. She chased after him.

"That's the point. I'll be able to prove to my father once and for all that I'm meant to ride alongside him as my brothers do; that I'm meant for something more important in this life than being a simple healer."

"You're no match for what lies ahead," Christian said.

Lily's face flushed with anger. "Oh really? I'll take you on." She pulled her sword, challenging Christian. "I win, I get to go. I've bested you, what, ten times now?"

Ethan rolled his eyes. The girl never did anything the easy way. She had to have a decision by combat.

"You didn't beat me." Christian winked at Ethan. "I always go easy on the girls."

"If you say so." Lily slid her sword into her scabbard. "But either I come, or these go back with me." She took the winsa pair from Ethan, put them in her bag, and closed it. With her back turned to them, she said, "Beware, Ethan Makkai. Glatisant is a beast who likes to get what she wants."

Don't do it. Ethan pressed his lips together. *She's bossy and annoying.* With the smile of an angel, and the temperament of a German shepherd. She hadn't liked him from the moment she met him, and would probably stab him in his sleep if he pissed her off, but for some idiotic reason he didn't want her to leave. She had saved his life after all. "I think Lily should come."

"You've lost your mind," Christian retorted.

Yes. It was painfully obvious he had lost his mind, but still, he wanted her along.

"It's all settled then." Lily grinned then started for her horse.

Christian waved his index finger in Ethan's face. "Fine. But you'll have to explain her death to her father." Annoyed, he marched to his horse, climbed on, and trotted to the path.

"Shall we?" Wasting no time, Lily hopped on her horse and followed Christian.

Ethan rushed to Devlin, shoved his left foot in the stirrup and stamped down, then tossed his other leg over while yanking himself up with the help of the pommel. It wasn't graceful, but at least he didn't fall off in front of Lily.

He caught up to her, while Christian took the lead as they headed deeper into Bramblewood.

"You know, your father said he'd confine you to your house for two weeks if he caught you out again."

Lily glanced sideways at him. "Not quite. He said if he found me on the castle grounds. These are not the castle grounds."

"You like to live dangerously, don't you?"

"Always." She kicked her horse, moving ahead, and then looked back over her shoulder. "Come, Ethan Makkai, let's live dangerously and find Runyun Cooper."

❧ ELEVEN ❧

As Christian led Ethan and Lily deeper into Bramblewood Forest, Ethan noticed several warning signs on the trunks: STAY ON PATH, NO CAMPING, and then KEEP CLEAR. The last sign turned downright ugly: NO TRESPASSING BY DECREE OF THE COMMIS. ANYONE FOUND BEYOND THIS POINT WHO IS NOT A NATURAL INHABITANT OF BRAMBLEWOOD WILL BE PUT TO DEATH.

Ethan wasn't sure who the Commis were, but he had no interest in being put to death. "Christian, are you seeing these signs?"

Christian glanced back but kept moving. "You want to find Cooper, right?"

"Yeah."

"Then what's a little lawbreaking?"

"It'll be fine," Lily tossed out.

Ethan had a bad feeling Lily's words were going to come back to haunt them but clicked his tongue, giving Devlin the signal to continue.

Shortly after, Christian gave the order to find a place to make camp. Lily spotted a small clearing just off the path. As the horses came to a stop, the sun peeked over the trees. They'd ridden through the night.

Utterly exhausted, Ethan had no idea that getting down off a horse could be worse than getting on in the first place. Every muscle from his midsection to his calves was stiff, and his knees were locked in a semi-permanent squat. Worse, he seemed to be the only one with this problem.

Lily gave him an amused grin as she reached out and took Devlin's reins. "I'll take care of him."

"Thanks." Ethan walked stooped over, like he had a painful rash between his thighs, to a log with the hopes of sitting down, but his legs refused to bend. He leaned against a tree instead.

"Come. We need firewood," Christian said.

Maybe Christian was used to riding horses all night, and being attacked by a large, snake-headed monster out to find a new husband, but Ethan wasn't. He couldn't even remember the last time he'd slept. Not to mention he was starving. "It's all good. I'm not cold. You cold, Lily?"

She gave him a droll stare. "I'll go."

"No! You can't go by yourself," Ethan said, instantly regretting the outburst.

Lily stormed over to him until her face was inches from his. "And why can't I go by myself?"

Because you're a girl, and I can't let anything happen to you. But Ethan wasn't dumb enough to say that out loud.

Fortunately, Christian answered for them both. "Because it's too dangerous."

Lily took a step back to glare at both of them. "Don't be ridiculous."

"We're deep in Bramblewood Forest, and even though we're still in Landover, the border of Primland is very close. We all go," Christian ordered. He unsheathed one of the two swords he carried on his belt, flipped it around, holding it by the blade, and offered it to Ethan. "You need a weapon."

With a black grip and crescent moons on either side of the hilt, Ethan recognized it immediately. It was the one that had hung over the fireplace in his room at Weymiss. "But that was your father's."

"He would've wanted you to have it."

Stunned Christian would've brought this for him, Ethan waved his hand over the pommel then wrapped his fingers around the grip, fisting it. When he tried lifting it in the air, the tip fell, striking the ground.

"Well done." Lily patted him on the back.

Ethan glared at her. "I'm starting to regret asking you to come along."

"Don't worry. You'll be battling with the best of us in no time," Christian reassured him. "Pass me your belt and I'll put the scabbard on."

"That's the article that holds the sword," Lily added.

"Yeah, I got that."

Once Christian had Ethan properly armed, they started into the woods. Sunshine broke through the tall trees, and the branches rocked in the breeze, casting dancing shadows on the ground. The cool air smelled of damp wood and rotting leaves. So many tree roots broke up the ground, it was hard to walk without stumbling.

The forest brimmed with life. Birds chirped loudly, and families of rodents that looked like chipmunks, only much bigger, scrambled with each step they took.

"We need to find some food too," Ethan mentioned, holding his aching stomach. He'd eaten all the bread and fruit Scully had packed for him before Glatisant's attack.

"I've got a whole sugarloaf in my satchel. It's much better when it's warm, though," Lily said.

"Your aunt's sugarloaf? With bilberries?" Christian asked, perking up. Lily nodded.

Christian rubbed his hands together and walked with renewed vigor. "Let's hurry!"

Over the next few minutes, Lily picked up several pieces of wood from the ground and dropped every one. "This wood is too wet. Let's try over there." She moved to the right, hopping over the tree roots.

Ethan followed but stopped when he noticed a small wooden sign hanging between two trees, suspended twenty feet up. On it, in white, was the word MEIDHREACH. "What does that mean?"

"'Happy.' There's a village of tree sprites who call Bramblewood home," Christian explained. "Try not to wake them up. They're not as *happy* as the name of their little town would have you believe."

Exhausted, Ethan yawned. "Do we really need a fire?" His legs were cramping with each step. "I bet cold sugarloaf is delicious." He laid his hand on one of the larger trees, hoping to rest for a minute, when the bark gave way.

"Whoa . . ." Ethan cringed as his hand sank into a pool of gelatinous slime. He tried to pull it out, but the hole closed around it, trapping it inside. *Uh-oh.* "Guys?"

But before anyone could help him, a pint-sized woman, maybe a foot tall, with fall-colored wings as long as her body, and vine tattoos spiraling up her legs and arms, flew out of the branches overhead, screeching. Her tiny hands balled into fists, she plummeted straight down, stopping only inches above Ethan's forehead.

"What do ya think you're doin'? Breakin' into me house?" she shrieked. Her tiny, pointy ears poked through the long auburn hair that reached down to her waist. Ethan looked into her furious brown eyes, until she leaned forward, gifting him with a view of her extremely well-endowed chest.

Averting his gaze, he used his legs as leverage and ripped his hand out of the tree, taking a big piece of bark with him.

"Ahhh! Me house!" she screamed. "You're destroying it!"

Ethan's arm started to heat up. His fingers throbbed like he'd been stung by wasps. "What is that stuff?" He waved his hand, hoping for some relief, but it only made it worse.

"Stinging sap. Perfect deterrent for thieves—like you!" she snapped.

"I'm not a thief." Ethan wiped the slime off on the front of his jeans, but his hand still ached.

"It won't last much longer," Lily said, examining the damage.

Ethan didn't know if it was the sap's effects wearing off or the fact that Lily was holding his hand, but she was right, the stinging subsided.

A group of at least twenty sprites, in matching brown uniforms, dropped out of the branches and surrounded Ethan. Their three-inch-long arrows were already nocked and aimed at his head.

"Shoot him!" she bellowed.

Bows stretched and Ethan wasn't sure if he should duck or run.

"Hold!" Christian ordered. At the sight of his cousin, the sprites relaxed their bowstrings, but kept the arrows pointed at Ethan.

Christian stopped next to Ethan. He noted the missing bark on the tree then smiled at the offended sprite. "Suffie, Ethan simply made a larger door for you."

"You're not funny, Christian Makkai. This imp is going to pay for breaking into me house!"

"First I'm a thief, now I'm an imp?" Ethan was about to tell her off when Christian set a hand on his shoulder, silencing him.

"This is the way you act when the Makkais come to Bramblewood?"

"Forgive me manners, Master Christian," Suffie said in a thick sarcastic tone. She started a midair curtsy, but paused with a bent knee. "Wait, did you say 'Makkais'?"

Christian didn't respond. He lifted his hand off Ethan's shoulder and pursed his lips together. Lily's mouths dropped open. Her father's orders were clear. No one was to know about Ethan.

"He did. He said Makkais," one of the other sprites exclaimed.

Ethan stepped back behind Christian and yanked his arm, pulling him close enough to whisper in his cousin's ear, "What are you doing? I was supposed to be a secret."

"You are . . . ," Christian said. Glancing up, he saw Suffie directly above, listening. Christian cleared his throat loudly. "This is my cousin, Ethan. He's . . . visiting from Coventry."

"What cousin? You haven't any cousins. Unless . . ." Suffie moved to hover at eye level with Ethan. As she examined every facet of his face, her wings flapped double-time, making a sound like a spinning helicopter blade. "Caitríona? Yes. The whispering branches were telling the truth."

"Whispering branches?" Lily asked.

"For more than thirteen years the trees have told a tall tale about the day Princess Caitríona left with Captain Bartlett. That she was with child, and that the child would return to save us all. Never would've believed it if I hadn't seen the boy for meself. It seems that the tale was anything but tall." Suffie pointed her index finger at Ethan and pressed the tip to his nose. "Kind of like you."

"You're one to talk," Ethan tossed back.

"I'm . . . the . . . tallest . . . in . . . me . . . family!" She poked his nose with each word, then she stopped and sighed loudly. "I've lost my way. Now, where was I? Oh yes. Caitríona has a son," she sang, "and you possess radharc."

"We have a king," another sprite said.

"We don't!" Lily said.

"We do," Christian countered.

"Christian, what are you doing?" Lily fumed.

"Show me! Can you rustle up the spirit of me mum?" Suffie balled her fists again. "There are a few things I'd like to say to her!"

"Do it." One of the uniformed sprites flew down next to Suffie.

"This is me sister, Leah."

Leah could have been Suffie's twin except her hair was cut to her shoulders. "I have a few things I'd like to tell Mum too!"

Confused, Ethan glared at Christian. "You told her on purpose. Why would you do that?"

"Because the people of Landover need someone to believe in," Christian confessed. "They're scared and without an heir. At least they were."

Ethan didn't know why, but Christian's words unnerved him even more than riding a horse. "But General Niles—"

"The general was wrong. I know what our people need," Christian insisted. "Tell them. Let them know there is hope."

Needing a second opinion, Ethan turned Lily. "What do you think?"

For the first time since he'd met Lily, she looked indecisive. She raised her a brow and shrugged. "I suppose Christian's right. There has been no hope of an heir. Everyone has been panicked since King Tearlach's death, with rumors of invasions by Primland running wild. Maybe it's better the people know."

"Wonderful!" Suffie rose up several feet. "Hey! Wake up, ya sots!" she yelled, and flailed her arms. As tiny lights flickered on in the trunks of the surrounding trees, Ethan stomach twisted. She'd woken up the entire village.

"Suffie McEntire, what's all the bloody noise about?" a male sprite piped up, sounding a little like Captain Bartlett. "Now quiet down!"

An older, buxom sprite, also in a nightgown, popped out of a tree and came next to Suffie. "What—" She was interrupted by a yawn. "What's going on? It's not morning yet, is it? You know how Orin gets upset when you make such a fuss." She whipped around and examined Ethan's face. "And who might you be?"

"Myrna, this is Ethan Makkai, Caitríona Makkai's son. He's real. And he does have the gift. He's about to prove it."

Sprites poked their heads out of every visible tree and sped toward them, piling up in a mob behind Suffie, Leah, and Myrna.

"No, wait," Ethan said, holding his hands up.

"Oh, come on, boy," Myrna pressed.

Lily watched Ethan intensely, while Christian slapped him on the back, showing his support. "Go on now."

"Look, I can't just call up a ghost. I only see them when they show up."

The crowd groaned. Leah folded her plump arms over her chest and scowled at him. "That doesn't sound like radharc. You sure he's the right one?"

Disappointed, Suffie sighed. "That won't pass the test."

"What test?" Ethan asked. "No one said anything about a test."

"In Coventry, before all of our people and the Council of Kings," Lily explained, "Landover's heir must call upon the ancient monarchs to answer a question, a question only they can answer. It is the test of our true king."

"Or queen," Suffie added.

"Hasn't been one of those in a while, has there?" Myrna chimed in.

"Oh, get on with it!" a sprite yelled from the back of the mob.

Ethan had never been able to make a ghost appear. He couldn't just call one. "I-I don't think I can do that."

With sorrowful eyes, Lily placed her hands on her hips. "Are you sure?"

For some unknown reason, Ethan could actually *feel* Lily's disappointment, and it hurt. His chest tangibly ached from her emotions. It was debilitating. Heartbreaking, even. Why would it matter to her if he could or couldn't conjure up a ghost on the spot? According to her, she didn't think much of him as a king anyway. She had called him a diminutive.

Ethan pinned her with a gimlet stare. "I'm sure."

With that, all of the sprites but Myrna and Suffie left. Ethan sighed in relief.

"Have you tried before?" Suffie asked.

Ethan shoved his hands in his pockets. "No."

"Give it a go. I'm sure you can do it! If you're Caitríona's son, then I believe in you. She could do anything, and so can you," Suffie urged. "You've got to concentrate! Think about me mum. She was thrice as plump as Myrna here, with thick calves." Suffie yanked her eyelids, making her eyes freakishly bug out. "And scary big brown eyes."

"Who are you calling plump?" Myrna protested.

"Not you, Myrna, me mum! Sheesh!" She turned back to Ethan. "She had gray hair and a gloomy miserable scowl."

"And why do you want to see her again?" Ethan asked.

Before Suffie could answer, an arrow whizzed by, skimming Ethan's ear and spearing the ground next to him.

"It's Mum from the spirit world!" Suffie cried, and clasped on to Myrna's waist. "Protect me!"

"I've gotcha, luv." Myrna dropped behind Ethan with Suffie still clinging to her.

"Get down, Ethan!" Lily stumbled over several tree roots before landing facedown on top of him.

"Good idea." Suffie let go of Myrna and hovered above them. "He's a bit scrawny."

Under normal circumstances, Ethan might have enjoyed Lily falling on top of him, but these were not normal circumstances, and he wasn't about to take that lying down. He shoved Lily off, yanked out his sword, and scrambled behind a nearby tree, when another arrow sailed past, barely missing Myrna.

With a high-pitched squeal, she flew as fast as her wings could carry her plump body into her trunk, and slammed the door.

Ethan came around the tree, trying to figure out where the arrows were coming from. Lily and Christian took up positions on either side of him so that he was caged against the trunk.

"Hey! I can take care of myself." Straining, Ethan hefted the sword into the air.

"Stop talking!" Christian yelled. "You're giving away our position."

Another arrow pierced the tree—dead center.

"I think that was you who gave away our position," Lily shot back.

"That's not Mum!" Suffie bellowed. "Bloody Runyun Cooper. I see you. Stop shooting at me house! You heartless scoundrel. There are young here!"

Hearing his father's name, Ethan's chest heaved. *Holy shit!* The man really was alive, and trying to kill him.

Another arrow sliced into the tree behind them.

"I took a wee tiny bit of cheese from the man's staples, and what does he do? You monstrous . . . Ahhh!" Suffie flew into her home and shut the door just as another arrow stabbed it.

"Suffie, come back!" Ethan called. "We need to find him."

"Are you mad?" she bellowed from inside.

"Yeah, I guess I am . . ." Ethan slid the sword in his scabbard and took off, heading straight into the line of fire.

"What are you doing?" Lily called, running after him.

"Ethan! Stop!" Christian yelled. But he didn't stop. Christian groaned. "Suffie, I need you!"

She cracked the door and peered down at him. "Oh—" Suffie started, but stopped when she noticed two of them were missing. "Where is the heir?"

"Where do you think?" Christian retorted. "Running after Runyun Cooper. You move a lot faster than I do. Go! Please!" Christian didn't wait for her response. He took off after Ethan and Lily.

"Do I look like I have a death wish?" Suffie called after him. She shook her head in disgust and flew after them.

Hurdling roots, Ethan ignored the pain in his thighs and concentrated on not tripping. Another arrow soared at him. Ethan fell behind a tree just as it struck dead on. Runyun Cooper was a good shot, too good. At this rate Ethan would end up dead before he got to meet him.

"Impetuous boy!" Suffie buzzed by with a huff. "Follow me."

It wasn't easy to keep up with her. She flew about twenty times faster than his legs could run.

Gasping for breath, Ethan stopped when he caught up to Suffie. She circled above a small pond. The sprite moved toward the trees a few feet in front of him until an arrow tore through the back of her nightgown.

Suffie spun around and furiously flapped for home.

Ethan scanned the trees but didn't see anyone. "Ru . . . ," he said, and gasped, so winded from running, he couldn't get the name out.

Lily appeared next to him. "Have you lost your mind? That man is a dangerous vigilante."

"Yeah, and he's also my father."

"What?" Lily exclaimed, moving to face him. "Are you sure?"

Ethan gawked at the audacity of her question. "My mom might have lied about a lot of things, but she was pretty clear on that subject."

Lily winced. "Sorry. That was rude." She glanced left. "I'll look over here."

Ethan's heart pounded so hard against his chest, he was positive he was going into cardiac arrest. He was about to meet his father. That is, if the man didn't kill him first.

◧ TWELVE ◧

The air stilled and the birds fell silent. The knot in Ethan's stomach cinched tighter with each passing second, making him feel like he was about to puke. Where was he? How could he have just vanished?

"Runyun Cooper." It felt so strange to say his name out loud.

"I'm going to check the other side of the pond. Stay there," Lily bellowed as she ran off.

Ethan kept a careful eye on the trees Suffie had pointed at, but there was no movement. The only sound came from Lily's footsteps.

An eerie feeling settled over Ethan, as if he was being watched. He set his hand on the hilt of his sword, fisting the grip.

"Li—"

An arm grabbed Ethan around the neck, cutting him off. He struggled but stopped when he felt a cold blade press against his throat. His much taller captor placed his other arm firmly over his chest, locking Ethan's arms against his side. He couldn't move.

"Lay down your weapon." The man enunciated each word in Ethan's ear.

It wasn't going to do him any good anyway, so he dropped his sword.

Lily sprinted around the pond, heading back to Ethan, but slowed the minute she saw the knife at his throat. With her sword raised, she looked from Ethan to his captor. She gave a single nod, letting him know they had found who they were looking for.

"Runyun Cooper." Christian emerged from the woods.

Ethan tried to wrestle free, but Runyun tightened the grip on the blade against his neck. "Hold still," he hissed in his ear, then spoke to Christian and Lily. "Both of you, drop your swords." Runyun sounded calm. Too calm. He was toying with them.

Lily laid her blade at her feet.

"Kick it a little farther, young one."

She glared at Runyun and then did as he asked.

"And you, Christian Makkai? You'll not yield for the sake of this boy?"

Christian stepped to the right, wearing a curious smile. "You recognize me."

"I never forget a Makkai," Runyun spat.

Christian twisted his wrist, swinging his sword in a circle, then leaned on it, using it like a cane. "I don't think you'll hurt him."

"You're trespassing on ranger land, an act punishable by death. This is not a play area for children. This is the border with Primland. I'd have thought the son of a king would know that. Or perhaps . . ." Runyun paused, letting the word hang in the air.

"Perhaps?" Christian asked in a pompous tone.

"You came looking for a fight." It sounded like an invitation.

Christian's lips curled into a smile. "Not today."

"Then do as I say, or this one will pay for your impudence."

Christian made no move to let go of his sword. Instead he flashed a cocky grin at Runyun. "Everything you say is true, Runyun Cooper. However, seeing as how the one you're holding a knife to is your own son, I believe the odds are good we'll live another day."

"What kind of a trick is this?" Runyun gripped Ethan tighter, scraping his knife against his neck.

Ethan felt the sting of the blade's edge cut him. A trickle of blood ran down his chest. Father or not, this was beginning to tick him off.

While Runyun focused on Christian, Lily inched toward her sword. She rolled and seized the grip, then lunged, shoving the tip against Runyun's back.

"Drop the knife and let him go!" she demanded.

He glanced over his shoulder at her, and the blade loosened but only slightly.

"I said drop it!" Lily nudged Runyun.

He dropped the dagger and lowered his arms, releasing Ethan. Christian quickly picked up Ethan's sword, making sure it was out of Runyun's reach while Ethan scooped up the knife and turned to face him.

Well over six feet tall, Runyun Cooper oozed a defiant self-confidence. His brown leather tunic, worn over a white shirt and brown leather pants, bulged on both sides, probably hiding an entire arsenal of weapons.

When Ethan finally had the courage to look at Cooper's face, he was stunned at how much he looked like his father—the dark blond hair, the shape of his face, even the dimples.

Runyun's frown turned into a guarded grin. He must've seen the resemblance too. He stepped closer and stood over Ethan with his hand held out. This was it. Ethan reached out his trembling hand, ready to shake his father's.

"Give me that knife before you hurt yourself."

Apparently, Runyun Cooper cared more about getting his knife back than meeting his own son. Ethan's heart fell five floors, crashing into his shoes.

"Now!" Runyun added sharply.

Startled, Ethan took a giant step backward. Father or not, the man had that knife to his throat a few seconds ago. Did he dare give it back to him?

"Christian?" Ethan said.

Runyun raised an eyebrow and slid his glare from Ethan to Christian.

With a jerk of his chin at Ethan, Christian came around him to stand protectively by his side.

"Here." Ethan slapped the dagger's handle into Runyun's hand, hard.

Runyun locked his eyes on Ethan's, and watched him with an intimidating scowl while he blindly slid the blade into his boot. Ethan didn't move. He didn't breathe. He glared right back at him, refusing to show any signs of fear.

Runyun tilted his head in thanks and then started to leave.

Shattered, Ethan struggled for control as a million emotions battled inside him. How could the man walk away? He wasn't sure what to say or do. He felt the weight of Lily's stare and glanced back at her, hating the pity he saw in her expression.

Flushed with anger, Lily tightened her hand around the grip of her sword. She hurried around Ethan and reached out as Runyun passed, grabbing his elbow, pulling him to a stop. "Wait!"

Runyun spun hard, forcing her arm to drop. "What?"

"Mr. Cooper, I'd like to introduce you to your son, Ethan."

"Why do you keep saying that?" Runyun glared at Ethan. "I don't have a son."

"You do," she insisted. "This is Ethan Makkai, Caitríona's son."

Runyun's eyes grew wide with fury. "Caitríona? Is this some sort of a joke?"

"It's no joke," Lily fumed, standing her ground. "He really is her son, and yours."

Runyun's steel-gray eyes studied him, and for a moment, Ethan swore he saw a hint of recognition. But then Runyun pushed him out of the way to get to Christian. "Is Caitríona with you?"

"Yes and no," Ethan answered.

Runyun glared back at him. "That's not an answer."

Ethan folded his arms over his chest, trying to keep from strangling the asshole. The man just found out he had a son, and he had absolutely nothing at all to say to *him*. He'd pushed him aside like he meant nothing. Fine. *Screw him*. He didn't need a father.

There was just one little problem. They did need him to lead them to Sawney Bean's cave. He summoned every ounce of willpower he had left, trying to rein in his temper. "You want answers, you'll have to follow us. Oh, and pick up some firewood." Then Ethan turned his back on him, shoved his hands in his pockets, and started walking.

Ethan and Lily walked fast enough to keep a good distance ahead of Runyun and Christian. While they retraced their steps to camp, they picked up small sticks and a few fallen branches that were light enough to carry along the way. The pain in Ethan's legs from riding all day was nothing compared to the stomach acid that was burning a hole in his gut, and the raw sting of the cut on his neck, all thanks to Runyun.

He paused to wipe the abrasion with his shirt.

"You all right?" Lily asked.

Ethan looked down at his shirt. "Bleeding has stopped."

"That's not what I meant."

Unable to meet her eyes, he stared into the dense forest. "I honestly don't know."

She nodded and started walking again. Ethan was grateful for the silence, and the companionship. He was glad she'd come with them.

Once at the clearing, Ethan dropped the wood next to Christian, who immediately started building the fire. Lily went to get the sugarloaf out of her saddlebag. Runyun leaned against a nearby tree, silently exchanging awkward glances with Ethan.

A minute later, a steady stream of smoke billowed and they all huddled around the flames. Lily placed the sugarloaf on a small pan and set it next to the fire for warming. Runyun sat across from Ethan, studying him. Ethan let his hair fall in front of his face, shielding his eyes from his father. He ran his fingers through the dirt, picking up dried leaves and tossing them into the fire.

"How old are you?" Runyun asked Ethan.

"Fourteen."

Runyun brushed his palms together as he warmed them over the fire. "I guess it's possible. There is a slight resemblance."

"A slight resemblance?" Lily chimed in, unable to hide her anger. "He could be your twin."

"Ethan." Runyun shifted uncomfortably. "That's your name?"

When Ethan didn't respond, Runyun continued to stare at him. Whatever. He could stare all he wanted. Ethan had no intention of answering. A man should remember his own son's name.

Christian sat down next to Ethan and stretched out his legs. "Glad to see you two getting acquainted."

Ethan clenched his hands into fists but resisted the urge to punch his cousin.

Lily sliced the warm bread into fourths and held the pan out to Runyun. "Sugarloaf. It'll fill even the belly of a savage beast."

He took a slice, then held it up like he was making a toast. "The savage beast thanks you."

Lily held the pan out to Ethan, but he waved her away. It smelled sweet and nutty and would have been delicious, but he'd lost his appetite.

After Christian and Lily had taken their slices, she set the pan next to Runyun and came to sit on the other side of Ethan, so that she and Christian had him boxed in.

A sudden chill ran up Ethan's spine. A ghost was close. Shivering, he stood up and scanned the area.

"What's wrong?" Lily asked.

Runyun eyed him suspiciously.

When Ethan didn't see anyone, he sat back down and leaned closer to the flames. "Nothing."

Runyun took a bite of the loaf. "I followed you to your camp and found a few pieces of firewood to boot. Now, where is Caitríona?"

"She was taken, by Ravens. They're headed to Sawney Bean's cave," Christian explained. "General Niles said you knew the way. We need your help to get there first."

"Julius Niles sent you to find me?" Runyun shoveled his last piece of loaf into his mouth. He picked up the pan and held it out to Ethan. When he didn't take it, Runyun shrugged and started to eat the last piece.

"Not exactly," Ethan said.

"Well then, what exactly is all this?" Runyun fumed with a mouth full of sugarloaf.

Lily and Christian both looked at Ethan to respond. When he didn't, Runyun rolled his eyes and answered his own question.

"Fine. Then I'll tell you what it is . . . rubbish. All of it. You three show up in my woods and tell me that I have a son. And his mother, who vanished more than fourteen years ago, has been kidnapped by Ravens and is now on the way to the prison cave of a murderer? That doesn't sound a little far-fetched to you?" He tossed the empty pan back at Lily. "Thank you. That was quite good."

"At least you have manners, even if you are insufferable," she said. "But I didn't cook it. The compliment belongs to my aunt Morgan."

That seemed to catch Runyun's attention. "Morgan McKenna? Are you one of Riona's?"

"Riona Niles was my mother."

"She was quite a talented sorceress."

"She was a healer, not a sorceress," Lily insisted.

"Oh, is that what Julius told you? Lies, lies, and more lies. He's been in the service of the Makkais too long."

"Excuse me?" Christian said.

Lily's face turned white. She dropped the pan, barely missing Ethan's foot. "You're saying my mother was a sorceress?"

"She was *the* sorceress, the most powerful one Landover ever had. But she was no match for Sawney Bean. No one is."

Lily's breath caught. "My mother died falling off a horse."

"She didn't," Runyun replied, his angry expression turning melancholy.

"How do I know you're not lying to me?" Lily argued.

"Because I have absolutely no reason to lie."

Sadly, Runyun was right. But Ethan understood better than anyone how she felt. That indescribable heartbreak when the one person you trusted more than anyone in the world has lied to you. And not just a small insignificant lie, but a huge, life-changing whopper of a lie. It was earth-shattering.

Maybe Runyun was right about the Makkais and those who served them. Too many lies.

And yet, looking over at Runyun, Ethan couldn't decide who he felt more sorry for, Lily or himself. At least General Niles acknowledged her existence.

Lily flung a stick in the fire with such ferocity that chunks of charred embers spewed in all directions. "Are you saying that Sawney Bean killed my mother?" Teary-eyed, Lily knit her eyebrows and sat frozen like a statue, waiting for Runyun's answer.

"I am. But I believe I've said more than enough." Runyun stood up to leave.

"Wait." Christian jumped up and stepped in front of him, blocking his path. "If you could just help—"

"Move," Runyun snarled.

"We simply need you to lead us to the cave . . . ," Christian tried again.

"No, Christian." Ethan stood and turned to face him, keeping his back to Cooper. "He can just tell us where the stupid cave is, and we'll leave him the way we found him. Alone. We don't need him to come along. In fact, I don't want him."

Christian didn't move. "It's not that simple, Ethan. Only he knows the way. It's deep in the mountains of Gransmore. And even if we found the path leading to the cave, it's full of traps, ones we cannot get past without him."

"Why not?" Ethan asked.

"Because I set them," Runyun tossed out.

Frustrated, Ethan had had enough. He stormed down the path toward the tree sprite village, but as he came to the sign marking the entrance, an icy gust struck his chest, knocking the wind out of him. He fell to his knees, struggling to catch his breath as a musty smell, like old, dusty books, settled under his nose. The spying taibhsí by the fire had followed, but he still couldn't see it.

On all fours, he whispered, "Who are you?"

Leaves rustled from the direction of camp. Heavy footsteps approached. Certain it was Cooper, Ethan forced himself up and slipped behind a tree, out of sight.

"Ethan!" Christian barked, sounding worried. He'd just passed the tree when Ethan stepped out.

"What?"

Startled, Christian spun around. "Get back to camp before you get yourself killed."

"I can take care of myself." Ethan started walking again, but Christian followed.

"You've twice proven that's not the case."

"Yeah, well, why is it up to you to keep me safe?"

Christian ran ahead, and stepped in front of Ethan, taking his arm and forcing him to stop. Ethan tried to get around him, but Christian refused to let him pass. "You know why. Landover needs—"

"I don't care what Landover needs! I needed . . ." Ethan choked on the word "father" and shook his head. "But obviously I was wrong. Did you hear him back there? How could he not want to help her? Help *me*?" With a lump in his throat, and an ever-tightening chest, Ethan wasn't going to hold it together much longer. "I just want to be alone." He shrugged against Christian's hold, but Christian held tight.

"Of all people, I know what it's like to have a father let you down."

Runyun ambled toward them, mockingly clapping. "Touching, really."

Had he been watching the whole time? Mortified and majorly pissed off, Ethan felt the butterflies in his gut morph into dive-bombing vultures.

Christian released Ethan's arm, and turned with an angry snarl on Cooper. "What do you want?"

Runyun kept his eyes on Ethan. "I'd like to speak to the boy alone."

"The boy" wasn't sure he wanted to speak to the arrogant jerk *alone*.

Smirking at Christian, Runyun added, "That is if you don't mind, your grace."

Christian gripped the hilt of his sword. "I don't think that's wise."

Sizing up Christian's threat, Runyun arched a brow and unsheathed his sword. Christian pulled his in response.

Ethan shook his head at the egotistical stupidity of this entire situation. "Yo, people. Put the weapons away before someone gets hurt." Ethan touched the top of Christian's blade, then pressed, trying to lower it as General Niles had done with Lily's, but it didn't work. His cousin was too strong.

Runyun flipped his sword over and stabbed it in the ground. "I'm not going to hurt him." He took a step back and held his hands high to prove his point.

Christian looked at Ethan, who gave him a hesitant nod.

"Call if he gets too close." Christian sheathed his sword and started back to camp.

In a nonchalant manner, Runyun leaned his back against a tree and slid down the trunk until he was sitting. Ethan remained standing, straddling a root. He shoved his hands in his pockets, and lowered his head so his tousled hair fell over his eyes and he didn't have to look at him.

Instead of speaking, Runyun reached inside a pants pocket at his ankle and pulled out a small pipe. He chomped down on the end of it, holding it in his mouth. There was no tobacco in it. No way Runyun had to light it. Long seconds of silence only made Ethan's stomach tighten more. Runyun lifted the pipe out then chomped on it again. Was it a prop? Something he used to unnerve his opponents? Because it was working.

Through clenched teeth, Runyun said, "A piece of advice. That trick, covering your hair with your eyes, it's a good one. Your foe can't tell what you're thinking." Runyun tilted his head sideways, as if trying to peek under Ethan's protective shield. He lifted the pipe out of his mouth and pointed the mouthpiece at Ethan. "Only problem is you can't see what he or she is thinking either, or subtleties of their movements, both of which are extremely vital to *your* survival."

Runyun lowered his eyes to his boots. Without Ethan noticing, Runyun had extended his foot on the tree root Ethan straddled. He stomped the heel of his boot and a blade slid out of the tip that was well positioned directly underneath Ethan's most vulnerable body parts.

Ethan carefully stepped his legs together. "Yeah. I know that." He ran his fingers through his hair, pushing it out of his face. "It's just getting a little long, that's all."

"Of course. Should've thought of that." Runyun bit the mouthpiece of his pipe again. "So, tell me. That soon-to-be king over there put you up to this? If he thinks I'd ever believe a thing he has to say—"

"Why do you hate my mother's family so much?"

Runyun stared at Ethan. "Caitríona is truly your mother?"

Ethan opened his mouth to respond but Runyun raised his hand. "Never mind. I know the answer. She's there, in your eyes." He yanked the pipe out of his mouth and snapped it in half. "Unbelievable."

"No . . ." A woman's frightened cry whispered through the trees. Ethan immediately recognized the sound of his mother's voice. He looked right, then left, scanning the dense woods for any sign of her.

"The Makkais have a long history of turning my life into shi—"

"Shhh!" Ethan snapped.

Angry, Runyun stood up. "Don't you tell me—"

"Did you hear that?"

Runyun looked around. "I didn't hear anything."

"No. Please," his mother cried again.

Runyun's eyes grew wide. "Caitríona . . ."

Her voice was coming from the same direction as the pond. Ethan took off without looking back.

"Ethan, stop!" he heard Runyun yell.

A-plus for remembering my name, dickhead, but that's never going to happen. Ethan stuck to the path, passing the place where Runyun had cornered him with his knife. "Mom! Where are you?"

"Please . . ." Caitríona's plea echoed through the trees.

He could tell she was crying. "Leave her alone or I'm going to make you pay!"

You must go no farther, Ethan!

Ethan wasn't about to stop, not even for a ghost with a Scottish accent that sounded like Sean Connery with a mouth full of marbles.

You will listen! another angry voice screeched, sending chills down Ethan's spine, but still he didn't stop.

Brilliant white energy shattered the blue skies. It spun into a ball. With a loud crack it shot straight down, hitting him in the center of his chest.

Ethan fell forward, landing hard on his hands and knees. His back ached, and his lungs seized with each breath. He wanted to scream but the intensity of the pain was too much. It felt as if the bolt were rattling around inside him, and when it traveled into the pit of his stomach, the energy beat his insides, making it impossible to get up.

"Stay away from—" Caitríona's words cut off.

"Mo—!" He gasped. He had to get up. With a deep breath, he pushed the pain out of his mind, and somehow willed his legs up to standing. Then he started running.

More lightning balls materialized in the sky directly above, threatening to strike. In all the years he'd dealt with seeing, feeling, and hearing ghosts, they'd never been able to interact with him like this. Never tried to kill him. *What has Tara done to me?*

Inside his head, voices screamed his name over and over again, demanding he stop or they'd have no choice but to force him to. He thought his eardrums were going to explode from the volume. His brain ached, but even disoriented, he kept going.

Ethan zigged and zagged, but the swirling energy matched his moves.

Ethan. Enough! This voice he thought he recognized. It sounded like the voice at Weymiss when he and Christian made a break for it.

"Leave me alone!"

But the taibhsí had other ideas. The energy bolt slammed into the ground in front of him. It was a warning shot. A good one. Ethan stopped and looked up. If they hit him again, he'd be too hurt to keep going.

His chest heaving with fury, Ethan felt a surge of energy travel from the pit of his stomach, down his arms, until his hands shook with a powerful feeling he recognized. It was the same one he had when Lily touched him after Glatisant attacked. On instinct, his body reacted. He threw his hands forward and yelled, "Dul amach!"

Feral energy burst from his palms, and hurled into the sky.

Noo—! The ghosts' cries ceased as the sky exploded.

Ethan wasn't sure where the words came from, but the unwanted visitors were gone.

Relieved, he'd just started running again when the path abruptly ended, and the landscape changed. Gone were the morning sun and blue skies peeking through the leafy green hardwoods. Instead, a ceiling of gray clouds hung over a forest of the tallest pine trees Ethan had ever seen. The air was thick with the familiar minty fragrance, making it smell eerily like Christmastime at home. A heavy layer of black fog hovered between the timbers, making it impossible to see more than a few feet in front of him.

"Ethan! No!" Caitríona's voice echoed from somewhere ahead, deep in the pine forest.

Ethan stepped into the mist. The ebony vapor swept over his shoes, consuming him up to his ankles. The soles of his feet grew hotter and hotter like he was standing on a bed of hot coals, then the scorching sensation moved up his legs.

Ethan winced as his heart filled with an all-encompassing dread. The weight of what had happened to him over the past forty-eight hours hit him like a Mack truck. *My life is over. I've lost everything.*

But as Ethan stared helplessly into the thick, black vapors hovering over his feet, he remembered what Christian had said about a mysterious cloak of darkness draped over Primland, and how it had turned Fenit Traynor into a mindless zombie.

Ethan must have stepped into Primland. The mist was invading his thoughts.

Panicked, he tried to move back into Landover, but searing pain shot up the backs of his legs again, knocking him off balance. He threw his arms out, struggling to resist falling. If his hands became stuck too, he was doomed for sure.

"Mom, where are you?"

Runyun appeared behind him, careful to stay out of the mist. "Don't take another step! Turn round. Turn round now!"

"I can't get back."

"Leave him alone!" his mother pleaded from somewhere ahead.

"Caitríona!" Runyun yelled into the pine forest. "Where are you?"

"Runyun! Run!" Caitríona screamed.

"Ethan, take my hand," Runyun said, reaching out.

Ethan twisted until Runyun managed to grab his left hand. He pulled so hard he nearly ripped Ethan's arm out of the socket, but it didn't work. Even Runyun's strength wasn't enough to break the grip of the mist.

The drifting darkness suddenly rose to Ethan's waist. He clutched his chest and gasped at the despair, as if the will to live were being sucked out of him.

Long, thin shadows drifted between the tops of the tall pines of Primland, gliding with a fatal grace in his direction. Ravens. One led in front, and the other two followed, carrying his mother.

"Kill the boy! He cannot get in our way," one of the Ravens hissed.

The two carrying Caitríona slowed as they descended and then vanished in the darkness.

The leader headed straight for Ethan.

Ethan cursed and reached for his sword. He tugged the grip, but it wouldn't budge. It was glued to his side.

"Ethan!" Runyun pulled his sword, flipped it over, and tossed it hilt first at Ethan, who caught it. The hook-shaped grip was thin and worn down, tarnished black from use, and the double-edged blade curved to a jagged point that could cause some serious internal damage. The weapon felt perfectly balanced in his hand, a vast improvement from the sword Christian had given him.

Ethan looked back, hoping Runyun had some kind of plan, only to see him darting back into Bramblewood. "Runyun?" Ethan yelled, but he didn't stop. First the man calls him a liar, then he deserts him when he's about to be clawed to death by a psychotic shape-shifting bird. *Forget him.*

With a deep breath for courage, Ethan turned to face the Raven alone.

Christian appeared and skidded to a stop a few feet from him. "Cooper?" Christian called after Runyun.

Lily burst out of the woods, and ran past Christian.

"No!" Ethan yelled at her.

Thankfully, Christian caught her around the waist.

"Let go!" She wrestled to get away but he pulled her against his chest.

"Lily, stop!" Christian ordered. "The mist will take you!"

Lily fixed her eyes on Ethan. "Get back here!"

"Don't you think I've tried?"

The Raven let out a war cry that pierced the eerie silence, sending a shock wave through him.

"To hell with it." Ethan raised Runyun's sword. If he was going to die, he was going down fighting.

THIRTEEN

T he Raven descended from a hundred feet above to kill him. With shaking confidence, Ethan reached the blade back, preparing to strike. It was all about timing, like a batter waiting to swing. He had to focus and patiently wait for the perfect moment.

He heard Lily say, "Take a deep breath and think about something happy."

"You've got to be kidding me." He glanced back at Lily and saw her green eyes glowing a brilliant yellow.

Lily didn't react to his ire. Instead, she stayed laser-focused on the black mist that had surged, reaching his chest. She ran her fingertips over the surface, careful not to touch it. It swayed, dancing with her movements. Somehow, *she* was controlling it.

Christian came next to her. "Lily, whatever you did, do it again!"

"I'm trying but—" Lily slid her eyes to Ethan. "I'm serious, Ethan. Think of a warm, safe, happy place."

The whole thing sounded ridiculous. He had a dive-bombing Raven heading straight for him and she wanted him to be happy?

"Ethan!" Lily snapped, as the Raven's screech grew louder.

A safe place. A happy place. Ethan thought about his apartment in Los Angeles, but it didn't feel safe anymore, not after what those Ravens did to it. There was one place, or rather one moment in time. That Sunday afternoon he and Sky decided to watch the original *Friday the 13th*. Ethan hated slasher films but Sky loved them. It wasn't so bad; your typical he dies, she dies, until Jason's decomposed kid-body rose out of the lake and yanked the girl under. Sky screamed and crushed Ethan's hand so hard, he swore she broke bones. Then she clung to his chest, hiding her eyes in the warmest embrace he'd ever known.

"Good," Lily said, like she was channeling Ethan's feelings. "Put yourself in that place."

Ethan remembered the warmth of her hand and the way her hair smelled like strawberries from her shampoo. No one had ever hugged him like that, except his mother.

"It's working." Christian sounded astonished.

Ethan opened his eyes. The mist had retreated all the way to his knees.

But the Raven was less than twenty feet away, and with claws extended, she was out for blood. They were running out of time.

"Hurry up!" Christian pressed Lily.

Runyun reappeared, striding to the border with a predator's gait. He held his bow with an arrow nocked and ready to shoot. In one smooth move, he took aim and fired.

The arrow sliced through the trees with a slow hiss before it hit the Raven with a thwack in the right shoulder. She cried out and slowed, but didn't stop.

A glistening halo danced around Lily's head as her eyes lit up again. She held her palms up, and the vapor rolled back farther, releasing Ethan's calves.

"We need more time," Christian groaned.

Runyun fired two arrows at once, but this time the Raven saw them coming and dodged both. But Runyun didn't give up. He shot another arrow, nailing the injured Raven in the other shoulder, slowing her down. But again, she kept coming.

The Raven was so close, the wind from her flapping wings whipped Ethan's face. He feinted and then stabbed the sword, hitting the Raven on the arm.

With a loud shriek, the half-morphed Raven hissed and flew straight up, topping the trees.

Ethan had overswung and was forced to drop the sword to keep from falling into the mist. He didn't dare reach down to pick it up.

The Raven dived with stretched legs, aiming her three-inch talons at Ethan's heart.

"Lily!" Christian sounded the alarm.

With a frustrated growl, Lily pushed against the mist. It sank beneath Ethan's shoes, but not before the Raven struck, the tips of her claws piercing his chest.

Runyun fired another arrow, striking her abdomen as Christian grabbed Ethan's right hand, and yanked him back into Landover.

The Raven's eyes wild, she ripped the arrow out of her and tossed it at Runyun. With a last hiss, she retreated, heading back into Primland to the other Ravens, who had disappeared into the mist with Caitríona.

"Mom!" Ethan listened, hoping, praying that she'd answer, but it was no use. She was gone. "Damnit! How do we get around this?"

"We don't." Runyun stared into the dense pine forest. "Bean's shadow is too strong. It ensnares anyone or anything that enters. And it allows Lachlan Traynor's guards to see everything and everyone in the realm. There's nothing that escapes it or them. We're lucky Primland guards are not here already."

The dark vapor gently drifted in the breeze, making it look deceptively harmless. Maybe that's how Bean liked to play it, like a sleeping giant with the power to kill.

Christian stared at Lily. "How did you do that?"

Lily held out her hands and turned them over. "I don't know. I could sense the aura in the mist, and when I reached out, I could feel its fear of my touch. But it was drawing on Ethan's emotions, feeding from his anxiety, making its hold on him stronger. Once Ethan's thoughts turned to something warmer, the mist retreated, and let go."

Christian nodded. He paced the edge of the forest, pointing at the black fog that had settled under the taller trees that were clearly not in Primland. "Cooper, the mist has crossed into Landover."

Runyun gave an ominous nod. "It's crept into Landover at the edge of Bramblewood Forest in three places, and is moving toward Gransmore. Since Tearlach's death it has progressed quickly. It's preparing. Primland is preparing, but for what, I do not know."

Christian pinned him with a fateful stare. "I will speak to General Niles as soon as we return to Weymiss."

"And when will that be?" Runyun asked.

"After we find my mother," Ethan answered. He rubbed the small puncture wounds from the Raven's claws. They hurt, but not nearly as bad as having lost his mother again. "I should've let them take me. Maybe I could have fought them off and freed her."

"That would have meant certain death." Runyun slung his bow over his shoulder. "If they're trying to find Bean's cave, they have a very long way to go. First, Primland. Then into Gransmores, where they'll have to move at night to avoid being seen. Fomorians have a deep-seated hatred of Ravens. King Fearghus will kill them if they're spotted. And even if they get as far as the mountain where the cave is hidden, they'll have to traverse on foot. Protective spells keep anything from flying overhead. In fact, charms make it impossible to get up the road to the cave at all."

"That's what General Niles said," Ethan commented.

"And the Ravens haven't hurt Caitríona, so they must need her for something," Christian added.

That made sense. "What?"

"I don't know," Christian responded.

Runyun scooped up his quiver. "No matter. First course of action is to get to the cave before they do. We can easily beat them there."

"Hold on." Ethan eyed Cooper. "We? You're going to help us now?"

"A man can change his mind, can't he?" Runyun clapped him on the back, hard. "Head back to your camp. I'll be there in a few minutes."

As soon as Runyun was gone, Christian started walking, but Ethan didn't move. He needed a minute to himself to think. His mother's frightened cries still haunted him. How was he going to get her away from the Ravens? Cooper was coming with him. That was a plus, but also terrifying. Ethan had no idea how to talk to him, and from what he'd seen so far, the guy was cold, grumpy, short-tempered, basically an asshole. But what choice did he have? He needed Runyun, and from the looks of it, Runyun wanted to save his mother too.

A series of pounding knocks on Maggie's front door startled Bartlett awake. Groaning, he rolled over on his side. Someone had better have died for them to be knocking like that.

Bartlett reached for his eye patch as two identical heads with mops of red hair and beady little brown eyes poked in his bedroom door. After being gone for almost fifteen years, he'd come home to find his only daughter, Maggie, had not only married, but was now mother to five, the youngest of which was a pair of identical twins of whom Bartlett could remember only one of their names.

"One of those heads belongs to Owen," Bartlett grunted, sliding on his patch.

Two boys in blue pants and yellow shirts crawled into the small room roaring like wild animals.

"I'm Owen," the one on the left said, thumbing his chest.

"And I'm Ronan," the one on the right added.

Bartlett arched a brow. Mirror twins. "Well, forget it. I'll never know which is which so I'll call you both Roo-wen."

The boys screwed up their faces, shrugged, and then went back to roaring and snarling.

With a sigh he felt all the way to his core, Bartlett sat up and glanced around the room. This had been his son Jesper's childhood room, but nothing remained from those days, only clean white walls and wooden floors. Maggie had packed up Jesper's things and put them who-knows-where. Not even the rug Bartlett brought back for his son from his one trip to Cantolin remained. There was only the bed, a night table, and a small wardrobe, none of which had been there when he left.

Part of him was grateful Mags had the courage to make use of the room; another part was furious. He would've preferred the comfort of seeing his son's room left untouched.

"You can't go back there!" Bartlett heard Maggie shout from the kitchen.

The boys snarled again loudly as they tackled each other on the floor next to the bed.

"Hush!" Bartlett ordered the twins.

"I've told you. My father is sleeping," Maggie said sternly.

"I understand, but we must see him. It's urgent." It was General Niles.

"H-hi, Seamus," the oldest girl said. Bartlett couldn't remember her name either. Perhaps he shouldn't have had that last pitcher of ale last night.

One twin turned to the other. "Why does Danielle say hi like that to Seamus Niles?"

"Because she l-likes him," the other one answered, imitating Danielle.

"Ewwww," the first said, and then made gagging noises.

Bartlett scoffed. He could make a fortune off these two in television if they lived in Los Angeles.

"Danielle, go get breakfast for the twins," Bartlett heard Maggie say. "Ronan? Owen? Now where did they go?"

The twins scurried out the door, slamming it shut behind them.

Bartlett kicked off his perfectly warmed covers and stretched his arms over his head. Every limb ached. Yawning, he raked a hand through his matted hair. Tangling with Nucky had sapped every bit of strength he had left.

Tea. He needed very strong tea.

He stood up and peeked out the window at the height of the sun. Early morning. Not yet eight.

"He's absolutely exhausted and needs rest, General Niles."

Hearing his daughter's whipping tongue, Bartlett knew he needed to rescue the general. He shuffled to the bedroom door, cracked it open, and bellowed in a gruff voice, "General, what's all the hoo-ha?"

"Excuse us." General Niles and Seamus pushed past Maggie and hurried through the kitchen toward the hallway, and Captain Bartlett's room.

Maggie didn't give up. Her temper flaring, she stormed after them, her flour-covered yellow dress sweeping the floor, her long red hair tied back in a ponytail, bouncing with each stomp. "General!"

As they approached his room, the captain noticed Seamus held an ice sack to the back of his head.

"What's the little scrapper done now?" Bartlett huffed, opening the door wide.

Niles approached with a stern frown. "He escaped, and is on his way to find his father."

Bartlett pressed the thick of his palm to his visible eye. "Impetuous. Didn't I warn you, General?"

"You did," Niles said, sounding contrite. "But the boy is smart. And bold. And truthfully, will likely make a good . . ." The general paused. He glanced over his shoulder and saw Maggie within earshot. Giving her a slight smile, he returned his gaze to Bartlett and said, "Leader one day. That is, if he lives that long."

"He do that to you, Seamus?" Bartlett asked.

"No. Christian . . . I think," Seamus said through gritted teeth.

"Seamus caught Ethan when he came through his window but was knocked unconscious. Christian's horse is gone, as is Ethan's," Niles explained. "Captain, I know Maggie needs you here, and you likely have much to catch up on in regard to the fleet, but I believe it would be best—"

"If I came with you."

"When we catch up to them, I can send Ethan home with you and I'll continue on with Cooper."

Bartlett nodded. "But when I get my hands on that lad"—Bartlett tensed his hands, choking air—"his mother coddled him too much."

"Perhaps. Although I'm utterly astonished that Christian would do something so foolhardy," Niles added.

"At least Christian is well trained. He'll be some help in keeping Ethan safe, that is . . ."

"That is what?" Bartlett asked Seamus.

"Unless they manage to actually find Runyun Cooper, and the man leads them into Gransmore to the cave before you two can catch them. King Fearghus will not be pleased with the trespass. He'll likely lock Ethan up."

The general swore before glaring at Seamus.

Bartlett nodded. "I'll get dressed."

"You will not!" Maggie parted Seamus and the general, entering the room. She held a wooden spatula in her hand like it was a weapon and waved it at Bartlett. "You promised to be here. The king is dead. There is no heir. No king. Or queen. And no sorceress. All of Landover is in a tizzy." She was practically shrieking. Bartlett had never seen her so frightened, and his Maggie was never afraid of anything. "The people are massing in Coventry. My husband, as well as the other members of Landover's Commis, is there, trying to keep the peace in the panic-filled streets. Not to mention if the rumors are true, it's only a matter of time before Primland invades."

Maggie took a deep breath, folded her arms over her chest, and glared at Bartlett. "Now, I don't know who this Ethan is, but for sure the general can manage to find him without you."

"Maggie, you shouldn't be listening to private conversations," Bartlett huffed.

She set her hands on her hips. "This is my house. I'll listen to any conversation in it."

General Niles grimaced at Bartlett. "Seamus and I'll wait for you in the kitchen." The two hustled out of the room before succumbing to any more of Maggie's wrath.

Once Bartlett was alone with his daughter, he turned a sincere eye on her. "Maggie, I have to go."

She shook her head as tears formed in her eyes. "You promised to stay."

"I know I did. But the boy—"

"You're saying this person is more important to you than the safety of your own grandchildren? Duncan can't come home until after the Council meeting. If Primland invades, I can't protect . . ." Maggie choked, unable to finish her sentence.

Bartlett pulled her to him and hugged her. "Mags, I will be back before anything happens. I will be here for you and my grandbabies. But I must go with General Niles."

Maggie took a step back, wiped her tears, and cleared her throat. "Who exactly is this Ethan?"

Bartlett glared out the window with fury in his eye. "A foolish young man. And if he is still alive when I find him, he's going to wish he wasn't."

FOURTEEN

It took only minutes to stomp out the fire and pack up. Runyun returned with two long swords sheathed on his back forming an X. A foot-long thin scabbard hung from his waist, and was tied with a leather strap to his right leg. The grip looked like a set of brass knuckles, and the cross-guard's edges curved to a sharp point, forming a U shape that was half as long as the blade. It was the strangest sword Ethan had ever seen.

His horse carried four bows, four quivers packed with arrows, and two more long swords mounted on each side of his saddle, and a tarnished and dented silver shield. Unlike General Niles, nothing on Runyun Cooper marked him as being from Landover.

The four mounted their horses and turned to Runyun, waiting instruction since he was the only one who knew where they were going.

"We've got a day's ride through the backside of Bramblewood to the border of Gransmore. Follow me closely. I'll move quickly until we get to the paths that lead away from the Primland border." He kicked his horse and, to Ethan's dismay, took off at a full gallop.

"After you, Ethan." Christian smacked Devlin's backside and Ethan's horse sped off after Runyun.

"Christian! I'm going to kill you!" Ethan bent over and clung to Devlin's neck, praying not to fall off. General Niles hadn't been kidding. The horse could haul ass.

Lily galloped her horse until she came beside him. "You've fought off

Glatisant, and Ravens, and even stepped over the border of Primland into the dark mist!" she shouted over the pounding hoofbeats.

"And your point is?" Ethan shouted back.

"How can you be afraid of a galloping horse?"

Furious at her, he was even madder at himself. They needed to hurry, but he had no idea how he was going to stay on Devlin at a trot, let alone a full gallop.

To Ethan's chagrin, Runyun turned his horse and came back. Once he was close enough, he grabbed Devlin's reins, and with an elongated "ho" pulled him to a stop.

"Thanks," Ethan said, relieved.

"Sit taller!" Runyun smacked him on the back, hard.

"Cut it out!" Mortified, Ethan shuffled one hand at a time up Devlin's neck until he sat upright.

"How can Caitríona's son not know how to ride a horse? She was a better rider than I," Runyun scoffed, igniting Ethan's anger, not only at Cooper but at his mother as well.

Maybe if she had bothered to tell him that riding would be important one day, he would have stuck with the lessons. None of which he was ever going to say to Runyun Cooper. He'd called Ethan Caitríona's son. The man still didn't believe Ethan was his. "I don't need to explain anything to you."

"Fine, but you do need to move at a faster pace than a walk if we're ever going to get where we're going." Runyun bit his lower lip, trying to keep his own temper in check. "Keep a tight grip with your knees, relax your upper body, and lean slightly back with the horse's stride. I'm going to pick up the pace. If you come behind me, your horse will follow mine. Focus on feeling the horse's rhythm. You won't need to worry about steering. Understand?"

Irritated, Ethan nodded even though he still wasn't entirely sure what the guy was talking about.

Runyun kicked his horse, and as if Devlin had understood their conversation, he fell in behind Runyun's without Ethan having to prod him. Runyun stayed at a canter, one gear slower than gallop, which to Ethan's surprise was actually pretty comfortable.

As they headed south, away from Primland, the path twisted around the base of several tall mountains, and the trees spread farther apart.

A frightening high-pitched stuttered whine rang out from the branches above. Another howl responded. Seconds later, several sets of big round red eyes peered down at them.

"Runyun?" Ethan called.

"Keep quiet," he snapped. Runyun threw on his cloak and raised the hood, covering his head while he kept a steady pace.

Coming out of the shadows of the leaves, an animal similar to a baboon, with a long, thin snout and rust-colored fur, climbed down the trunk and growled in Ethan's face, revealing a mouth full of razor-sharp teeth.

Startled, Ethan flinched.

Metal scraped leather as Christian and Lily pulled their swords.

"Don't react. They won't attack unless provoked. Put the weapons away," Runyun instructed, trying to keep his voice low.

The animal in the tree leaped to the next, following them.

"What are they?" Ethan asked.

"Milcai. Spies for Gransmore. They keep watch from the trees on the border, and report back on anyone they believe to be an enemy."

Ethan hunkered down. "Should we all cover up?"

"Have you done something to offend Gransmore?" Runyun asked, his tone thick with sarcasm.

Since Ethan had been in Tara for only one day, he was reasonably sure he was in the clear. "Don't think so."

"How about your grace or you, daughter of Julius and Riona? Offend King Fearghus or Queen Cethlenn?"

"I didn't," Lily answered.

"Not that I know of," Christian responded

"Good. Then you won't raise suspicion."

"But you would?" Ethan asked.

Runyun glanced over his shoulder at Ethan. "Let's see if we can't put some distance between us and them." Runyun turned east, leading the horses off the path and into the dense woods, heading farther into Landover, away from the Milcais' prying eyes.

As the air grew chillier, and the skies darker, Runyun led them into a small clearing. "We'll stop here for the night."

The twenty-foot circular space had a rock ring in the center that was three feet across and filled with old ashes. Large logs were set fireside. There was even a small mound of hay for the horses to eat and a wooden bin filled with rainwater for them to drink.

"It looks like the spot belongs to someone," Lily commented.

"It does. It belongs to me," Runyun responded. "Now, if there are no other questions, let's get the horses settled."

The man had all the warmth of a rattlesnake.

After the horses had been taken care of, they set their saddles on top of one of the logs and started to make camp.

"Lily, got any more of Morgan's sugarloaf?" Runyun asked.

She shook her head.

"There's a stream over there." Reaching behind one of the logs, he pulled out a long stick with a sharp point and held it out to her. "See if you and Christian can manage to catch us a meal."

Lily folded her arms across her chest, refusing to take it. "I don't eat meat."

"Then I guess you'll starve," Christian said, snatching the spear.

"Why don't you eat meat?" Ethan asked her.

"Because it's barbaric!"

"You don't eat meat, but you have no trouble waving that thing in people's faces?" Ethan pointed to her sword.

Lily tossed him a teasing smile. "I like animals."

"Sorry. Should've guessed. Go with Christian. You'll find stonecrop along the river's edge. But stay together." Runyun narrowed his eyes on Christian. "Don't know what might be lurking."

Christian nodded, and fisted the grip of his swords as he and Lily walked off, leaving Ethan alone with Runyun.

"Lily descends from Druids. That's why she doesn't eat meat," Runyun explained, gathering small sticks to build a fire.

He continued when he saw Ethan's confused expression. "The Druids were what the high priests and priestesses were called during ancient times. They had magic. Morgan and Riona, both Druids, come from an extremely skilled family, and those who wield magic don't use it to take lives."

Ethan started piling blankets next to the logs. "Maybe someone should explain that to Lily."

"That would be a futile task. Although she's looks deceptively like her mother, she seems as stubborn and bullheaded as her father."

"Hey. Back off. Yeah, she's stubborn and bullheaded, but she's saved my life more than once since I got here."

Runyun stopped and looked up at Ethan with an infuriating grin. "I didn't realize I'd struck a nerve."

"You didn't strike a nerve." Not wanting to continue this conversation with Runyun, he diverted the conversation. "You just don't like General Niles."

"Julius and I agree to disagree, on everything. His way of dealing with an idiot king is to do whatever he's told."

"And your way of dealing with an idiot king?"

"I believe my banishment to the Primland border is a clear indicator that I tend to make my opinions known." Runyun placed a handful of sticks into the center of the rock circle.

Ethan sat down on a stump and stretched his sore legs. "You said Druids don't use magic to kill. Bean is a sorcerer, and they say he's killed many."

"That's what makes him so dangerous." Runyun stacked the sticks into a pyramid shape. "He doesn't adhere to Druid law. I don't believe he's Druid at all."

"Then what is he?"

Runyun tilted his head to look at Ethan. "Don't know. I've seen him slit the throats of his enemies, cut out their hearts and eat them with ritualistic lust. On his last jaunt through Landover, he almost got mine." Runyun lifted the left side of his shirt, revealing a long jagged scar than ran the length of his pectoral muscle, directly over his heart.

Shocked, Ethan's mouth fell open.

"Being turned is much, much worse."

"Turned?"

"When he wants to keep someone alive for his use. They call it caod. Neither alive, nor dead. His touch is like the aura over Primland, only a hundred times worse, filling captured souls with absolute terror and indescribable pain before he takes over their minds." Runyun stared at the sticks in his hands. His eyes glossed over as if he was reliving something. "We were lucky to get him locked away when we did."

"What if we're not in time and the Ravens let him out?"

"There are only two who know how to open the cave. One is dead."

"And the other?"

"You're looking at him." He tossed Ethan a cocky grin. "He won't get out." He sounded a little too sure for Ethan's taste.

As Runyun layered on more twigs, he glanced over at Ethan. "This fire won't build itself. Make yourself useful. Find some larger pieces of wood."

"Sure." Ethan scrounged the perimeter of the clearing, collecting an armful. He stacked the wood next to Runyun, before sitting back down.

Runyun began stuffing dried leaves into the center of the teepee of twigs. Ethan kneeled down to help, when Runyun stopped and eyed him. "You do look like me."

It sounded like an accusation. Or was that Runyun's pathetic attempt at acknowledging he was Ethan's father? Like Ethan's physical appearance somehow validated that Runyun was in fact the sperm donor? That Ethan hadn't been lying this whole time?

Either way, it didn't sound like he was too happy about it. Ethan wasn't all too happy about that fact either at the moment. Shaking his head, he sat back, pulled his knees into his chest, and rested his chin on his kneecaps.

Runyun struck two rocks together, trying to make a spark, but then stopped and stared at Ethan again with a pained expression. After a few more seconds of deafening silence, Runyun dropped the stones. "I don't know what to say to you."

"So how about we stick to silence." Ethan picked up the stones and whacked them together over and over, but all he managed to do was smash his fingers repeatedly.

After his hundredth try, Runyun's face softened. "Give me those."

Ethan set the stones on the ground and scooted back.

"Have you ever used a flint before?" Runyun scooped them up and got down close to the leaves.

"No, but it didn't look like you were having much luck."

Runyun ignored Ethan's harsh tone. "Watch." Using the sharp edge of one rock, he struck the other with skilled precision, producing sparks. The sparks made contact with several leaves. Seconds later, tiny puffs of smoke began flowing steadily from within the tiny teepee. Runyun gently blew on it and the smoke ignited. Once the teepee was ablaze, he set several larger pieces of wood on the flames.

The fire began to radiate a soothing heat, taking the chill out of the night's air, but when Runyun sat down right next to Ethan, any feelings of comfort fled his body.

Runyun took a deep breath before he said, "When Caitríona left she didn't tell me about you."

"I think that's obvious." Ethan reached out toward the fire to warm his hands.

Runyun clenched his teeth together. "Not going to make this easy, are you?"

Ethan let out a disgusted laugh. "No. I'm not. So far you've been an outright prick."

"Excuse me?" Runyun's eyes grew wide with anger.

"Let's set aside the fact that you called Lily a liar when she told you who I was—that I might be able to forgive. But all you've done since I met you is tell me how much you hate my mother, and her family. So no, I don't intend on making this easy because I don't trust you. Let's do us both a favor and not talk to each other until Christian and Lily get back."

"Are you always this stubborn?"

"Really? Going to keep talking, huh?"

Runyun lowered himself to the ground, rested his elbows on the log, and frowned at Ethan. "I plan on having this conversation whether you want to or not. So hold your sharp tongue or I'll force you to."

He'd probably do it too. "Fine. It's your migraine."

Expecting anger, he was surprised when Runyun shook his head and seemed mildly amused. "Caitríona didn't tell me she was leaving. She never told me anything. I showed up on our wedding day, the whole town gathered at the gates, and her brother cheerfully tells me she's gone."

Apparently, Runyun had something he wanted to get off his chest. If he was looking for a sympathetic ear, he wasn't going to find one. "Why? What did you do?"

"What did I do? What did I do? Nothing! I don't know why she left." He flung a stone at the fire. "But when we find her you can be damn sure I'm going to ask."

They both sat staring into the crackling flames.

"I guess that's one thing we've got in common. She never told me anything about anything either. Not this place, not who her family was." Ethan paused and looked at Runyun. "And she said you were dead."

"Dead?" Runyun sounded insulted. "Isn't that just fitting? Where have you two been all this time? Oh wait, let me guess. Balmore Fortress?"

Having no idea where Balmore Fortress was, Ethan shook his head.

"Wait! Don't tell me . . ." Runyun held up his hand. A second later he said, "Those clothes you're wearing. White Islands at Windsbreath House."

Lost again, Ethan shrugged.

Runyun took that to mean he was right. "How appropriate. While I was forced to defend the borders of Landover, the beautiful princess Caitríona was on holiday at the shore for fourteen years, living in her family's sea-side home and being pampered with servants waiting on her every need. Spoiling you. I mean look at you, you can't even ride a horse."

"How dare you?" Ethan stood up, clenching his fists, trying not to give in to the overwhelming urge to slug him. "We weren't in any beach house with servants. Mom was a servant. She spent all day, every day, cleaning other peoples' houses to pay the bills and watched over me like a hawk. And for your information, she tried to get me to take horseback-riding lessons, but I hate horses." The man knew nothing about who Caitríona Makkai was or what she was made of; no wonder she never told him that she was leaving.

Runyun gave Ethan a stern look of warning. "Sit."

Still fuming, Ethan sat crossed-legged beside him and tossed sticks into the fire, trying not to look at him.

"Where could you possibly have been in Tara where she would've passed as a servant? Everyone knows Caitríona."

"We weren't in Tara. We were in Los Angeles."

Runyun sat up, and a small crease formed between his eyebrows. "Outside of Tara? Caitríona lived as a Shadowwalker? But why would she take such a risk?" Runyun grabbed his right arm.

"Hey." Ethan yanked, but Runyun held firm. He examined his wrist, then slowly let go. "I don't understand. You don't bear the mark."

Ethan rubbed his wrist. "I wasn't born in Tara."

Runyun let his gaze drift to the treetops. "Caitríona, a servant." He said it like he didn't believe it, and then lowered his eyes to Ethan. "Alone in a strange place and acting like a responsible adult. That doesn't sound like the Caitríona I knew at all. The woman could barely take care of herself. She always followed her impulsive heart rather than her head."

"That doesn't sound like Mom at all. I never saw her do anything impulsive, not once."

From the look on Runyun's face it was clear he didn't believe a thing Ethan was saying. "Caitríona threw caution to the wind. I should've guessed she was living in Los Angeles. One afternoon, she brought me a map of the world from the library at Weymiss. She closed her eyes, and struck it with her finger, pinning the city. She wanted to run away, leave Tara. She said it would be the journey of a lifetime. I was the one who told her she was utterly insane, that it was way too dangerous."

"Are you sure we're talking about the same Caitríona Makkai?"

"That's how we met. On one of her adventures. She'd run away from the castle to camp in the woods with the sprites. She pretended to be a farmer's daughter so no one would tell her brother where she was."

"What happened?"

"Julius Niles found her a couple of days later, but not before I'd fallen in love with her, and she with me." Runyun turned his eyes to the crackling fire. "Or so I thought."

The way Runyun said those words made Ethan wonder aloud, "You don't really hate my mother, do you?"

Runyun met Ethan's gaze. "I never said I did. Her family is another story entirely."

"You still love her. That's why you came with us."

Runyun folded his arms over his chest, stuffing his hands tightly under. "I never knew love until I met your mother, but when she left"—Runyun winced—"those overwhelming emotions turned angry and sharp, opening a wound that has never healed."

The raw honesty of that statement hit Ethan hard, softening his resolve to stay mad at the man. No one, not even his mother, had ever spoken to him like that.

"I understand."

"You're too young to understand love."

"Maybe. Maybe not." Ethan thought about his feelings for Sky and the nagging affection he was beginning to feel for Lily. Maybe neither was real love yet, but they sure tugged at his heart and other body parts enough to make him lose his mind.

"Well, since you are my son, let me impart some advice in that department. Be cautious. Think carefully. Once you give your heart, you don't ever truly get it back."

Ethan gazed into the fire, wondering how his mother could've changed so much. She became a completely different person when she found out she was going to have him. She'd changed her entire life to keep him safe in a place far from her home.

The leaves stirred in the trees above, signaling a subtle change in the wind. Runyun closed his eyes and sucked in a deep breath. A second later, he stood up, and looked in the direction of the horses.

"What's wrong?" Ethan asked.

"Something follows us."

Ethan stood up too. "Milcai?"

Runyun took a long sniff. "No. Whoever or whatever it is carries the distinct smell of burned ash, as if it had bathed in a river of molten rock."

"Is it close?"

"Not yet. But it's moving fast. We'll need to leave at dawn." The way Runyun said that made Ethan think he'd left off a very important end to that sentence. *We need to leave at dawn or we may never leave at all.*

◙ FIFTEEN ◙

Sawney Bean dipped his quill in the inkwell to his right and returned to the large leather-bound book in front of him, but it was useless. With no light, he could barely make out his own handwriting.

"Shite!" Bean slammed the quill on the rock table. He wanted to snap it in half but didn't dare. It was his last.

What's wrong? Having a little trouble seeing? Perhaps old age is catching up to you, Mr. Bean. A woman with long curly brown hair draped over her shoulders and wearing a floor-length lacy black dress floated toward him from the shadows in the back of the cave.

Bean lifted his eyes to meet hers as she came within inches of him, wearing a mischievous grin. With pale skin and flawless features, Kiara, the daughter of Fuamnach, the goddess of malicious envy, was even more beautiful in death than she was in life, and equally as annoying.

Trying to ignore her incessant babble, he got up from the table and walked the few feet across to the overstuffed bookshelves. He snatched a bowl from the top shelf, then sat back down. There were no windows inside his prison-hovel. The morning sun came through the cave opening, but by early afternoon there was nothing but damp darkness.

There was only one way for him to manufacture light in this hole—with his own blood. With each recent and frequent pour, he'd grown weaker, but time was growing short and if he didn't finish, he wouldn't be ready. That was unacceptable.

Bean rolled up his sleeve and held his scar-riddled forearm over the bowl. He slid a shiv out of his boot and without flinching made a deep inch-long horizontal slice into his flesh.

Kiara threw her ethereal hands over her eyes. *Disgusting! Must you keep doing that?*

A curtain of darkness draped over the whites of Bean's eyes until they were solidly black. "It's not a good day for idle prattle, Kiara, so shut your trap before I destroy what's left of your maddening soul."

Kiara backed away from the table to the middle of the cave and hid behind a column. *No need to take that tone. I was merely going to point out that so much blood loss isn't good for you.*

"I'll keep that in mind." Dropping the blade on the table, he squeezed his arm, forcing his iridescent black blood to ooze from the wound and drain into the bowl.

Once the bowl was half full, he closed his eyes. The upside-down triangular black mark that started at his hairline and ended with the point plunging between his eyes began to spread, driving down his nose, his cheek. It then slid off his face and down his neck, until it vanished under his shirt. A second later it appeared from underneath his sleeve, raced over his forearm, and covered the wound. The skin knit back together, raising another scar.

He held his hand over the bowl, and snarled, "Fuilgooladh."

The color drained, until his blood had transformed completely into the clear vital oil he needed. Bean dipped his right thumb into the bowl, and whispered the word "Dotheain," igniting it.

Look at that. Such talent, Kiara chided.

Bean sniffed at her taunts. He should've gotten rid of her the day she showed up to his cave, but after so many years of talking to himself, he'd gotten sick of hearing his own voice and foolishly thought having her around might be a good thing. "Woman, I need a moment of peace and quiet. If you wish to get out of this cave anytime soon, then shut your trap."

Kiara came behind him. She scoffed as she stared over Bean's shoulder to his writing on the page. *You've been saying that for months.*

Bean rolled his eyes, but refused to look at her. If he ignored her, she generally found something else to do, like a petulant child.

As the black mark that had stretched down his arm receded to its original triangular shape, Bean got back to work. He picked up the quill again, and stared down at the very last page of the book.

After a few minutes, Kiara grew inpatient. *Fine. All work, no play makes you a very dull boy, Sawney Bean.* Her voice trailed off as she drifted into the darkness in the rear of the cave, finally giving him a moment of precious silence.

Bean made several carefully calculated strokes of the pen, then set the plume gently on the stone table, and smiled. He raked his hand through his greased-back black hair, and let out a bitter laugh. "This is it."

It was done.

And it would work.

The last page of the book meant the last spell for Primland. Not that it mattered. Bean would soon have another scáthán to control.

There was one last confirmation to make. Bean closed his eyes, set his open palms down on the table, and reached out with his powers, tapping into the lifeline of the king who had opened his doors to him almost a century ago. His eyes shuttered as his thoughts crisscrossed the dark tangled web of ethereal planes, spinning to a stop on the Isle of Mord, searching for Fenit Traynor.

Circling the island, and dropping into the only existing shelter, a damp cavern under the volcano, Bean's mind's eye twisted and turned, avoiding the sharp stalagmites and stalactites until it found the once great king.

Traynor let out a painful cry and gasped as Bean's powers grasped the king's soul. His heartbeat sped up to an unnatural rate and his head swam. Bean warmed at the fear he felt in Traynor's body.

A man who had once exuded a formidable strength, Fenit Traynor now sat pathetically slumped over his Galgan, the deliciously vicious generals who had done a magnificent job ravaging Landover. *One, two, three. . . . All six were present and accounted for.* A slow leer spread over Bean's face. Traynor had found them all.

When the final battle of the war was over, the thousands of Primland soldiers who had fought and died for Gransmore were left on the isle with Traynor. In a fit of rage, Tearlach Makkai refused to allow them to be properly interred. Instead, he ordered them left in piles on the island's surface.

And being on an island of stasis, neither Traynor, nor they, had aged. Their bloody and disfigured bodies had never decayed, and unburied, their souls had not been able to move on to the Otherworld. They were left in a perfect state for Bean's plan.

Fenit continued his melodramatic bellyaching.

Bean hissed, *Calm down. I see the Galgan are all present and accounted for. You've done well.*

Th-thank you, Traynor stuttered, his body still trembling. The king had not known that when Bean performed the ancient ritual of Náilanam, touching his soul, that it would permit them to stay in contact, forever indenturing Fenit Traynor to him. Bean had left that little tidbit of information out.

The Ravens succeeded.

They have the heir? Traynor sounded more concerned than excited.

The man was so weak. *What's wrong, Fenit? Losing your taste for Makkai blood?*

Never, Fenit argued. *I only hope in death Tearlach can see everything he saw in life, because I will personally kill one of his people for every day he's had us imprisoned.*

Bean smiled. *There's the bitterness I was missing, sire. Remain at the ready. The hour will be upon us very, very soon.*

Bean let go of his connection to the king. His eyes flew open, and his lips curled into a gratified smirk. Traynor was a fool, yet faithful, and that meant something.

Bean gathered up the loose pieces of parchment on the table that held his notes on what he planned. Once free, there could be nothing left behind to clue his enemies in on what he had in store for them. One at a time he crumpled them up and pitched them at the only opening in the cave. As each piece crossed the threshold, the paper ignited and burst into flames.

When he threw the last piece, Kiara came out of the shadows, pouting, to annoy him once more. *You locked me in here. The least you can do is talk to me.*

Bean lifted his eyes to meet hers as she settled in front of him. "I did not lock you in here. You did that to yourself. And very soon, this will all be over, for us both."

How do you figure that? Those worthless birds lied to me. They said you had my ring.

Bean glanced at the pitiful woman. "Yes. The operative word being 'had.'" He pushed out his lower lip like a moping child. "But, sniff, sniff . . . I no longer do. And without it . . ." Bean sucked in a hissing breath and shook his head, then sobered. "But you gave yourself to me freely. A woman with magical talents such as you have, or had—I never understood why you would do that."

You know why, Kiara said in hushed tones.

"Your precious Torin. And yet, he left you for another woman, just like your worthless father left your pathetic mother. Did you learn nothing from her mistakes? Did he ever return to her, even after she turned his new wife into a puddle of water?"

Kiara cringed at his painful reminder of what her father, Midir, had done to her beautiful goddess mother, Fuamnach, and what her husband had done to her. But Torin was nothing like her father, and she was nothing like her mother. *Torin wants me, Sawney Bean. He just doesn't know it yet. I learned from my mother's mistakes. The woman who tricked him into leaving me is still among the living, while Torin and I are both dead. They can no longer be together, but he and I can. And he will reunite with me because I love him.*

Bean guffawed. "*Love.* Such a noble cause." He rolled up his left sleeve and turned his arm over so the soft flat underside of his forearm faced up. Then he grabbed his feather pen, dipped the tip in the ink beside the book, and began copying words from the open page onto his arm.

"Have you ever noticed that both 'love' and 'hate' are four-letter words? On opposite ends of the emotional spectrum, and yet connected at their very core. In order to fully understand hate, one must have felt love. And if love is a noble cause, isn't hate then just as noble? Harnessing hatred for those who tossed you out and considered you worthless? Is there any more noble a cause? And thus by default, isn't revenge the proper course of action, rather than reconciliation?" He paused his scribbling and turned to face her. "Revenge on Torin should be what you seek, Kiara, and yet, you, even in death, continue to seek love."

With a furious glower, Kiara floated around the table to face him. *I gave up my life to bring you that book and your father's beloved weapon.* The ghost's green eyes glowed with power as she looked from the book to a three-foot-long club that sat to Bean's right, next to the cave's opening.

Irate, Bean set the quill down. He stood and held up one long index finger in front of her scowling face. The tip of the triangle that now sat at the end of his nose spread until it completely masked his face. "Don't you ever mention that man again or I will destroy what's left of your pathetic soul. That club belongs to me."

The power emanating from his hand forced her to the ground, where she cowered, nodding. Only after he'd sat back down did she move.

Continuing to copy the words from the book onto his arm, he took a long breath. "However, so you'll stop the incessant whining, know that you will have what you want when I get what I want. The ring is on its way here."

What? With a hopeful expression, Kiara stared down at the empty fingers on her left hand. *And with a Raven and your help—*

Bean paused his copying to pin her with a stern frown. "The Ravens and I will be long gone by the time the ring makes its way inside the cave."

Then how will I get out?

"They have a female with them."

Incensed, Kiara waved her hand over the table, causing a gust of wind that fanned the book's pages from the one he was working on. *But if you're gone, how—*

Bean held his hand out, cutting off her grating voice, and flipped the pages back. "You only need to draw the girl to the back of the cave. Force her in front of the mirror I set out for you this morning. She must look at her reflection. Her soul will be exchanged for yours, and you will have her physical form to slip the ring Torin gave you on your finger. The rest you know. Kill the girl and you will be pulled to him. You will be reunited and free."

Kiara glanced to the back of the cave. *You have Lugh's Mirror?*

"Let's just say the Shining One should have been more careful with his shining things," Bean said, his tone thick with jealousy.

Kiara shook her head and tsked. *Making the sun god angry. I didn't think you had it in you.*

Bean checked his arm to be sure the spell from the book had been perfectly copied. Although he planned to take the book with him, he knew better than to trust that he'd get out with it while fleeing. Runyun Cooper was always full of surprises.

He touched the dried ink on his arm. Riona Niles. Tearlach Makkai. Both dead. And last, but certainly not least, would be Runyun Cooper. On his way here, all in the name of love. He would lose everything that he held dear, and Bean would finally have his revenge.

◧ SIXTEEN ◧

Dawn came way too fast. Runyun relentlessly bellowed for Ethan to get up, but Ethan's body refused to do what his brain asked anymore. Every muscle ached, and he had no idea how he was going to spend yet another day on a horse.

"Last time I'm going to ask nicely." Runyun dropped something hard on Ethan's chest that bounced off. "We leave in *five* minutes."

He opened his eyes and turned his head to see something that resembled an apple in the dirt next to him. It hardly looked like the breakfast of champions. More like the breakfast of fugitives, or Hobbits on the road to Mordor, but he figured complaining was a bad idea. Runyun might never feed him again, and Ethan didn't know which fruits and berries in Bramblewood were edible, and which would kill him.

He picked up his meager ration and wiped it off on his shirt. As he pulled the blanket off, he realized he wasn't alone underneath it. Stunned and afraid to move, he felt his his heart hammering against his chest as Lily sat up, yawning. She looked beautiful. Her long, silky blond hair hung loose for a change, and when it dusted his arm he knew he had to sit up before he gave in to the urge to touch it.

"Good morning," Ethan said.

Lily's eyes grew wide with panic. She hopped up to sitting on the log behind them. "Dear gods! I'm so sorry. I move in my sleep. I must have been cold when the fire died." Her cheeks burned bright red.

"I didn't mind."

Lily gave him a subtle smile that took the chill out of the crisp morning air, until Christian picked up his saddle off the log behind Ethan, startling them both. "I'm sure you didn't," Christian said to Ethan. "If you two lovebirds are done, I could use help with the horses. Cooper is threatening to leave without us."

Lily started to follow Christian but stopped, and glanced back. She opened her mouth to say something but bit her lip instead. When she did it a second time, it drove Ethan over the edge.

"What?"

"Please don't take this the wrong way. You could use a bath." She wrinkled her nose.

That was unexpected. "A bath?"

"The river is just beyond those bushes. I won't let Runyun leave without you." With that, she made a quick exit.

Ethan took a whiff of his armpits and almost gagged. He was seriously ripe. Not wanting to be yelled at by Runyun, he hurried to the river. From bank to bank it wasn't more than twenty feet wide, but it looked pretty deep in the middle, where the rippling currents seemed to move faster. He had never swum in a river before. Only in the ocean at the beach close to their home on the few days off his mother took every year.

He tore off his clothes and dived in. A second later he burst through the surface, exhilarated. He submerged again and swam across to the other bank, letting the current wash off the layers of dirt on his skin.

Standing up a few feet from the opposite shore, he sucked in a deep breath, tasting the cool, earth-scented breeze, relishing a moment alone. The sun peeked over the trees while birds chirped morning songs. He was about to return to camp when a chill ran from his fingers, up his arms, and settled in his gut. A taibhsí was close.

Runyun Cooper is not a man to be trusted, the ghostly stalker from Weymiss warned, spitting his father's name.

Shivering, Ethan rotated a full three-sixty, trying to find him, and then glanced down. He was stark naked. Panicked, he lowered his hands to cover the important parts.

A deep chuckle resonated in his cranium. *You don't have anything I haven't seen before.*

"Well, you haven't seen mine and I'd like to keep it that way. Who are you? And more importantly, where are you?"

I am your Muincara. The man had an air of supreme arrogance. *I alone can teach you how to unlock the powers of radharc that have been bestowed upon you.*

"Last I checked, I didn't have any powers except being bothered by ghosts, no offense."

And yet that is offensive. Radharc is much more than seeing spirits. It is what sets you apart from everyone else in Tara, and in the universe. Your powers tap into the very essence of life, the Brícath. A formidable gift and one you've already tapped into, much to my chagrin.

Ethan couldn't believe what he was hearing. He'd never had any power other than seeing ghosts, except . . . come to think of it, when he ran toward the Primland border. He remembered the sudden gut-wrenching surge that had spiked his blood pressure and exploded out of him. "When I got rid of you and those fire-blasting taibhsí by saying Dul—"

Don't! Don't say that again! Don't even think it, his Muincara snapped.

A slow smile spread across Ethan's face. This ghost might actually be of some use to him. "Does that work on the living?"

The essence includes everything that has life. A life force is a life force no matter its plane of existence. It drives both emotional and physical responses, all of which you should, at some point, hopefully, be able to see, feel, and manipulate. But only when your powers have been released and you've learned to control them.

This sounded too good to be true. "So release them."

You're not ready.

"No! I am ready! My mother is in big trouble, and those powers could help me save her."

You are my only concern. I told you to remain at Weymiss. If you're the slightest bit intelligent, which I'm beginning to question, you will return, now.

Ethan snorted. "First off, you whispered something about not leaving. I barely heard you."

As you are learning to tap into your gift, I am still trying to understand mine. I was having a hard time communicating with you.

"Not my fault. And I'm not going back to Weymiss. Since you know my name, can you at least tell me yours?"

My identity must remain a secret. I should not be communicating with you, not until after the Council meeting. This is a matter of death. Specifically mine. I am trusting you, something that is particularly difficult considering the circumstances. But I fear for your life, and if it is lost, so is Landover.

"So let's see if I got this straight. I'm not supposed to tell anyone a nameless, faceless ghost is speaking to me . . ."

Exactly.

"Not a problem."

Good. Now, I cannot leave the boundaries of Landover. Once you cross into Gransmore, you will be on your own. Remember that Runyun Cooper's priorities are his, not yours or Landover's, and they never will be.

That was disconcerting. Runyun was rough around the edges and a bit acerbic, but he was his father. Ethan suddenly had a bad feeling. Wouldn't it be advantageous for an enemy to try to drive a wedge between them? Particularly one with magical powers? "How do I know you're not Sawney Bean playing head games?"

A skeptic? Good instincts. You tell me. Lesson number one! Close your eyes, tighten your fists, reach deep down inside while focusing on what you want to ask. Hold the question in your mind, and then ask me again if I am the hated sorcerer, and you will sense if I'm lying.

This sounded too good to be true. Ethan slammed his eyes shut, fisted his hands, took a deep breath and released it slowly. He saw the question in his mind's eye, and when he spoke, his voice carried a deep resonance he'd never heard before. "Are you Sawney Bean?"

I am most definitely not.

A blue pin-light appeared behind Ethan's eyelids, radiating a sense of calm. Without a doubt, he knew the ghost was telling the truth. Ethan opened his eyes. "You're not lying."

Very good. You can be taught— His voice abruptly cut off. *On your left!*

Out of the corner of his eye, Ethan saw a Brownie sneak out from behind a row of bushes on the bank in front of him. Ethan jetted behind a large rock on the river's edge. It was the same guy he had seen at the market at Weymiss by the potions stand. The one who had refused to help when Glatisant attacked. Ethan had been right. He was following them.

His curly brown hair shot out in all directions. He had on the same outfit, a formal brown vest and matching pants, only he looked like he'd been in a fight and lost, badly. His face had a long, deep scratch from his fore-head, down his left cheek, to his neck.

He removed his muddy shoes, set them neatly on a fallen log next to the bank, and then returned to the river's edge.

As the Brownie walked into the water, Ethan reached for his sword, only to remember he'd left it on the shore, along with his clothes.

"Ethan?" Lily called from the opposite shore. "What is taking so long? Runyun is fuming."

Hearing her, the Brownie slid a knife out of the waist of his pants, set it in his teeth, and dived under the water, heading straight for Lily.

Naked or not, Ethan had to do something. He swam, freestyling across the river, and caught up to the Brownie. He latched on to his midsection, pinning his arms against his sides, but he was too slippery, and before Ethan could secure him, the Brownie head-butted him in the nose.

"Gah!" Blood drained from his left nostril, leaving a salty metallic taste in his mouth.

"What's going on?" Lily came out of the bushes on the bank and saw Ethan wrestling with the Brownie. She ripped her sword out of its scab-bard and, without hesitation, stormed to the river. "I'm coming."

The Brownie struggled, but Ethan wrapped an arm around his neck, snaring him in a chokehold. With the other hand, Ethan grabbed the knife's handle, yanked it out of the Brownie's mouth, and dropped it into the river. It fell to the bottom, out of reach.

"Ethan, bring him here," Lily said.

Reluctantly, Ethan dragged him closer to Lily. *Please don't let her see me naked.* Between the cold water and chill from the ghostly interaction, it could be really, really embarrassing.

Lily placed the tip of her sword under the Brownie's chin, forcing him to look at her. "I know you. You serve the Traynor family. You're Alastair."

"Traynor?" Ethan yanked him against his chest, and was overtaken by the smell of burned ash. It was Alastair who Runyun had smelled last night.

"Not true. I left them long ago." Alastair tried to wiggle free, but Ethan tightened his hold.

"That's impossible! Brownies can't just leave. They're tied to their mon-archs forever," Lily exclaimed.

"You've been following us for a while, haven't you?" Ethan asked.

Furious, Lily pressed the tip of her sword against the Brownie's chest. "Why are you following us?"

"I wasn't following you. Let me go!" Alastair lifted his hands, holding them up in surrender. "I can pay you. . . ." He slipped a finger into the pocket on his vest and came out with a small gold ring, hanging above his knuckle. He waggled it at Ethan. "For my freedom and your silence."

"I don't want your ring. I want information. You know something about what's going on with my mother, Caitríona Makkai, don't you?"

"I don't know anything about your mother. I don't know anything about anything!"

Take the ring, his Muincara ordered.

"Why?" Ethan asked, annoyed at the intrusion in his head.

"Why what?" Lily asked. When Ethan didn't answer, she moved the tip of her sword over Alastair's heart. "Let's take him back to camp. Runyun will make him talk." She snatched the Brownie's wrist.

Christian came around the brush on the far side of the river's edge. "Ethan, Cooper is threatening—" His words cut off as he took in the scene. "What's this?"

Alastair yanked his wrist back from Lily, brushing his finger on her hand, and the ring slid off into the murky water. With a snarl, he slammed his eyes shut, and lowered his hands on the surface of the river. The current picked up and the water level rose until they were completely submerged.

Lily tried to swim to Ethan, but she was in the fastest part of the current, making it impossible.

The Brownie spun, kicked Ethan in the chest, knocking the last bit of breath out of his lungs, and broke free, heading for the opposite riverbank from their camp. Ethan kicked off the bottom, and swam as fast as he could. He had the back of Alastair's shirt within reach when his Muincara had other ideas.

Get the ring!

Startled, Ethan cursed underwater as Alastair slipped from his grasp.

Now. Hurry. Before the waters carry it away.

Ethan found himself at a crossroads. If Ethan went for the ring, Alastair would definitely get away and he couldn't let that happen. But then again, the taibhsí was supposed to be his mentor, and he had to place his trust in someone.

Ethan surfaced for breath then dived under, kicking against the raging water. It took every ounce of strength he had not to get swept away as he ran his hands through the soft mud where he'd thought the ring had fallen. His lungs straining, he still hadn't found it.

Why hadn't he listened to his instincts? The ring had to be gone by now. He'd let the Brownie go for nothing.

Frustrated and raging, Ethan was about to surface when a beam of light burst through the top of the water, illuminating a small spot right next to his foot. A touch of gold flickered under a large rock. The ring. Ethan slid it onto his pinkie and then broke through the surface, gasping for air. He scanned the area for the Brownie, but he was long gone.

Ethan started toward Christian, who stood on the riverbank holding his jeans out to him, but stopped when he saw Lily glaring at him from only a few feet away.

"Would you mind?" Ethan asked.

Fuming, she flipped around.

Only then did Ethan come out of the water. "Where's Alastair?"

Lily stood with her hands on her hips, staring in the other direction. "He got away, thanks to you."

Christian tossed him his jeans. "Runyun's tracking him, but he won't catch him. On land, Brownies are much too fast and can change color to blend into the surroundings."

Ethan zipped his fly. "Okay. I've got pants on. Commence the verbal thrashing."

Lily didn't waste any time. "Where were you?" She took several long, angry steps in his direction.

"I went after the ring."

Horrified, she sneered at Ethan's clenched fist. "What? I needed your help."

"What ring?" Christian asked.

Ethan passed it to him. "The Brownie tried to give it to us as a bribe to let him go. He didn't want anyone to know we'd seen him. He told us he left the Traynor family."

Christian examined it carefully. "Impossible. Brownies are tied to their families." He passed it back to Ethan's outstretched hand.

"A servant of the Traynor family is lurking near our camp, and he happens to have a ring in his pocket? Then he conveniently leaves it behind. Why would he do that? This is all part of Traynor's plan. That ring is likely cursed," Lily insisted. "Drop it in the water. Let it go."

"I don't know about that," Christian said.

Lily turned her glower on him. "Well, I do!"

She did have a point. The ring could be cursed, and Alastair might be working for the Traynors or worse, Bean. But his Muincara said he needed it.

"Did you hear me?" She took a long step in his direction. "It's dangerous. That Brownie works for the enemy."

"He *worked* for the enemy!" Ethan backed up until he was knee deep in the water.

"Your trousers are getting wet. Riding all day in wet clothes will be very, very uncomfortable," she pointed out, wearing a goading smirk.

"Yeah, well, they needed a bath too." Ethan moved back until he was waist deep.

"Fine. I'm already wet." She stormed into the water, closing the distance between them. "Drop it."

Christian walked to the water's edge, and laughed. "This is getting interesting."

This argument was going nowhere fast, and they needed to get a move on. "Fine." Ethan held up the ring between his index finger and thumb then let it fall into the river. It shot straight down and settled on the bottom, next to his foot. "It's gone." As he opened his hands to emphasize his point, Ethan stepped on the ring, squishing it between his toes. "Happy now?"

"I would've been happier if Alastair was our prisoner. And I would've thought you would be too."

Runyun came through the trees on the bank across from them. "He got away. I tracked him as far as I could, but his footprints vanished. Now, if you're through with your bath"—Runyun pinned Ethan with a cross stare—"let's get a move on."

Cooper swam to the other bank and continued to camp. Lily followed him, but Christian made no move to leave.

"It's cool. I'll be right there. Just gonna get my shirt and sword," Ethan said.

"Perhaps I should wait." Christian's eyes swept the other bank.

"I don't need a babysitter."

"Don't be long." Christian started back toward camp.

Once he was out of sight, Ethan reached into the water, scooped up the ring, and examined it. In the center of the small gold band was a set of rubies in the shape of a star. It was way too small for Ethan's large fingers. It must've belonged to a woman.

"What's so important about this ring?" Ethan asked his Muincara.

"Ethan!" Runyun yelled from camp, startling him.

There's no time. Keep it safe. You'll understand soon enough. Good luck. I truly hope to see you in Coventry at the Council meeting. There was something very unsettling in his Muincara's last words.

An hour later they crossed the border into Gransmore. The horses came to a full stop at the base of a ten-foot-tall statue of a pale blue man. For armor, he wore only a breastplate with a tree carved into it. The fingerlike branches rose upward while the thick roots extended down, each weaving into a braided border that circled the trunk.

Sticking out of a short-sleeved shirt were arms as thick as Schwarzenegger's during his Conan years. A braid-patterned tattoo wound down the statue's arms from his shoulders until it disappeared into thick cuffs on his wrists. The statue held a sword as long as Ethan was tall, the tip buried in the ground.

"What is that?" he asked the others.

"That is a Fomorian. They're the inhabitants of Gransmore. To give you a little insight into their moral compass, in the war, they refused to fight with us against our enemies, but were more than happy for our men to die for their freedom," Christian said. "Once strong and fierce, their clans became soft after the move to Tara."

Runyun raised an eyebrow at Christian's estimation of the Fomorians. "They no longer believe in war, but don't underestimate them. They're still dangerous."

"Wealthy, they're full of pomp and circumstance, parties and ceremony, but no real courage," Christian retorted.

"Are they really blue?" Ethan asked.

"They are. A remnant of their life centuries ago when they lived under the sea. Father says they can breathe underwater and on land," Lily explained.

Runyun cleared his throat. "I should make you three aware of something. The Fomorians and I have had a few run-ins in the past."

"The Milcai," Ethan commented.

Runyun grimaced. "Last time I was in Gransmore I lost a rather large wager."

"And let me guess—you still haven't paid it," Christian surmised in a disapproving tone.

Runyun didn't reply, which Ethan took as an affirmative. "And the cave is where?"

"On the tallest mountain, across the plains, west of here. We should be able to get through without being seen so long as you follow me closely. The only thing I haven't worked out yet is how to get past the guard who will be blocking the entrance to the path up the mountain, but all in good time. Are we ready?"

Ethan touched the bulge in his pocket. Was the ring meant to pay off Runyun's debt? Or to bribe the guard on the path? It would have been nice if his Muincara had been a little more specific about what he was supposed to do with it. Conflicted, Ethan decided to ask for a group vote and lifted the ring out of his pocket.

"Ethan Makkai! You lied to me!" Lily snapped.

"Not exactly. I simply executed an elaborate ruse to get what I wanted."

"Ethan, what is that? Give it to me." Runyun held out his hand.

Once in his hand, Runyun turned it over and over. "Curious." He checked the inside of the band for markings. Then bit it. Then held it up to the sun. It seemed like he was sizing it up for what it was worth. He looked back at Ethan. "Did you get this off Alastair?"

"Yeah. Can I have it back?" Ethan reached for it only to have Runyun slip it into a small pocket on his tunic.

"I'll hold on to it for now." Without so much as another word, he kicked his horse and headed into Gransmore.

"Runyun, hold up. I need that back," Ethan called.

"I'll keep it safe," his father bellowed back at him.

"He'll use it to pay off his debt." Christian shook his head in disbelief. "Let's go before he gets too far ahead and leaves us behind." With a click of his tongue, he kicked his horse and took off after Runyun.

Lily followed, prodding her horse into a cantor.

"Let's go, Devlin. Canter, boy." Ethan imitated Christian's moves, but the annoying horse started walking. "Come on. A little faster." He kicked again. Groaning, Devlin moved into a hesitant trot.

Ethan rode past the sleeping statue and could've sworn its eyes opened, but he was so far behind the others he didn't dare go back to check.

The border between Landover and Gransmore was more than a simple dividing line. On one side were the much shorter trees of Landover, which had teardrop leaves with frayed edges. On the Gransmore side, the trees were five times larger and mirrored the mark etched in the breastplate of the statue. They had long, thin branches and fingerlike leaves. It was as if the land had adjusted to fit the Fomorian footprint, but since Landover and Gransmore were so close together, the difference had to have been caused by more than evolution.

Ethan caught up to Lily, but Christian and Runyun were nowhere in sight. She peered back at him then slowed her horse, waiting for him.

"Hurry up," she scolded. "Or we'll never"—the ground began to shake—"catch up . . ." Lily's voice trailed off.

Ethan followed her sight line to the trees behind him, on the left. Milcai. One after another dropped from the weeping trees, heading straight for them.

◨ SEVENTEEN ◨

The Milcai pack was huge, way bigger than the one in Bramble-wood Forest. They let out high-pitched, stuttered screeches as they'd done before, only now they turned up the volume and frequency, sounding the alarm.

"Lily, go!" Ethan yelled, and kicked Devlin hard. The two horses took off, and for a second, it looked like they were going to get away, but the Milcai were way too fast. They knuckle-walked faster than the horses could move and in no time had them surrounded.

With glowing red eyes, the Milcai shrieked and hissed, baring razor-sharp teeth and frothing at the mouth, yet they didn't attack.

With an annoyed growl, Lily ripped out her sword and swung it at them as they snapped at her legs.

The ground trembled again, but unlike the chaotic tremors of the Milcai, it shook rhythmically. The trees to the left rustled and a Fomorian emerged from the trees. Sword drawn, he stormed toward the chaos.

At least ten feet tall, with short brown hair, he wore a short-sleeved muted yellow shirt with a bronze breastplate that covered his abdomen. It bore the same mark as the statue, and a similar tattoo ran down his pale blue arms and dived under his etched cuffs.

Ethan turned to Lily. "Go. Find Christian and Runyun. I'll distract him."

Before she could protest, Ethan kicked Devlin as hard as he could.

The horse leaped forward into the pack of horrifying monkey kin. The Milcai attacked, latching on to the horse's legs, sinking their teeth into his flesh.

His ears pinned back against his head, Devlin roared. He reared up, causing Ethan to fall forward and wrap his arms around the horse's neck to stay on.

Lily rode around the pack and into the open field, heading after Runyun and Christian as an enormous arm wrapped around Ethan's abdomen. It yanked him off Devlin and into the air.

Ethan flailed his legs. "Let go!"

The Milcai continued screeching while the forearm squeezed his gut so tight, Ethan was positive his internal organs were going to pop out his nose.

Seeing the melee, Lily headed back into the pack of Milcai. She raised her sword at the Fomorian guard, which looked more like a butter knife next to him. "Put him down."

When the Fomorian didn't respond, she said, "Didn't you hear me? I said to put him down."

"Oh, I heard you. . . ." The guard shifted his gaze to her. He reached for a whistle that hung from a string around his neck, lifted it to his mouth, and blew. A ear-piercing deep tone escaped and the Milcai fell silent.

"Good work, mo carse," the guard commented in a baritone voice fit for opera. Unlike the thick Irish accents Ethan had heard from most everyone in Landover, his was more highborn English.

"Patrol." With another blow of the whistle, the Milcai spun around and knuckled back into the woods.

The guard squeezed Ethan harder as Lily continued to wave her weapon.

"Can't breathe . . . ," Ethan protested.

Lily stabbed the Fomorian in his right thigh.

"Rar!" he hissed then backhanded her, knocking her off her horse. She crashed down on the ground, clutching her stomach.

Ethan saw red. He glared up at the Fomorian. "When I get free, I'm going to kick your ass for that. And if you touch her again, I will kill you!"

The guard picked the blade out of his thigh and tossed it on the ground.

"You are in no position to threaten me, Celt. I am Fomorian." The arm wrapped around Ethan's gut tightened even more. The guy was literally squeezing the life out of him. Ethan couldn't speak. He couldn't breathe.

"Phalen, stop!" a female voice shouted from behind them.

Phalen let out a sigh of supreme annoyance at the sight of the guard who was headed in their direction. "Always getting in the way," he mumbled.

She was on them in seconds. Wearing the same uniform as Phalen, she had a thin face and a long, lean body that stretched almost to Phalen's height. Her long blond hair was loose except for two small braids that hung from each temple. The letter "T" was woven into the tattoo that wound down her arm.

"Teighan Bryg," Phalen said, and lowered his head.

"What's going on here?" Bryg asked, looking from Ethan to Lily. "Why are you squeezing this one to death?"

"They're trespassing," Phalen explained. "Crossed the border."

"I see." Bryg sighed. "What have you to say?" she asked Ethan.

"We were—" Lily began, but the Fomorian held up a large hand, silencing her.

Bryg brought the tip of her blade under Ethan's chin. "I was speaking to you."

Ethan's mind went blank until he looked down at Lily and, like an idiot, said the first thing that came to mind. "Trespassing?" Ethan feigned a laugh. "No. My girlfriend and I were—"

Lily huffed, cutting Ethan off. "Girlfriend, well, that's quite presumptuous of you, isn't it?"

Ethan rolled his eyes and tilted his head to Bryg. "Okay. It was a first date. A guy can dream, right? I mean, look at her." He gestured to Lily, who bit her lower lip, trying not to react.

"Anyway," Ethan continued. "We heard there was happening stuff going on in Gransmore, so we thought, hey, we'll come for a visit, and then your annoying pets attacked us. Really, you should put them on leashes. Not good for tourism."

Bryg arched a disbelieving brow but slid her sword into her scabbard as Ethan continued rambling. "And your pal Phalen here nicely called them off, so don't be so hard on him." Ethan gave Phalen a man-pat on the shoulder.

Phalen tossed Ethan to the ground. Bryg seized his arm, then grabbed

Lily with her other hand. "You two have been traveling the Landover–Primland border for several hours. Why?" Bryg's eyes shifted from Ethan to Lily and back again. "And where is the rest of your party? The taller, dark-haired one and Runyun Cooper?"

"Nice play." Ethan shook his head. "Damn. Those Milcai are good."

A cocky grin spread across Phalen's face. "Yes, they are."

"Now tell me where Cooper is and we'll take you two back across the border to Landover," Bryg said.

"I have no idea where he is," Ethan said.

"Too bad. With the queen's celebration at Brimouth Castle, you'll have to wait for it to be over to see the king. That won't be for a couple of days, and oh, wait, maybe a few more for the king and queen to recover from too much food and drink to have an audience, right, Phalen?"

Phalen ran his hand along his chin. "Probably four or five days."

Ethan struggled against her hold. "You can't—"

"Oh, but I can. You see I am the teighan in Gransmore. The head of the armies, in charge of the safety of this realm. Runyun Cooper and you by association are a threat." Bryg lowered her head so that her face was only a few feet from his. "I can do whatever I want with you both."

Ethan bit Bryg's hand hard at the same time Lily ducked and slid out of her grasp, breaking free. But Bryg didn't let go of Ethan. Furious, she kicked him to the ground.

Ethan landed on his stomach and smacked his chin on a rock, biting his tongue. His mouth filled with the taste of blood. Before Ethan could get up, Bryg buried her enormous boot in his back, pinning him to the ground.

"You little—" Bryg started, but stopped when she heard a horse racing in their direction. Ethan flipped his head to the side. With his horse at a full gallop, Christian headed straight for them. Alone. There was no sign of Runyun anywhere.

"There's the other one," Phalen said. "Now where is Cooper?"

Ethan was wondering the same thing.

As soon as Christian arrived, he dismounted and placed a hand on the hilt of his sword. "I'm so glad you found them."

"Are you now?" Phalen said with a sarcastic chuckle. "We're equally glad to have found them. And you. Thank you for making it so easy."

"And now that you've arrived, you're under arrest for trespassing," Bryg added.

"Excuse me? Have you any idea who I am?" Christian asked stiffly.

"A dimwit from Landover with a bigger mouth than this one," Bryg said, stomping down on Ethan's back.

"Ow!" Ethan yelped.

Christian sneered at the Fomorian. "I am Christian Makkai, heir to the throne of Landover."

Ethan was stunned. Why would he claim to be the heir when he was so ready to tell Suffie and the rest of the sprites that Ethan was the next king?

"And the one you're stepping on happens to be my cousin, Ethan Makkai, and this"—Christian pointed to Lily—"is Lily Niles, the daughter of General Niles, leader of our armies."

Phalen laughed. "Sure you are."

Bryg pulled Lily closer to her. "Julius Niles is your father?"

Lily nodded.

"They're lying, Teighan Bryg. Why would the next king of Landover travel without protection, and into another realm without prior permission, no less?" Phalen turned to Christian. "How daft do you think we are? Runyun Cooper used you as a cover to get into Gransmore, didn't he?"

"If it was a cover, it certainly didn't work, now did it?" Lily tossed out.

Bryg folded her arms over her chest and leaned on her bent knee, adding more weight to the heel in Ethan's back. She glared down at Lily. "Mr. Cooper is nowhere to be found, if you haven't noticed. It seems to have worked very well."

Christian set his hands on his hips. "We were using him."

"As a guide," Ethan choked out.

"That still doesn't explain why you'd be traveling all this way unprotected," Phalen said as he moved to stand over Christian.

"I don't need protection." Christian pulled his sword. "Now let them go." His tone dropped five octaves on the word "go," making it sound like a threat.

"Heir or not . . . ," Phalen said, and slid his sword out. He held it point down over Christian's head, preparing to skewer him. "Go on. I dare you."

"Stop!" Bryg exclaimed. "Phalen, put away your weapon."

Phalen clenched his teeth.

"You heard her." Christian smirked.

Grumbling, Phalen lowered his sword but didn't put it away.

"Where were you going?" Bryg asked Christian.

"With the Council meeting in less than a fortnight, I am on my way to pay my respects to King Fearghus and Queen Cethlenn. Before you lock any of us up, I demand to see the king."

Bryg set her free hand on her hip and raked Christian with a look of disbelief. "Very well. If what you say is true, the king will be very glad to see you. But if you're lying"—Bryg lowered her eyes to meet his—"then know you'll be locked up way too long to make the Council meeting." She turned to Phalen. "We'll take them to Brimouth. Let King Fearghus decide their fate."

Bryg lifted her foot off Ethan's back. Finally able to take a deep breath, he rose slowly.

"Mount your horses. You're to ride together." Phalen glared down at Ethan, and added, "I'll be bringing up the rear, so don't get any big ideas about trying to get away because if you do . . ." Phalen ran his finger across his neck.

"I still owe you for hitting Lily, so maybe it's you who should be watching his step." Ethan didn't wait for a response. He walked over to Devlin and climbed up.

After Lily mounted, she brought her horse next to Ethan. "You do know I can take care of myself."

Ethan nodded. "Yes, but no man, or Fomorian, has the right to hit a woman. Ever."

They rode behind Bryg as she walked swiftly down a hill. At the bottom, they joined a path that traveled south along the forest line to the left. On the right was a huge hill that blocked their view of the rest of Gransmore.

With Bryg and Phalen a good ten feet from them, Ethan figured they wouldn't hear him if he talked softly. He reached over and smacked Christian on the arm. "Why are you the heir in Gransmore, but I'm the heir with Suffie in Bramblewood?"

"You heard Teighan Bryg. King Fearghus may choose to lock the heir up because he's trespassing, but a cousin he may overlook. You"—he pointed to Ethan's chest—"must be at the Council meeting. So keep quiet."

Ethan gave a disingenuous nod. There was no way he'd let Christian take the fall for him. As they continued, Ethan scanned the forest for Runyun but didn't see him. He thought about asking Christian, but feared saying his father's name with the Fomorians so close.

After a short time, Bryg led them up a hill and into the heart of an enormous ornate town. Varying in heights, the tall buildings were stacked side by side, and all made out of similar pale yellow limestone with intricate black ironwork framing the large rectangular windows.

A wide river ran through the center of the town, dividing it in two. It looked like the pictures Ethan's mother had shown him of Paris, the one city she desperately wanted to visit but never had.

"Where are we?" Ethan asked.

"Quinsberry Gorge," Bryg replied. "This is our largest city. And that"—she pointed to the river—"is the River Shannon."

"That's the name of the longest river in Ireland," Ethan said without thinking.

Bryg turned a suspicious eye on him. "You sound as if you've been."

"No. Geography class. Had to regurgitate every major river in the United Kingdom and Western Europe for a test three weeks ago." Which was the truth.

That answer only made Bryg more curious. "A bit of useless information unless you plan on leaving Tara, don't you think?"

Ethan nodded. "Yes. I totally agree and plan on letting my teacher know that the minute I get back. Unfortunately, they teach a lot of useless information, and probably some useful too, but it's hard to tell the difference."

Bryg's scowl broke into a hesitant grin. "I understand. Although we were taught that there were many similarities between the new Tara and the old country, we were given no more detail than that. I always assumed it was because they didn't want us interested in the outside world."

"Did it work?"

"Most definitely not," she said with a wink.

They continued down several blocks, all similarly laid out, and all empty. The place was deserted.

"Where is everyone?" Lily asked.

"At the Brimouth for the celebration. Today is a holiday for the queen's birthday," Bryg explained.

Leaving the city, Ethan noticed three large mountains on the right. Two were completely covered in trees, while the third, and tallest, transitioned from forest to steep, rocky surfaces midway to the top.

Goose bumps spread up Ethan's arms, and his heart filled with a cold dread, the same hollow fear he'd experienced when he'd stepped into the mist in Primland. He couldn't explain how he knew, but he was one hundred percent positive the cave of Sawney Bean was at the top of the bald mountain.

With an ever-tightening chest, he had the sudden feeling that something bad was about to happen. Yes, they'd probably end up prisoners of Gransmore, but it was more than that. He had no idea why, maybe it was his powers sending him warning signals, but he had the horrible feeling that Sawney Bean not only knew he was coming, but was waiting for him.

EIGHTEEN

For the rest of the ride, Ethan kept a sharp lookout for Runyun, hoping he would turn up and prove he hadn't abandoned them. But he didn't. He wasn't coming to help. Runyun had taken the ring and gone to pay off his debts. His Muincara was right. Runyun Cooper only cared about himself.

"Where is your father, Ethan?" Lily whispered.

"He's not coming back." There was a harsh tone in his voice he hadn't meant for Lily.

Christian gave Ethan a single nod, agreeing.

Ethan leaned toward them, trying to keep the Fomorians from hearing the conversation. "First chance we get, we head to the mountains to the west." Ethan pointed right. "Bean's cave is on top of the bare mountain."

"How do you know?" Christian asked.

"Trust me. It's there."

They rode through the open gates of a thirty-foot-high black iron fence with patterns of intricate lacy scrollwork and leafy vines. Inside, the lawn was so manicured it looked like a soft green carpet. The path was lined with bushes as high as the fence that had been sculpted to look like Fomorian soldiers. The castle sat a few hundred feet away, and looked like it belonged in Bel Air, except in Bel Air the bushes would've been sculpted into cutesy animals, not armed guards.

Bryg led them past a large crowd of Fomorian men, women, and children dressed in extremely posh outfits, waiting in line for the largest buffet table Ethan had ever seen. Most men wore long collarless leather jackets with matching pants. The women and girls were in long brightly colored dresses with jewelry that looked like it belonged to the Queen of England. As the horses walked by, the Fomorians took notice of the scruffy visitors from Landover.

"Dismount," Bryg ordered.

Obeying, they led the horses right into the middle of a huge party. On one side, a musical group played a fast-paced Irish jig–meets-rock that reminded Ethan of "Some Nights" by the band Fun. In addition to acoustic guitars and something that looked like an upright piano but had three stacked rows of keys, musicians played short flutes and a row of circular drums with curved sticks, rather than the straight ones Ethan was familiar with. The partyers danced with an unbridled sense of happiness and warmth that Ethan had experienced when he'd found Gransmore on Bartlett's map.

Brownies roamed, serving drinks and cleaning up plates of food left on tables just fast enough for another group to sit down to eat. The air was filled with the aroma of roasted meat and sweet desserts, making Ethan's mouth water.

Behind the courtyard was the palace. As grand as the rest of Gransmore, it was shaped like a tiered wedding cake, with three square levels, the largest on the bottom and the smallest on top. A checkered flag of blue and red squares waved from the top of the castle. Each floor had balconies with black iron railings that matched the exterior gate, and the ones in Quinsberry Gorge. The castle was at least ten times wider and taller than Weymiss, which made sense considering the size of the royal family living there.

To one side of the castle was a pool the size of a giant lake, with a fountain in the form of a female Fomorian with slithering eels for hair and a long tail, like a mermaid's. Water spewed out of her huge hands.

Unlike Weymiss, no moat isolated the castle from the grounds. No soldiers stacked cannonballs on top of the wall. In fact, there were no weapons of any kind except in the hands of the stone sculptures of soldiers placed against the fence. Another sculpture by the lake jumped out at him. It was of a girl sitting cross-legged, reading a book.

From a distance, the castle doors appeared open, with carefree Fomorians strolling in and out. The windows were made of stained glass that, like his mother's sketches on their wall at home, depicted a redheaded girl at different ages.

Bryg signaled to another guard, who approached and abruptly took the three horses' reins, then led them back out the gate. *This is bad.* Without their horses, they were in deep, deep trouble.

Phalen remained with them while Bryg approached a nearby table that was covered with large plates of food. A thick bald Fomorian with a well-groomed red beard sat and chowed down on an enormous plate of meat.

"King Fearghus, I presume," Ethan said to Christian.

He nodded. "How could you miss him?"

"Hold your tongue," Lily warned. "He could hear you."

King Fearghus let out a loud belly laugh and smacked the much thinner Fomorian next to him who had short, spiky white hair that was set off against his pale blue skin. He wore a look of disgust as the king stuffed another piece of dripping meat in his mouth.

"And the other one must be his sorcerer," Ethan surmised since he wasn't eating the meat.

"Name's Rhisiart. Father called him the Enforcer," Christian replied. "Gransmore's sorcerers have used transformation as punishment for crimes for centuries. Rhisiart is particularly talented in that area, and once changed, his victims generally remain in their animal state for the rest of their natural lives."

Ethan had a horrific thought. "The Milcai."

"Very good," Phalen interjected.

"Don't you know it's rude to listen in on people's conversations?" Ethan snapped.

Phalen stood over him, snarling, making Ethan regret his outburst, but stopped when he heard King Fearghus.

"Visitors? From Landover?" The king sounded annoyed at the intrusion. Setting down the piece of bread in his hand, he slowly got up and padded in their direction, squinting in disbelief, with Bryg and the other Fomorian following.

As he approached, King Fearghus brushed bread crumbs off his dark gray leather tunic. His black pants were tucked into ankle-high black boots, and a crisp white shirt peeked out from underneath his tunic. Adding to his slick look was a thin braided-knot tattoo that circled the middle of his neck, running over his Adam's apple.

Rhisiart wore a long-sleeved white shirt, with ruffles down the front and sleeves that poofed out at the shoulders. As they stopped in front of them, his chiseled face mimicked the same annoyed scowl as the king's.

"Who do we have here?" King Fearghus's voice was so deep, he could have given James Earl Jones a run for the role of Darth Vader and won.

"Your majesty, I present the visitors from Landover." Bryg waved a hand over Ethan's, Lily's, and Christian's heads.

"You mean trespassers," Phalen said.

Bryg didn't argue with him. "This one, Christian Makkai"—Bryg set her finger on Christian's shoulder—"claims to be the heir and said he has come to pay his respects."

King Fearghus looked down on Christian with disdain. "I see. Ah well, I remember him."

Ignoring the king's slight, Christian smiled. "King Fearghus, I appreciate you allowing us to visit your realm."

"I've allowed nothing," the king replied. "It is you who have come on your own accord, and although a diplomatic mission is to be commended, it seems like an odd time for one. You come without your Commis, without your general, or even a guard escort."

"As I said to Teighan Bryg, I prefer to travel alone," Christian said through gritted teeth.

King Fearghus tilted his head to Ethan and Lily. "But you're not alone. Who are these other two?"

"This one"—Bryg touched Lily on the shoulder—"is Lily Niles, Julius Niles's daughter. The other is Christian Makkai's cousin."

The king stepped toward Ethan and fixed his squinting gray eyes on him. "Are you now. What's your name?"

"Ethan."

"Ethan who?" the king pressed.

Christian cleared his throat loudly. "As I told your guards—"

"I was speaking to him." He poked Ethan in the chest. "What is your surname? Your father's name?"

That was a loaded question. Ethan certainly couldn't tell him Cooper or they'd string him up from the tallest tree. He decided to try the truth, sort of.

"I don't use my father's last name. In fact, I don't even know who he is. I use Makkai."

As he squinted at Ethan, King Fearghus's cheeks filled with air, making him look like a blowfish. "Makkai? Your mother?"

"His mother is the princess Caitríona," Lily added.

King Fearghus rounded on Lily. "Caitríona Makkai? Did you say Caitríona? How is that possible? No one has seen Caitríona for more than fourteen years. How could she have had a child? There has been no announcement. I don't understand." He turned back to Ethan. "Where has she been? Where did you come from?"

Ethan locked eyes with Christian, who shook his head. The cross-examination was making his cousin as uncomfortable as it was Ethan. It was time to go. He leaned his head toward the open gates and locked eyes, first with Christian, and then with Lily. "King Fearghus, thanks for the big welcome. It's been a sincere pleasure. "

Ethan spun, and the three took off, racing to the exit. Weaving through the crowd, Lily latched on to Ethan's hand but they quickly lost sight of Christian. Ethan looked back to see if he'd been captured and plowed into an immovable wall. He crashed to the ground, taking Lily with him.

"Leaving so soon?" Bryg asked.

Before they could blink, she had hold of Ethan's wrist in one hand, and the other on Lily's. She dragged them back to King Fearghus. Next to him, Phalen had Christian, his arms restrained behind his back.

A slow tic worked in his jaw as King Fearghus bent down on one knee and glared at Ethan. "Let's try this again, shall we? Your mother was a dear friend of my daughter, Dratsuah. Now I'm simply asking where she is. Out of respect, answer my question and perhaps"—the Fomorian king glanced over his shoulder at Christian—"I'll let you and the others return to Landover."

With a determined gaze, Christian shook his head once.

If he told King Fearghus the truth, they'd be locked up for trespassing, and if he refused to answer, they'd also be locked up for trespassing. Ethan wrenched his wrist out of Bryg's hold and took several long steps backward.

"I wouldn't do that. You run and they will suffer the consequences,"

Fearghus warned. He nodded to Phalen, who pulled his sword and set the tip against Christian's neck.

The king folded his arms over his chest and narrowed his eyes on Ethan. "Answer me."

"Your majesty, the only thing I can tell you is that my mother is in danger, so please let us go."

"In danger how?" Fearghus huffed.

"Ethan," Christian warned.

"Shut it!" Phalen snapped.

"In danger how?" Fearghus repeated.

What choice did he have? He could never let Christian or Lily get hurt because of him. "She's been kidnapped, and if we don't get to Sawney Bean's cave, we may never get her back."

"Bean?" Rhisiart hissed.

"No one is going to that bloody cave!" Fearghus shoved Ethan. He fell against Rhisiart, who grabbed hold of him.

"You three interrupt my wife's birthday celebration for Sawney Bean?" He turned to Bryg. "I will not listen to any more of this nonsense. Take them to the dungeon."

"No!" Ethan kicked and wrestled, but it was no use.

Fearghus smacked Rhisiart on the back, and pointed to Ethan. "And if this one gives you any trouble, turn him into a Milcai. Let him spend his lifetime in a pack, patrolling our borders."

After shackling their hands behind their backs, Bryg, Phalen, and Rhisiart escorted them to the dungeon. Ethan had made a calculated bet, and lost. Big-time. But it wasn't over yet. He'd find a way for them to get out of here, or die trying.

Bryg took the lead, carting their confiscated swords under her arm, heading around the back of the castle, through a deserted field, toward a cone-shaped keep that was surrounded by a wide moat. Standing side by side, Christian kept shifting his eyes to Ethan and shaking his head, making him feel even worse.

Crossing the wooden bridge that spanned the moat, they reached the tower's entrance. Bryg nodded to the single guard standing in front of the barred door. He stepped aside as she lifted a skeleton key off her neck.

She slid it into the lock, and twisted, until they heard the clank of the bolt dethatching. With a strong pull, the door creaked open, revealing nothing but darkness.

Lily and Christian followed Bryg inside, while Ethan paused outside the door and stared up at the top of the tower. He took a last look at the outside of the dungeon for any possible escape. It had to be a hundred feet high, and with no visible windows, this door appeared to be the only way out.

A blunt force knocked Ethan so hard in the back that he flew ten feet and skidded to a stop at Lily's feet. Wincing, he leaned on his side, praying the sharp pain in his back wasn't a cracked rib. Having had one before courtesy of an embarrassing altercation involving a taibhsí and a doorknob, he knew that would seriously slow him down.

Lily glared at Rhisiart. With the flexibility of a gymnast, she popped her shoulders back and stepped through her bound hands, moving them in front to help Ethan.

She pushed his back, helping him roll up on his knees, and he got his first look at a real dungeon. The only ones he'd ever seen were in movies or on television shows, and they were always underground with long tunnels that were damp and lit by torches.

As frightening as those looked, they were nothing compared to the reality of this one. The bleak dark tower prison had a single central circular staircase that wound up to the only light source, a tiny hole at the very top. A thin beam streamed down from the opening through the center of the staircase all the way to the ground, where it left a circular yellow spot. There was a putrid odor of sewer gas and BO and, strangely, the place was dead quiet.

"We the only ones to piss King Fearghus off recently?" Ethan asked.

"You're not. There are several here," Phalen said without elaborating.

Bryg dropped their weapons on the ground under the stairs, and then returned.

"You do realize that by locking us in this place, King Fearghus has declared war on Landover," Christian spit at Bryg.

Smirking, Bryg set her hands on her hips. "And what do you think my uncle would say in retort to that?" She held up a finger in his face. "Oh, wait, I know. Your trespass is tantamount to declaring war on Gransmore, is it not?"

Christian took an aggressive step at her, but Phalen caught his bound hands and yanked, practically ripping his arms out of the sockets, forcing him to his knees.

"Get off!" Christian growled.

"You've just earned yourself a little time alone," Bryg snapped. "Phalen, take him to the third floor." She lifted a set of keys off her belt and handed them to him.

Ethan panicked at the idea of being separated. "He didn't mean anything by it, did you, Christian?"

"I most certainly did, cousin!" Christian said to Ethan, but kept his gaze locked on Bryg. "General Niles will be on their doorstep with a thousand men if we're not released. I promise."

For the first time, Ethan saw hesitation in Bryg's eyes. She pressed her lips together as if contemplating her next action carefully. Her eyes darted to Lily, then Ethan, and lastly Rhisiart, who frowned and shook his head.

Taking a large step back, she looked at Phalen, and jabbed her chin. Without hesitation, Phalen lifted Christian over his shoulder and started up the steps.

Bryg walked into the darkness ahead of them while Rhisiart came forward and placed firm hands on the backs of Ethan's and Lily's necks. Lily shrugged, trying to get him to let go, but he didn't. Instead, he clamped down harder on Ethan, pressing him to his knees.

"What the—" Ethan winced.

With rage in her eyes, Lily struggled against his hold. "What is wrong with you?"

"If *you* can't behave, he will pay the price. He is, after all, an obvious weakness of yours," Rhisiart hissed.

Lily placed her hand on the top of Ethan's head, adding to the painful pressure the Fomorian was putting on the back of his neck.

"Lily—" Ethan choked. A surge of power burned deep inside him, catching his breath. From the look on Lily's face, she felt it too.

She released Ethan, and breathed the tiny word, "Te."

"Gah!" Rhisiart cried out, ripping his hands off them. He blew on his fingertips, scowling at Lily. With wide eyes, he rounded on her, grabbing her shirt in his fist. "What did you do?"

"Let her go!" Ethan warned.

Bryg rushed back. "What's wrong?"

Rhisiart didn't answer.

Bryg stared at the sorcerer. "Rhisiart? What happened?"

The sorcerer glared at Lily with tightly pressed lips. It was obvious Lily's magic had surprised him. For a moment Ethan worried Rhisiart would tell Bryg what had happened, and they too might be separated, when a wave of emotion washed over him. Ethan had to hide his grin. Lily had one-upped him, and Ethan literally sensed his mortification. This emotional sensing was new, but was coming in handy. He only wished he knew how to control it.

"Nothing is wrong. I tripped," Rhisiart snapped. "I need to return to the king. Lock them up."

Bryg's eyes darted among the three of them. Without a word, she dragged Ethan and Lily forward, and shoved them into an open cell, then slammed the iron-barred door shut.

As Bryg placed the key in the lock, a wave of panic tore through Ethan. If they didn't find a way out of this mess, he would never be able to save his mother, and Landover would have no king. "Please don't do this," he pleaded.

"Make yourself comfortable."

With a turn of the key, Ethan and Lily's fate was sealed. Bryg turned her back on them. With Rhisiart by her side, she walked swiftly out of sight.

◈ NINETEEN ◈

Phalen's footsteps pounded the stairs, getting louder, until they stopped altogether. Ethan's stomach tightened as he heard the outside door slam shut and the clink of the bolt being thrown.

Raging, Ethan grabbed on to the door's bars and furiously shook them. He wanted to be shaking the crap out of the Fomorians, but since he couldn't, this would have to do.

"Don't waste your energy, Ethan. It's locked," Lily said.

"You don't always have to state the obvious."

Lily's mouthed the word "oh." "My brothers are the same way. Go on then. Beat the bars until your fists are bruised and broken. I'm sure that will make you feel much better." Her tone was thick with irritating sarcasm.

He pressed his head against the cool bars and scanned the dark cell, unable to make anything out. A second later, a glistening sunbeam dropped through the hole at the top of the tower, throwing off enough light for him to see the cell was empty. There wasn't a stool to sit on, a bed to sleep on, or even a toilet to pee in. He glanced down at the brick floor and wondered exactly how many people had been locked in here, and for how long.

"I wouldn't sit down," Ethan said.

Lily wrinkled her nose. "I was thinking the same thing." She came next to him and pressed her forehead against the bars.

"This is all my fault," Ethan groaned.

"Much of it is, but it doesn't help that Christian is pretending to be the king and threatening war either." She sighed. "Your father is our only hope."

"Like I said, I wouldn't count on him. We've seen the last of Runyun Cooper. At least he got us this far. I saw the mountain. I know where the cave is. We just have to find a way out of here."

"Let's scour the cell. You go left. I'll go right."

They split up, venturing into the darkness in the rear. It was impossible to see anything. Ethan ran his hands along the wall, using it as a guide, touching everything he could reach, but the place was sealed shut. There wasn't so much as a loose brick.

"Lily?" Ethan called in the darkness.

"Right here," she answered, then whacked him in the face.

"Ooh," Ethan moaned. She'd hit him in the nose in the exact same place Alastair had head-butted him.

"I'm so sorry!" She reached out again, nearly poking him in the eye.

"Ow! I know you hate me, but honestly, there are better ways to finish me off."

Without a word, Lily made her way back to the front of the cell, setting her back against the bars. Ethan came next to her, pinching his nose, hoping it wasn't bleeding.

"Why do you think I hate you?" Lily asked with a furrowed brow.

"The first time you saw me, you waved your sword in my face," Ethan said, "even after your father told you who I was."

Lily tried hard not to smile. "My father embarrassed me. To have him speak to me the way he did in front of you . . . of all people. I wanted to kill him for that. I took it out on you. I'm sorry."

The apology was completely unexpected, and Ethan wasn't sure what to say. His eyes met hers, then his gaze drifted to her soft lips and his mouth watered. *God, she's beautiful. . . .* Here they were, caged like animals in an abandoned zoo, and all he could think about was kissing her.

His eyes drifted back to hers and he found her staring at him with the same intensity he was at her. He contemplated giving in to the impulse. His mouth hovered mere inches from hers. His head dipped, her breath warming his cheeks, when a sharp warning chill ran up his spine, distracting him.

An ethereal Fomorian girl with long curly red hair floated through the bars into the cell, causing him to uncontrollably shiver, interrupting what might have been the best moment of his life. He stepped back and leaned against the bars to keep from falling over.

"Ethan, are you all right?" Instead of backing away, Lily touched his hand. "You're not. You're absolutely freezing." She rubbed his arms, creating friction, causing Ethan's body to quake for a totally different reason. His heartbeat shifted into high gear. If she was going to do that every time he shook from ghostly interactions, he might start to believe radharc was a gift.

The Fomorian ghost wore a white formal gown with glistening sequins that ran up the long sleeves, over the shoulders, and down the front, forming a V that ended at her waist. It was hard to tell how old she was because Fomorians were so much taller, but if he had to guess, he'd say she was older than Christian, but not by much. Staring at her, he realized that a ghost was exactly what they needed.

The taibhsí looked from Lily to Ethan, a crease forming between her brows. *Hmmm . . . Landover or Primland?*

"L-L-Landover," Ethan stammered.

"What are you saying?" Lily asked. "Who are you talking to?"

Stunned, the girl's mouth fell open, and she closed the distance between them. *Can you see me?*

"Yes." Ethan nodded.

"Yes, what?" Lily looked over her left shoulder. "What are you looking at?"

How many fingers am I holding up? She balled her right hand into a tight fist and reached back like she was about to pound him in the nose.

"Don't hit me." He'd end up convulsing on the feces-covered floor.

"I wasn't going to hit you, Ethan," Lily said, offended.

The taibhsí laughed. *Your girl thinks you're speaking to her.*

"That's not funny."

"What's not funny?" Lily popped him on the shoulder.

"Ow! What was that for?" Ethan rubbed his arm.

"Tell me what's going on."

He held his hands up before she could hit him gain. "There's a ghost in here," and as he said it, it dawned on him he'd seen this girl before. He stared at her. "Are you the girl in the statue and the stained-glass windows?"

Father had the windows done every year since birth until I was seventeen . . . then, he had the statue made . . . as a memorial . . . Her voice trailed off. She turned her sorrowful eyes on the ground.

Seventeen. She was only a few years older than he was when she died. "What's your name?"

Dratsuah.

"Ethan? Do you know what it's like to listen to a one-sided conversation? No. You probably don't. Important pieces of information are left out," Lily said.

"The king's daughter is here."

Lily's jaw dropped. "Dratsuah."

"You know her?"

"Not personally. No one knows what happened to her."

A single ethereal tear ran down Dratsuah's cheek as she lowered her head, unable to look at them. Ethan's chest tightened, making it hard to breathe. Dratsuah's melancholy was somehow entering him. He really needed to ask his Muincara how to shut off this sensing-emotion thing. He had no idea how to control it and it was killing him right now. Dratsuah was guilt-ridden and distraught, over what, he didn't know. He took a deep breath, trying to dispel the heart-wrenching emotions.

"So you d-decided to take up residence in the d-dungeon after you died? Let me guess, you l-like sparse décor."

Dratsuah wiped her tears with her sleeve. *No. Because it is what I deserve.*

Glancing around the dismal tomb, Ethan grimaced, unable to stop his teeth from chattering from the cold. "I d-don't think anyone d-deserves this."

"You're positively freezing." Lily placed her warm hands over his.

Dratsuah frowned. *She's right. I should leave.*

"I'm f-fine. Please don't go." Ethan had to find out how to get out of here, but first he needed Dratsuah to trust him. He took a deep breath and forced himself not to think about the cold. "Why do you think you should be imprisoned?"

She floated around the room, then through the walls, vanishing, only to come back through the bars, and settle next to him again. *I betrayed my father. I let Dragomire in.*

"Who is Dragomire?" Ethan asked.

"Dragomire of the Fomorian clan Gobar. The Gobar family sided with Primland in the war," Lily chimed in.

Dratsuah nodded. *Once the war was over, they were considered untrustworthy. All their lands and money were taken from them. I met Dragomire when he was fishing in the river on the castle grounds. It's forbidden. He begged me not to turn him in. Told me his family didn't have enough to eat. He looked so hungry. So I kept his secret and brought him home with me to give him something to eat. I lied to Mother about who his family was.*

Dratsuah moved into the darkness and hovered next to the cold cell wall. Ethan looked at Lily's hands still on him and smiled. "Give me a second, okay?"

She nodded, and then let go.

Ethan closed the distance between Dratsuah and himself.

"What happened?" Ethan asked.

Every week, for months, he'd come. Dratsuah looked down at the ground. *I fell in love with him. Then one day Father discovered him in the kitchen with me, and threw him out. He forbade me from seeing him. He threatened to kill him if he ever found him in the castle again.* A tear dripped down her nose. *That night Father and Mother went out. Dragomire came back to see me. I couldn't believe it. I thought he would've hated me for what my father had done.* Her voice was filled with longing and guilt. *I stupidly snuck him past the guards to the upstairs chambers.* She finally looked back at Ethan. *Dragomire asked to see the Conbata. I should've known what he was up to.*

"What's that?"

A golden rod with magical powers that is passed down from ruler to ruler in Gransmore. I led him into Father's private chambers, where it was locked up. But he wanted more than to see it. He asked to hold it, and I let him. Once he had it in his hands, Dragomire told me he was taking it. When I tried to stop him, he stabbed me in the heart with my father's own blade. She placed a hand over her heart and rubbed. *It still hurts.*

"He killed you? How could he do that?"

He did.

"Did he take the Conbata?"

No. Worried I was still angry with him, Father left Mother at the party and came home with Rhisiart earlier than expected. He caught Dragomire as he tried to leave the castle with it.

"What did your father do to him?"

Dragomire rots in this very tower. On the third floor, in the cell next to where they tossed your friend. He hangs from his long hair or upside down by his ankles, depending on Father's mood.

"I'm surprised King Fearghus didn't kill him. I'd like to wring his neck with my bare hands."

Dratsuah gave a wry smile and looked at Ethan's hands. *He's a Fomorian. Your hands wouldn't fit around his neck. Besides, Gransmore is a civilized society. Criminals are never put to death. They are imprisoned and tortured for centuries.*

"Oh yeah. Sounds much more civilized."

Dragomire swears his father put him up to it. Such a coward. Can't even take responsibility for his actions.

Ethan cupped his hands and blew warm breath into them. "Dratsuah, I still don't understand why you're here. Why not move on?"

Because my father can't move on. He blames himself for my death. He punished the guards on duty that night, and blames himself for not insisting on more security in the castle, believing it was easy for Dragomire to break in. I've never been able to tell him the truth. To take responsibility for my actions.

Her words cut through Ethan like a knife plunging into his gut. He could still see the hurt in his mother's eyes when she'd told him she trusted him more than anyone in the entire world. What had he done? Left her to be kidnapped. What kind of a horrible person, horrible son, does that? Sure, she'd kept so much from him, but he'd abandoned her, and he would never forgive himself.

"We all make mistakes, Dratsuah."

But I betrayed my father, three times. First I let Dragomire in. Then I led him to the Conbata. And then . . . I died. Ethereal tears trickled down her cheeks, disappearing as they hit the cold floor. *Dragomire's father confessed they were going to sell it to Lachlan Traynor, Primland's king. He'd been using me all along. He never loved me.*

Lily approached and squeezed Ethan's hand. She leaned over, her lips right next to his ear. "Ask her how we can get out of here."

"I was just getting to that," he said to Lily.

Getting to what?

"Dratsuah, my mother was kidnapped and if we don't get out of here, she's going to die. The Ravens who took her are on their way to Sawney Bean's cave with her right now. If they reach there before we do, I have a feeling we're all going to be in big trouble."

Even if you could escape the tower, the western border of Gransmore is guarded by the strongest and best guard of my father's army, tested like no other. No one has ever gotten past him, and those who try generally lose their heads to his axe.

Ethan touched his neck. "That's not good."

"What's not good?" Lily asked.

"I don't think you want to know. I wish I didn't," Ethan answered.

Who is your mother?

"Caitríona Makkai."

Caitríona? Dratsuah stared at Ethan, scanning his face. *I haven't heard her name in so long. She was like a sister to me. She had the most endearing spirit.* Dratsuah smiled. *One she passed on to you. I can see it in your eyes.* She floated closer, until they were only a few inches apart. Her eyes filled with tears again. *A favor for a favor then?*

"Anything," Ethan promised.

You promise to tell my father that I'm so, so sorry. That my death was my fault, not his, and I'll not only lead you out of here, but give you the one thing that will get you past the guard.

"So I'd have to talk to him again?"

Lily tugged on his arm. "What exactly are you promising, Ethan Makkai?"

Ethan looked back at Lily, wondering if this promise was going to get them out of here, or get them killed. *You're playing with other people's lives now.* It was true, but he had to get out of here, even if it meant risking everything.

⊠ TWENTY ⊠

Getting out of the dungeon was going to be a lot harder than getting in. Ethan never thought he'd count on a ghost for anything. If Dratsuah could help them get out, then the only other thing keeping them from reaching Bean's cave, that Ethan knew of, was the guard on the road up the mountain.

"What would get us past the guard?" Ethan asked Dratsuah.

The Conbata. The possessor gains the power of persuasion. Simply by holding it, you can make anyone do anything you ask.

Ethan couldn't understand why she would offer something so sacred, something that got her killed, for his use. "Why would you—"

Caitríona. She is special. I do this for her. But you must promise to return it to the guard before you leave. It cannot leave Gransmore.

"I promise."

"Ethan, you're making me very nervous," Lily chimed in.

"Me too." Ethan gave her hand a tight squeeze. "Where's the Conbata now, Dratsuah?"

"The Conbata?" Lily sounded surprised.

Still in my father's private chamber. Do we have a bargain? I show you out of here and to the Conbata, and you talk to my father for me?

How could he do that? The king would lock them up again, but what choice did he have? It was their only way out. "Yes. We have a deal. But it has to be all of us. Christian too."

Is that the dark-haired one screaming obscenities on the third floor?

"That would be him."

She let out a groaned sigh as if getting him out wasn't going to be easy. *Very well. Give me a moment to check on him.* Dratsuah floated through the bars and up the staircase, vanishing.

While the ghost was gone, Ethan explained his conversation with her to Lily.

"While I'm all for getting out of here, how can you speak to King Fearghus on her behalf without winding up right back here?"

Ethan shrugged. "Yeah. Haven't figured that out yet."

Lily rolled her eyes. "Of course not."

Dratsuah flew back in through the bars and shuddered. *I hate going to that floor.* She then floated outside the cell again and pointed to the floor. *Underneath me, there is a trapdoor to a tunnel that leads into the castle. All you have to do to open it is pull this step*—she touched the back of the fourth step from the bottom of the spiral staircase—*and it will release the latch. But first, we must get your cell door open, then release the one on the third floor, and come back down, all without the notice of the guard outside.*

"And how do we open the door?" Ethan asked.

That's the part I have to figure out. My cousin Bryg is the only one with a key. My father is skeptical of anyone not family.

"Great." He turned to Lily. "You think your recently acquired magic skills could open the door?"

Lily eyed the lock. "I can try." She set her dainty hands on the square lock plate.

"Quietly," Ethan pressed.

Lily looked back at him with a hard grimace. "Oh right. Like I can control what I'm doing."

She closed her eyes and whispered, "Cas."

Ethan yanked on the bars, but the door was still locked.

"It seems to work better when I'm touching you."

Ethan bit his lip, trying to hide the sheer happiness coursing through his veins from her declaration. "So touch me."

Lily arched a brow at that, set a hand on his shoulder, and pinned him with a knowing smile. "You're enjoying this, aren't you?"

"Not at all," he lied.

She set her other hand on the lock, and closed her eyes, concentrating. "Cas."

There was no click. No hiss. No sparks. Ethan shook the bars again, but the door were still firmly locked.

Lily let out an aggravated growl. "I have no idea how this lock works. If I could see the inner workings, perhaps the logic of what I'm asking it to do might make better sense and it would work."

Ethan carefully examined the back of the door. "What about if you focus on popping out the hinges? The door would still be held in place by the lock, but we could probably leverage enough space for us to squeeze out."

Lily moved next to Ethan and studied the hinges. "Brilliant. Let's try again." She touched his shoulder and took a deep breath. "Ardaitheoir." A golden halo ringed her pupils and widened, covering the green of her eyes, and the three hinge pins on the left side of the door rose, shimmied, and shook, lifting completely out of the knuckle, then fell to the ground.

"I could kiss you!"

Lily smiled. "If we get out of here, I may let you."

"Motivation and now incentive." Ethan moved around Lily until he was facing the unhinged side of the door. With the right side still hanging by the lock mechanism, he kicked the other side and it swung open a few inches.

"You first." He leaned his shoulder into the gap, opening it enough for her to slide out, and scooted through after her.

Excellent, Dratsuah said. *Let's get the other one and get out of here.*

Grabbing their weapons from underneath the stairs, they quietly came up the steps until they reached the third level. There was a simple two-foot-wide ledge that circled the cells. One wrong step meant falling twenty feet down the center of the shaft in the spiral staircase to the unforgiving ground below.

"Christian?" Ethan whispered.

"Over here," Christian's anxious call came from the other side of the circular floor.

Ethan took the lead, coming off the steps, and scooting around the ledge, while holding on to its bars. Lily followed.

"This one."

Ethan saw Christian wave from a cell opposite to where he and Lily were standing. He'd only made it a few steps when he heard Lily scream.

"Let go!" she demanded.

"Please let me out." A Fomorian pressed his face against the bars of the cell in front of her. Ethan saw his hand wrapped around Lily's wrist. "I didn't mean to hurt her. It was the mist."

This had to be Dratsuah's murderer. "Get off!" Ethan kicked Dragomire's hand, forcing him to release Lily.

The Fomorian yanked it back through the bars, and clutched it against his chest, wincing. His long, dark hair was matted to his head. He hid his face in the crook of his elbow. What was left of his clothes was shredded and the smell coming out of the cell was enough to make Ethan gag.

Dragomire lifted his frightened eyes to meet Ethan's furious scowl. "Please. I didn't mean it. I loved her. . . ." His voice trailed off as he backed up, disappearing into the darkness of the cell.

It's always the same. He loved me. He didn't mean to kill me. He blames the mist. Dratsuah's heavy eyes narrowed on him. *Coward. Tell the truth.*

As if sensing her presence, Dragomire looked directly at her. "I love you, Dratsuah."

Ethan's powers took control of him again, flooding him with Dragomire's true emotions. He was telling the truth. But that could never change the fact that he'd killed her.

I can't stand it. Meet me downstairs. Dratsuah vanished through the floor.

Ethan pulled Lily to him then continued to Christian, but couldn't stop thinking about what Dragomire had said. The mist. Bean's mist. Could it really drive a person to kill?

Within minutes, they were free, and heading through an elaborately designed tunnel, with high arches and lit torches, that supposedly led directly into the upper floor of the king and queen's chambers. Along the way, Ethan and Lily filled Christian in on their plan.

The tunnel ended at a very tall wooden door that opened into a storage room filled with oversized spare chairs and tables. Dratsuah led them through several empty halls. So far, entering the castle had been simple, which worried Ethan even more.

Moving down another empty corridor, Ethan couldn't help the feeling they were walking into a trap. "Where is everyone?"

Outside, at the party, except . . . She paused at the next corner.

Ethan held up a hand to stop Lily and Christian.

Dratsuah peered around the corner. *The guard. My cousin Ulric.*

"Cousin?" Ethan saw a single guard outside a set of double doors.

As I mentioned, my father only trusts family, especially after what happened to me. His private office is behind those doors.

Ethan turned to Christian. "I'll distract him, then you take him out like you did Seamus."

"What do you mean, 'like you did Seamus'? What did you do to him?" Lily whispered harshly to Christian.

Without answering Lily, Christian glared at Ethan. "That is a Fomorian. We can't simply knock him out. I can't even reach his head."

"You knocked Seamus out? You know he's going to kill you for that." Lily gripped the hilt of her sword. "That is if I don't first. No one hurts my brothers."

"Kill us later." Ethan looked around the corner at the guard. "First, figure out how we get rid of him."

"There is no way to get rid of him. Let's get out of here and we'll deal with the guard on the path later," Christian pressed.

Peering out at Ulric, Ethan had an idea. A dumb one. Probably one that would land him right back in the tower, but it was all he had. "Dratsuah, where is the Conbata exactly?"

Once through the doors, it is in the room to the right. Encased in a binding spell. You will need to say, "Saoirse agus fírinne," and the spell should release.

Ethan repeated the instructions to Christian and Lily.

"Where do you think you're going?" Christian asked in a fatherly tone.

"To fulfill my promise to Dratsuah. Get the Conbata and find the horses. I'll meet you there."

Ethan came around the corner and into the guard's sights before Christian or Lily could stop him. He padded down the hallway, taking in the paintings along the walls.

"Where do you think you're going? Party is that way." The guard pointed the other direction.

"I'm actually not here for the party." Ethan approached the guard. Seeing a set of keys on his waist, he snatched it and took off running as fast as he could.

"Shite!"

Ethan looked back and saw Ulric sprinting after him. Fortunately, his size actually worked to Ethan's advantage. With wide halls and tall ceilings, Ulric moved quickly, but Ethan turned faster. He wove up and down the passageways until he found a huge marble staircase, and started down.

The guard's boots pounded the staircase behind him, getting closer and closer. His heart pounded so hard he swore it was going to pop out of his chest, until he finally reached the bottom.

The place was filled with partyers. Ethan did his best to blend into the much taller, much bluer crowd. He heard Ulric asking people to move out of the way, but still he hadn't found him.

When Ethan saw Ulric heading back up the steps, he whistled loudly, catching his attention, as well as most of the crowd.

"Catch." Ethan threw the keys over Ulric and didn't wait to see where they landed. He sprinted out the front doors and into the grand castle grounds, trying to find the king. It didn't take long. King Fearghus stood with Bryg, both glowering into the crowd. They must have figured out the three had escaped.

With a deep breath for courage, Ethan approached. As soon as Bryg saw him, she tried to grab him, but Ethan ducked under her reach and spun toward the king.

"King Fearghus, please. I need to speak with you about Dratsuah."

Before Ethan could say another word, Bryg was on top of him, with her knee grinding into his back.

"What is it with your overwhelming need to crush my rib cage?"

She leaned over, adding more weight. "I'm about to crush more than a few bones. And the only thing you'll be doing is going back to the dungeon with the others. Where are they?"

"Wait!" King Fearghus bellowed. "Let me speak to him."

"Uncle—" Bryg started to argue.

"I said I want to speak to him. Let him up," the king ordered.

As soon as Ethan stood, King Fearghus wrapped a hand around the back of his neck. He looked at Bryg. "You, go after the other two."

With an angry glare at Ethan, she nodded and left.

Fearghus dragged him to a chair, and sat down so he could meet Ethan's eyes. "Know this, young Makkai, my patience is gone. If you are using my daughter's name to gain sympathy—"

"Dratsuah wants you to know that what happened with Dragomire was her fault."

The king's face turned deadly serious and he blinked continuously. "What? What did you say?"

"She told me to tell you that she made the mistake that cost her her life. She let Dragomire into the castle even after you told her not to. She loves you, and doesn't want you to keep blaming yourself."

A hint of fragile shock washed over King Fearghus's face. "She let him in!" he roared; then, breathing heavily through his nose, he calmed. He gazed up at the blue skies, as if looking for divine intervention. "I don't care. I want her back." His voice shook. Then Fearghus leveled his eyes on Ethan's. "Radharc was passed to you, not your cousin."

Ethan nodded. "With the assassination of my uncle . . . Christian was trying to keep my secret. Please don't tell anyone until after the Council meeting."

"Is Dratsuah here?" King Fearghus stood up. "Can I speak with her?" He sounded so hopeful, as though being able to talk to her again would fix everything.

Ethan looked around and found her by the banquet table, watching them as party guests walked through her. Ethan waved and she floated over, wearing a tentative mask. As she came next to Ethan, he started to shiver.

King Fearghus glanced down at him, frowning.

"I'm fine. It's the cold that comes with ghosts," Ethan explained. "She's right next to me." He pointed to his right.

King Fearghus looked to his left and then back at Ethan. "Is . . . is she all right?"

"Yes. She's just worried about you. She doesn't want you to wallow in grief over her death."

He cleared his throat and wiped at his eyes. "My lovely had such a wonderful heart. She always cared more about our feelings, or her friends.

Our home feels so empty without her." His heavy hand draped over Ethan's shoulder. "Is it possible for you to tell her something for me?"

"You can tell her yourself. She can hear you."

King Fearghus swallowed hard, then looked at the seemingly empty space where Dratsuah stood. "Dratsuah, your mother and I are fine, but we miss your beautiful face." He sang the word "beautiful." "I wish I could go back and be there that night. I never would've let him hurt you."

And I wish I hadn't been such a fool. I love you, Father.

"She knows. And if she had to do it over again, she wouldn't have let Dragomire in or let him come between you, ever. She says she loves you."

Ethan really wished King Fearghus could see Dratsuah, but that's the thing about life and death. Once loved ones are gone, they're gone. Death is the permanent great divide.

Most believe anything left unsaid tends to remain unsaid. But that's not true. Dratsuah could hear the king; but he couldn't hear her, and for the first time, Ethan felt like radharc was a gift. He could help King Fearghus and his daughter have closure, and go on with life and death in peace.

"We love you too, my pre—" King Fearghus choked on the word "precious."

Dratsuah tried to hug him but her arms slid right through him. King Fearghus didn't seem to feel it. That kind of contact would've put Ethan on life support.

"My queen and I would give everything we have for one more day with Dratsuah."

"And I would give anything for another day with my mother."

King Fearghus's face softened. "I understand. I do. But you cannot go to Bean's cave. It's too dangerous. You'd likely never make it there alive, and if you did, and he was to get out, we'd all pay the price. But you have my word I will tell no one that you are the heir." King Fearghus set his hands on his hips. "I don't have the heart to lock you up any longer. I'm sure you're hungry, as are the others. Come and eat, then I'll have Bryg and Phalen escort you over the border, back to Landover."

Ethan nodded, knowing nothing he could say would change the king's mind. Out of the corner of his eye, he noticed Christian and Lily hurrying through the crowd, heading for the gate.

"I think I'll grab something while I wait for them." Ethan walked toward the table filled with platters of food.

King Fearghus kept an eye on him until the queen caught his attention, giving Ethan his out, and he took off. He spun through the throng and ran out the gates, finding Lily and Christian mounted and holding Devlin's reins. Christian gave him a confident nod as Ethan got on Devlin. He had the Conbata.

Things were finally looking up, until Bryg, Phalen, and several other Fomorian guards came out of the gates, swords in hand, heading straight for them.

"Go!" Ethan yelled.

Bryg and Phalen were fast, but the horses proved faster. They galloped west, passing through field after field, until they reached the base of the tallest mountain. There was no visible path up and they were forced to slow down.

"What now?" Lily asked.

Ethan trotted left, into a large tuft of trees, searching, but there was no way up the mountain.

"We've got them," he heard Bryg bellow.

She was right. If they didn't find this mysterious path and soon, they'd end up back in the tower, bloody and chained like Dragomire.

TWENTY-ONE

Ethan could hear the Fomorians closing in on them. It was over. Forget locking them up; King Fearghus was going to let Rhisiart turn them into Milcai.

The thrumming of a galloping horse drowned out the pounding of Ethan's heart. Runyun emerged from the trees to the right, his horse moving at lightning speed. Bryg, Phalen, and the other Fomorians came through the trees, pausing as Runyun pulled up directly in front of them.

"Cooper, so very nice of you to turn yourself in," Phalen said.

"Not today." Runyun gave a cocky grin and threw a round object no larger than a baseball at the ground. A brilliant green light spread in all directions, creating a barrier that extended as far as the eye could see.

Phalen raised his sword and brought it down, striking the barrier with such force, the entire mountain shook. With a loud hiss, the end of his blade broke off.

"Good to see you again, Teighan Bryg," Runyun said.

"I wish I could say the same." Her voice sounded far away.

"Give my regards to King Fearghus." Runyun raised his sword, saluted, then swatted Ethan on the back, and said, "Follow me."

As pissed as Ethan was at Runyun, he wasn't dumb enough to stick around. Who knew how long that force field would last?

Following Runyun deep into the forest with Lily and Christian, he offered nothing as to where he'd been, and that was fine with Ethan. There was no explanation good enough to assuage his anger over his own father abandoning him. He'd taken his ring, paid off his debt. Done exactly what his uncle said he would do: what was good for Runyun, not Landover, or Ethan. He had been better off when he'd thought Runyun was dead.

They'd been riding south, hard through the tree line at the base of the tallest mountain, for more than thirty minutes when Runyun turned onto a narrow path. The others followed, single file.

As they rode up a steep incline, a painful chill stabbed Ethan's side, then spread, firing every nerve in his body.

Lily was riding ahead of Ethan, and took the sharp left first. "Mother of the gods!"

He caught up to her quickly, and gasped at the gruesome scene. The head of a man was set on the top of a twenty-foot wooden post, but there wasn't just one. Post after post, topped with heads with terrified expressions, lined the path. Behind each post stood the aura of a body, all men draped in black cloaks.

"Primland soldiers trying to get to Bean," Christian said.

Ethan trembled uncontrollably. "They've b-been t-trying for a while," he surmised, based on the number of heads.

"Ethan, don't tell me you're frightened. They're dead. They can't hurt you," Runyun admonished.

Ethan rolled his eyes. If the man only knew . . .

As Ethan passed, each spirit reached out to him, unable to speak without their heads, but still his powers sensed their hopelessness. Primland soldiers or not, he felt sorry for them, but there was no time to stop.

The farther they trudged up the mountain the more and more decomposed the heads grew until there was nothing but skulls, and yet, their spirits still stood steadfast behind even the most decomposed, the ones who had been there the longest.

As they neared the last post, a high stone archway over the path came into view. Chiseled into the stone were the words, BÁS DÓIBH SIÚD A PAS A FHÁIL.

"'Death to those who pass,'" Lily read.

It wasn't the words that twisted Ethan's stomach into knots. It was the Fomorian standing in the center. With a helmet that covered his head and nose, a black leather jerkin with the tree mark of Gransmore stamped in the center, the guard was taller than the statue at the border. His eyes narrowed as their horses slowed to an apprehensive walk. In one hand, the big guy held an axe with a blade large enough to slice them into shish kebab meat in seconds. In the other hand he held a large metal shield that was rectangular except for the bottom, which came to a point, making it the perfect weapon for cracking skulls.

"Suppose the direct approach is best at this point." Runyun, still on his horse, moved forward a few paces until he was under the Fomorian. The guard, who'd been clocking their every move, stared down at him with an expression that was completely unreadable.

"We need to pass."

"No one passes." The guard's axe sliced downward, burying itself in the ground inches from Runyun's horse's front hooves. The horse reared up on its hind legs twice.

Ethan gasped and started to slide off his horse to help him, but Christian caught his arm. "He doesn't need your help."

"Whoa, boy." Runyun was completely unfazed. When the horse calmed, he backed him up next to Devlin.

"That was a warning," the guard bellowed. He lifted his axe, preparing to strike again. "Leave!"

"Let's go," Runyun said.

"We can't just give up," Ethan said.

Runyun turned his horse one hundred and eighty degrees. They followed. He headed back down the hill and around the bend until they were out of the guard's view, then stopped. He slid off his horse, taking a bow and a quiver of arrows with him.

"What are you doing?" Ethan asked.

"I think that's obvious," Christian commented.

"An arrow won't kill a Fomorian, especially not one that size," Lily said.

"A well-placed arrow will kill anything," Runyun disagreed.

"No." Ethan dismounted and turned to Christian. "Let me have it."

"What do you mean, 'no'?" Runyun said, miffed.

Ethan padded to Christian, who yanked a foot-long golden rod from underneath his saddlebag, and placed it into Ethan's waiting hands. It was heavy, but not as large as he would've expected, considering the size of the Fomorians.

"Is that what I think it is?" Runyun asked.

"Yep," Ethan said.

"Give it to me," Runyun demanded.

Ethan shook his head. "I got this."

Lily dismounted and came beside Ethan. "I'm coming with you. I had to shrink it. I'll need to make it bigger, but once I do, you won't be able to lift it."

Ethan locked his gaze on hers, sick at the idea of her walking out before a Fomorian ready to take their heads off. For several gut-wrenching seconds he didn't think he could do it, but he needed her magic to return the Conbata to its proper size.

Runyun snatched another bow and quiver from his horse and held them out to Christian. "Can you use a bow?"

Christian dismounted and took them from Runyun. "I think I can manage."

"We'll hit high from both sides, keeping the guard's focus off the ground." He looked at Ethan. "Hopefully, that will give you time. As soon as the first arrow has launched, go." Runyun pointed to the trees twenty feet beyond the edge of the path, and then looked at Christian. "You, there. I'll take the right."

Everyone moved.

Carrying the Conbata behind his back, Ethan and Lily started around the bend and hid behind the last tree, waiting.

"Did Dratsuah tell you how to make it work?" Lily whispered in his ear.

Ethan shook his head.

"Next time, will you please include me more in these conversations?"

"Now is not the time to get snippy," Ethan whispered back.

"I'm not being snippy. I'm trying to keep us alive." Lily's fiery green eyes met his as the first arrow soared from the right, over their heads, and bounced off the Fomorian's shield.

The guard scanned the trees, but didn't leave his post.

"Let's go." Ethan and Lily rounded the bend and crept toward the archway.

Another arrow soared from the left, then one from the right, and arrows continued raining down, all plinking off the metal shield, until one struck the guard in the upper arm. He grimaced, yanked out the arrow, and threw it on the ground.

Lily and Ethan ran to within a few feet of him. As soon as the guard saw them, he lowered his axe to their neck height. "Another step and I add your heads to my collection."

A barrage of arrows rose over the trees, baring down on him again. The guard raised his shield, covering his face, giving Ethan and Lily the opportunity they needed, that is, until the arrows abruptly stopped.

The guard gave a wicked laugh. He raised his axe over Ethan. But before he could swing, Lily waved her hands over the stick. "Driom ar ais."

With a high-pitched whine, the Conbata stretched at both ends until it reached its original length, forming a ten-foot-long staff. Embedded jewels reflected the sunlight, giving off a shimmering colored light show that danced on the guard's shield and chest plate. Ethan buckled under its weight, and it fell to the ground with a loud clank.

Stunned at the sight of the Conbata, the guard froze. He cocked his head, but recovered and swung down. Ethan shoved Lily out of the way, and then wrapped his hands around the shaft of the Conbata.

"Stop!" Ethan yelled.

The guard's eyes glazed over and the axe stopped inches from Ethan's neck.

"Raise the axe," Ethan said.

The Fomorian did as he requested, his eyes fixed on the Conbata.

Ethan fisted the golden staff even tighter. "Now, you will let us through."

"I will let you through." He took two steps to the left, opening a large enough space for them to get through the arch.

Ethan and Lily exchanged triumphant looks. Keeping his hands on the Conbata, Ethan added, "And you will tell the guards coming up the path that you sent us back down the mountain."

"You went back down the mountain," the guard repeated Ethan's words.

Runyun and Christian appeared with the horses.

"You will stand silently and not move from your position for twenty minutes," Ethan added.

The guard nodded.

"Ethan, let's go," Christian pressed.

Ethan and Lily ran to their horses and mounted quickly, but Runyun slid off his horse and walked to the Conbata. He tried to lift it, but it was way too heavy. "Ethan, we should take it with us. Lily, shrink it back down."

"No. It must be returned to King Fearghus," Ethan said.

"You can trust that it will be returned safely after we find Caitríona," Runyun replied.

"Ethan, he's right. This would come in very handy on the journey ahead," Christian agreed. "We should take it."

Yeah, right. Do I look like a complete moron? He'll return it like he returned the ring. "No. It belongs to King Fearghus. I promised it wouldn't leave Gransmore, and I don't break my promises."

Ethan rode back to the guard. The ground began to tremble. He heard Bryg and Phalen's angry shouts calling out to the Fomorians pounding up the path with them.

"We're out of time!" Runyun called.

Ethan slid off Devlin, and gripped the shaft of the Conbata. "You took this from us and it must be returned to King Fearghus's chambers as soon as possible."

The guard reached down and lifted the golden staff up easily. "Return. Yes."

"Ethan, hurry!" Lily cried.

Ethan dashed to Devlin, and climbed up, barely getting a leg over the saddle before the horse started after the others. But as he looked back, Ethan saw another big problem. "Lily, can you cover our tracks?"

"I can try." She held out her hand. "Scrios."

Loose dirt filled in the horses' hoofprints. The ground looked undisturbed, as if they had never been there.

It occurred to Ethan that the last two times Lily had done magic, she had done it on her own, without touching him. Her powers were growing.

They galloped up the path until the horses were so winded they had to slow down. The ground was still. They could no longer hear the voices of the Fomorians. Ethan breathed a sigh of relief, stunned that his plan had worked.

The trail took a sharp turn to the left and began to wind up the mountain, leaving a steep drop to the right.

Ethan dared to glance down. Bad idea. He wasn't afraid of heights, but death by falling off the steep side of a mountain was something else entirely, especially since his fate was left to Devlin's strategic climbing skills.

As they rounded the next bend, Runyun started talking to himself: "Cailleadh anáil. Fearg gheimhridh. Imeall scian. Dragain dóiteáin."

"What's he doing?" Ethan asked Lily.

"Releasing charms," she explained. "Lose breath. Winter's anger. Knife's edge. Dragon fire."

Lovely. Ethan supposed he should've been grateful to have Runyun along after all. Otherwise, judging from the sounds of those charms, he'd have ended up strangled, frozen, butchered, and set on fire.

After a short time the path widened a bit and Runyun slowed his horse, coming next to Ethan. Ethan kept his eyes focused on the path ahead, trying to hide how angry he was at the man.

"What I would give to march our army through Gransmore for the insult they dealt us," Christian said.

"What insult?" Runyun asked.

"You missed it all. They locked us in the dungeon, unwilling to let us out until after the Council meeting. They were going to allow Landover to go without an heir all because we crossed the border without permission," Lily replied. "Oh, and because we were traveling with *you*."

Runyun glanced over at Ethan, who remained silent. If he started yelling at Runyun for disappearing on them he wasn't going to stop.

"And they'll pay for it," Christian commented.

"That's not for you to decide," Lily said to him.

"It is after the Council meeting," Runyun pointed out.

Christian pressed his lips into a hard thin line. "It's not, actually."

Son of a bitch! Ethan looked at Christian, who shook his head. When he turned back, he saw Runyun had been watching the exchange.

Wide-eyed, his father stared at him. "You . . ." He paused. "The shivering on the path leading to the arch. All this time . . . Radharc was gifted to you." His father's eyes narrowed. "When were you planning on telling me?"

Ethan met Runyun's gaze. "I wasn't." He kicked Devlin, forcing him to pick up his pace.

"Ethan!" he heard Runyun yell. "Ethan, stop where you are!"

No. He wasn't going to stop. He needed a minute to himself to think. Really, was that so much to ask for?

"Ethan, wait!" Runyun ordered.

Apparently it was. Twisting to the left, the path continued to a ravine. The steep sides were covered in thick vines.

Devlin hesitated.

"Come on, boy," Ethan prodded. With trepidation Devlin took a few steps between the rocky walls as a small yellow bird flew overhead, and chirped. "See, Dev, it's not so bad."

A vine whipped into the sky, captured the bird, and dragged it into the thicket.

"Uh-oh." Not wanting to end up lassoed and choked to death, Ethan tugged on Devlin's reins. "Back up, Dev."

Before Devlin could move, thick green vines launched from the walls and ensnared all four of his legs at once. He let out a high-pitched whinny and struggled as they constricted.

Panicked, Ethan dismounted and tried to pull the vines off, but they only tightened. He reached for his sword and more tendrils dropped from above. They lassoed Ethan's hands, binding them together. He flailed and the vines yanked, lifting him off the ground several inches, leaving him dangling.

"Lily . . . Christian . . . get back!" Runyun yelled from above.

An unwelcome sense of relief washed through Ethan at the sound of his father's voice.

"Ethan, don't struggle. It will only make things worse."

Don't struggle? Was he kidding? He twisted his wrists, attempting to free his hands, but the plant constricted then snaked around his legs and over his shoulders. *Okay, two points for Runyun. Struggling, not a good idea.*

Runyun leaned over the edge of the steep wall above Ethan's head. He swung his sword downward, severing the thick vines from the wall.

"N—" The plant coiled around Ethan's neck, choking him.

Runyun pulled the small knife from his boot and threw it with deadly precision, slicing through the vine binding Ethan's hands before it lodged into the rocky wall next to him. Ethan slid one hand between his windpipe and the choking vine in an attempt to hold off death while he stretched the other to retrieve the knife, but it was too far. His head swam from lack of oxygen.

With vines wrapped around his legs, Ethan slid a foot against the wall and pushed with every bit of strength he had left, straining for the knife. His fingertips slid against the handle, pulling it toward him, until he could wrap his fist around the grip. He pulled it out of the wall and cut the vine around his neck.

Gasping, Ethan coughed while he cut his legs free. With each slice, the dark green vine turned black and shriveled.

A low whine came from Devlin. The vines wrapped around his neck, constricting tighter and tighter, pulling him toward the walls thickly layered with the deadly plant. Before Ethan could reach his horse, Runyun dropped into the ravine and cut Devlin's legs free.

Ethan slid his hands between the ropes and Devlin's neck, and sliced the vine. He turned back to see that the plant had retreated, taking refuge against the walls.

"Ethan, Cooper?" Christian called from above.

"Should we come down there?" Lily bellowed.

Ethan tried to respond but his neck was so sore he coughed instead.

"Stay where you are!" Runyun lifted Ethan's chin, inspected his neck then released him. "You'll live." Runyun pointed to the knife in Ethan's hand. "The metal in this blade and my sword were mined on the island of Cantolin where the mumfree vine grows."

Again, the vines shot out, this time twisting around Runyun's ankles. Without looking, he swung his sword, killing it, and continued his explanation. "It is the only known metal that can kill it. For us to get out of the ravine it will all have to be killed. Work swiftly, or it will snare you again."

Side by side, they chopped and cut for more than thirty minutes. When it was done, Runyun slid his sword into the scabbard on his belt and stared at the piles of the wilted plant.

"All that work to plant, and I end up taking it out myself." He turned to Ethan with a stern frown. "Follow me."

Leading Devlin, he trailed after Runyun up the path he'd missed to Lily and Christian at the top of the ravine.

"You went the wrong way," Christian pointed out to him with a sarcastic grin.

"Figured that one out on my own, thanks."

"You two," Runyun said to them, "tie the horses to that tree. We walk from here. And you"—Runyun grabbed Ethan's arm, hard—"over here. Now."

Ethan's arm had been whipped so many times by the vines that Runyun's grip burned. "Hey!" He tried to break away, but Runyun held tight.

After a few more steps Runyun finally let go and stood over him. "When I tell you to hold up, you listen. Or you and your friends can turn back and I'll proceed on my own."

Ethan stared at the ground, rubbing his sore arm, unable to meet Runyun's eyes. It was embarrassing enough to have walked into a trap. He didn't need the man yelling at him. "Fine."

"Fine? That's all you have to say? You could've been killed!"

Ethan's eyes darted from the ground to Runyun and back again. The man was seriously pissed. Was it possible to trade radharc in for another power? Invisibility would be so choice right now. "I get it! I made a mistake. But now you're trying to act like my father, and you don't have that right."

Runyun glared down at him, confused. "Exactly what is that supposed to mean? I am your father. Am I not?" When Ethan didn't respond, Runyun yelled, "Answer me!"

"Yes," Ethan shot back. "You are."

"Be glad I am. If you weren't my son, I'd have knocked you upside the head for putting your life in jeopardy like that, not to mention mine. You have to be smarter than that." He flicked Ethan's forehead.

Ethan opened his mouth to argue but stopped. He was right.

"And so you know, I would've returned the Conbata to King Fearghus. I may be a bit of a gambler, but I would never betray your trust."

"Really? You expect me to believe that when you left us? Where did you go anyway? To pay off your debt with the ring?"

Letting out a loud sigh, Runyun reached in his pocket and came out with Ethan's ring. He held it up between his index finger and thumb. "I needed to get the bolbasa, the ball that produced the shield we used on the Fomorians. I thought you and your girlfriend were dawdling. Christian volunteered to go back and get you. When none of you had returned a minute later, I rode back, but they had you headed to Brimouth."

"But why didn't you come to Brimouth? We needed your help."

Runyun folded his arms across his chest. "The king wasn't going to kill you even if you were trespassing. He's too soft for that. And knowing you,

I thought you might figure a way out, so I chose to give you a bit of time. I went to get the bolbasa, and waited for you at the base of the mountain, figuring you would have seen it on the ride to the castle. Two hours later, you and the others showed up."

Ethan raked his fingers through his hair, pushing it out of his face. "Oh."

His whole life Ethan begged for freedom, and the first time Cooper gave it to him, he berated him for it. Ethan stuffed a hand in his pocket and gripped his mother's necklace. "I should've told you about me, and radharc, but . . ."

"But you didn't trust me. I understand that better than most."

Ethan gave a hesitant smile, and then held out Runyun's knife. "Thanks for the loan."

Runyun pushed his extended hand back. "You keep it. I've yet to meet anything the metal in that blade couldn't cut."

"Thanks." Ethan slid the knife into his belt. "Runyun, do you know whose ring that is?"

"I don't. It was once in Bean's possession. When we locked him away, Tearlach took it. I don't know how Alastair came to have it. I simply wanted to keep it safe." He held it out. "But it'll be safe with you."

Ethan took the tiny ring and slid it into his pocket.

Runyun patted his shoulder. "This was the last barrier. We need to hurry—"

Loud screeching caws rang out from the clouds above, and Ethan's heart sank as three Ravens flew overhead.

Runyun's eyes shot up. "Dear gods, what have I done?"

◪ TWENTY-TWO ◪

Time stopped. The mountain fell silent. The only thing Ethan could hear was the thrumming of his heartbeat as he ran as fast as he could in a futile attempt to keep up with his father.

Runyun blew past his horse, snatching his bow and quiver, then sprinted up a short hill until he came to the cliff's edge. He huddled behind a tall, thick tree trunk as Ethan came to a stop next to him. Lily and Christian brought up the rear.

"What—" Lily started, but Runyun looked back at her and held a finger to his lips, silencing her.

Ethan peered out. Beyond the edge was a one-hundred-foot drop to the river below. On the other side of the twenty-foot-wide gorge was a steep rock wall that mirrored the side they stood on, except for the small cave opening. Sawney Bean's cave.

The only thing linking the two sides was a makeshift bridge: four ropes that spanned the gorge, leading directly to the ledge outside the cave.

It was quiet, too quiet. There was no sign of the Ravens or Caitríona.

"Where are they?" Christian anxiously scanned the skies.

"Waiting. They can't get in without—" Runyun's sentence was cut off by a gruff, irritated voice that echoed from inside the cave.

"Soith! Give me that!"

"No!" Runyun growled, and raced to the bridge. Everyone followed. "They've opened the barrier. It's the only way we could be hearing him." Runyun looked back at Ethan. "You three, stay here!"

"You're not going alone." Christian pushed past Runyun, leaped onto the ropes, and moved swiftly across.

"Christian Makkai, do you have a death wish?" Runyun bellowed, chasing after him.

"Cooper! We're out of time," a woman yelled from inside the cave. Three Ravens emerged from the small opening and stood on the ledge, scowling at them, but didn't attack. All were in their human form, except their arms, which were still feathered wings.

A black-hooded figure slipped effortlessly through the opening, onto the ledge, facing the gorge. Sawney Bean. The man was at least six foot five. With dark vapors rising from his shoulders, he gave off an aura of unbridled anger that Ethan could sense from twenty feet away.

Under his long cloak, Bean had on a black leather jerkin, black pants, and ankle boots, but instead of a sword mounted on his back, there was a three-foot-long club. In his right hand, he carried a small cauldron.

"Can you smell it, my lovelies?" Bean said to the Ravens. "That's the smell of fresh air and freedom."

Christian leaped from the ropes, landing on the ledge behind Bean, and pulled his sword. Bean spun. With a bitter laugh, he hissed and threw his arms out. Christian flew into the rock wall beside him so hard that he fell to the ground, unconscious.

Runyun kneeled, dropping below Bean's immediate sight line. He steadied the ropes with his knees at the same time he swept two arrows from the quiver on his back, which he nocked and released.

With a resounding caw, a Raven swooped down from a few feet above the cave, whacking the arrows off course and causing them to miss Bean and slam into the rocky surface behind him.

Bean's eyes locked on Runyun, his face contorted with unbridled hatred. Ethan's radharc senses shifted into overdrive, causing his chest to heave from the painful sting of Bean's overwhelming need for revenge. Ethan bent over and latched on to his knees. He had never felt anything more painful in his life.

"What's wrong?" Lily grabbed his arm to steady him.

"I'm okay." But he wasn't. Sawney Bean was free and his mother was nowhere. He took a deep breath, willing the pain to yield, glanced up at Lily, and said, "Stay here." Then he leaped onto the ropes.

And to his dismay, Lily ignored him and followed.

Ethan shook his head as the two moved across the ropes toward the cave.

Runyun flipped off the makeshift bridge and onto the ledge, somersaulting and rolling up in front of Bean.

Bean yanked the club off his back. A slow lethal smile spread across his face. "Bás def toirt!"

Shocks of white light mixed with stark red crackled in the sorcerer's eyes. He let out a wicked cry and a blast of energy burst from his hand, traveled the length of the club, and shot out from the top, heading for Runyun.

With catlike reflexes, Runyun dived back onto the bridge, grasping the bottom left rope with both hands. The shot missed and struck the bottom of the gorge with such force that it exploded the trees. It sent a reverberating blast straight upward that was so powerful it snapped the ropes, which fell, taking Runyun, Ethan, and Lily with them. They managed to grab hold of separate ropes, then swung into the cave side of the cliff.

Peering over the edge at them, Bean clutched his chest as if performing the magic had somehow injured him. Runyun twisted his ankle, wrapping the rope around his leg, and set the other leg on the knot for balance. He lifted out his bow, pinned an arrow, and released.

Bean stepped away from the ledge and the arrow missed. He raised his left fist and spun his wrist. In the gorge, wind began to whip, shaking the ropes. All Ethan, Lily, and Runyun could do was hold on.

Christian stirred and picked up his sword. Bean turned his head and with a low snarl thrust his club at him, keeping him from coming forward.

"Time for you to go!" a Raven cried from above the cave. "We'll take care of them."

Bean settled his club into the holster on his back as the Ravens took hold of his arms and legs and lifted him into the air. He continued to rotate his wrist, stirring the wind.

"Goodbye, Cooper. It gives me great pains to know we won't be seeing each other ever again. You've been such a worthy adversary." Bean flicked his wrist hard, slamming a gust into Runyun's back.

Runyun slipped.

"No!" Ethan cried.

His father fell to the very bottom of his rope, barely catching himself with the toe of his boots on a tiny rock that stuck out from the wall.

The Ravens carried Sawney Bean over the mountain's crest and then dropped low, vanishing from view. The wind fell to a gentle breeze, but it was too late. It had taken every bit of energy Ethan had to hold on, and now he was slipping.

"I can't hold on," Lily cried out.

Christian appeared at the top of the ledge.

"Pull them up," Runyun bellowed.

"Lily first," Ethan added.

Christian grabbed her rope and heaved, while she scaled the wall, slowly making her way to the ledge. Runyun released his feet, set them against the wall, and started climbing. Ethan tried to imitate him but at this point, it was all he could do to just hold on.

Christian helped Lily over the edge while Runyun slid up. As he reached for Ethan's rope, Ravens appeared in the sky and circled the gorge.

"You two, get him up!" Runyun ordered Christian and Lily, while he lifted his bow off his shoulder. He nocked two arrows, and fired. With a resounding thwack the arrows struck the two Ravens in the center of their chests. Their loud strangled cries echoed as they fell into the charred trees at the bottom of the gorge.

Christian hoisted Ethan over the ledge as three more Ravens in full bird form dive-bombed them. Two headed for Runyun, while another went for Lily with extended talons. Lily dived to the ground as the Raven dipped, barely missing her.

The Raven landed on the ledge next to the ravine only a few feet from Ethan. An arrow whizzed past his head and sliced into the Raven's chest. The bird fell backward off the edge of the cliff.

Ethan nodded a thanks to Runyun as three more Ravens swooped down, this time heading straight for Ethan. With both hands he swung his sword at the birds, but each time his blade came close, the Ravens lifted up, out of range. Christian and Lily came up behind him to help as Runyun fired two more arrows, roaring, "Incoming!"

Christian shoved Lily out of the way, then rolled out of the line of fire as the arrows struck two of the Ravens in the chest, dead center, killing them. But the third was still coming for Ethan, talons extended, prepared to strike.

"Duck!" Runyun yelled.

Ethan glanced over his shoulder and saw Runyun's arrow aimed at his head.

"Are you insane?"

Runyun released his arrow. Ethan managed to duck but the Raven's long, sharp claws clamped down hard on his shoulder, piercing the skin. Ethan cried out as Runyun's arrow struck her so hard it knocked her claws out of Ethan. He fell to his knees only inches from the edge.

Droplets of blood rained down on him from above. He looked up and saw the injured Raven hovering directly overhead. She coughed as she landed in front of him in bird form. Ethan stood mesmerized as the Raven's wings pushed forward, morphing into arms, and her body stretched into the shape of a girl not much older than he was.

She was draped in two pieces of cloth that would barely qualify as a bikini. Her hair and eyes were black as night, and her skin white as the clouds. She grabbed hold of the shaft of the arrow protruding from her left shoulder and winced.

"Move," Runyun ordered Ethan. He notched another arrow, aimed it at the Raven's heart, and walked to her with a determined gait.

He was about to fire when Ethan said, "Wait!" He grabbed Runyun's arrow and stared into the Raven's hooded gaze. "Where is Caitríona?"

Her head tilted jarringly, in a birdlike fashion. Her frightened eyes darted to Runyun. With a loud hiss, her arms morphed into wings again and she lifted up a few feet, but was too injured to fly.

Runyun pushed Ethan's hand out of the way, and pulled his bowstring taut.

Before Ethan knew what the Raven intended, she circled behind him. "Don't let him kill me."

Christian moved at her from the other side, startling her. The Raven slipped over the edge, but not before she latched on to Ethan, her long, thin nails cutting into his shoulder again, taking him over with her.

"Ethan!" Lily ran to the edge with Runyun and Christian right behind her.

Ethan managed to grab on to a small branch, stopping his descent, but the injured Raven had latched on to his leg and was weighing him down. The branch wasn't going to hold them long.

"Don't let go!" Lily ordered.

"I wasn't planning on it," Ethan shot back.

Runyun picked up his bow, nocked an arrow, and took aim, but Ethan was in the way. "I can't hit her without hitting you."

"Then don't hit her!" Ethan yelled.

"Use your knife, Ethan! Get her off you before you both fall!" Lily yelled, panicked.

Christian leaned over the side, but he couldn't reach.

With a tiny cry, the girl's hands slid to Ethan's ankles. He glanced down. Her terrified eyes swung up to meet his. Lily was right. He should hurt her the way she did him. Let her fall to her death, it was what she deserved, but he couldn't. He had to try to save them both.

"Hold on!" Ethan called to her.

The Raven gave one last remorseful look as one by one her five fingers slipped off and she fell into the gorge below. She was gone, and there was nothing Ethan could do. Horrified, his arms trembled from the strain as he tried to hang on too. His left wrist ached, and started to slip.

Runyun tried to get to Ethan, but Christian was in the way and already reaching down.

"Use the façade," Runyun instructed.

Ethan immediately understood. With one hand on the branch, he leveraged his feet against the wall and hoisted up, stretching his free hand as far as he could. He swatted Christian's open hand but slipped and dropped back down.

"Ah!" Ethan managed to grab hold of the branch again. "Oh god. I don't think this is going to work."

"Move!" Runyun shoved Christian out of the way. He looked down at Ethan. "Again!" Runyun lowered his arm.

Planting his feet on the wall, Ethan used every ounce of strength he had left and pushed up. His arm smacked Runyun's; he latched on to Ethan with both hands. Christian added his, and the two hoisted Ethan over the edge.

Numb from hanging for so long, Ethan could barely feel his hands.

"How did they find the cave?" Christian asked Runyun. "I thought you were the only one who knew where it was?"

"I am. The Ravens were following us. They used us to get past the traps," Runyun said, sounding irate. "I should've realized."

"Maybe." Ethan lifted the ring out of his pocket and looked at Lily. "Or maybe this was cursed. Maybe you were right, and they put some kind of tracking spell on it that showed them where we were, making it easy for them to follow."

"Definitely possible," Lily said.

At least she didn't say I told you so. Ethan slid the ring back in his pocket, wondering how he could've been so foolish. He knew how. He trusted the ghost at the river. Could he have been setting Ethan up all along?

The four stared at the cave entrance.

"How could they have let him out? Tearlach and I were the only two who knew the incantation to release the bacainn charm! And where the bloody hell is Caitríona?" Runyun growled.

"Ethan! Run!" Caitríona cried from inside the cave.

"Mom! She's in there!" Ethan had taken only a step toward the opening when Runyun pulled him to his chest.

"Don't cross the threshold."

"Why not?" Ethan struggled against Runyun's impossible hold. "Mom is in there and you're wasting time!"

"If you'll hold still, I'll show you." Runyun clamped down on Ethan even harder.

He calmed and Runyun slowly let go.

"Stay." Runyun kept a careful eye on Ethan as he picked up a leaf.

"You know I'm not a dog."

Runyun stepped in front of the cave entrance and tossed the leaf at the center of the opening. It drifted a few inches, crossing the threshold, and was suddenly grabbed by an invisible force, suspending it in midair. A spark lit at the tip of the leaf, and then with a flash, it turned to dust. "No. But you'd have been dead if you'd tried to go through. It's what I feared. The bacainn charm has been set again."

"Can we please just get in?" Ethan snapped.

Runyun moved next to Ethan. He leaned over so his mouth was right next to his ear. "There are times where quick decisions will save your life, but more often than not they'll get you killed. Learn from your past mistakes." He locked eyes with Ethan for emphasis then turned back to the cave entrance. "I'm going to release the charm but I want the three of you to stand back as I do."

Ethan's brain screamed, *Yeah. Whatever. Now let me in,* but he made sure not to let the words slip out of his mouth for fear that Runyun would hogtie him and leave him outside.

Runyun held his hand up to the opening. "Caithfid an madra codlata tar eis. Caithfid an madra codlata tar eis. Caithfid an madra codlata tar eis." He picked up a stick and flung it at the entrance. It passed right through without disintegrating. Runyun yanked a sword out from his back scabbard and stood, bracing for an attack.

When it didn't come, Ethan couldn't stand it any longer. "Let's go."

Runyun held a hand up, blocking the opening. "It'd be futile if I told you to remain out here, wouldn't it?"

"Completely," Ethan replied.

"This is most certainly a trap. He's left Caitríona in there with the knowledge we'd go in after her. Not to mention the dramatics of telling me he won't be seeing me again." Runyun turned and locked eyes with Ethan, then Lily, and lastly Christian. "Don't get killed."

Runyun lowered his arm, bent over, and crawled into the cave first. Ethan was next, then Lily. With a last glance over the ravine, Christian brought up the rear.

The inside of the cave was cold and dark. Ethan raised his hand above his head and stood up slowly, making sure he wasn't going to bonk his head.

"Lily, we need light," Ethan said.

"Solas," Lily whispered. Tiny flames burst from her fingertips. One by one she flicked them off, and they landed on several bowls of oil scattered around the room, dimly lighting the tiny hourglass-shaped chamber.

"Impressive," Christian commented to Lily.

She followed Ethan as he walked slowly around the front room, taking inventory.

Ethan wrinkled his nose at the fumes from the burning oil. "What is that smell?"

"Charred blood. The oil in that bowl comes from Bean's veins," Runyun explained. "I've seen him transform it before. It's the only way he would have had oil."

"Lovely." Ethan exhaled. "Mom?"

There was no answer.

In a caveman kind of way, it was a home. It had a small table with a single stone set up as a chair. Neatly stacked in the center were a dish, two chiseled stone cups, and a small cauldron.

Tapestries hung on the walls beside two filled bookshelves. Next to that were clothing shelves. Each article folded perfectly. Everything was put away in its place. For a narcissistic murderer, the guy was freakishly neat. There were no talking shrunken heads, no loose snakes, no zombified rats in cages—none of the things Ethan expected inside a sorcerer's prison cave—and yet the place still gave him bone-chilling creeps.

In the center of the chamber stood a round pillar at least three feet wide. Beyond the pillar it was too dark to see anything except the outline of a bed.

"Where did he get all these books?" Runyun wondered out loud. "The plenty cauldron"—he lifted the cauldron on the table—"for food and drink and clothing was left with him. But these . . ." Runyun set the cauldron down and lifted a book off the shelf, examining the spine.

"Mom?" Ethan called again.

"Runy—" Caitríona's words cut off.

Runyun's eyes darted to the bottom of the bookshelf. Ethan came next to him as he kneeled and held his sword out in front of him.

"Christian, on point," Runyun said without looking at him.

"On it," Christian responded and positioned himself so he could watch both the entrance and the rest of the cave.

"Caitríona?" Runyun said.

"Runyun—" Caitríona replied, and then added a frightened, "No!"

Ethan dropped to his knees beside his father. "She said that to you in that exact same way at the border of Primland. Remember?"

"Runyun . . . please . . . no!" Caitríona cried out again.

With a strong hunch, Ethan picked up a small upside-down bowl beside the books. A blood-red crystal about the size of Ethan's pinkie rolled off the shelf, landing on the floor.

"Runyun—" Caitríona's voice sounded from the crystal.

"What is this?" Ethan picked it up and handed it to Lily.

"I believe it's a memory crystal. I've never actually seen one before, only read about them." She held it up over the flames of a nearby bowl of oil. Ethan came next to her, took the crystal, and squinted at tiny letters written across the facets.

"What do those words say?"

"Your mother's words: 'Runyun, no, please, Ethan . . .'" Lily's voice trailed off.

"The Ravens must have captured her words in Bramblewood." Runyun stared at the crystal, the slow tic working his jaw and tightly pressed lips giving away his feelings.

"Ethan! No!" Caitríona called again, this time from Lily's hand.

Her haunting cries were more than Ethan could take. He grabbed the crystal from Lily, dropped it on the ground, and with a loud roar stomped it with the heel of his shoe, cracking it to bits.

Runyun scanned the cave. "Why haven't we been attacked? This has to be a trap."

"Let's fan out. See if there's anything that will give us a clue to where they've gone. Lily and I will check the back." Ethan lifted out his sword, almost dropping it on his foot.

Runyun arched a taunting brow at him. "Don't hurt yourself."

He made sure to toss Runyun a scathing glare before he and Lily started into the back of the cave.

Runyun went back to checking the books on the shelf while Christian examined sheets of parchment on the rock table.

The closer Ethan and Lily got to the center of the cave, the colder it became. White puffs of air wisped out of Ethan's mouth with every breath. There was a taibhsí. But more than that, as with Bean, he could fully sense the ghost's emotions. His powers were growing. And they sucked. A combination of anger and rage so palpable it was almost debilitating coursed through his body.

"What's wrong?" Lily asked.

"There's a ghost in here."

"Where?"

"I don't know. But I can feel her."

"'Her'?"

A very ticked off her. Ethan had the sudden urge to hold Lily's hand and pull her behind him, but knew she wouldn't find his chivalry chivalrous. She'd take it as an insult, like she couldn't take care of herself. Besides, if he really thought about it he'd be hiding behind her.

As they reached the column a threatening growl started in the rear of the cave, shattering the tense anticipation. Oh yeah, this was a trap. "Runyun? I think we've got company." Ethan swallowed hard at what sounded like fierce guard dogs preparing to make them their next meal.

"Everyone, out!" Runyun bellowed.

Before anyone could move, two creatures that looked like the demonic offspring of a Rottweiler and a dragon leaped out of the darkness. Almost as tall as Ethan, they had webbed batlike wings, short snarling snouts with protruding fangs dripping with saliva, and the largest paws Ethan had ever seen.

"Gargoyles!" Christian yelled.

Lily grabbed Ethan's arm and yanked him toward the front of the cave. One of the two gargoyles leaped over their heads and landed between them and their only way out.

The other gargoyle headed straight for Runyun and Christian. Wasting no time, they pulled their swords and went on the attack. Christian struck first, lunging at the gargoyle's neck, slicing it through the center until the tip burst through the other side, but it didn't stop. It didn't even flinch.

"Move!" Runyun yelled at him. "Your sword won't work."

But Christian refused. He ripped his sword out of the beast and rained a heavy blow on the back of its neck, but still it didn't fall. It darted right, around Christian, heading straight for Runyun like it was on a mission.

Runyun shoved Christian out of the way as the gargoyle leaped on top of him, knocking him to the floor. With sheer strength, Runyun rolled with the gargoyle until they slammed into the bookshelves.

The gargoyle inhaled deeply, then growled as its nostrils ignited, glowing a brilliant red. Trapped underneath, Runyun braced his elbow on the floor and used his free hand to shove the gargoyle's smoking nose away from his face as it unleashed holy hell. Fire sprayed the wall and the bookshelves erupted in flames. The cave immediately filled with smoke.

Christian kicked the gargoyle in the back. It jerked forward off Runyun, who spun up to stand next to Christian. The two cornered the gargoyle against the burning shelves.

In the middle of the cave, Ethan and Lily danced with the other gargoyle, spinning around the column. Smoke wafted from its nostrils, giving off a burned charcoal smell.

"Ethan, watch out!" Lily cried.

Fire hit the pillar, separating into two distinct streams, engulfing them in blazing hell. Ethan and Lily stood back-to-back, trying to keep from being barbecued. When the fire stopped, tiny whiffs of smoke billowed off the bottom of Lily's singed hair.

"I'm going to kill that beast!" she said, gasping for breath.

They rounded the column and together, ferociously stabbed at the gargoyle several times, making lethal contact, but again it had no effect.

"Why won't they die?" Lily bellowed.

"Ethan, use your knife!" Runyun yelled.

"Lily!" Ethan held up Runyun's dagger. "Can you distract it?"

"Oh sure. No problem," she muttered, then peeked around the column. "Over here!" Lily shouted, waving her arms.

Ethan gripped the knife tightly in his right hand and started around the other side of the pillar when he slipped on gargoyle spit, and fell flat on his back. The beast pounced on top of him but somehow he managed to hold on to his knife.

"Ethan!" As Lily rounded the pillar, Ethan flicked her the knife. With a vicious growl, she stabbed the bad boy in the neck. The gargoyle burst into pieces.

Runyun darted in and out, trying get a proper angle on the trapped gargoyle. It crouched a second before it leaped at Christian.

In one smooth move, Runyun did a forward roll and jabbed his sword into the gargoyle's neck. He yanked, slicing it open from stem to stern, and then spun away as the gargoyle exploded to dust.

Breathing a sigh of relief, Lily helped Ethan up.

"That wasn't so bad." Ethan leaned against the column, coughing up gargoyle bits, when a slow chill wound around his neck. "Uh-oh."

"Uh-oh?" Lily frowned at him.

Sada chra anosa, the taibhsí susurrated from the deep recesses of the cave.

The bits of gargoyle vanished.

"Time to go," Christian bellowed.

Before they could escape, the gargoyles reappeared as statues in the seated position, wings spread, and teeth barred, blocking the only way in or out of the cave.

They were trapped. And Ethan had a sinking feeling that the gargoyles were the least of their problems.

TWENTY-THREE

An uncomfortable silence fell as the last of Bean's books smoldered at Runyun's feet. While the gargoyles no longer appeared to be a threat, appearances could be massively deceiving. There was no way around them. No way out of the cave. And yet there was something even more terrifying than the gargoyles close-by: an angry ghost who could do magic.

Runyun moved next to Ethan and Lily. Christian stalked the other side of the cave, scanning everything, but finding nothing.

Now that I have your attention, let's have a visit, shall we? The ghost's strong Irish cadence was so melodious it was almost hypnotic.

Ethan alone spun around to stare into the back of the cave. He could barely make out the taibhsí's outline until she floated out of the darkness and into the dim light of the smoldering bookshelves. The woman had a round pale face, long curly brown hair, and eyes so black he couldn't see a pupil at all. Her long black lacy dress was so low cut that Ethan had no idea how she kept it on. Krazy Glue?

"Ethan, what are you looking at?" Runyun asked.

Her cleavage actually, but no one needed to know that. "A ghost. She's the one who trapped us here. She controls the gargoyles."

The woman glared at Ethan with raised eyebrows and a sinister smirk. She floated within inches of him, and when her icy breath touched his face it sent a chill down his spine. She leaned over next to his ear and said, *Boo.*

"Boo yourself," Ethan replied.

"Bloody hell," Runyun whispered. For the first time since Ethan had met the man, Runyun looked noticeably shaken. "You're speaking to the ghost?"

Ethan nodded.

The ghost threw her head back and cackled. *Isn't this perfect? You can see me. Oh, my, my, my, if only the gimp knew.*

"What's a gimp?"

"A fool," Christian answered.

"Good word. And who would that gimp be? Bean?" Ethan asked her.

Tsk. Tsk, she said. *Not important.* She waved her hand over the destroyed bookshelves. *You've made quite a mess. He'll be most upset. But then again, he won't be returning, will he?* She let out a sadistic laugh.

"Neat freak, huh?"

Oh, more than that. Gods forbid, if one thing is out of order the idiot throws a hissy fit like a three-year-old demigod.

"Sounds like some serious OCD. Probably not a good affliction when you have a thing for cutting out people's hearts."

You're funny. I like you. The woman winked at him.

"Gee. Thanks. Why did you say demigod? Is Bean a demigod?"

"Demigod?" Runyun repeated. "What's she saying?"

And clever too. Perhaps. But his secrets are not for me to tell. She raked Runyun with a disgusted scowl.

"Who would tell his secrets?"

No one. Unless they wish to have their soul obliterated from existence.

Interesting. "You his wife?"

She laughed. *Now that is funny.* She flew past Ethan without elaborating and stopped behind Lily. *And I believe you have something that belongs to me. A gold ring with rubies in the shape of a star.*

Shocked, Ethan took a step away from the ghost. "How did you—"

Oh goodie. He wasn't lying. You do have it. Her lips curled into a smirk. *And look at her.* She stared down at Lily in a way that made Ethan very uncomfortable.

"I'm going to ask you again. Who are you?" Ethan paused between each word for emphasis.

You may call me Kiara. And what is your name? She floated back toward him, stopping only inches away with her hands placed on her hips.

"Ethan Makkai."

Oh . . . this is too good to be true. She stared into Ethan's eyes. *The Makkai heir.*

"Ethan, who is she and what is she saying?" Runyun asked, annoyed.

"A woman named Kiara. Do you know her?"

Runyun shook his head. "Does she know where Bean and the Ravens went?"

Oh yes, but I'll not tell him. For that betrayal, Bean would spend eternity hunting me down. That man—she pointed to Runyun—*must die.*

"No. I won't let you do that."

"Do what?" Christian and Lily asked simultaneously.

Ethan held a hand up, silencing them.

Why would you care about him? What is he to you?

"My father."

Runyun shifted so his shoulder was protectively in front of Ethan.

She positively beamed. *This just keeps getting better. Runyun Cooper is your father? The heir's father? Oh, if only I could see Bean's face when he finds out. But alas, I will be long gone, reunited with my Torin.* She lowered her eyes on Ethan's. *If you want him to live, tell Cooper and the other tall one to stand by Bean's pets. I wish to speak to you*—she paused to look at Lily—*and the pretty girl, alone.*

"She needs to talk to me . . ." Ethan caught Lily's eyes, and added, "And Lily."

"What?" Lily asked, confused. "Why?"

"I don't know yet," Ethan answered. "But there is only one way to find out. Runyun, you and Christian wait by the entrance."

Lily started for Ethan, but Runyun grabbed her arm, stopping her. "I don't think so. I want you both behind me now. This woman is—"

"A ghost," Ethan interrupted. He pinned his father with a confident look. "I got this."

Reluctantly, Runyun let go of Lily's arm. She made a beeline for Ethan. The woman watched Runyun closely as he took several steps back, moving Christian with him, until they stood to the right of the frozen gargoyles.

"Kiara, did the Ravens have a woman with them? She would've had the same hair color as you, only not curly."

The ghost didn't answer. Instead, she roared a second before she jabbed her left fist into Ethan's right shoulder. *You don't get to ask questions.*

Gasping, Ethan fell to his knees. The right side of his body paralyzed, he leaned his left hand on his thigh to keep from falling completely over. "P-p-please . . ." Ethan was in too much pain to even say "stop."

"Ethan, what's wrong?" Lily asked, trying to help him up.

Concerned, Runyun and Christian came toward them.

Tsk. Tsk. Tell them to stay where they are! Kiara snapped. She ripped her fist out of Ethan's shoulder.

Relieved, Ethan panted and held a hand up to Runyun and Christian, yelling, "St-stop!"

Shaking his head, Christian ignored Ethan's request and started for them, but Runyun threw out an arm, holding him back.

"Give him a chance," Runyun said, his own chest heaving from worry.

Lily grabbed Ethan's arm and swung it over her shoulder, lifting him to standing.

"P-please, she's my mother. I need to know if she's okay and where they took her."

Do you know how long he's had me trapped here?

"No. But maybe if you tell me where Bean went I can help you leave."

Oh, such a sweet, handsome thing, and a wonderful son. You can help me. Kiara's sickening sweet tone was an obvious prelude to something that was going to make Ethan very unhappy. *I simply need my ring. Give it to me.*

"Your ring for information," Ethan insisted. "Or turn the gargoyles back on and we'll fight our way out."

You'll die, Kiara huffed.

Ethan shrugged with a nonchalance he didn't feel. "Better to go down fighting."

He pulled Lily closer, lifted out his knife, and started for the statues when Kiara held up her pale, bony hand. *Wait!* Ethan froze. *Fine. You free me and I'll give you the one thing that will answer all your questions. Where Sawney Bean is going, and why.*

She was probably lying. But Ethan was pretty sure that getting past those gargoyles was going to be impossible, so he decided to tempt fate.

Maybe, just maybe, Kiara had something that would help them. "Sounds like a fair trade."

Tell me, Ethan Makkai, what are you willing to sacrifice to get your mother back? Or should I say who? Kiara folded her arms over her chest and lowered her eyes on Lily.

"Excuse me?" Ethan asked.

She raked Lily with a pitiful frown. *This lovely girl,* she said with a hint of envy, *won't be leaving.*

"You stay away from her!" Ethan stepped in front of Lily. "Runyun, take Lily!"

"What? Why?" Lily asked.

Runyun grabbed Lily's arm. He raised his sword while pushing her at Christian. With a wave of Kiara's hand the two gargoyles came alive. They inched forward, baring their teeth and growling.

That may not be enough. Kiara waved her hand again. The fanged beasts split in half. Each missing side regrew instantly. Where there had been two, there were now four, then eight.

"Ethan! Whatever you're doing is making things much worse!" Christian snapped.

Christian, Runyun, and Lily stood back-to-back-to-back with swords raised as the gargoyles circled.

Bring the girl to the back or they attack.

"Never," Ethan said, holding his knife up. "Bring it on."

Kiara huffed. *I simply want to show her something, silly boy.*

She was lying, but two could play at this game. Ethan lifted the ring out of his pocket and held it out on the palm of his hand.

There it is. . . . She closed the distance between them.

"How stupid do you think I am? You need her body. Corporeal form, don't you? So you can put the ring on. What's back there? Something that will allow you into her body?"

"What?" Lily said, flabbergasted.

Kiara winked at him.

Enraged, Ethan grit his teeth. "But what happens if your overgrown mutts kill us? She won't be of any use to you then. You'll spend eternity staring at the ring on the floor of this cave, trapped."

"Ethan, I don't like where this conversation is going," Lily said, her eyes wide with panic.

The ghost smirked a grin. *You are clever. Landover might even have a chance at surviving Bean's plans with you leading, but, alas, we seem to be at an impasse.* Kiara held up an index finger. *Oh, but maybe not. You see, I do know where they've taken your mother.* Kiara locked her eyes on his. *The lovely Caitríona Makkai. I know everything they're planning. It's all in the book hidden in this cave. I managed to keep that louse from taking it with him . . . all because I knew you were coming. I thought it might come to this.* Kiara moved in front of Ethan. *You help me with the ring, and the girl, and I'll tell you where the book is.*

Ethan looked back at the stalking gargoyles that were about to make a meal out of his father, his cousin, and the girl he wanted to kiss so badly it hurt.

Choose quickly, boy. Your mother or the girl?

There was no choice. Even if Kiara were telling the truth, he'd never let her hurt Lily. He'd never let anyone hurt her. Not in a million years.

Too long!

The gargoyles attacked. Two jumped Runyun, one attacked Christian, and the last stalked slowly at Lily, who walked backward in Ethan's direction.

The remaining four blocked the exit.

There was no escape.

Runyun sliced the head off one and it turned to dust, but the other bit his shoulder, hard, and dragged him across the floor toward the gargoyles guarding the exit.

Runyun dropped his sword with a clank. Metal scraped leather as he pulled both knives from his boots. He stabbed the gargoyle clamped on to his shoulder right between the eyes. It turned to dust, only to reappear again right beside him.

The last gargoyle backed Christian into the smoldering bookshelves. It lunged and clawed at his chest, leaving deep bloody scratches down his torso.

Ethan's heart filled with dread. There was no way this was going to end well. "Stop!"

Kiara waved her hand and the gargoyles froze midstep. Eyes wide with excitement, she floated over the bed, into the darkness beyond it. *Good boy. Now follow me if you want them to live.*

As Ethan watched Kiara vanish into the back of the cave, his stomach tensed and his mouth filled with acid. His mind raced, trying to come up with a plan. There was only one thing he could think to do. It probably wouldn't work, but at this point anything was worth a shot.

"What's going on, Ethan?" Christian demanded.

Ethan ignored him and walked over to Lily, who now stood behind the pillar. He stared into her warm green eyes. She didn't look nearly as scared as he felt. "Do you trust me?" He reached out his hand to her.

She looked down at it and took it without question.

Runyun watched, his faced etched with worry, but didn't say anything. He gave a nod of encouragement to Ethan, and turned to Christian. "We have to trust him."

Christian arched a brow but said nothing.

Ethan led Lily into the back of the cave, following Kiara's path. The temperature plummeted. Uncontrollably shivering, he interlaced his fingers with Lily's, and gently squeezed.

Wonderful. You've chosen your mother. Wise boy. There's always another girl. Kiara commented. *Bring her here.*

As they walked the short distance to the very back of the cave, the ceiling height decreased until it was only a few inches above their heads. The only light came from three tea light candles set before a round mirror that sat on a tall wooden stand. The aged glass had a tarnished gray ring on the outside edge.

The minute Ethan saw it he flipped Lily around so she didn't accidentally look in the mirror.

Kiara floated closer until she hovered next to Ethan. *Place the ring on the stone.*

Hesitating, Ethan let go of Lily's hand and set the ring next to the mirror.

Kiara spun around and moved so that she was positioned before the mirror. *Well done. All that's left is for her to look at her stunning reflection.*

Ethan's heart slammed against his chest. *There are times where quick*

decisions will save your life, but more times than not they'll get you killed.
Runyun's words haunted him. Was this a rash decision? Could this plan
even work?

He nodded to Kiara and made as if he were going to move Lily in front
of the mirror, but then stopped, and glared at Kiara. "I think you're forget-
ting something."

Very well. Kiara floated over to the wall on the other side of Lily and
waved a hand over a small, darkened spot. *Touch here, and say "siorse." The
slab will open and you'll find the book.*

Ethan started for the wall.

Wait! First, tell her to look in the mirror! Kiara shrieked, her tone taking a noticeable downward shift.

Ethan glanced over his shoulder to check on Runyun and Christian.
The two were still close to the bookshelves, surrounded by gargoyles that
sat ready to pounce.

This was it. Go time. A slow smile spread across Ethan's face as the words
his Muincara told him never to say came out of his mouth. "Dul amach!"

Nothing happened.

Kiara arched an eyebrow. *Nice try.* She tapped her bone-white finger
through Ethan's nose.

"Bah!" He winced as the pain shot through his brain, making it feel like
an IED had exploded in his head.

Kiara yanked her finger out of his nose. *You are no match for Sawney
Bean. His magic is all-powerful. He imprisoned me, and only my ring and
your girl can break his charm.* She floated back in front of the mirror again.
*Don't waste another second of my time or I'll turn the gargoyles on your
father and force you to watch as they gut him from—*

Ethan held his hands up, surrendering. "No need to go there." He let
out a long exasperated breath. So it was down to this.

"Runyun, Christian? Remember what happened when I stepped in the
mist?" Ethan bellowed.

"What are you doing?" Christian asked with a dreadful tone.

"I'm about to step in it again." Ethan positioned Lily next to the wall.

Fear not, Kiara said, *there is no mist in the cave.*

With his left hand, Ethan reached for the stand that held the mirror,
and carefully picked it up.

What do you think you're doing? Kiara snapped.

"I don't trust you. You don't trust me. It'll all happen together, on three."

I like it! Kiara clapped her hands together in approval. She moved beside Lily so that when Ethan held the mirror up, she would be in position. *Yes, yes. Do it!*

"One," Ethan said loudly. He turned to Lily and mouthed, "Get the book."

"What?" Lily mouthed back.

He locked his wide eyes on hers, then shifted them left, at the wall behind her, hoping Lily understood.

Could you count any slower, nitwit? Kiara snapped.

"Two!" Ethan bellowed. He took one last look at Kiara, and then yelled, "Three!"

"Soirse!" Ethan slammed the dark spot on the wall with his right hand, and rocked the stand in his left forward. A piece of the wall slid open, revealing an old leather-bound book as the mirror tumbled, crashing to the ground, shattering into a million pieces.

With a cry so loud it shook the ceiling, Kiara turned to the gargoyles. *Kill them all!*

Lily grabbed the book while Ethan went after the ring.

Small flakes of rock crumbled where the book had been and fell to the ground. The walls fissured, forming small veins that spread. The place was caving in.

"Get out!" Ethan yelled as he and Lily ran out of the recesses, and into a nightmare.

The gargoyles were all over Runyun. One bit his injured shoulder, the other had fangs in his leg. With a knife in each hand, he slammed one into the head of the gargoyle on his leg and the other into the cheek of the one over his shoulder. Both turned to dust, but reappeared and went on the attack.

A loud boom from under Ethan's feet reverberated through the chamber. A crack started in the floor at the back of the cave, then spread, opening up a bottomless sinkhole.

Lily shoved Ethan against the table to keep them from falling in, but Christian wasn't so lucky. His legs slipped out from underneath him and he fell. Somehow he grabbed on to the ledge with one hand, but his fingers strained from his weight. He wasn't going be able to hold on for long.

Ethan ran to the ledge, reached over, and latched on to Christian's forearm with both hands. Lily set the book next to the exit, then grabbed on to Ethan's waist. With their combined strength, they managed to pull him up as six more gargoyles stalked from the rear of the cave.

Lily took the knife from Ethan's hand, and struck the first gargoyle right between the eyes, but before it turned to dust, it sank its fangs into her arm and she dropped the knife. "Ethan!"

Ethan tried to pick it up, but Kiara dived into Ethan's body. He fell to the ground, convulsing.

Give me my freedom!

The walls quaked. Any second they were going to collapse. The gargoyles circled, clawing Ethan's legs. He tried to move but he couldn't feel his body. It had gone entirely numb.

With the gargoyles focused on Ethan, the cave entrance was finally accessible. Runyun shoved Christian out, but Lily refused to go. She raced toward the gargoyles, retrieving Ethan's knife, with Runyun following. With one lethal blow, Lily stabbed a gargoyle in the back, then another. Runyun tossed Lily his sword and picked up Ethan in his arms. They backed away from the gargoyles toward the opening with Lily holding the knife and sword, ready to strike.

Ethan writhed in pain from Kiara's occupation.

If Cooper takes you across the threshold with me inside your body, we will both die!

Christian reached inside the cave, ready to take Ethan from Runyun.

With every bit of breath Ethan had left, he yelled, "W-w-wait!"

Runyun paused at the threshold.

There was only one thing Kiara wanted, her freedom, and without the ring he was holding, she'd never have it. Ethan lifted his head. "Kiara?" He held up the ring. "Fetch!" With all the strength he could muster, he threw it in the back of the cave.

My ring! Kiara dashed out of his body after the ring, leaving an ethereal trail that was immediately crushed from both sides by the collapsing walls.

Lily dived through the hole while Runyun carried Ethan out, barely making it before the rocks filled the opening, sealing it shut.

Runyun set Ethan down. "What happened to you?"

Ethan set his hands on his knees and tried to catch his breath. "Kiara decided to take up a new residence . . . inside me. I'll be fine in a minute."

"Christian?" Ethan said, staring at his shirt, which was shredded and covered in blood. "You gonna live?"

Christian winced as he pulled what was left of his shirt off his abdomen. The claw marks were deep and seeped with blood. "I will. Looks worse than it is. Lily can fix me up when we get back to the horses, right, Lily?"

Lily didn't answer. She returned the weapons to Ethan and Runyun then picked up the book. "Do you know what this is?"

Ethan leaned over her shoulder and stared down at it. Burned into the leather cover was a shield made from Celtic knots with a double-edged long sword down the center, woven into the pattern. "No."

"The scáthán of Primland," she said.

"What?" Shocked, Christian lifted the book out of Lily's hands and examined it. "What's it doing here?"

"Kiara said that whatever Bean was planning was spelled out in it." Ethan reached over Christian and yanked the cover, but it didn't budge. "Great. It's locked."

Runyun took a turn next, but couldn't open it either. It was as if the book were glued shut.

"What now?" Lily asked.

Ethan walked to the cliff and stared out across the ravine, in the direction Bean and the Ravens had gone. "We keep going."

"Agreed, but where?" Christian asked.

Runyun ran his hand along his jaw. "We follow them." He lifted a thin, rolled-up twine out of the inside of his jacket. He tied the end like the first part of a shoelace, and with two more moves, made a lasso. He spun it above his head and threw it high in the air, looping it smoothly over one of the stumps on the other side of the ravine. He pulled the twine taut and tied it to an enormous rock close-by.

"Lucky shot," Ethan commented.

"There is no such thing as luck. It takes practice, as does using a sword."

Runyun glanced at the scabbard hanging from Ethan's belt before he latched on to the rope with both hands. He lifted his legs up and wrapped them around it, making sure it could hold his weight.

Ethan had the sudden urge to knock him off the rope into the ravine below. He'd almost died. Did the man have to insult his less-than-poor medieval fighting skills?

Runyun lowered back down to the ground. "Who's first?"

Having had enough, Ethan latched on to the rope, lifted his legs up, and pulled himself backward across the ravine without looking back.

Once across, they hustled to the horses and made their way down the back of the mountain. Menacing clouds gathered, darkening the skies, and unleashed sheets of rain. They trudged through, following the direction Bean and the Ravens had gone, straddling the Gransmore–Kilkerry border, but after a few hours of riding, they were soaked, starving, and exhausted. The temperature had dropped so low, Ethan could see his breath. He had been forced to wrap his only blanket around him, and it too was drenched.

"We need to find shelter," Ethan bellowed.

"Two choices really," Christian said. "Gransmore. But, the Fomorian guards will be expecting us. They know we have to pass through to return to Landover. Watches have likely been set up along the border. We'd surely be captured and returned to the tower, but we'd be dry."

"And Runyun would be dead," Ethan retorted. "Besides, the Ravens headed west. So should we."

"West is—" Lily started.

"Kilkerry," Runyun blurted out, making it sound like a curse word. "I know a place." His stern eyes locked on each of them. "Keep your wits about you. Fomorian guards tossing you in a dungeon will feel like a warm welcome compared to the reception we may run into in Kilkerry."

TWENTY-FOUR

The rain ceased as the group crossed the border into Kilkerry. Steady cold winds over rocky terrain slowed the horses to a walk. Without cover of forest, Runyun found a spot to camp in a canyon. They were blocked from the wind, but there was nowhere to take cover if something unfriendly found them. From above, they were completely exposed.

They settled the horses and Runyun went foraging for something to eat. Christian kept a lookout while Lily and Ethan built a fire from sticks and dried leaves they had gathered along the way.

Once the fire was going, Ethan sat down to examine the book.

Christian held out his hand. "Give it to me."

"Don't," Lily answered for Ethan.

"What do you mean, 'don't'?" Christian asked. He walked to the fire and stood over her.

"I don't trust your judgment with something as dangerous as Primland's book of magic," Lily snapped. She stood up and turned to face him with a heated glare. "You've proven in Gransmore that you're not to be trusted with the safety of the realm. For all we know Gransmore's guards are tearing through Landover. You threatened King Fearghus with war!"

"They were locking us up! He had no right to do that," Christian retorted.

Lily leaned over so their faces were inches apart. "And you had no right to start a war for Landover. To start something that would get our soldiers, our people, killed!"

Things were getting entirely too weird. "Let's all calm down," Ethan said, stepping between them with his arms out.

"You're right," Christian said to Lily, startling both her and Ethan. "I don't. But he does." Christian pressed a finger on Ethan's chest. "So, cousin, what do you say to all this? Was the insult King Fearghus dealt us enough to prove his ill intentions toward Landover? No friend of our realm would lock up our heir until after the Council meeting. Would they?"

Ethan could see both sides. On the one hand, Lily had a point. Wars cause people to die. Soldiers to die, and her father and brother were soldiers. But on the other hand, if Ethan hadn't gotten away, would King Fearghus have let him out before the Council meeting or would he have benefited from Landover having no heir?

"I don't know," Ethan answered. "My guess is Fearghus would have let us out before we were due in Coventry, but there is no way of knowing. Now, if you're both done flipping out over things we can't change, can we focus on the task at hand? How the hell do we open this book?" He passed it to Christian. "Give it another try."

Christian nodded respectfully. "Your knife?"

Ethan pulled it from his belt and handed it to him. Christian tried to slide the knife tip into the pages, but couldn't. The blade came within a quarter inch of the paper but was unable to penetrate whatever shield Bean had sealed it with. He tried twice more before letting out an aggravated sigh, and dropping the book into Lily's waiting hands. He handed the knife back to Ethan.

"It's impossible," Christian huffed.

Lily ran her hand over the emblem on the cover. "This book is weighted down with an evil essence so powerful it seeps through the shield Bean placed around it. I can feel it." Lily set the book on the ground. "Maybe we should go back to Landover. My—"

"No," Ethan said, cutting her off.

"But my aunt might have a good idea of what magic is binding the pages together."

There was no way Ethan was turning back. "Forget about your aunt. What kind of spell do you think Bean used?"

Lily frowned at the book. "I don't know." She picked it up and tried to pass it back to Ethan, but he refused to take it.

"Yes, you do. Lily, you just said you felt dark magic inside. So Bean's a powerful sorcerer. I have a feeling you're a whole lot smarter than he is."

Lily glared at Ethan and shoved the book into his hands. "He was smart enough to kill my mother."

He hadn't meant to offend her. "And we need to stop him before he kills anyone else." Ethan handed it back to her. "Put the fear of what's inside out of your mind."

"Easy for you to say." Lily ground her teeth together while she examined the front cover, the back, then turned the book on its side and inspected the edges. With each inspection, she opened her mouth to say something then closed it, until one corner of her mouth curled. "It can't be that simple."

"What?" Ethan asked.

"Bean was the sorcerer of Primland, right?"

"A redundant question, if ever I heard one," Christian said, tossing her a droll stare.

She rolled her eyes at him. "He likely used the book quite frequently. Like my aunt. She has one particular book that she refers to constantly. It's filled with spells and magic that are family secrets and she keeps it locked with a binding spell."

"What's that?" Ethan asked.

"It's a rather simple spell, designed for quick access. The release of the spell consists of a word." Lily closed her eyes and touched the book on both sides. "Yes. I'm positive. It's a binding spell. We just need to figure out what the word is."

"Like a password." Ethan thought about all the passwords he'd ever used. He had one for his iTunes account, one for his e-mail account, the combination on his locker, and they were all the same—he always used his birthday. Bean wouldn't have made it that simple, but Ethan was positive he'd use an unforgettable word, one likely tied to something personal. "Does anyone know anything about Bean's life?"

"They say he had a wife," Christian said.

"Old Black Agnes. Legend says she was a horrifying woman. Warts covered her face and her arms, one for each person she cursed," Lily added. "Seamus used to tell me she haunted his room to keep me out."

Ethan leaned over and whispered, "Black Agnes," while tugging on the cover, but the spell remained in place.

Runyun came back carrying five large fish impaled on an arrow and set them next to the fire.

"Runyun, what else do you know about Sawney Bean? Did he have a favorite pet? A favorite song?" Ethan asked.

"Hold on now. It's not like we were mates. I spent years hunting the man down."

"That silly rhyme . . . ," Christian said. They all stared at him. "'There was once a warlock named Sawney Bean, who ate his son and killed his queen. . . .' My mother was fond of that one."

Lily screwed up her face. "He ate his son?"

"I repeated it many a time while beating the sense out of General Niles. Threw him off," Christian gloated.

Runyun patted Christian on the back. "I like any man who enjoys beating the sense out of Julius Niles, no offense to the Niles present."

"Offense taken," Lily shot back.

She wasn't the only one offended. For some reason, the fact that Runyun would tell Christian that he liked him didn't sit well with Ethan. All he ever did was pick at Ethan, telling him exactly what was wrong with him. He couldn't ride a horse, or use a sword, or build a fire. Pick. Pick. Pick. But Christian, he liked, and why not? His cousin had trained since birth. He was, to Runyun, what a perfect son would look like.

Trying to move on, Ethan asked Runyun, "What was the son's name?"

"When we wrestled him into the cave, he wore a leather strap with strip of gold hanging from it. Engraved on it were the letters 'D-A-N-Y,'" Runyun said. "I bet his name was Dany."

Ethan took the book from Lily, turned it over so the emblem was facing up, and whispered, "Dany."

A foul scent exhaled with a whistle from the binding. Ethan tugged and the cover lifted. He flipped through the book until he found a page in the back marked by a black feather, but he couldn't understand the writing.

"What language is this?" He held up the book so everyone could see.

"All spells are written in some form of ogam, an ancient alphabet used by the Druids," Lily said. "Let me see."

Ethan handed Lily the book.

Runyun and Christian leaned over her shoulder as she read aloud.

"It's a potion. Namhaid spiorad beo—'Enemy spirit alive.'"

That didn't sound good. "What does it do?" Ethan asked.

"Raises the dead. But not any particular dead, the dead of an enemy," she explained.

"His plan is to create an army of Draugar?" Runyun asked. "But how?"

Christian stood up and pinned Ethan with a nervous frown. "Traynor's soldiers were left on the Isle of Mord."

"What!" Runyun exclaimed. "Tearlach left them? Unburied?"

"Why would we bury the dead of an enemy?" Christian replied.

"I don't know, decency?" Runyun barked.

Memories of the countless souls who remained by their decapitated heads along the path to the arch in Gransmore flooded Ethan's mind. "More than that, if their bodies were left unburied their souls would not have moved on. Those souls are still on the isle, with their bodies, ready, likely willing, and soon able to fight for Traynor and Bean again."

Christian bit his lip and stared into the fire. "Hadn't thought of that."

"Apparently, your father, with all his radharc powers, hadn't either," Runyun quipped.

True. His uncle should've known, but his father shouldn't. How was it Runyun Cooper knew so much about death? Ethan would've asked, but Lily spoke first, catching everyone's attention.

"Bean needs three things to brew the potion: three cups of water bubbling up from Fiddler's Well, three crushed leaves from the vivificus tree, and . . ." Lily's breath caught and she stopped reading. She pursed her lips and closed the book.

"And what?" Ethan demanded.

"Freshly spilled blood from the person whose deceased enemies you wish to raise."

Stunned, Ethan's chest filled with dread. "My mother's blood. That's why they took her. They're going to kill her."

"You're sure about what it says, Lily?" Runyun asked.

She looked up and nodded.

He sat down next to Ethan. "It says 'freshly spilled.' That means they can't hurt her until they have all the other elements," Runyun surmised.

"What if they have the other two now?" Ethan picked up a thick twig and snapped it in half, then tossed it into the fire. "What if freeing Bean was the last step?"

"Fiddler's Well is in the mountains of Algidare. The Bugganes would never help the Ravens or Bean, and the well is heavily fortified. The Ravens could not retrieve the water without Bean's help. The Bugganes would rip them apart," Runyun explained.

"Bugganes?"

"Inhabitants of Algidare. The most vicious of all cultures in Tara," Christian replied.

That was comforting, at least a little.

"One more thing," Lily chimed in. "I don't believe there are any more vivificus trees. The leaves had been a major component in dark magic for centuries. Aunt Morgan told me they were all burned after the last war."

"If that's true, then why go after a potion that's impossible to make?" Ethan asked.

"I don't know, but it seems that our next stop is Fiddler's Well," Christian replied.

Lily stood up. "Have you lost your mind? You want to lead Landover's heir into Algidare?"

"I don't see any other way," Christian responded.

Neither did Ethan. He stared into the crackling fire, unable to get the images of Bean killing his mother, and an army of dead soldiers tearing through the market at Weymiss out of his mind. How could he let that happen when there was a chance to stop it? "We're going."

Lily glanced at Runyun for support.

"Fiddler's Well. Bugganes, Ravens, and Bean. Sounds like a death trap. I love a challenge," Runyun said with a wicked grin.

The horses began to whinny and stamp their hooves.

"What's up with the horses?" Ethan asked.

A high-pitched howl echoed through the canyon. It sounded like a coyote fighting laryngitis. A chorus of louder, deeper howls answered, coming from all directions. They were completely surrounded, but by what?

"Efin Faoladhs! That was fast." Runyun stood and unsheathed his sword. "Get behind me and let me do the talking."

"You're planning on talking with that?" Ethan asked.

"I mean it, Ethan. Quiet," Runyun ordered.

Ethan opened his mouth to argue but decided against it when three wolf-men leaped into the small canyon, snarling and growling. Like the ones Ethan had seen at Weymiss, they were covered in black fur, a few inches taller than Runyun, walked upright, wore loose-fitting pants, and had dual swords mounted on their backs.

Two of the three had the same white circles around their brilliant green eyes, making them look as if they were glowing. But the tallest's face was entirely black, right down to the color of his eyes, cloaking him completely in the shadows.

Without hesitation, the Faoladhs attacked. The tallest one ran to Runyun and with one hard swat knocked Runyun's sword out of his hands. Then again Runyun didn't seem to be putting up much of a fight. The Faoladh easily whipped him around, kicked him to the rocky ground, and held him facedown by the neck. "Runyun Cooper, you've come across our border without permission, and you're not welcome here."

Was there any place the man was welcome? Ethan pulled his sword. With blades in hand, Lily and Christian stood with Ethan, anticipating yet another fight for their lives.

"Put those away," Runyun said calmly. He wasn't struggling at all. Christian put his away first, then Lily, but Ethan glared at the Faoladh, conflicted.

"Ethan!" Runyun barked.

With trepidation, Ethan slid his sword into its scabbard.

"Leader Maul, forgive the intrusion. I am but a servant to these young folk. They seek refuge," Runyun said.

Maul glanced at each of them then pressed harder on Runyun's neck. "Clever, Cooper. You know our laws well. We don't kill children, not even the children of our enemies, but you . . ." He lifted his paw, extended his razor-sharp claws, and brought them next to Runyun's neck. "The last time you came into Kilkerry you took something most precious from my lair. I want it back."

"I simply returned a stolen item to its proper owners," Runyun choked out.

"The Fiery Arrow of the Triple Goddess was given to my ancestors as a gift from the Fomorians," Maul growled, his sharp canines only inches from Runyun's jugular.

"The Fomorians had no right to give it to anyone. It belongs to the tree sprites in Bramblewood Forest and has since been returned. You'll have to bargain with them if you want it."

"I think I'd rather kill you, Runyun Cooper." A low rumble grew in the back of Maul's throat as he reached his claws back to strike.

"Stop!" Ethan yelled.

Leader Maul looked up at Ethan, accidentally loosening his grip on Runyun's neck. Runyun rolled out of his grasp and jumped to his feet.

Maul lunged at Runyun, but Ethan stepped between them, his hands at shoulder height, trying to separate them. "Don't touch him."

Howls combined with laughter echoed from everywhere. The glare of the fire against the night sky made it impossible to see exactly how many Faoladhs stood on the rocks above, but it sounded like way too many for Ethan and the others to have any possible chance of escape.

Moving lightning fast, Maul snatched Ethan's shoulder, the same shoulder the Raven had stabbed, and dug his sharp claws into his chest. Ethan's breath caught as excruciating pain flooded his chest and circles of blood pooled on his shirt, ringing each puncture wound.

"Move, unless you'd like to join Cooper."

"You said your laws forbid hurting children," Lily exclaimed, trying to push Maul off Ethan, but the Faoladh didn't budge.

"I said we don't kill children," Maul corrected. "But in this one's case, I might be willing to make an exception."

"All three of you, get back now!" Runyun ordered. "This is not your battle to fight."

"Listen to him," Maul warned.

"I don't think so." Christian pulled his sword and moved at Maul, aiming his long blade at the Faoladh's leader's chest. "You get back."

The other two Faoladhs skulked toward him.

"I said, get back!" Christian demanded. "All of you!"

They jumped him. Christian spun, catching one on the arm with his blade, but the other bit him on the calf. They knocked Christian's sword out of his hand and pinned him to the rocky ground. Runyun moved to help Christian, but Maul seized him again, hurling him down as well.

Ethan yanked his sword, but if Christian and Runyun went down so easily, what hope did he have of fighting them off? There was only one way out of this. "Lily, do something."

Lily's eyes widened with panic. She raised her hands and shouted, "Buail!"

For the first time, nothing happened. Her magic didn't work.

"Lily!"

"Don't you think I'm trying!" She reached for Ethan, but two more Faoladhs leaped out of the darkness, and before Lily and Ethan could even turn around, they had their hands behind their backs and had tossed their weapons in a useless pile next to the fire.

"Maul, what are you doing?" Runyun asked.

Maul kicked Runyun in the side, hard.

Runyun spit out the side of his mouth and tried to breathe through the pain. "You don't want to do this, Maul."

"Oh, but, Cooper, I do. I've been waiting to do this for a long time," he snarled.

Four more Faoladhs leaped out of the darkness. They took hold of Runyun while the others tied his hands and feet then gagged him.

"Damnit! Get off!" Ethan snapped. The Faoladh clenched his arms tighter. Where was a 007 miracle when you needed one? Or SEAL Team Six? Heck, he'd even take T. C. from *MI:5*. No one was coming to rescue them.

Ethan's heart sank as they rolled Runyun up to standing.

Maul slid his sword out. He set it against Runyun's throat. "Let them see what happens to those who steal from Kilkerry!"

It was over. Runyun Cooper was going to die, and there was nothing Ethan could do to save him.

TWENTY-FIVE

Wait!" a commanding voice boomed from above.

Maul cocked his head, and sniffed the air, trying to catch a scent. His eyes shifted to the sound of the voice, darting right. Hissing, he turned back and let out a high-pitched whistle as General Niles appeared at the top of the canyon and walked his horse down the rocks and into the cavern. As he approached, he noticed Lily and his eyes grew wide in shock.

Captain Bartlett, clean-shaven, followed him. Ethan wouldn't have recognized him except he was in the same muddy coat and pants.

"I never thought I'd say this, but I'm really happy to see you," Ethan told Bartlett.

"That happiness may be short-lived," Bartlett replied.

Maul shifted to face them, keeping Runyun, and the men holding him, out of their reach. "General Niles, Captain Bartlett. You're a long way from home. What business do you have in Kilkerry?"

"Seems some of our young decided to go on a quest without proper security and permissions," General Niles replied, frowning at Ethan.

"We've come to fetch them." Bartlett clutched Ethan's sore shoulder and squeezed. Ethan swallowed the urge to cry out, refusing to even wince.

Leader Maul nodded, and the Faoladh holding Ethan's arms let go. They released Christian and Lily too, but not Runyun.

"Very well. You may leave with the three, but Cooper comes with us."

"No!" Ethan slid his knife out but only made it a step before Bartlett whipped an arm over his chest.

"Let go!"

"Keep still!" Bartlett growled in his ear.

Ethan rolled his foot around the back of Bartlett's knee, and yanked his leg forward until Bartlett went down.

Before Ethan could reach Runyun, Maul's long arms grabbed his legs. Ethan fell forward on top of Runyun, which was exactly where he wanted to be. With one well-placed slice, he cut the ropes binding Runyun's hands.

With a frustrated snarl, the Faoladh leader lifted Ethan up over his head but didn't notice Ethan let the knife fall. Before the Faoladhs could stop him, Runyun had freed his feet and scooted to his sword, picking it up.

"Put him down," General Niles demanded to Maul.

"We're not going to ask again, Maul. Put him down." Bartlett held his hand on his eye patch.

When Maul didn't, Lily threw her hands out and whispered, "Cosaht."

Maul's hold on Ethan wavered, and he was forced to let go. As soon as Ethan hit the ground, Maul grabbed his head, turned it so Ethan could see him, and then raised his arm, baring his claws. "We may not kill children, but I'll give you something to remember to never to cross me again."

Runyun, General Niles, Christian, Lily, and Bartlett came at Maul. The Faoladh leader pulled Ethan to standing and held him in front of him as a shield. Maul howled, and at least twenty more of his kind rushed down from the darkness.

The general's face fell.

"Cooper, unless you want them all to die . . ." Maul didn't need to finish his sentence. The threat was clear.

Locking eyes on Ethan, Runyun let his sword fall.

"No!" Ethan struggled against Maul's hold, but it was no use.

Two Faoladh lunged at Runyun and pressed his arms behind his back. Runyun was forced to his knees as they wound rope around his wrists again.

Maul threw Ethan at Bartlett, and turned to his men. "Bind Cooper tightly. Feel free to cut his circulation off. He won't need his hands anymore."

"Let him go!" Ethan yelled.

"What do you think you're doing?" Bartlett asked Maul as he stretched an arm across Ethan's chest.

"I told you. He's coming with us. Now go unless you all want to die. I'm tired of these games."

Ethan elbowed Bartlett in the rib cage, and slipped out of his grasp. He grabbed Runyun's sword with both hands, and stepped between Runyun and Maul.

With a strength he'd never felt before, Ethan brandished the long blade in the Faoladh's snarling face. "I'm Ethan Makkai, heir to the throne of Landover."

Ethan half expected Maul to laugh. Some kid dressed like an alien announces himself as a king, that's pure comedy. But Maul didn't. No one did.

Maul took a step back. He raised his eyes to meet General Niles's, who nodded.

"Runyun Cooper chose to camp here to keep the three of us safe," Ethan told Maul. "He didn't care about himself. He probably knew you'd find us. That doesn't strike me as the kind of person who'd steal. If you really had something that belonged to the tree sprites you have no right punishing him for your crimes." Ethan took another step toward Maul. "And if you want to take him, you're going to have to kill me first."

"Ethan, let's not be melodramatic," Bartlett chimed in, and reached for his eye patch. "If he's planning on taking Runyun, he'd have to kill us all."

No one said a word. The only sound Ethan heard was his heart pounding against his chest.

After what seemed like an eternity, Maul took a step back and raised an arm, signaling to his pack to move back. Without a spoken word all but two took off, climbing the rocks in seconds, disappearing into the night.

Relieved, Ethan cut the ropes binding Runyun and helped him stand up.

Leader Maul stood inches from him. "Runyun Cooper, I will spare you this one time. But if I find you here again, you will not be so lucky."

Runyun nodded.

"Thank you," Ethan said.

"Now, Ethan Makkai, heir to the throne of Landover, what quest could be so urgent that you'd put your life in jeopardy before you've been confirmed at the Council meeting?" Maul asked.

"Sawney Bean and a bunch of Ravens kidnapped my mom. We're going to get her back."

"Bean is imprisoned. He could not have kidnapped anyone," Maul said.

"Unfortunately—" Runyun started.

"He escaped?" General Niles asked.

"Afraid so," Runyun confirmed.

"What?" Maul growled.

"This is Landover business," Christian said. He positioned himself between Ethan and Maul. "We'll need you to leave, now."

"You are in my realm. You do not tell me to leave. And Sawney Bean is everyone's business," Maul snapped, raking him with an angry sneer. "We will sit, and you will tell me everything."

Christian glanced at General Niles, who gave a slow subtle nod. Only then did Christian move.

As they settled next to the fire, Lily attacked Ethan with her spit-paste, smoothing it over the wounds in his chest and shoulder. She offered to help Christian, but he was still angry with her, and refused.

General Niles had brought four of Morgan's sugarloaves. After eating an entire loaf, Ethan understood why Christian had been so happy in Bramblewood when he found out Lily had some. It was nutty and sweet, like banana bread without the bananas.

Captain Bartlett reached for one of the fish that hung over the fire, but Maul lifted the arrow and bit the head off. He ate it, eyeballs and all, and then sat down next to Ethan, still chewing.

"Your mother is Caitríona, Tearlach's sister?" Maul asked.

Ethan nodded.

"I can see her in you." Then he glanced at Runyun but said nothing.

Lily sat down next to General Niles and stared into the fire, trying to ignore the disappointed frown her father was giving her.

"Leader Maul, until the Council meeting, I'm hoping we can ask you to keep Ethan's existence and identity a secret. It is the only way I can guarantee his safety," General Niles said.

"I'm not sure I'd want to have to guarantee this young man's safety. He's rather impetuous," Maul responded.

"You do know I'm sitting right here," Ethan tossed out.

"Of that we are all aware." Maul cast Ethan a hooded stare before answering Niles. "You have my word. Now I want to know how Sawney Bean was released, and I want to know now."

Runyun set a hand on Ethan. "Why don't you fill them in on what we've learned?"

Ethan started with the trip into the mountains of Gransmore. Based on the looks coming from the general and Bartlett, Ethan thought it best to leave out pretty much everything before that.

"Primland's scáthán was in the cave of Sawney Bean?" Maul asked while examining the book. His ears twitched with curiosity, then he handed it back to Lily.

"Yes," Christian said.

"There was a spirit in the cave," Lily started. "My aunt told me that those with the gift of sight"—she glanced at Ethan—"can touch the various planes of existence in a metaphysical way. Meaning she somehow made it to the cave and was carrying the book with her, and died getting through the barrier; the book could have survived if it had been protected. She may have brought it to him."

"Who was she?" General Niles asked.

"A woman. Kiara. She was trapped there, by Bean," Ethan answered.

"Kiara? Did she speak of a man named Torin?" Bartlett asked.

"How did you—" Ethan said.

Bartlett let out a short whistle. "Daughter of the goddess of jealousy and hate, Fuamnach. She might have been powerful enough to enchant the book and bring it through the barrier charm to Bean."

That made sense to Ethan. "She was a goddess's daughter?"

Bartlett nodded. "Be glad you got out of there in one piece. She's not one to be messed with. In life or in death."

"But that still doesn't explain how it came to be in her possession and not in Primland," Christian commented.

"Lachlan Traynor," Runyun said.

General Niles nodded in agreement. "He had to have given it to her. Too like his father. Not to be trusted."

"If Bean manages to raise the dead, it'll mean war again," Christian added.

"We knew this was coming with Primland. We're prepared to fight a living army. But battling the undead . . . ?" General Niles's voice trailed off.

"Why is it that Landover and Primland cannot maintain the peace?" Maul questioned.

"You think we brought this on?" Christian asked, unable to hide his contempt.

"I'll remind you that it was on the blood of our ancestors that your territory remained untouched by Primland in the last war. And if Landover falls, what prevents Primland from invading Kilkerry?" Niles argued.

"Traynor wouldn't dare cross our borders. We'd tear them apart and they know that." Maul picked the fish out of his teeth with a twig.

"Not if Bean is leading them," Christian remarked.

Maul arched a brow and tossed the toothpick into the fire.

"Have you been to the border recently?" Runyun spoke up. "The mist has moved well beyond their territory. Its tendrils have slipped into Gransmore, Landover, and Kilkerry. My guess is Algidare too. Do you know what that means? The darkness is on the move. Bean is up to something, something that began with Tearlach's death."

"Why would we accept the word of a thief?" Maul accused.

"He's not a thief," Ethan countered.

"He was banished by King Tearlach," Maul pointed out.

"He was sent to protect the border," Captain Bartlett corrected.

"I think the truth lies somewhere in the middle," Runyun said, wearing a cocky smirk. "But believe me, the darkness is coming. They're coming. And we'd all best be prepared."

Maul stood. "The Council meeting is in three days. We'll confront Lachlan Traynor and find out the truth."

"But Bean is free!" Christian exclaimed.

"If Bean's gone to the mountains of Algidare, the Bugganes will not allow him into Fiddler's Well. It is sacred ground. He will not succeed. We wait for the Council meeting," Maul concluded, and started to leave.

Ethan stood, facing him. "You're scared."

Maul turned on him with a vicious snarl and lowered his head to within inches of Ethan's face.

Ethan didn't flinch. He didn't move. He met Maul's glower with one of his own. The Faoladh leader's anger faded and he let out an irritating laugh.

"Nice try, but unlike the men of Landover, we can't be baited into doing something foolish. Goodbye, Ethan Makkai. I hope to see you in three days' time in Coventry. It would be a shame if Landover had no heir." His final words carried heavy sarcasm.

The three Faoladhs leaped out of the canyon and vanished into the night.

The fire crackled, sending wispy sparks into the darkness, breaking up the uncomfortable silence. Lily was slouched over, nervously rubbing her knees. She glanced questioningly at her father. It had been obvious from his expression when he arrived that he didn't know she had gone with them.

"Saddle up. We're going home," General Niles commanded.

"Julius, if they've gone to Fiddler's Well, we can catch them," Runyun said.

Niles shook his head. "There's no way you can get in and out of Algidare, even with our help. In the process, you'll be risking your son's life and Landover's future. Can you not see that?"

"Fine. I'll go. You take Ethan back to Landover." Runyun swept up his bow on his way to the horses and lashed it to the pack on his saddle.

"No way." Ethan turned to face the general. "I came here to get my mom back, and that's exactly what I'm going to do, Council meeting or not."

Niles abruptly stood, and started for him.

Ethan held his hands up, halting him. "General, you and Bartlett can try to drag me back to Landover, but you know I'll just get away again."

"I'm in." Christian gave a nod to Ethan then mounted his horse.

"Anyone else in for a fun-filled adventure through the aforementioned unfriendly and dangerous realm of Algidare?" Ethan asked.

"General, if what they found out is true, and we can stop Bean before he gets any further with his plans . . ." Bartlett locked eyes with Niles.

Lily started to stomp out the fire.

"What do you think you're doing?" Niles asked her.

"It's obvious, isn't it? We're all going to Algidare."

TWENTY-SIX

Caitríona Makkai woke from a nightmare, screaming. It was always the same. Sawney Bean was free. He stormed into Weymiss Castle, his powers sizzling from every part of him, preparing to kill her family. Only it wasn't her father, or mother, or even her brother he was out to kill. Bean had already done that. It was Ethan and Runyun.

Her head ached above her right temple. She tried to touch the spot to see if it was bleeding, only to find her hands bound behind her back.

Darkness blanketed the woods, letting her know it was still night. Not that it mattered. Since being taken by the Ravens, the days and nights had blended together into a blur of worry for her son.

The blinding pain began to subside, but her heart still ached, knowing Ethan was in danger. She could still hear the Ravens attacking him, and Runyun's voice with him. Then the Ravens latched on to her and carried her farther into Primland, above the trees that lined the borders of the other realms.

After one night of rest, the flock separated with only two coming with her. The others traveled into Gransmore, spewing rubbish about freeing Sawney Bean.

But how had she injured her head? Oh. Right. One of the Ravens, the big one, had hit her when she'd tried to escape again. With only two Ravens guarding her it seemed like the odds were with her, so she ran. But the birds were too fast. She'd barely made it a hundred feet when they took to the skies and found her, but that wouldn't stop her from trying again.

Caitríona used her bound wrists to push herself up to sitting. She tried using her shoulder to scrape off her matted hair that was stuck to the side of her face, but it was no use.

"Finally awake." Relieved, Cyra wiped Caitríona's forehead with a damp cloth. She gently pushed the hair off her cheek, weaving it behind her ear. "I thought Hersi's blow might've killed you." She had been the only Raven to speak to Caitríona since her capture. While the others stayed in their bird form, Cyra, the smallest and youngest of the Ravens, seemed to prefer her human form, and Caitríona's company.

A babbling brook could be heard in the distance. Something else could be heard as well. Something that made Caitríona's heart sink to a new low. The angry swears of Sawney Bean. Her nightmares had turned into her reality.

"You've released him?" Caitríona bemoaned.

The Raven looked only a few years older than Ethan, maybe seventeen. With crystal-gray eyes and long black hair that hung to her waist, Cyra was truly beautiful. She had been nothing but kind and warm. Caitríona couldn't understand how she could be helping a murderer.

Cyra's waried look was answer enough. "Please. Don't run away again."

"Why? Because Bean will kill me? If that is to be my fate, then so be it. I'll not stand to be a pawn used against my home by Sawney Bean or Fenit Traynor."

Caitríona leaned her back against a thick tree trunk, resting her throbbing head. She looked down at her clothes. At least she wasn't in her bathrobe. She'd managed to throw on a sweater and pull on her jeans when she heard Ethan sneak out of the apartment. She should've seen it coming. Caitríona herself would never have put up with the kind of confinement she'd instituted for her son, but she'd needed to keep him safe.

Now, her heart ached to see him again, to hold him. To let him know that she loved him, even though she'd told him that every day of his life.

And then there was Runyun. . . .

Caitríona had always dreamed that one day Runyun would know he had a son. Even though she knew he would never forgive her for having left, and for keeping Ethan's existence a secret. Hearing their voices together, even if it was only for a few fleeting moments, gave her some solace that if she died, Runyun was with him. She knew Runyun would protect him.

"If you were to die, Bean would kill me," Cyra whispered.

If she was looking for sympathy from Caitríona, she'd come to the wrong person. "He'll kill you anyway. You must know that. How in the world could the Ravens get involved with such a murderer? How could *you* get caught up in this?"

"I follow my aunt, Mistress Muriol's, orders," Cyra said with a hint of regret.

"And I followed my brother's and look where it has gotten me," Caitríona huffed, but then immediately felt guilty for the insult. She'd learned from Cyra that Tearlach had been murdered in the same fashion as her father. Poisoned. Although she and her brother never got on well, she would never have wished that on him. She hadn't seen her brother since the day Tearlach had ordered her out of Tara, the day she'd realized she had been expecting Ethan and that he possessed radharc. She knew it the second she'd conceived him, his powers so strong they emanated through her.

She remembered the day like it was yesterday. Tearlach was furious with her when she told him the child within her was his heir, Landover's heir. He'd always thought it would be Christian. Never before had the heir been identified so young. But the goddess had chosen her son. Caitríona didn't have to tell Tearlach. She could have hidden the fact that she was pregnant until after she and Runyun were married, even until after Ethan was born, but she'd told him out of fear for her son's life.

She'd lost her father and she was worried her son would suffer the same fate. Now her brother was dead, murdered the way her father had been. When would all this hatred end?

The ground rustled behind the tree where Caitríona rested, startling her. She had no idea what it was going to be like to look into the eyes of the man who killed her father. As Sawney Bean stepped out from behind the trunk, the anger tasted bitter. If only her hands were free.

Caitríona had been in his presence only once when she was sixteen, the day Sawney Bean came with that traitorous Fenit Traynor to ask her father for her hand in marriage. Bile rose from her stomach at the mere memory. The pair of them, standing in her father's private chamber, Primland's mark well represented on their spiffy new cloaks, plastered grins on their faces. She worried her father would give in, attempt another marriage for peace, but he didn't. When she refused Bean, he stood by her. So the bastards poisoned him.

Bean's narrowed black eyes moved from Caitríona to Cyra. The young Raven lowered her head and moved back a few steps, but was still close enough to hear their conversation.

Bean stepped in front of Caitríona and dropped down on one knee, so that he was at eye level with her. "You should know that if you escape again, whether you are successful or not, they'll all die." Bean nodded at the Ravens in bird form who stood on a log next to a small fire, a few feet away.

Caitríona wanted to tell him she could care less if they died, and she didn't care about most of them, but she felt sorry for Cyra. The girl was as much a pawn as Caitríona was in these games.

Bean produced a cup Caitríona hadn't seen before and held it to her mouth. "It's water."

Caitríona turned her head and pressed her lips together, refusing to drink.

"You'll not die on me," he said calmly.

Caitríona had no intention of dying. She wouldn't give him the satisfaction. But she wasn't going to make it any easier for her captors either. The longer it took for her to eat or drink added to the time it took for them to travel with her, and that was more time for Landover and Ethan to prepare for whatever Bean was planning.

He set the cup down. "If you'd agreed all those moons ago to be my wife, none of this would be necessary."

Caitríona glared at at him, but refused to respond.

"Having second thoughts?"

She spit at him.

He gave her a sardonic grin as he wiped it off with his sleeve. "Not that it would matter. You'd likely be using your incredible allure to save your life, and then try and kill me. Then I'd have to kill you, and in the end we'd be right back here." He sighed and slid his knuckles down her cheek. "Oh, but you are a rare beauty, Caitríona Makkai. It's beyond comprehension why you'd waste your time with Runyun Cooper."

Her breath caught at the mention of Runyun's name.

Bean leaned over and whispered in her ear. "Struck a nerve, did I?"

If he knew about Runyun, was it possible he knew about Ethan too? "You don't know anything about me. You've been locked away—"

Bean grabbed her by the throat, choking her. "I know everything about you! And your precious Runyun Cooper, but that's all over now."

Caitríona struggled, but with her hands tied, there was nothing she could do. After several long, terrifying seconds, Bean let go.

As she writhed, coughing and gasping, a stoic mask covered the ire she'd seen on Bean's face, giving her hope that he was done with her for now. He passed the cup to Cyra. "Make her drink." Then he stormed off toward the Ravens near the fire.

Cyra set a reassuring hand on Caitríona's leg. "I won't let them kill you, Caitríona. They only need a few drops of your blood, then my aunt said we can let you go."

Caitríona choked a laugh. "Foolish girl, Bean never lets anyone go. But wait, I don't understand. What is this about my blood? You said I was being held as a hostage to exchange with Landover for Fenit Traynor."

Cyra kept her eyes on the ground and shook her head. "I didn't know. I thought that was the plan."

"Why does he need my blood?"

"I can't tell you."

"Why not? Who am I going to tell?"

Cyra considered her words. She leaned over, making sure no one heard her. "He's working on a potion. Your freshly spilled blood is one of the requirements. So you see, he won't hurt you, but he will kill me so please don't try to escape again."

"If you're so concerned with me escaping, why not lock me up somewhere? Is it really necessary for us to follow Bean until he gets all the ingredients he needs?"

Cyra pressed her lips together as if holding back information. "The only thing I can tell you is that time is of the essence. We all need to stay together."

Time is of the essence. Caitríona's blood needed to be freshly spilled. She needed to be there when he had all the other components, but still, why not hide her somewhere? Unless the location of the last piece of his puzzle was in a place Bean couldn't easily hide her. There was only one place

Caitríona could think of, Landover. Was it possible the final ingredient he needed was there?

Caitríona lowered her head, and leaned in to Cyra. "You have to let me go."

Cyra glanced nervously back at the other Ravens and Bean, and shook her head feverishly. "I can't."

"You can come with me."

"I can't!" she snapped. Realizing her tone, Cyra's face softened. "But I promise you that once this is all over, and there is a new king in Landover, you will not be hurt."

"A new king in Landover?" Caitríona scoffed. "You think Fenit Traynor, Sawney Bean, and Primland can invade Landover again and win?"

Cyra nodded. "They will and as the heir, if you support them, the people will follow your will."

There it was, the answer she needed. Bean didn't know about Ethan. They believed she was the heir. "Let's presume for the sake of argument that they do somehow win. The people of Landover will never support Fenit Traynor."

Cyra shook her head. "Another will rule."

Caitríona was even more confused than before.

Cyra held the cup to Caitríona's lips. "Please drink."

Caitríona turned her head to avoid Cyra pouring a drop of it in her mouth. "I'd rather be dead than see my people sacrificed for Primland. Without my blood, this potion won't work, will it?"

Cyra's eyes fell to the ground, and Caitríona knew she'd guessed right. The potion wouldn't work without the heir's blood and as long as they believed her to be the heir, that potion would never be a threat to her people, to Ethan, or to Runyun.

Caitríona shuffled her legs, trying to keep them from stiffening, when Bean grabbed her from behind and dragged her to standing. He came around to face her with his hand holding tightly to her jugular.

"This is getting old," Bean hissed.

"Take her soul," one of the Ravens cried. "Force her into servitude." The other Ravens cawed in agreement. All except Cyra, who shrank even farther away from them.

"Shut it," Bean snapped. "We cannot risk changing anything about the heir, not yet." He turned, wide-eyed, to Caitríona. The tip of the upside down, triangular mark on his forehead inched down his nose and spread over his cheeks, separating at his mouth as his lips curled into a snarl. "There's only one way to keep you alive if you won't eat or drink. Please. Tell me you see Landover's pathetic ancients? Maximus? Tearlach? I want them to watch as you fall to caod."

Caod. Tears welled in Caitríona's eyes. She twisted and turned, trying to shake off Bean's hold. Many soldiers of Landover's fell to caod, trapped in Bean's hollow darkness. When they finally awoke, most were never the same again. Then again, if they put her in caod she would be left unconscious, and unable to walk. "You'll have to carry me. That'll only slow you down."

"It will. But it seems to be the smartest thing to do anyway. We can't have you trying to escape, or talking our young and stupid"—he slid his eyes to Cyra—"into helping you or Landover."

Bean held his hand over Caitríona's forehead. His fingertips sizzled with an energy that felt cold and had the foul smell of sulfur. Bean lowered his crackling hand over her face. Caitríona shook her head back and forth, trying to keep him off, but he smacked his palm against the bridge of her nose, slamming her head into the tree behind her, then spread his fingers over her face.

Black mist formed tentacles that extended from his hand to her eyes and into her ears, filling her mind with a haunting darkness. Dread turned to anguish, then to hopelessness, and finally to thoughts of death, wrenching her body and soul.

As the black mist dampened her senses, Sawney Bean yanked Caitríona forward so his mouth was right next to her ear. "Oh, and I thought you should know: Runyun Cooper and the rest of his traveling party died today."

TWENTY-SEVEN

The horses couldn't go into Algidare. Runyun said horse meat was a delicacy for Bugganes. Yet leaving them behind wasn't going to be easy. Ethan had a much better view of the terrain riding. On foot, he felt much more vulnerable.

Bartlett reached into his saddlebag, yanked out a blue wool cloak and hat, and tossed them at Ethan.

"What's this for?"

"You've never seen cold like you're about to, California boy."

In fact, everyone donned extra clothes except for Runyun. The only thing he brought with him from his horse was a bow, a quiver full of arrows, and his shield.

After only a few minutes in Algidare, Ethan understood what Bartlett meant. The temperature in Los Angeles never dropped much below fifty degrees Fahrenheit, and even having ghosts invade his body wasn't enough to prepare him for this kind of cold.

The temperature plummeted. Unlike with internal ethereal cold where he couldn't move or think straight, his body was in constant painful motion. His mouth and nose ached with each twitch from the freezing wind. He wiggled his toes in his shoes and fisted his hands, trying to keep feeling in them.

Runyun led and General Niles brought up the rear. From their exchanged glares, they had done that on purpose so they wouldn't have to speak to each other.

After trudging in silence for a while, Lily decided to pepper Ethan with questions about life in LA. She didn't think the idea of living in an apartment building with so many other families would be a particularly good time, especially considering the size of her home, but music coming out of something small enough to fit in your hand intrigued her.

"I don't understand. How does it get in there?"

"The digital files are stored in it."

"What's a digital file?"

"Um, yeah, this is the same planet, right? How come there's no technology in Tara? I mean, everywhere else on earth we call people on phones by using satellites in space and have computers that send electronic files back and forth. If we were in Los Angeles, we'd be riding in a helicopter or plane and would already be landing at this Fiddler's Well. It's like Tara's still in the Dark Ages or something."

"What's a phone?" Christian asked.

"A small device they use for communicating," Bartlett tried to explain. "They walk around with it glued to their ear, talking and talking. If they only thought as much as they spoke, they'd have fewer problems."

"If you've got that much to say, why not visit?" Lily asked.

"Exactly," Bartlett agreed. "Ethan, helicopters and planes cannot fly near Fiddler's Well. They can't fly in Tara at all. It's protected airspace."

"Protected by who?" Ethan asked.

"The gods," Christian answered.

Bartlett grunted in agreement. "And to answer your next question, bombs and guns wouldn't stop Sawney Bean or the Ravens, and they would destroy the land in Tara if they were used against him."

If bombs and guns wouldn't stop his mother's kidnappers, how were they supposed to? He kept that thought to himself.

"What's so special about the water in Fiddler's Well?" Ethan asked Lily.

"Some call it the fountain of youth. It can turn the old young, the dead into the living."

"Dead into living?"

"But the well is sacred, and those who drink from it may live forever or come back to life, but it is a cursed life."

General Niles cleared his throat loudly.

Ethan noticed Lily shoot him an angry glare over her shoulder. He leaned over to whisper in her ear, "Are you going to talk to him about your mother?"

"What about her?" General Niles asked.

"Oops." Ethan grimaced.

Lily whacked him on the arm, hard.

Ethan held his hands up. "It was an accident. I swear."

The general fell in next to Lily. "What about her?" His gentle tone gave away just how blindsided he was going to be.

Lily took a deep breath, and met her father's gaze. "Mother was Landover's sorceress and died fighting Sawney Bean."

There was no denying the girl had guts.

Niles's face flushed with anger. "Runyun Cooper, how dare you!"

"How dare I?" He scowled back at him. "You knew I had a son, and where he was hidden, didn't you? And you never told me!"

Niles showed no remorse. "I was under orders from the king."

"There's justification for you," Runyun retorted. He turned to face the road ahead. "Did you know your daughter possesses magic, just like Riona?"

Niles chuckled. "That your way of getting back at me? To lie to me about my daughter?"

"General, Cooper is telling the truth," Christian said. "I've seen her skills several times with my own eyes."

His breathing suddenly ragged, General Niles pulled Lily to a stop, causing everyone else to stop too. "What's he talking about?"

Lily sighed wearily. "Ever since Ethan came to Landover, something inside me is different."

He set his hands on the pommels of his swords. "What's different?"

"I'm not sure I can explain it. A growing energy that builds, and then releases on my command."

The general's cold red cheeks turned ashen. He tilted his head to pin Ethan with an irate glare. "My daughter will not be Landover's sorceress."

"Excuse me?" Fuming, Runyun dropped his bow and quiver on the ground, and came back to confront Niles. Bartlett stepped in front of him and held him back. "But Ethan will be king?" Runyun argued. "He can risk his life for Landover but she can't?"

General Niles didn't back down. "As always, you misinterpret what I'm saying."

"No, comrade," Bartlett interjected. He slowly released Runyun and turned to face the general. "He understands perfectly."

"Can someone explain to the new kid what's going on?" Ethan asked.

Christian crossed his arms over his chest. "I told you. To each kingdom, there is a monarch, a sorcerer, and a scáthán."

"The three together make up the trinity granted to each kingdom by the god of the sea," Captain Bartlett added. "Landover has its monarch, and it seems it may soon also have its sorceress."

"Soon?" Ethan asked.

"As the heir, you will be presented with a sign," Captain Bartlett explained. "You will see her Rónd Solais, her ring of—"

"I'll hear no more of this," General Niles interrupted, and stormed ahead.

Captain Bartlett didn't need to finish. Ethan knew what he was about to say, and he'd already seen it, but he kept that to himself. There was no reason to make things worse by telling General Niles, not yet anyway.

Lily followed her father. It was her turn to pull him to a stop. Ethan couldn't hear what she said, but every time she opened her mouth, her father put a hand up. It was clear she was losing the argument until finally she grabbed his fingers and lowered his hand down. Through clenched teeth, Lily had the last word.

When the conversation was over, Runyun walked past General Niles, taking the lead again. Everyone continued, but Ethan slowed so he and Lily could talk, hopefully without being overheard this time.

"You okay?"

Lily nodded. "Had to remind my father that I can make my own decisions." A gust of wind from behind blew Lily's hair in her face. She pulled it back and wrapped it into a ponytail.

"Not too happy about that, huh?"

She clenched her hands into fists. "Doesn't matter."

Ethan wrapped his hand over her fist. "It matters to me. I don't want him angry at you over something I've done."

She glanced down at his hand on hers, and almost smiled. "You didn't do anything. None of us can change who we are."

Over the next hill, a sea of undisturbed white snow covered the open landscape. The air was crisp and void of any real scent. Ethan stretched out his palm and watched as delicate flakes with intricate patterns landed and melted. He'd never seen snow before. It was really beautiful.

After two more hours of trudging, Ethan had lost feeling in every extremity, important one included. "How much longer, Runyun?"

"Not far. On the other side of that mountain." Runyun extended an arm to the tallest in the range, and fortunately the closest.

A ray of sunshine broke through the blanket of gray skies. With laser precision, the beam melted a path from the mountain to a few feet ahead of Runyun, as if someone was granting them permission to enter.

"What is that?" Christian asked.

"The sacred light of Fiddler's Well. It leads the way," Runyun answered.

"I thought the Bugganes wanted to keep seekers of the well out," Ethan said.

"They do," Runyun replied.

"So this path is a trap," General Niles said, looking to Runyun for confirmation.

"It is, but there's another way in." Runyun continued, pounding through the snow.

As they followed, Niles turned to Bartlett. "Do we have enough gold?"

"For what?" Ethan asked.

"The Bugganes," Bartlett said with digust. He reached into his coat and pulled out a burlap sack the size of a baseball. "This should do it, right?"

General Niles took it. He lifted it up and down, assessing its weight, then passed it back to Bartlett. "Let's hope. Their passion for gold is rivaled only by your passion for spirits."

"Now that you've met the heir, you can't deny my need for a wee bit of relaxation."

"I'm standing right here, you know?" Ethan reminded them yet again.

"Oh, we know," Bartlett retorted.

* * *

The sun grew brighter, sending a shower of light that bounced off the white snow, making it impossible to see much beyond a few feet ahead. Runyun led the way around the base of the mountain, trudging through the packed drifts, following no clear path.

The farther they hiked, the stronger the wind became. Ethan could no longer feel his face or his feet, but didn't think it wise to complain. It was his idea to come to this godforsaken place.

Glancing up, he tried to see a possible way up the steep mountain, but was blinded by a sunburst. Seeing spots, Ethan blinked, trying to regain his sight. "The Bugganes don't want you to look up."

"Should've mentioned that," Runyun quipped. "But there's no need to." He held up a hand, stopping everyone. Then he dug his hand into the snow-covered base of the mountainside. When he pulled it out, his hand was coated with moisture that must have been warm because it instantly turned into a small white cloud. "This is it. Lily," he called.

"Runyun—" General Niles started to protest.

"I need your daughter to help me, Julius." Runyun reached a hand out to her. She stepped around her father and Ethan and came to Runyun's side. "Set your hands on the snow, Lily. Then say these words. 'Taspeain dom an bealach.'"

After a quick glance at her father, Lily removed her gloves, sliding them under her armpit, and set her palms on the snow. "Taspeain dom an bealach."

The ground rumbled and the snow peeled off the mountainside in one long sheet, heading straight for them.

"Lily!" Niles called.

Ethan shoved Lily into Runyun, knocking them out of the way. He landed on top of Lily, who was on top of Runyun. When the snow settled, Ethan rolled up and looked back at the mountainside. The entrance to a cave had materialized.

"Quickly! Inside before it vanishes again," Runyun ordered.

The damp cave tunneled through the mountain. When they emerged on the other side, they came to a shallow valley. There was a murky lake the size of a baseball field with a tiny island in the center.

On the deserted muddy shore, the temperature rose and the air became hot and sticky. It was as though they had walked through a seasonal doorway, thankfully leaving winter behind, and coming out in the middle of summer. A gentle breeze warmed Ethan's frozen cheeks and he felt like he was stepping on needles as his feet thawed from the long walk in the snow.

The group moved toward the far side of the lake where lit torches threw off golden trails of light on the water leading to the island, coming together in the center. Beyond the torches was a small wooden shack.

Christian scanned the lakeshore. "Perfectly inviting," he whispered. He was starting to unsheathe his sword when Runyun put a hand out to halt him.

"Keep still. We don't want to notify the entire land of Algidare we're here."

"Where's the well?" Ethan asked.

"On the isle, but first we must bargain for boats." Runyun turned a set of wary eyes on the shack. A row of wooden rowboats sat aground next to it. Hanging on the door was a sign with a circle and a diagonal line through it.

"What does it mean?" Lily asked.

"In my world that's the universal symbol for keep out," Ethan said.

Captain Bartlett lifted out the burlap sack filled with gold from his inside jacket pocket.

Ethan didn't hesitate. "I'll go." With two hands, Ethan heaved the bag of gold from Bartlett, hoisted it over his shoulder, and walked tentatively to the shack. There were no windows; only a single door. In front of it was an old-fashioned scale with two wooden plates suspended from opposite sides of a beam. One plate held a large rock and rested on the table. The other one hung in the air, empty.

It seemed obvious to Ethan. He placed the sack of gold on the empty dish. The other plate with the rock bobbed in the air until they both hung evenly suspended. It was perfectly balanced.

A square board on the bottom of the door slid sideways.

Startled, Ethan stepped back as a huge hand draped in a metal fingerless glove popped out. With a high-pitched shung, knifelike claws extended six inches from the thick dark-skinned digits, stabbing the bag of gold and yanking it inside. Then the door slammed shut.

When nothing else happened, he looked back and shrugged. "I guess we can take a boat now."

Runyun walked around the shack to the boats and tried to lift one, but it wouldn't budge.

The door swung open, smacking the side of the shack. Out stepped one of the scariest species Ethan had ever seen. It stood a foot taller than Runyun and was as thick as a gorilla, with its body covered in dark brown fur, except for its chest, which was smooth leathery skin. It had monstrously large canines that protruded straight up from its lower jaw. Hanging from its waist was a thick belt with an apron. He carried a poleax with a four-foot wooden shaft and a steel head that was an axe on one side, and a spike on the other.

"Buggane?" Ethan mouthed to Lily.

Her mouth hanging open, she nodded.

Its large round green eyes narrowed as they found General Niles. The creature tossed the sack of gold back to him and snorted. Runyun stepped forward and raised his weapon-free hands. He answered the Buggane with a series of stunted clicks.

The Buggane ran his hand over a long, deep scar in his left cheek.

"For the boy," Runyun said, nodding to Ethan.

Confused, Ethan felt the weight of the Buggane's stare.

When it returned Runyun's click with one of its own, he grimaced at Bartlett. "We need more gold."

"That's not enough?" Bartlett huffed.

"It appears not," General Niles answered.

Bartlett grimaced as reached into his coat and lifted out another, equal-sized sack of gold. "Greedy buggers." Reluctant, he tossed it to the general, who handed it to the Buggane.

"What did you say to him?" Ethan asked Runyun.

"I told him we needed to take you out to the isle to pray to Sulis, the life-giving goddess of the sun, for Caitríona's safe return. This is her blessed well, so when we get out there, say a quick prayer so I'm not a liar. Wouldn't want her wrath down on me."

"Got it. One prayer to Sulis coming up."

The Buggane hefted the gold sacks in its hands, weighing them, and then walked back into the shack. When it came back out, it hissed, and handed two small pebbles to General Niles.

Runyun made a similar noise, and the Buggane responded with a grunt.

"We've been given permission to row out but also a warning: Do not enter the well."

"And the Ravens? Did we beat them here?" Christian asked.

Runyun followed the Buggane back to the shack. When he returned, he said, "No one has taken boats across."

"But that isn't the way Ravens would get to the island, is it?" Ethan commented.

General Niles placed the pebbles into a slot on the side of the pole the boats were tied to. A few feet away, two of the boats slid down the short decline and into the water. Christian grabbed one.

He motioned to Lily and Ethan. "Get in."

Bartlett, Runyun, and the general piled into the other.

Hurrying, Christian inserted the oars in the oarlocks and started rowing. With each stroke, bubbles burst through the surface of the water, expelling rancid gas that smelled like rotten eggs, turning his stomach even more than it was already. He had a very bad feeling they were rowing into a trap. Ethan felt his powers surge. He closed his eyes and lifted his hand, releasing the energy. It stretched from his fingertips and wrapped around the island twice, searching for any signs of Bean or the Ravens, but found nothing. No emotional presence at all.

They'd gotten here first, and with the team they'd assembled they had a good shot at stopping Bean. Ethan only hoped that this time, his mother would be with them.

The boats kept pace, sliding up on the island's shore at the same time. Christian, Ethan, and Lily jumped out. Christian had just yanked the boat up on shore when the wind picked up.

A white fog blew in from the opposite side of the island, heading for General Niles, Runyun, and Bartlett. A moment later, it blanketed them then moved toward Ethan, filling the air until it smelled sickeningly sweet. With one breath, Ethan grew light-headed. After another, words swirled in his head but couldn't find his mouth, and his limbs grew heavy.

He turned to see Runyun and Bartlett drop to the ground, unconscious. Then Niles fell to his knees and collapsed on top of Bartlett.

"Da!" Lily called.

Ethan set a hand over her mouth. "Don't breathe!"

Christian dived into the lake. He was right. The water was their only hope. Holding his own breath, Ethan grabbed Lily's arm, dragged her to the shore, and dived in.

The water was as warm as a bath, and as dark as the La Brea tar pits, which Ethan found out when he made the mistake of opening his eyes. A gas bubble exploded in his face, causing his eyeballs to feel like they were on fire. He slammed them shut and tried to keep from panicking. The only sound was the throbbing beat of his pulse banging against his eardrums. With his eyes burning and his lungs bursting, he held on to his lifeline, Lily's hand, gripping it tighter.

She tugged on his arm. She needed air. Ethan needed it too, but they had to be sure the fog had cleared. Seconds later, Christian yanked Lily upward with Ethan in tow.

Bursting through the water, Ethan rubbed his eyes and took a slow breath, testing the air. They watched one another, waiting for someone to pass out, but nothing happened. The air was clean.

"You think they're already here?" Ethan whispered to Christian.

He shook his head. "That was more likely one of the goddess's tests to reach the well."

Ethan looked up at the sky. "Goddess Sulis, we're just trying to save my mother. We promise we won't touch the water in the well. Please, no more tests." It was more of a plea than a prayer, but it would have to do.

Swimming back, they walked slowly out of the water. Runyun, General Niles, and Bartlett lay motionless on the ground, but at least they were breathing.

"Come on," Ethan said.

The three crept toward a low rock wall that surrounded a grass area, anticipating another test that thankfully never came. Crouching, Ethan took inventory of the surroundings. Large boulders of varying sizes circled the base of a twenty-foot-high tower that appeared to have only one small opening.

"Ethan, where's your sword?" Christian asked, alarmed.

Ethan reached for it, but it was gone. All he had was Runyun's knife.

"Must've lost it in the water," Ethan replied.

Christian shoved him. "You lost it!"

Lily rolled her eyes. "It's only a sword."

"I'll get you a new one!" Ethan said, shoving him back.

"Besides the fact that it was irreplaceable, you're going to need—"

Loud caws and beating wings echoed from all around the lake, interrupting Christian's idiotic tirade. Winged shadows skated over the grass as Ravens descended from every direction. Sword or no sword, the battle had begun.

TWENTY-EIGHT

E than sprinted for cover with Lily in tow, hurdling the wall and div-
ing behind a large boulder. Christian followed as four Ravens
dropped from the sky. The birds spread out along the rock wall
facing the opening in the tower.

Ethan frantically looked for his mother but didn't see her anywhere.
Since she hadn't been at the cave when the Ravens let Bean out either, they
must've hidden her. Which meant she could be anywhere. A realization
that hit him hard. Not only might he never find her, but he had put everyone's lives in danger for nothing.

Soaking wet, Sawney Bean stomped out of the water, carrying a heavy
sack over his shoulder. He glided over the low rock wall, heading straight
for the tower. When he reached the opening, he set the sack down on the
ground. He lifted his club out of its mount on his back, lowered his hood,
and peered through the arched entrance.

The smallest bird hopped off the wall. Its wings spread and with a flash
morphed into two arms, while its sticklike feet grew into a full pair of
legs. The feathered head and beak were the last to morph, and when the
transformation was done, a girl with long black hair and a midsection still
covered in feathers walked with trepidation to Bean. Even in her female
form she only reached Bean's chest.

Ethan felt an elbow in his back. He looked over his shoulder and found
Christian using him for support to peer out. It wasn't the fact that he

wanted to see what was happening that struck Ethan as strange. It was his stunned expression.

"Do you know her?" Ethan whispered.

Christian set a finger to his lips, silencing him.

The Raven placed her hand on the sack. "I'll watch her. You get the water."

"Very well, Cyra." Bean leered at her. "Keep an eye on the water's edge for the brats and tell the others to kill the sleeping. I don't know how Cooper escaped my pets, but I don't ever want to see his smug face again. If he's still alive when I come out, they won't be."

Cyra moved to deliver his orders, but Bean grasped her arm and yanked her toward him. His eyes glowed red and the tip of the upside-down triangle on his forehead came down his nose and spread over both sides of his cheeks, filling in every inch of pale skin, until his face was completely covered. Cyra cried out as her arm underneath his hand blazed red. "Her life is more valuable than yours. She'd better be here when I get back."

Her eyes on the ground, Cyra nodded. Bean stepped into the tower, while Cyra paused next to the sack. She lifted it up and leaned it against the tower, then slid back the canvas.

Mom.

Ethan's breath caught. She looked awful. Her shirt was shredded on the bottom in long, thin tears, and she had scratches on her cheeks and across her forehead. She didn't move or blink. Her open eyes stared straight ahead like she'd been hypnotized. His heart ached. She wasn't moving. He wasn't even sure she was breathing. His face flushed with anger. The Ravens and Bean were going to pay for what they'd done to her.

"Try to get to your father," Ethan whispered to Lily. "Christian, go with her. Wake them up before the Ravens get there. I'm going after my mother."

"Don't be a fool, Ethan," Lily whispered back. "Christian—"

Christian shook his head. "He's right. Bean's in the well and there's only one Raven guarding Caitríona. Ethan can take care of her. But your father is in danger, Lily." Christian turned to Ethan. "That club Bean carries, it's said that it can kill nine men with one strike. Don't let it touch you." With that last bit of advice, Christian took off. Lily raced after him.

"Good to know." Ethan pulled his knife.

Cyra left Caitríona to deliver Bean's orders. A moment later, the three Ravens leaped into the air, heading for Runyun, Niles, and Bartlett.

Christian and Lily sprinted as fast as they could, but the Ravens proved faster. They were still too far away to help.

"Captain! Da! Wake up!" Lily shouted.

At the sound of her voice, Bartlett stirred, but not General Niles.

Spreading out, the Ravens landed a few feet from each of them, and transformed into women, their bodies, like Cyra's, still covered in feathers. Two of them had straight black hair and black eyes, but the one next to Runyun was different, with curly red hair and pale eyes that looked almost white. Eyeing Runyun's shield, she cocked her head and with ease hurled it into the black lake. Light-footed, she moved gracefully behind him, and pulled one of his two swords from his back holster.

"Cooper!" Christian yelled.

Runyun's eyes flew open as the Raven reached back, preparing to strike.

"Damnú air!" He rolled, knocking her legs out from under her. She fell to the ground, still holding on to the stolen sword, and stood up quickly.

On his feet, Runyun yanked out his remaining sword as she lunged. He deflected her blade and went on the attack.

Another Raven stalked Bartlett, who lay on the ground next to Niles, stirring. Before she could get his sword, Bartlett lifted his eye patch and blasted her in the chest, leaving a hole where her heart used to be. Her feathers burst into flames as her lifeless body fell to the ground.

The third Raven danced around General Niles, dodging Bartlett's repeated blasts.

"Get your father up. I'm going back," Christian called to Lily. Lily waved her sword, letting him know she had heard him, but Christian was already hurdling the wall.

Ethan had moved from boulder to boulder unseen, and was about to pounce on the Raven when Christian came at the tower, catching Cyra's attention. She turned to face him, giving Ethan his chance.

Ethan was within an arm's length of his mother when Bean exited the tower. His breath ragged, his heart pounding against his chest, Ethan fisted the grip of his knife. With one well-placed strike, he could end this, now. He thrust the blade at Bean's back, but his arm froze in midair.

With one hand magically holding Ethan's knife off of him, Bean lifted his club out of its back holster with the other, and turned to face him. "What do we have here?"

Bean lowered his hand, releasing Ethan's blade, setting it on Caitríona's shoulder. He waved his club, sizing him up, while keeping Ethan from getting to his mother.

Ethan's eyes drifted to the dripping pouch tied to his waist—the water from Fiddler's Well. He lunged, trying to slice the string as Bean swung. Before the club could make contact, Christian knocked Ethan out of its reach.

Bean remained at Caitríona's side, his club in hand. The whites of his eyes drained to red. A sizzling power surged down his arms and into his weapon. "Bás du toirt!"

The spell blasted out the top, heading straight for Ethan and Christian.

Both rolled, and Bean's spell hit a rock only a foot from Ethan's head. The rock exploded into a million tiny pieces.

Scrambling to their feet, Ethan and Christian took cover behind a boulder.

B artlett didn't see another Raven drop from the skies. Claws extended, it struck him in the back, knocking him away from General Niles, giving the other Raven her shot. She slid out one of the general's swords.

"Da, get up!" Lily's cry startled him awake. He opened his eyes just in time to see the Raven double fist the grip, raise it over her head, and with a vicious screech, strike.

Before Niles could react, Lily blocked her blow. Blades locked, she thrust the hilt, and using the crossbar like a hammer, struck the Raven in the head, knocking her out.

Stunned, Niles took Lily's extended hand and let her help him up. Before he could stop her, she slapped the grip of his sword in his hand and headed for Ethan.

Still in a heated battle with the red-haired Raven, Runyun rained blow after blow down on her, beating her back, until she fell to her knees, gasping.

Runyun lunged again. She leaped to her feet, gripped her weapon with two hands, and raised the blade, thrusting an uppercut. She hadn't seen

Runyun pull his smaller sword. He trapped her blade in the U-shaped crossbar, then kicked her back.

The Raven hissed as she flipped through the air backward ten feet, landing next to Runyun's bow and quiver. With a wicked grin, she picked it up, slid an arrow out of his quiver and nocked it before Runyun could reach her, then let it fly.

Runyun dived out of the arrow's path, and ripped a dagger out of his boot. He threw it with lethal aim, striking her in the chest.

With a hateful glare at him, the Raven yanked the knife out and let it fall to the ground, then crawled into the water. She rolled over and expelled a last breath.

Runyun's gut wrenched as he got his first glimpse of the nightmare happening around him. Captain Bartlett, General Niles, and Lily were on their way to the tower where Bean was blasting spells at Ethan and Christian.

"Bean!" Runyun yelled. "You want me, you'll have to come and get me yourself, you coward!"

Bean frowned. "Éin damnaigh! Worthless!" He barked at Cyra. With a wave of his hand, Raven reinforcements dropped from the skies, dive-bombing Runyun, General Niles, Captain Bartlett, and Lily, leaving Ethan and Christian to battle Bean alone.

Cyra grasped Caitríona's shoulders, but Bean shoved her off. He pulled the sack over Caitríona's head and threw her over his shoulder, making for the water.

"No!" Ethan couldn't let her get away. Not again.

"Ethan! Don't!" Christian shouted as Ethan dodged his outstretched hand, heading straight for Sawney Bean.

Winded, Ethan reached the sorcerer quickly, keeping his eyes on the club. "Put her down!"

With his back to Ethan, Bean tsked. "Why would I do that?"

Whispering a spell, Bean turned to face him with the tip of his weapon held out. Ethan ducked under his club with his knife in hand. He lunged and sliced a deep gash in Bean's thigh, then did a forward roll, moving out of his reach.

Sawney Bean roared in pain, giving Christian the opening he needed.

He ran to Ethan but Bean recovered, and with a wave of his hand sent Ethan flying into Christian, knocking them both to the ground.

Ethan got up and was headed straight for Bean with fierce determination when Christian grabbed his arm.

"Stop. We can't beat him, Ethan. We'll both die trying. Let him go. We'll fight again when we have reinforcements. Our army stopped him once before—"

"No! This ends here!" Ethan wrestled his arm away from Christian, but Bean was waiting for him.

"Bás def toirt!" The power exploded from Bean's club, quaking the ground as the spell barreled at Ethan.

There was no escape. A loud boom rang out. Eyes wide, Ethan flinched but there was no pain. Cyra rocketed behind Christian, landing at his feet. It took a second for Ethan to realize that the spell hadn't hit him. The Raven had stepped in the way of the blast, saving his life.

Ethan raced to Christian and helped carry Cyra behind a boulder. Christian kneeled by her side. His face contorted with anguish, he cradled her head in the crook of his arms. Blood drained from the corners of her eyes as she touched Christian's cheek and then let out a long breath. Her last.

Cyra's spirit floated out of her body. It stayed in the same statuesque form and then spun, transforming into a beautiful white dove. The dove looked down on them, and then flew to the skies, dissolving into the white clouds.

Stunned, Ethan couldn't move.

"Why would she have done that?" It should've been him lying on the ground dead, not her.

Before Christian could answer Bean shuffled closer, dragging his wounded leg, carrying Caitríona. Filled with a palpable anger Ethan could feel from twenty feet away, the sorcerer wanted revenge. "Come out from behind that rock."

Christian shook his head. "Don't you dare."

His cousin was asking him to choose between his mother and Landover. In that, there was no choice. Clutching his knife, wearing the strongest glare he could muster, Ethan stepped out. He didn't know if the burning hatred inside him was coming from Bean or himself, and honestly he didn't care. "Put her down."

Bean aimed his club at Ethan's heart. "I don't think so."

Before Bean could release his spell, Lily came around the tower. Surrounded in a golden aura, she threw out her arms. "Nei bhogann!"

Bean's arm holding the club fell to his side. The sorcerer tried to raise it, but couldn't. His legs wouldn't move either. With a frustrated growl, he glowered at Lily. "Ar ais!"

The spell shot from his eyes, blasting Ethan and Lily back ten feet.

Black mist streamed from underneath his fingernails and rolled over his body until it coated his hands and feet, freeing him.

"Is this Landover's sorceress? Little girl, a little piece of advice," he spat. "You've got to say it with feeling. Nei bhogann!"

Ethan tried to push Lily out of the way, but they both got hit and were frozen side by side, midstep. Ethan couldn't move or speak. He could barely breathe.

"Run!" General Niles yelled. He threw the Raven who'd latched on to his back over his shoulder and stabbed her, leaving the blade in her, pinning her to the ground.

Runyun nocked two arrows, setting the shafts on opposite sides of the arrow rest, then released. The arrows spun into the sky, striking two of the dive-bombing Ravens. "Ethan! Get out of there!" Runyun hurdled the wall with Captain Bartlett right behind him.

Bean threw his hand out, sending Lily hurdling into General Niles. They both flew backward into the wall.

Ravens screeched an alarm from above. Bean held his arm up, twisting at the wrist, chanting, "Goath! Goath! Goath!"

Wind picked up, spinning faster and faster, forming a cyclone barrier between them and Bean.

Ethan's eyes watered, making it impossible for him to see as his legs lifted out from under him. He raked his fingers into the grass, but it was no use. With the next gust, he spiraled out of control and slammed into Christian. The two careened into the tower, Runyun and Bartlett crashing next to them.

Two Ravens swooped down and lifted Caitríona into the air while Bean strode into the water. His body sank lower and lower, until the only thing above the surface was his hand. He crossed the lake, whipping the wind. It wasn't until he'd reached the other side and vanished into the trees that the cyclone finally stopped.

Christian, Runyun, and Bartlett got to their feet but there was no sign of Lily and General Niles.

Panicked, Ethan raced around the tower, relieved when he found them huddled next to the wall.

"You two okay?" Ethan called.

"Not bad. Only scratches and bruises," answered Lily as she and General Niles stood up and dusted off.

Christian paced to the group, holding his left arm.

Ethan glared at the black lake. For the first time since this journey had begun, things felt hopeless. He slipped his hand in his pocket, pulled out her picture, and unfolded it. It had gotten wet so many times the creases were worn thin, and the pencil strokes smudged, but he could still make out her warm smile and his. Bean only needed to find the leaves of the vivificus tree. Once he had them, he was free to kill his mother.

Runyun set a hand on Ethan's shoulder and started at him with it. "You saw her? Did she say anything?" Runyun sounded as choked up as Ethan felt.

Ethan shook his head. "She was in some kind of a trance." From the look on Runyun's face, he knew that wasn't a good thing. "What's going on?"

"Caod." Bartlett said it like a curse word. "Your mother is strong, Ethan. She will be fine." He sounded like he was trying to convince himself.

Ethan carefully folded up the picture and put it back in his pocket. "What exactly is caod?"

Lily closed the distance between them before answering. "It's a form of stasis. Bean's vapors fill the mind, forcing the soul to live in the shadows between life and death. Although the soul can return, sometimes the mind is lost from the sheer terror of the experience."

"We've got to go after them!"

"Ethan, we'll never . . ." Lily's voice trailed off.

"Never what?" Ethan asked, picking up his knife. "Lily . . . ," he began, but when he looked back at her, he knew exactly why she'd stopped midsentence. Several rowboats brimming with Bugganes headed for the island. They raised their poleaxes and hollered high-pitched screams that grew louder and louder the closer they came to shore.

Bartlett, General Niles, Christian, and Runyun formed a circle around Lily and Ethan.

"We've not entered the tower," General Niles said.

"Bean did," Ethan replied. "He took the water."

Runyun let out an exasperated sigh. "So he did. Fiddler's Well was violated, Bean has gotten away, and we've been left to pay the price."

"They're coming from everywhere," Lily added to Ethan's dismay. By his calculations there were at least twenty Bugganes and only six of them.

"We've got no way off the island," Christian groaned.

Runyun ran to the water's edge and hooted in the Bugganes' native tongue. They returned a message of their own. Based on Runyun's expression, it wasn't good news.

"And there it is. They're not going to let us out of here alive. We're going to have to fight our way out." Runyun slid his sword into his scabbard and picked up his bow and quiver. "Ethan, Lily, Christian, as soon as they step foot on the isle we'll clear a path for you to that boat," he said, indicating the one directly behind Ethan.

"I'll get them to it," Bartlett assured Runyun. He looked back at Ethan, Lily, and Christian. "You three, head for shore as fast as you can."

General Niles continued, "When you get there, don't stop and don't look back. Run to the horses and head for Landover. Do you understand?" He pinned Christian with a confident gaze. "Ethan must be at the Council meeting."

Christian nodded.

Lily shook her head at General Niles. "I'm not leaving you."

She was right. "We're not running away," Ethan agreed.

Niles met Ethan's defiant glare with a determined one of his own. "Ethan Makkai, your destiny lies elsewhere. If you're hurt or worse, Landover has no hope. My family has no hope! Do you hear me?"

The Bugganes reached the shore, ending the conversation. They leaped out of the boats and huddled together, howling and beating their chests like a pack of wild gorillas. They smacked their poleaxes against their circular shields, the clanks coming together into one unified death chant.

Bartlett brandished his sword. "Gentlemen, shall we?"

Runyun stretched two arrows in his bow at once and let them fly. They struck two Bugganes who'd snuck up behind Ethan. The oversized apes roared and ripped them out of their chests.

Runyun took off and they followed. The rest of the Bugganes split into two groups. One tearing after Runyun as well, and the rest headed straight for Ethan and the others.

The Bugganes were bigger and stronger, but not faster. Fighting three at once, General Niles stabbed one, then spun and struck another. That was when the third pounced. Axe swinging, the Buggane forced Niles to retreat behind a rock. "Get out! Now!"

Christian shoved Ethan and Lily, then started running. They'd only gotten a few feet when two Bugganes came from opposite sides to block their exit. They opened their mouths wide and howled, then attacked.

One swung his poleax at Lily, but, holding her sword with two hands, she struck the wooden shaft just below the steel head, blocking it. The Buggane released his six-inch claws. With swift precision, he grabbed Lily's sword between the hooks, gave a strong twist, and snapped the blade in half. The Buggane reached for Lily. Ethan was about to stab him between the shoulder blades when one of Runyun's arrows struck the Buggane in the chest. His eyes rolled into the back of his head and he fell over.

With a fury of well-trained moves, Christian deflected several Buggane attacks. As he faced the biggest one, Christian spun out of his poleax's reach and kicked him in the side. Enraged, the Buggane dropped his axe, unsheathed his claws, and lunged at Christian. The Buggane would have killed him if two red blasts hadn't hit him in the back, igniting his fur on fire.

"Go!" Bartlett yelled.

With their path to the boat clear, the three took off. With Bartlett covering their escape, they made it to the boat quickly. Lily and Ethan hopped in, while Christian pushed off, and leaped over the side.

Even though General Niles had said not to, Ethan looked back and his heart filled with dread. Four Bugganes had Runyun boxed in, their axes raining blow after blow around him, giving him no chance to recover. It was only a matter of time before he ran out of steam and they struck him down.

Niles and Bartlett fought two at a time. Even with Bartlett's fire-shooting eye, there was no way they were getting out of there, not without help. Ethan threw one leg over the side.

Christian latched on to his arm. "What do you think you're doing? You heard General Niles."

"Living up to my reputation!" Ethan pushed Christian off and slid into the water. Lily dropped in next to him, and they swam back together.

Christian immediately dived in after them.

A Buggane tackled Runyun. With superhuman strength, he lifted Runyun over his head and threw him to the ground. Grimacing, Runyun rolled, but there was no escape. He was surrounded.

As soon as they reached the shore, Lily, Ethan, and Christian immediately separated.

With three Bugganes chasing him, Christian turned, and with an angry growl, slashed the first across the middle, then punched him. The Buggane fell over, and now he was fighting two. They brought their axes down on Christian. With well-timed moves, he dodged out of the way, and went on the attack.

Lily ran toward her father.

"Lily, get back!" General Niles yelled, but both were instantly surrounded.

"Ar ais!" Lily yelled, throwing her arms out. She hit one of the two, knocking him to the ground, unconscious. But he was quickly replaced by three more.

As Ethan sprinted to Runyun, he noticed a Buggane sneaking up on Captain Bartlett.

"Captain, look out!"

Bartlett turned too late. The Buggane stabbed his elongated claws into his leg then kicked him squarely in the chest, dropping him on his back on the ground. The Buggane held his axe over his head and hooted in celebration as he stepped on Bartlett's chest, pinning him.

Christian ran at Ethan. "Cousin!" he cried, tossing him a Buggane axe, and then went to help Bartlett.

With the axe over his shoulder, Ethan ran to Runyun, but by the time he got there, the Bugganes had his hands behind his back.

Ethan watched in horror as they shoved Runyun at Bartlett, General Niles, Lily, and Christian, who were now completely surrounded.

As the Bugganes closed in, forcing them into the center of their seething troop, Ethan saw no way out. They were all going to die. Coming to Algidare was a huge mistake, one that was entirely his fault.

◈ TWENTY-NINE ◈

From every direction, the Bugganes hooted and beat their chests as they closed in on them. Captain Bartlett still hadn't gotten up. He lay on the ground, holding his injured leg, writhing in pain.

Ethan glanced over at Runyun. He was bleeding from his nose, mouth, and neck. "We're going to die, aren't we?"

"No one can escape death. In the end, it comes for us all."

"Inspiring. Really." Ethan held the axe out in front of him.

When the two Bugganes in front of Ethan reached for him, a startling gust of wind blew them back. Dark clouds swept over the shores. They moved over the lake, speeding on top of the water, then rolled on the island, forcing the wall of ape-men to part, leaving an open trail that ended at Ethan. The Bugganes' panicked wails echoed off the banks.

For a moment, Ethan thought it was Bean's mist, coming to finish them off. He raised his axe, unsure if it would have any effect. The rolling darkness circled, then transformed into five midnight-black unicorns.

Ethan lowered his axe. Continuing to circle, the unicorns dipped their heads, and used their spiraled silver horns to drive the Bugganes back. With a loud crack, lightning flashed in the sky and struck their horn tips. The blinding power spread through their bodies, emanating from their hooves, radiating over the ground, heading for the Bugganes.

With stunted, high-pitched hoots, the Bugganes made a mad dash for their boats.

Stunned, Bartlett, General Niles, and Runyun stared openmouthed at their saviors.

"Well, I'll be . . . ," Captain Bartlett said.

"Thank the gods," Christian added.

General Niles touched Ethan on the shoulder. "You called for them?"

"I'm not exactly sure. I think they knew our lives were in danger."

General Niles shook his head. "Not our lives. Your life. You have brought the unicorns back to Landover."

"Does that mean something?"

General Niles petted the neck of the unicorn nearest him. "It means everything."

Ethan touched the unicorn closest to him and a black saddle appeared on its back, then on the others' as well.

"I think they're offering us a lift," Ethan said, dropping the axe.

The unicorn next to Bartlett kneeled, making it easier for General Niles to help him on. With the others mounted, Runyun circled with his bow drawn and an arrow nocked. But the Bugganes didn't come back.

Before mounting, Ethan checked on Bartlett, who sat slumped over the unicorn, his leg bleeding and his skin even paler than usual.

"'O Captain, my captain,'" Ethan said, quoting his favorite line from *Dead Poets Society*. "You still alive?"

"Unfortunately for you, yes," Bartlett groaned.

Niles and Christian mounted. That left two unicorns remaining. One for Runyun and the other . . . "Ride with me?" Ethan asked Lily.

Gifting him a smile, she nodded.

The powerful steed lowered to its knees, making it easier for Ethan to slide onto its back. Ethan reached a hand down to Lily and she swung up behind him. "Oh god . . ." His stomach tightened as he realized he had just voluntarily jumped on a horse that moved a million times faster than a normal one.

"It's okay." Lily wrapped her arms around his waist, sending his heart into some serious cardiac arrest. If she did that the whole way back, she was right. It was absolutely going to be okay.

With an excited snort, Ethan's unicorn leaned back on his haunches and jumped into warp speed. Ethan hunkered down, and gripped so tightly to the edge of the saddle that his knuckles turned white, praying he wouldn't fly off and take Lily with him. But as he shifted his weight, he couldn't move his legs. They traveled so fast he was glued to the saddle. Lily squeezed his stomach, and her warm breath tickled his neck. As the unicorn leaned, turning left, she laughed in his ear.

He was glad one of them was enjoying this.

The wind made Ethan's eyes water. Forced to close them, he was haunted by images of Bean getting away with his mother. Ethan knew in his heart that once Bean finished making his potion, he was going to kill her. And this time, Ethan didn't have a clue where to start looking for her.

Blinking his eyes open, through blurry vision, he saw they'd crossed into Kilkerry.

Ethan pressed on the unicorn's neck, getting his attention. "Stop at the horses."

They found them right where they'd left them, but there was also someone else there: Mysty, the shape-shifting Cat Sidhe from Bartlett's crew. She stood next to Devlin in human form, stroking his neck.

"What are you doing here?" Ethan asked.

"I've been trying to find the captain for days."

Bartlett lifted his head from the unicorn's neck. "Mysty, what's going on?"

Hearing his voice, she padded toward him, holding her head low. "It's my fault, Captain. I should never have done it. It was forbidden, but I wanted her to have something special."

"Mysty, what are you bloody talking about?" Bartlett slid off the unicorn. Ethan ran over and lifted Bartlett's arm around his shoulders so he could support him.

Mysty's gaze moved to Bartlett's wounded leg. "Captain, you're hurt."

"Good observation. And it hurts. I'm in no mood for long-winded speeches. Tell us what you're talking about before I lose my temper and fry your arse."

Mysty arched a brow at him. "I took the last vivificus sapling from Cantolin when I left and gave it to Caitríona. She planted it somewhere on the castle grounds, but I don't know where. And those vile Ravens are there now, searching for it."

Lily's frightened eyes darted from Ethan to Christian. "The last element."

"Damnit!" Ethan knew there had to be one out there somewhere, otherwise why would Bean have bothered trying to make the potion? But at Weymiss? Memories of the packed courtyard flew through his mind. "We've got to get back there!"

"Get me back on that unicorn, Ethan!" Bartlett ordered. With Niles's help they slid him back on. Mysty climbed on behind Christian.

Ethan set a hand on Devlin's side. "What do we do about our horses?"

"Untie them. They know the way back and will travel much faster if they don't have us to carry," General Niles explained.

Runyun ripped the horses' reins from the tree, removed their bridles, shoving them in their saddlebags, and got back on his unicorn. "Let's go!"

"Lily, Primland's scáthán," Ethan reminded her.

Lily rushed to her saddlebag and lifted the book out. She swung up behind Ethan, and pressed the book between his back and her stomach, securing it.

As the unicorns sped toward Weymiss, Ethan was horrified at the thought of what he might find when they got there, and as hard as he tried to push the images of Caitríona's lifeless entranced expression out of his mind, he couldn't. And he knew this was his last chance. He was going to save his mother or die trying.

THIRTY

Voices echoed as the unicorns slowed outside of Weymiss. A cloud circled above Ethan's head. At least he thought it was a cloud. It turned out to be an ethereal fog made up entirely of spirits, all reaching out to him.

Save my family.

Stop him. Be strong where we could not!

Don't let them take Landover.

Somehow they knew he could see them, that he was the heir. As the cloud fell over him, every inch of his body shivered.

"You're cold." Lily pressed her front tighter against his back, sending an entirely different kind of chill up his spine.

For there to be this many taibhsí in one place . . . "Something's happened," he said to her. "Something terrible."

The unicorns came to a stop near the path outside Weymiss's castle wall. The flower-filled fields Ethan had ridden through on his first day here were now littered with injured people and Landover soldiers attending them. Next to the path lay a row of covered bodies. The dead.

With a heavy heart, he let Lily dismount first then slid off. The unicorns took off, vanishing in the same blur in which they had appeared.

"What happened?" Lily gasped. Her fingers brushed against to Ethan's hand, and lingered.

The answer was obvious. "Bean."

Smoke rose from the market inside the castle wall. The smell of charred flesh settled into Ethan's nose. He had witnessed death since coming to Tara; only this time it wasn't Ravens who'd been killed. It had been his people, the people of Landover, and they'd been attacked in the one place they should've been safe, in the middle of his family's protected fortress.

Bartlett leaned against a tree, holding his leg and speaking to Mysty. A second later, she glanced at Ethan, concerned, then she flashed into her panther form and took off.

Runyun walked to a group of Landover's soldiers who seemed to know him, while two others in scratched leather chest plates approached General Niles and Christian. One Ethan recognized—Seamus. Lily's brother eyed Ethan and Christian as blood dripped from a long thin scratch on his forehead down the side of his face.

"Adam, Seamus, what happened?" General Niles asked.

"Bean and a legion of Ravens attacked," Adam reported. He looked younger than his brother, but stood taller than both the general and Seamus.

"Ethan, you've met Seamus. This is Adam, another of my sons," General Niles said.

"Sire," Adam said to Ethan, lowering his head.

"Let's hold off calling him sire until after the Council of Kings meeting." General Niles checked to see who was in earshot of their conversation. "His identity must remain a secret for as long as possible."

"Where is my mother?" Christian asked.

"Not sure. We had more than twenty men in the castle with her when they attacked. Seamus and I were patrolling the wall. I'm sure they have her hidden." Adam turned back to the general. "We cleared out as many merchants and folk as we could. We were just on our way back in."

"I need to find her," Christian said, and started away, but General Niles pulled him to a stop.

"One minute. I don't want you going alone."

Christian hesitated before nodding his consent.

Lily approached Seamus to examine his wound. "What are you doing here?" her brother asked.

"Never you mind," she replied. "Do you need help with that?"

"This is nothing." He wiped the blood with his sleeve before it dripped into his eyes.

"Where is Bean?" Ethan asked.

"Two reports suggest he and the Ravens headed that way." Adam pointed at the path that ran along the cliff's edge, the one Ethan had ridden on his first day in Landover from the dock to the castle. "We have teams scouring Weymiss and the road, but there's been no sign of him again."

"Let's hope he left. We need time to regroup," Christian chimed in.

"The only reason he would leave is if he found what he was looking for. So let's hope he's still here," Ethan countered.

"General, the sprites in Bramblewood informed us that Lachlan Traynor has nearly a thousand men positioned just over the border in Primland," Seamus added.

"That's not good." Going after Bean was likely a suicide mission. And if Ethan died, Landover would be left without an heir and Primland would attack. "We need to be prepared to stop them should they do something stupid."

"Agreed." Niles turned to Seamus. "Send Mullarchy and his fena of five hundred and have them hold their position until further orders."

"That's not enough," Adam retorted.

"I know. Have the rest camp at Dryden Lake."

"Dryden Lake?" Seamus asked.

General Niles's eyes shot to Ethan, then back to Seamus. "We know of Bean's plans and if he succeeds . . . just have them camp on the coast there."

"Yes, sir." Seamus marched off to give the order.

"That puts our men away from Weymiss and Bean is here," Adam argued.

Runyun walked back and stood next to Ethan with his arms crossed on his chest, wearing a forbidding expression.

"Runyun and I will handle Bean," General Niles said with a nod in Runyun's direction.

"For sure," Runyun boasted. "I've asked the men to move out any wounded who can ride. We need to clear as many as possible out of the line of fire, in case the Ravens and Bean return."

General Niles arched a brow at that, seemingly annoyed that Runyun would tell his men what to do, but nodded, then turned to Adam. "Where is Morgan?"

"On her way here," he replied.

"Get Captain Bartlett to Maggie's house, and have the men send Morgan there the moment she arrives. You'll need three horses. Lily will go with you."

"Father, I'm not going anywhere," Lily protested.

Shaking his head at her, Adam left to get the horses.

"This is not negotiable. Captain Bartlett needs you. The venom from the Buggane stab wound is spreading."

With a defiant glare, Lily walked to the other side of Ethan. "Aunt Morgan will tend to Captain Bartlett. My place is here."

If looks could kill, Ethan would be ten feet under from the one General Niles gave him.

Adam returned quickly with three horses and helped Bartlett up on one. He held another's reins out to his sister. "Lily?"

Lily shook her head, refusing to take them.

Niles opened his mouth to argue with her, but Ethan held his hand up. Much to Ethan's surprise, the general allowed him to speak first.

He looked over his shoulder at Lily. "Can I speak with you for a sec?" Without waiting for her answer, he walked to a small group of trees nearby, carrying Primland's scáthán with him.

Fortunately, she followed. When Ethan reached the first tree, he slipped behind the trunk, out of General Niles's direct sight line.

Ever the rebel, Lily folded her arms over her chest. "I'm not leaving you."

The way she phrased that statement hit Ethan like a Mack truck. She didn't want to leave him. He didn't want her to either, but her father was right. "You need to help Captain Bartlett. We're going to need him in this fight." Ethan held out the book to her.

Unfolding her arms, she took it.

"And you have to go through this book and find something to obliterate an army of undead soldiers."

Lily's eyes fell on the book, tracing Primland's seal. "You think it's going to happen, don't you?"

Ethan reached out and lifted her chin. "I honestly don't know. Better to be safe than sorry, right? And you're the only one I trust with this book, and saving us all if the nightmare happens."

With a conflicted stare, she clutched the book to her chest, and then stepped closer to him. Loose blond strands of hair fell around her face, tickling Ethan's neck. She leaned over, her lips next to Ethan's ear. He could feel her warm breath on his cheek, igniting a blazing fire inside him.

"Be careful," she whispered, and then closed her eyes.

"You—"

Lily pressed her lips against his, cutting him off. Stunned, Ethan couldn't move. He couldn't breathe. Her unique spicy lavender scent filled his head as her tongue swept his. Thank the gods of puberty, somehow, his mouth knew what to do, and he kissed her back. Even if he died battling Bean today, he'd die a happy man. Not that he wanted to die, especially since Lily had kissed him. *Shut up, brain. Don't think. Just kiss.*

"Ahem." Adam cleared his throat loudly.

Startled, Lily stepped back, her cheeks turning bright red. Ethan had the sudden urge to whimper like a puppy. He didn't want to let her go, but he knew he had to.

She flashed a tight-lipped smile at him then walked to Adam, who stood a few feet away, holding the reins out to her. After stowing Primland's book of magic in the saddlebag, Lily hopped up and headed off, riding beside her brother, with Captain Bartlett in tow.

Ethan hustled back to General Niles, who turned to Seamus and Christian. "Take Ethan to the castle. Get to his chambers through the hidden stairs on the west side. Lock him in his room, and then—"

"Lock me in my room? Not gonna happen."

Growing inpatient, Niles stood over Ethan, trying to intimidate him. "You heard what's waiting at Bramblewood. You must be at the Council meeting. Primland is going to invade."

"King Fearghus, Leader Maul, they'll never let that happen," Ethan said.

"You're suddenly an expert on Tara?" Seamus said.

Niles gave Seamus a look that shut him up.

Ethan glanced at Runyun, who had been abnormally quiet.

With a simple pat on Ethan's back, he said, "Trust me to find Caitríona."

Ethan wasn't sure he trusted Runyun, or anyone other than Lily and Christian. But there were other things to consider, like how to find where his mother planted the damn vivificus tree. That was where Bean would eventually turn up, if he hadn't found it already. Two people in the castle might have seen where she'd planted it, one in the land of the living, and one dead. "Of course. I get it. I'll go to my room. No problem."

"Really?" The general fixed his eyes on Ethan's like he was trying to read his mind. "That was too easy."

"General!" A soldier covered in scratches raced at them. "A flock of Ravens are on the east road. At least ten of them. I believe Bean is with them."

"Cooper?"

Runyun nodded. With a nod at Ethan, he ran off toward a group of saddled horses.

"Seamus, get Ethan inside, now!" General Niles bellowed on his way to his own horse.

Ethan's first instinct was to insist on going with them, but why would his mother have planted a tree on a road? Made no sense. The Ravens were trying to keep them off their trail while they searched. Bean was still at Weymiss.

O nce around the back of the castle, Seamus stopped. "Wait here."
    Three of Landover's finest stood a few feet away. After minimal conversation, Seamus headed into the tall thicket of trees circling the wall. The men moved next to Ethan.

"We're to watch you until Seamus returns," one of them said.

"Of course you are." Ethan grimaced.

Christian leaned over so only Ethan could hear him. "Seamus will be right back. I need to find my mother."

"It's all good. Go. Don't worry about me. I'm heavily protected," Ethan replied.

With a quick glance back, Christian started around the back of the castle.

The hidden door that Ethan and Christian had snuck out of squeaked opened, and Scully and Seamus came out of the bushes.

"Sire!" Scully looked terrible. His suit was shredded and he had a bloody gash on the top of his head.

"What happened?" Ethan asked.

"Bleedin' birds got the drop on me. Knocked me out with a rock. When I woke, the castle was empty."

"Men, return to the wall," Seamus ordered. He looked around for Christian.

"He went to find Clothilde," Ethan said.

Shaking his head, Seamus motioned for Ethan to walk through the door first.

Once inside the wall, Ethan couldn't believe the damage done to the place. The market was trashed. Not one wooden cart had been left standing. Their contents lay in piles, burning. What struck Ethan the most was the silence. The castle grounds emptied, the only sounds were the crunching of their footsteps, and the crackling of the smoldering fires.

As they moved cautiously around the inside wall, the bridge that extended over the moat had been blown to smithereens. His mouth filled with bile as they passed several men lying dead amid the destruction.

"Bean did all this?"

Scully nodded. "In short order."

Seamus stopped a few feet from the moat's edge. He bent down and pulled back a large section of grass, revealing a hidden door. Opening it, he led the way down a staircase, moving swiftly, with Ethan following. At the bottom, there were three damp dark tunnels, each leading a different direction. They waited for Scully, who had taken up the rear.

When the Brownie closed the outside door, everything went completely black. There was absolutely no light. Ethan could hear Scully's footsteps rushing down the stairs toward him.

Seamus wrapped his hand around Ethan's wrist, startling him, and squeezed.

"Yo, man, not so tight." Ethan twisted his arm, trying to get Seamus to loosen his hold, when he was yanked forward.

"Yo, man, next time you're told to stay somewhere, I expect you to listen," Seamus said, imitating Ethan's American accent. "And to not hit me over the head with the pommel of a sword."

Ethan had to jog to keep Seamus from ripping his arm out. "That was Christian."

"Helping you escape."

He has me there.

After a few seconds, Seamus said, "Mind the stairs down."

Ethan stumbled over the first one. Damn, he'd like to kick Seamus's ass. Sure, he was Lily's brother and she would be pissed at him if he started something. But it might have been worth it.

A minute later, they were on flat ground and Seamus finally let go of Ethan's wrist. "Hold."

"Hold what?"

"Hold still," Seamus replied stiffly.

"You could use the word 'please' now and then. People might like you more."

A door swung open, and light flooded into the tunnel. Seamus fisted his hands as he glared down at Ethan. "I don't want anyone to like me more. Especially not our soon-to-be-king who got me reprimanded when he ran off, and who kissed my sister."

Actually, she kissed him, but saying so wasn't going to help the situation.

"Nothing you can say will ever cleanse the thought of your lips locked to Lily's from my mind. Now, please, let's try to get to your room without talking."

"Fine." Ethan walked through the door and found the bottom of a well-lit stairwell. "We're inside the castle. The tunnel goes under the moat?"

"Yes. Thus the need for silence," Seamus whispered.

As they climbed swiftly, Ethan glanced at Scully. "Did you ever see my mom plant a tree sapling?"

"Many, sire. What did it look like?"

"I don't know, but it was a present from Mysty."

He thought for a moment. "I don't know where that particular sapling is. I'm sorry, sire."

"Shhh!" Seamus hissed.

Ethan nodded a thanks to Scully. The living person he had thought might know where the tree was planted couldn't help. Now he had to find the dead one.

When they reached the second floor, Seamus pulled on an unlit candelabrum in the center of the wall and twisted it counterclockwise twice. A door creaked opened. On the other side was the hallway leading to Ethan's chambers. Weymiss was full of surprises.

Once through, Scully shut the hidden door, which was camouflaged by a painting. Seamus led the way as they rushed down the hall and turned the corner, arriving at Ethan's room without running into any problems.

"Sire, I fear Christian will not find Madam Clothilde without my help. Do you mind if I—"

"It's fine. Go help him."

Scully shuffled off as Seamus opened the door. He scanned the room, then checked the closets and looked under the bed. "Good. It's all clear. I'll be right outside. Don't even think about going out that window again."

"Not a problem," Ethan said, holding his hands up.

Seamus quietly shut the door.

Relieved Seamus had left him alone, he glanced around the empty room. "Miss? Laaaady? Where are you? Come out, come out, wherever you are."

Ethan patted the bed, but the ghost wasn't there.

Heavy footsteps pounded in the corridor. Seamus opened the door, swept inside then closed it as quietly as possible, mouthing the word "Hide!"

They slid into the wardrobe just as the door to his room squeaked open. Ethan crawled to the back, behind the clothes. He immediately started to shiver.

Seamus held his finger to his lips. Ethan bit his lip hard, trying to take his mind off the fact he couldn't feel his fingers any longer.

"My sweet love, I know you're in here," they heard Bean say. "Come out, before I come in."

My sweet? He better not be talking to me. Ethan slid out his knife. He wasn't going down without a fight.

A charcoal fog crept in through the bottom of the wardrobe and settled next to Ethan. The taibhsí's frightened face materialized. Her wild red hair was singed off at her shoulders, the arms and front of her green dress shredded. She stared at Ethan, beseeching him with her bewildered, terrified eyes, to do what, he had no idea.

One thing was all too clear. Bean was the man who had killed her and kept her from leaving. *And if he's here searching for her now, she must know where the tree was planted.*

Ahhh . . . ! The ghost's aura was sucked out the bottom of the wardrobe.

"Hiding, from me? I told you, my love. All you have to do is tell me where the vivificus tree is," they heard Bean say.

Please . . . !

Ethan peeked through the crack between the panels.

"Sruthán." Pulses of white energy crackled from Bean's hands. He touched her shoulders. White smoke rose from the ghost as she shook from the pain Bean sent through her body.

Please! No more!

He released her and she fell to her knees before him. Bean lifted out his club and shoved the tip against her shoulder. Her face contorted, she opened her mouth to scream but nothing came out. A circular window the size of the club's head materialized in her chest. Then her entire aura grew more translucent. He was destroying her soul.

She frantically tried to move, but Bean's mist surrounded her, holding her in place. *Please,* she whispered.

"Last chance. Where is the bloody tree?"

Ethan accidently leaned too hard on the closet door. It inched open with a creak. Bean froze and looked back at the closet.

Ethan heard Seamus's sharp intake of breath and felt him stiffen. He held his own breath and pleaded with the ghost in his mind: *Please don't let him find us.* He didn't know if she could hear his thoughts, but it was worth a shot.

Bean shuffled toward the wardrobe. The closer he came, the harder Ethan's heart pounded against his chest. He was sure Bean could hear it.

It's the wind, the taibhsí said to Bean.

A glimpse of a Brownie appeared in the window behind her. But it wasn't Scully. It was Alastair. A sudden strong gust slammed the wardrobe door shut.

Bean limped away from the wardrobe, dragging his injured leg. Grabbing the ghost by the neck, he lifted her to standing. His hand sizzled with power while she whimpered, pleading with her eyes.

I loved you. Her words came out like a whisper.

Bean pulled her closer to him. His lips pressed against her ear. "We must all suffer for love."

Bean lowered the club against her arm. His energy crackled down the shaft and into her aura. Her face twisted from anguish, she didn't speak.

Ethan's radharc senses kicked into overdrive. A staggering pain ripped through his body. His heart ached in fear. He could feel her dying. Not the kind of release when a soul leaves a body, extinguishing suffering.

This ache was hollow. He could feel her soul being wiped out from existence, shaking the very fabric of the universe. Albert Einstein had said energy could not be created nor destroyed, but he had never met Sawney Bean.

"The sapling would've grown very tall by now with triangular leaves as soft as feathers," Bean said.

Ethan's lips curled. He knew where the tree was. He'd seen it when Bartlett's ship pulled into Brodik Bay. It grew out of the cliff next to the dock.

"Tell me now, or I promise I will take you apart piece by piece!" Bean snapped.

Please don't tell him! Please don't tell him! Ethan thought to the ghost.

The ghost's hooded eyes flickered to the wardrobe, then back at Bean. Her words stuck in her throat, she choked out, *Do-ck. Bro-d-ik Bay.*

Oh god! She'd done it. She'd told Bean where the tree was. How could she do that? *Freshly spilled blood,* Lily's voice echoed in his mind. Bean would have to bring his mother to the dock.

Bean gave her a wry smile and kissed her ethereal cheek, then thrust his club into her stomach. "Lúka!"

As the ghost screamed, Ethan felt every bit of her agony. His head spun with glimpses of her parents tending fields on a farm, and his body tensed at the loss of never seeing them again. The rest of her life force turned completely translucent then disintegrated. When Ethan felt nothing, he knew she was truly gone.

Seconds later, the door to the room creaked open and slammed shut.

Ethan crawled out with Seamus following.

"Who was he talking to?" Seamus whispered.

"A ghost. I never knew her name." Ethan couldn't believe what he'd seen. Bean had not only killed the woman, he'd destroyed her soul, her very life force. What kind of a monster does that? "We need to find your father."

"You're safer here. Bean won't come back."

Without a word, Ethan slid his knife into his belt and started for the door. He raced down the hallway, climbed through the secret doorway behind the painting, and rushed down the stairs with Seamus chasing after him.

"Slow down and let me catch up!" Seamus yelled.

Ethan ran faster until he hit total darkness in the tunnel. He was forced to slow a little, using the wall as a guide, until he literally fell onto the stairs that led to the exit.

Seamus caught up to him and grabbed his legs as Ethan attempted to climb out the open trapdoor. Ethan flailed and tried to punch Seamus, but the downward angle made it impossible.

"Calm down," Seamus said. "We'll find my father, but let me go first."

Seamus crawled over Ethan, lifted out his sword, and started up the steps.

Once outside the castle wall, Seamus hurried to the first soldier he saw. The bald man was a foot taller than Seamus, and three times as round in the middle. With his sword in one hand, he placed his arm on his chest, saluting. "Sir!"

"Where's my father?"

"Engaged with the Ravens on the path near Brodik Bay."

"Bean's on his way there now," Ethan told Seamus. To his right, Ethan saw three saddled horses tied to a post, grazing.

After a quick glance back at Seamus, he took off. Seamus ran after him, but Ethan beat him to the post. He untied the smaller of the horses, slipped his foot in the stirrup, swung his leg over, and prodded the horse.

Seamus hopped on another one and followed, cursing.

Rushing up the path that led to the dock, it didn't take long for them to hear the Ravens' battle cries. Halfway to the dock, they saw two enormous black birds plummet like spears from the skies, heading for General Niles. The Ravens landed and transformed into women while a third Raven soared above and dropped bows and arrows into their waiting hands.

Niles dived behind a thick tree trunk just as two arrows struck it.

With two arrows nocked, Runyun jumped out of a tree and let them fly. One Raven transformed into a bird and got away, but the other took a direct hit. She fell to the ground, dead. The other Raven was nowhere to be seen. The skies were clear, for the moment.

"Ethan, what are you doing here?" General Niles snapped. He turned to Seamus. "What's he doing here?"

"Bean knows where the tree is, and so do I. It's the big one with the feather-shaped leaves that grows over the dock in the bay," Ethan said.

"Let's go!" Runyun leaped up on the horse Ethan had been riding and reached down to pull Ethan up. General Niles grabbed Ethan's arm, holding him back.

"You cannot risk yourself!"

"General, I'd let go unless you plan on walking funny for the rest of your life," Ethan warned.

"Da, he's going to go whether you like it or not," Seamus argued.

The general growled, pulled Ethan toward him, and stared into his eyes. "You have a brave heart, Ethan Makkai. Be careful. We're all counting on it beating for a very long time." Then he let go.

THIRTY-ONE

On the road to Maggie Flynn's, Adam barely spoke two words to Lily until their destination was in sight.

"You have nothing to say?" Adam asked.

If Captain Bartlett hadn't groaned in pain Lily might have turned back for Weymiss at Adam's fatherly tone, but she couldn't leave him, not until she knew he was safely in the care of her aunt.

"About what?" Lily asked.

"Don't play games with me. Aunt Morgan panicked when she went to wake you and found an empty bed. Not even a note. What were you thinking?"

Lily tilted her head in his direction, but kept her eyes ahead. Truthfully, she hadn't been thinking at all. Annoyed with her father, she'd only thought to take a rogue jaunt around the castle when she saw Ethan and Christian sneak out.

She'd run home, packed her saddlebag, then made sure her aunt and father saw her go to bed, knowing no one would notice her gone until morning. A note might've been a good idea, or a really bad one. Ask for forgiveness instead of permission. A rule she lived by, one that had always served her well.

She'd gone because the Ríegre needed protection. She'd tested his battle skills firsthand. He hadn't had any. And at first, that had been all Ethan was to her, the heir, but not anymore. He was funny, even charming at times, and utterly annoying at others. Over the past few days he'd become her friend.

There were times when she wanted to punch him, and others, especially when he smiled, unleashing his dimples, when she wanted nothing more than to hold him close and kiss him. And she had kissed him, and even amid all the chaos going on, she wanted to do it again.

A horrifying thought occurred to her as she arrived at the Flynns' door. What if Ethan didn't feel the same way about her that she did about him? It had seemed like he wanted her to kiss him. But he didn't say anything after. Dear gods, what had she done?

The thought turned her stomach, until she saw her aunt waiting in the doorway with Maggie Flynn, looking everywhere except at Lily.

"Adam, bring him inside. Hurry!" Morgan ordered.

Adam dismounted, rushed to Bartlett, who was bent over the horse's neck, and helped him slide down. Throwing the captain's arm over his shoulders, he started for the house.

Maggie rushed out to take the captain's other arm. "Jesper's old room."

Adam nodded, and they vanished into the house. With a harsh glare, Morgan walked inside, refusing to even acknowledge her.

Lily let out a long sigh as she dismounted. She was prepared for her aunt to yell and threaten a lifetime of punishment, but between the anger in her eyes and the deafening silence, she wondered if their relationship had been irreparably damaged.

Lily led the horses to the corral. Once they were locked behind the fence, she hurried back to the house, carrying Primland's scáthán.

When she entered the kitchen, she found Danielle filling a bowl with hot water. Pieces of red hair popped out of her ponytail, and her yellow dress was covered in green paint.

"The twins have been busy, I see," Lily said.

Danielle rolled her eyes. "I really wish they'd never been born."

"My brothers probably say the same thing about me."

"Morgan asked for hot water and rags. Can you—"

"I've got them." Lily knew exactly where they were.

Danielle and Lily had been friends since they were little. She had even been there with her aunt when the twins were born, not that she'd ever want to witness childbirth again. What a mess. She wasn't sure she even wanted to have children after seeing that.

Sitting on the third shelf of the pantry, next to the lye and other soaps, was a basket of rags. She set the book on the highest shelf she could reach, picked up the basket, closed the pantry door, and padded down the hall with Danielle to Bartlett's room.

Danielle paused at the door before going in to shush Owen and Ronan. They sat with their backs against the wall, whining about not being able to see their grandfather.

Morgan had cut away Captain Bartlett's pants to expose the puncture wound, splattering blood on the white apron she wore over her blue dress. Adam stood in the back of the room, grimacing at the sight of Bartlett's leg. Around the two-inch holes the skin had turned gray-blue and yellow pus oozed from the cuts.

A few seconds later, Adam cupped his hand over his face and darted from the room. Lily would have given him grief for that but she was feeling a bit woozy herself.

"The poxmud is laced with cornswallow juice. It should counteract the venom, Captain. I will place it only in the puncture wound. But you cannot move. I don't want it spreading all over your body. Cornswallow isn't good for you either," Morgan explained.

His breathing ragged, Bartlett gave a slow nod.

"Did you bring the rags, Danielle?" Morgan asked, her attention still on Bartlett's leg.

Lily came around Danielle, and held out the rags. "They're here."

Morgan took them without looking at her.

Overwhelmed by mixed emotions, Lily decided to take the direct approach. "I'm sorry, Aunt Morgan."

Morgan shook her head. "Sorry for what? Running off in the middle of the night?" She returned to Captain Bartlett, and scooped a spoonful of poxmud from a small bowl on the nightstand. "Following Christian Makkai and his fool cousin on an idiotic journey that could've gotten you killed?"

"Ethan's not a fool," Lily exclaimed.

"Well, he certainly acted like one," Morgan countered.

Bartlett arched an agreeing brow at that.

"I'm not sorry I went. I'm sorry for making you worry," Lily explained.

Morgan paused over Bartlett's leg. "This will sting." She used her thumb to guide the clump into the wound.

Wincing, Bartlett growled and sat up slightly. "How long will this take?"

"You think you're going somewhere? You move from that bed and you won't have to worry about poison from Buggane claws. I'll kill you myself," Maggie threatened.

Owen and Ronan oohed from the hallway.

"I need another bowl of clean water," Morgan said.

"I'll get it." Lily was more than happy to leave the room, but as she started out the door, she felt a sudden sharp pain in her side. Her head swimming, she leaned against the wall and closed her eyes. There, in the darkness, she felt it. Then she saw it. Bean standing over Ethan, and in his hand, a bloodied knife.

Morgan walked over to Lily and shook her. "Lily, are you so tired you can't fetch a simple bowl of water?"

Her heart pounding against her chest, Lily eyes flew open and met her aunt's scowl. "I have to go. Ethan's in trouble. I should never have left him."

She started for the door, but Morgan beat her to it, slamming it shut and setting her back against it. "You're not going anywhere. Ethan is fine. He's with your father."

"He's not fine! I saw . . ." Lily choked on the words.

"Morgan, let her go," Captain Bartlett said in a soft voice.

"Da, I hardly think we need to be sticking our nose into their family matters," Maggie scolded. "I didn't even know Christian Makkai had a cousin. Who is this boy? Lily, what did you say his name was? Ethan?"

Bartlett sat up on his elbows so he could see Maggie more clearly. "Ethan Makkai is Caitríona's son, and Landover's heir." He turned his head and pinned Morgan with a stern stare. "And if he's in trouble, Morgan, you damn well better let Lily go because she is the one person who can save him."

Maggie's mouth dropped open. "You were with Caitríona Makkai all this time to protect her son because he is Ríegre? Why didn't you tell me?"

Bartlett ignored Maggie and dropped his head back on the pillow. "Morgan, let her go."

Morgan stared at him as if she were seeing a ghost. "What're you saying—"

"You know exactly what I'm saying. Your niece is—"

"I've raised her her entire life." Morgan blurted out. "She's never shown signs of magic."

"She has now. Trust me. I've seen it." Bartlett raised a fist in the air. "Do I have to get out of this bed and open the door myself?"

"I've got it. Céim." Lily eyes flashed yellow and her spell moved her aunt's foot away from the door. Lily yanked it open and darted into the kitchen, where Adam sat at the table, sipping water.

"What's happening in there?" Adam asked.

Lily didn't answer. She went to the pantry and grabbed Primland's scáthán from the shelf and dropped it in front of him. "I have to go. Please make sure this gets home. Don't let anyone near it. Especially not the twins."

"Is this what I think it is?" Adam pushed it away from him.

Lily nodded. "Please, do as I ask!" She ran out the front door and to the corral. She pulled one of the horses out, closed the gate, then started to mount when Adam caught her around the waist and held her six inches above the ground.

"I'm not letting you go back to Weymiss!"

"Put me down!" Lily struggled, but Adam had his arm tightly around her waist. "Do you want to have children someday? Because if you do—"

Adam grabbed her legs, scooping her up, rendering her immobile. "I do, actually. And you're staying here!"

Lily neither had the time nor the patience for this. She placed her hand on his arm around her waist. "Titallor!"

Adam's arm lifted and Lily fell to the ground. She hopped up and mounted the horse.

Stunned, Adam grabbed the horse's bridle, keeping Lily from leaving. "You're like Ma. Why didn't you ever tell me?"

"Because I've never been like this before. Not before Ethan came to Landover. Now let go of my horse."

"You can't do this, Lily. Not to me, and not to Da."

"Do what?"

A slow tic worked his jaw. "Die the way Ma did."

Lily glared at him. "I can't believe all of you lied to me. Especially you! Of all my brothers, you are the one I trusted the most."

"Da never wanted you to know. He didn't want you haunted the way we are. Please, Lily, I'm begging you. Don't do this."

"I'm sorry, Adam. It's already done." Lily kicked the horse, and as it took off, she ripped the reins from Adam's grasp.

Lily really was sorry. She didn't want to hurt her family, but she wasn't about to let Sawney Bean take Ethan from Landover, or from her.

THIRTY-TWO

s soon as Ethan started down the stairs, his heart stopped. Caitríona lay on the far end of the dock, not moving. Next to her, a tripod had been set up on a stone slab. Hanging over it, a small cauldron sat above a burning fire. And Sawney Bean kneeled next to the pot, holding a handful of leaves.

Ethan broke into a sprint, but Runyun and General Niles shoved past him, taking the lead. Seamus trailed close behind.

With the pounding footsteps, Bean glanced over his shoulder, but continued his work. "One." Bean placed a green feathery leaf into the pot. "Two." He added another. He was almost done. "Three."

Midway down, Runyun stopped and fired an arrow at Bean's back. Dead on, it sank and spiraled, moving with incredible speed. Without flinching, Bean swiveled and reached out, catching the shaft, then stabbed it in the dock.

"I'm getting a bit tired of these constant interferences, Cooper. Or did you come to witness the deed for yourself?"

Runyun held a hand out to General Niles, and they both stopped three steps from the bottom. "Julius, get to Caitríona. Wake her up and get Ethan out of here. I'll take care of Bean."

Before Niles could respond, Runyun leaped onto the dock. With narrowed eyes, he dropped his bow and quiver, slid out one of his swords, and headed straight at Bean.

Time stopped. Ethan's lungs seized. He tried to follow Runyun, only to have Seamus grab hold of him, keeping him on the bottom step. "Give them a chance first, *sire*."

The "sire" gave Ethan pause. Seamus used the term on purpose to remind him there was more at stake than this battle with Bean. Ethan acquiesced, but it was the hardest thing he'd ever done.

General Niles started for Caitríona. "Caitríona! Wake up!"

But she didn't move. Didn't blink. Ethan saw red and struggled against Seamus's hold, but the guy had him in a death grip.

As Runyun approached, Bean kept his back to him, but held his club of destruction inches from Caitríona. "Do you really think that sword will stop me, Cooper? You should have died in the cave. Let my pets have you. It would've been a much more pleasant death than the one I'm going to inflict on you now."

The tip of the upside-down triangular mark on Bean's forehead ran down his nose, spread to his scarred cheeks, then consumed his chin. His entire face was a swirl of black, except for the whites of his eyes. He rose and turned to face Runyun.

Runyun backpedaled a few steps, drawing Bean away from Caitríona, keeping a watchful eye on his outstretched club. "What a glorious day. Not only will I release an army so deadly that the people of Landover will beg to live in servitude to Primland, but I will have the pleasure of killing you myself."

Bean swung his club hard at Runyun's head. Runyun leaned back so far that Ethan had no idea how he stayed standing. Missing its target, the bludgeon swung with so much force that Bean's arm swept across his body. Runyun recovered and kicked Bean's hand holding the club. It flew twenty feet, dropping into Brodik Bay.

Wasting no time, Runyun swung his sword, but with a flick of his wrist, Bean deflected the blade before it reached him. With another wave, it flew out of Runyun's hands and spiraled into the bay.

Bean gave Runyun an arrogant smile. "Payback is a bitch."

Unfazed, Runyun pulled the remaining sword out of his back holster, and attacked, hoping to give Niles the time he needed to wake up Caitríona.

"Get up, Caitríona!" The general shook her shoulder hard, but she wouldn't wake up. He set his sword on the deck and tried to lift her, but he couldn't. Bean had somehow bound her to the dock. He tried to kick over the bubbling cauldron, but his foot stopped inches from it. It too was under Bean's spell. The only chance they had was to defeat Bean.

With his back to Niles, Bean was busy tossing spell after spell at Runyun and didn't see the general coming. Niles struck him in the upper right arm, slicing through his leather jerkin, then spun so he and Runyun stood side by side. Bean hissed and glanced down at his bleeding arm.

Seamus's hold eased. "Stay put, Ethan. With three, we'll have him."

Ethan gave him a nod and Seamus started down the dock. But as he reached them, Bean raised his left hand and called out, "Ar shiúl."

Niles, Seamus, and Runyun flew backward thirty feet, slamming into the cliff, knocking them unconscious. The blast was so strong, it blew the vivificus tree apart, igniting what was left.

"I should have led with that," Bean said to himself, sounding winded.

As the sorcerer hurried back to Caitríona, Ethan realized it was up to him and there was no time to waste. The last component Bean needed was his mother's blood. He picked up Seamus's sword, and came down the dock.

Before Ethan could get near him, Bean reached his arm out. His club rose out of the bay and flew into his hand. As he slid it back into its holster, he spoke to Ethan. "I let you live once. It won't happen again. You want her, you're going to have to get through me." Smirking, Sawney Bean turned to face him.

"You let me live?" Ethan sniffed. "Keep telling yourself that." He took several long steps and swung as hard as he could.

Bean sidestepped and leaned, easily dodging his blade. "Try again. Use both hands this time."

Ethan thrust again and again, but each time Bean danced out of the way, toying with him. "Cooper's son doesn't seem to have the skills of his father."

Ethan froze. "How do you know that?"

With a downward wave of Bean's hand, Ethan's sword was yanked from him and fell to the dock. Panicked, Ethan gripped the pommel and pulled, but it was stuck. Bean started for Ethan. He backed up, but hit something. Glancing over his shoulder, there was nothing there. Bean had put up some kind of shield.

With two long steps Bean stood inches from him.

"I know everything." Bean thrust his hand out, latching on to the left side of Ethan's chest, his stiff fingers flexed over his heart. Ethan felt a painful tug, gasped, and fell to his knees.

With his hand firmly in place, Bean leaned over so his mouth was right next to Ethan's ear. "I'm going to kill you now."

Before Ethan could react, Bean let out an ear-piercing cry. He dropped his hands to his leg. A small round metal object stuck out of the wound Ethan had given him in Algidare.

"Get away from him!" Runyun growled.

Bean stumbled back and Runyun tackled him. They both went down.

Ethan ran to his mother's side. He shook her and shook her, but she still wasn't moving. "Please! Wake up!"

General Niles turned to Seamus. "Reinforcements. Now."

Seamus immediately started up the steps.

Niles picked up Runyun's bow, pinned an arrow, and struggled to find a clean shot at Bean. Runyun punched the sorcerer in the stomach. Bent over, Bean threw a side punch into Runyun's rib cage then waved his hand at Niles, sending him twenty feet into the air. He crashed down into the water.

Ethan got up to help Runyun when he saw his mother's hand move.

"Ethan?" Caitríona called with a shaky voice. "You've got to get out of here!" Her eyes open, they had changed back to their normal blue. The spell was wearing off.

Ethan breathed a momentary sigh of relief. "Mom, I'm not leaving you." He headed straight for the cauldron, and kicked it, but his boot stopped inches from it. The invisible barrier was still up.

With an angry growl, Bean tossed Runyun far into the bay and stalked toward Ethan, limping more heavily on his right leg now.

"So not only is this boy Runyun Cooper's, but also Caitríona Makkai's. The bastard son of a royal princess and a third-rate piece of shite. You and I have more in common than you know, young man." Bean lifted the club off his back, gripping it tightly in his right hand. "If you won't leave her, you're both going to die."

Unseen by Bean, General Niles silently rolled onto the end of the dock.

Ethan inched closer to his mother, and the club of destruction.

"Stupid boy." Bean reached the club back.

Niles body-slammed Bean into the water.

Ethan pulled out his knife and stood over his mother, prepared to strike.

Bean levitated out of the water and onto the dock. Soaking wet, he focused on General Niles. A dark shadow fell over his pure-white eyes.

"Look out!" Ethan yelled.

"Ar ais!"

Niles dived into the water, dodging the spell. Bean scooped up the general's broken sword and limped to Caitríona and Ethan. "As much fun as this is, it's time to take what I need and be done with you!"

"Ethan, run!" Caitríona cried.

God! I need Lily! He could really use her help right now. Ethan fisted the grip of his knife, waiting for the right moment. "You want her, you're going to have to go through me!" Ethan said, tossing Bean's words back at him.

"That won't be a problem," Bean snarled. "Ar ais!"

The spell blasted Ethan over the cauldron, his knife slipping from his hand, falling next to his mother. He landed hard on his head at the end of the dock. For a few precious seconds, everything went blurry, spinning into a pattern of colors, gray mixed with red, then his heart seized as it became all too clear.

Bean had sliced Caitríona's hand with the tip of the broken blade and now kneeled over the cauldron, adding the necessary drops of her blood. The deranged sorcerer watched the boiling pot, wide-eyed. Suddenly his smug grin slipped into a scowl. He tilted his head, submerging his face in the smoke wafting from the pot.

"No!" he yelled so loud the dock shook.

A lone Raven landed in front of Ethan. She transformed into a tall, thin woman, her body covered in silver and black feathers. Her long gray hair dragged on the dock as she moved swiftly to Bean.

To Ethan's left, he saw Runyun's head pop up and lift a finger to his lips. Ethan nodded.

"What's taking so long? We've lost too many. We can't hold them off much longer!" the Raven hissed.

"There should be green, Landover's color, in the vapors. You were wrong, Dilga!" Bean's words sounded like a threat. "Her blood was the wrong blood!"

Dilga recoiled. "That's not possible. The Brownie—"

Dilga stopped as footsteps pounded the stairs. Ethan looked up and was relieved to see Christian heading for him as fast as he could. Unfortunately, he was alone.

As Christian reached the bottom, he pulled two arrows from a quiver on his back, nocked them in his bow, and yelled, "Get down!"

Ethan ducked so Christian had a clear shot at Dilga and Bean.

General Niles came out of the water and onto the dock. He closed the distance between Christian and him, who turned, aiming the arrows at the general instead of Bean. "Don't move."

Stunned, Niles's mouth fell open as he raised his hands in front of him. "Christian, what are you doing?"

Christian cast a quick glance down at Runyun, who bobbed silently in the water behind him. "Cooper, get up here or I'll kill Caitríona too."

Christian took a step back so he had a clear shot at Niles and Caitríona.

Cursing, Runyun climbed up on the dock.

"Christian . . ." Ethan's chest tightened to the point he couldn't breathe.

His eyes locking on Ethan's, Christian nudged Niles and Runyun toward Bean. "Don't look so surprised, little cousin. When my father was dying, he told me where Caitríona was hiding, and that's when I knew it was time to act."

"You told them where my mother was? How could you do that?"

"Simple, really. With Cyra's help, information reached Fenit Traynor and Bean. But what I didn't know about was you." Christian sniffed at General Niles. "But our good general here dropped you into my lap and conveniently left Weymiss."

Clenching his hands into fists, Ethan glared at Christian. "You told them how to get into the cave."

"I found that secret long ago, written on a scroll in my father's chambers. He never could remember anything. Always wrote things down. I didn't know where the cave was, but that part was easy too." Christian winked at Runyun. "Wasn't it, Cooper?"

"But why?" Ethan asked.

"Because I should be king, and when Landover falls to the army of undead, and Primland takes control, our great-uncle Fenit Traynor has promised to name me regent. I will rule Landover."

All this time, he'd trusted Christian. Told him everything. In seconds, shock led to fear and shame, but when all that was over the only thing left was anger. Christian was going to pay for this.

Ethan lunged for Christian, but Bean caught him, and wrapped an arm around his neck. He picked up Ethan's knife. "Time to kill the little bastard."

"Wait!" Christian snapped.

Dilga narrowed her eyes on him. "You're wasting time. What's going on here?"

"That's what I want to know. Bean killed Cyra!" Christian's voice cracked on her name.

Dilga's eyes widened. "What?"

"She got in my way." Bean cast a look to Dilga, reminding her that she could be next.

"Yes, well, Mistress Muriol will understand," Dilga answered stiffly.

"How can you say that? She was her niece!"

"Would you like to join her?" Bean threatened.

"You're a pawn in their game, Christian. You'll end up with nothing. Put the bow down," Runyun said.

With unparalleled speed, Dilga stepped around Bean, ripped the bow from Christian's hands, and fired. Runyun and Niles leaped backward into the water to avoid being hit.

"The mistress will want retribution for the loss of her niece. Kill the mother's boy," Dilga said to Bean.

"You can't!" Christian exclaimed. "Not yet."

"Why not?" Bean groaned.

"Because he is the heir! He possesses radharc," Christian said.

"Ethan, run!" Caitríona screamed, struggling to get up, but her legs still wouldn't move. Dilga stepped on her chest, holding her down.

Using the heel of his shoe, Ethan kicked Bean in his wounded leg. Letting out a painful cry, Bean lessened his hold. Ethan broke free and tried for the stairs, but Christian got there first, blocking his escape. He grabbed Ethan, placed him in a chokehold, and dragged him back to Bean and the bubbling cauldron.

Runyun and General Niles hoisted themselves on the dock by the smoldering tree, and had started for Ethan when Bean raised his hand and hissed, "Sciath!"

Runyun's frantic cries were cut off as Bean put up a barrier between Ethan and them.

Dilga's red eyes filled with anger. "Alastair said it was Caitríona Makkai."

"I told him before we left Weymiss that it was the son, not the mother. You were supposed to take him. The Brownie followed behind us every step of the way," Christian growled.

"That little traitor! I'll kill him," Dilga spat.

"When I get free, you're dead, Christian. I'm going to hunt you down!" Ethan thrashed, but couldn't get the turncoat off him.

Led by Seamus, Landover's soldiers stormed down the stone steps, but were forced to stop next to Runyun and General Niles.

Christian lifted a small knife out of his boot and moved it next to Ethan's jugular. He leaned over, his mouth next to Ethan's ear. "Don't you understand? Today you get to join the ghostly world you're so fond of, and once you're dead, the pathetic radharc power will die with you. Or better yet"—Christian hissed a laugh—"Clíodhna may finally grant it to the one who deserved it all along. And then Bean will have what he needs from me."

Before Christian could strike, Bean waved Christian's knife out of his hand. Holding the barrier in place with his left hand, and Ethan's knife in his right, Bean took two long steps and kneeled beside Ethan.

With a slight tilt of his head, Bean's eyes locked on Christian's. "Let's not count on that." He reached back and plunged the blade deep into Ethan's side. "You see, this way we both get what we want, Christian Makkai."

"No!" Caitríona cried. "Please no . . ."

Ethan felt nothing at first. Then Bean ripped the knife out. A blinding pain tore through his gut. It was raw and sharp and burned. Desperate to fight back, Ethan tried to move, but every time he even took a breath, it felt like he was being stabbed all over again. Christian let go and he collapsed on the dock.

"Ethan!" Caitríona screamed.

Runyun, Niles, Seamus, and every Landover soldier uselessly beat on the barrier. Ethan *sensed* their helplessness, watching him writhing in pain, which only added to the agony of the wound.

Through blurred vision Ethan saw Bean tap the handle of the knife three times, dripping Ethan's dark red blood into the pot. Wafting gray smoke turned a rich green.

"We're done." Bean stood.

With her foot still pressed to Caitríona's chest, Dilga let out a series of truncated caws. Five dark shadows glided down from above. Swooping over the dock, three took Bean, two Christian. Dilga shifted to her bird form, latched her claws on the bubbling cauldron, and flew away carrying the death of Landover with her.

THIRTY-THREE

The physical pain from the wound in Ethan's abdomen no longer registered. It had become white noise, background music to his panicked thoughts, which raced at Nascar speeds through his mind.

To tell the truth, he'd never given much thought to death. He'd seen ghosts every day of his short existence, and he knew life went on—in some form.

But I'm only fourteen. He hadn't driven a car or drunk his first beer, not that it smelled like it would taste very good, but still. . . . He only had his first real kiss that day. And he hated himself for thinking earlier that if he died today, after that one kiss, that it would be fine. It wasn't fine. He wanted more kisses, many more from Lily. More time to hold her hand and stare into those deep green eyes.

I don't want to die.

Not when he'd finally gotten his mother and his life back.

People were counting on him. Lily was counting on him, but that thought wasn't enough to stave off death.

Ethan's hooded eyelids dangled like a curtain starting to close. He struggled to keep them open, afraid that if they did shut, his soul would slip out of his body forever.

The barrier must have fallen when Bean left because Runyun and General Niles appeared beside him.

Ethan clutched his side and his fingertips went numb. The feeling traveled up his arms and into his chest. He was fully cognizant that the separation between body and soul had begun. His heartbeat slowed and it was impossible to take a full breath. The ringing in his ears grew louder, and drowned out the voices around him.

Caitríona's long brown hair dangled in his face as she set a hand on his forehead. Runyun bent over him, putting pressure on the wound, causing Ethan to wince.

"I'm so c-c-cold." His teeth wouldn't stop chattering.

"Do something!" Caitríona yelled at the others.

A slow apprehensive tic worked Niles's jaw. "Seamus has gone for Morgan."

"Mom, are y-you okay?" Ethan whispered.

"I'm fine." She grasped Ethan's hand in hers, and locked her tear-filled eyes on Runyun, who met her gaze with a frightened one of his own, and then pressed harder on the wound.

"Ah . . ." Ethan managed somehow to roll over. He didn't want his mother to see him like this. *She shouldn't have to watch me die.* And he was dying. Blood had filled his gut to the point he could taste it in his mouth.

As his eyelids fluttered, Ethan saw a glimmer of light come down the steps, heading straight for him. *Death.* He closed his eyes, refusing to look at it.

"Oh gods! I told you to be careful!" Lily picked up Ethan's knife from the dock, and kneeled beside him.

"Lily . . ." He said her name like a prayer, then let out a painful laugh. Only she would say I-told-you-so while he lay dying.

He forced his eyes open, wanting to see her face one more time. Lily clapped her hands, startling him. "Ethan, I need you to call for the unicorns."

"Wha—" Ethan's words were cut off as another wave of pain tore through his abdomen.

"Do as I ask! Call for them!" Lily beat the dock. "Please!" Water droplets dripped on his Ethan's face. She was crying. "Please, Ethan . . ." She took his right hand and laced her fingers through his. "I know you can do this."

Trying to focus, he closed his eyes. *Help! Please!* The words echoed inside his head but refused to come out of his mouth. He channeled what little energy he had left into his powers. His radharc senses reached out, touching everyone around him. Lily, his mother, Runyun, and General Niles, all filled with heavy hearts and dire anticipation.

But as the fingers of his power stretched up, climbing into the skies, Ethan felt peace, and it was in that state that he suddenly gained clarity, and *sensed* the ancient words he needed. Beini liom . . .

A second later a whipping wind skated over his face and the dock rocked.

"A unicorn!" Ethan heard someone cry.

He forced his eyelids to open. The unicorn pounded its front hoof.

With a gentle squeeze, Lily let go of Ethan's hand and hurried to the unicorn's backside. Using his knife, she sliced off a piece of her shirt, then set her hand on the unicorn's hip and made a small cut into the steed's hindquarters. The unicorn didn't flinch or whinny. It stood perfectly still as Lily soaked the cloth in the blue liquid oozing from the gash.

She carried the soaked cloth back to Ethan and lifted his shirt. "This may hurt a little." Then she twisted the fabric, dripping the unicorn's blood into his open wound.

"What the . . . !" Ethan thought getting stabbed was painful. This was ten times worse. It felt like he'd been stabbed with a hot poker, then the burning sensation spread throughout his entire body.

The blue unicorn blood mixed with Ethan's red, forming a purple layer on top of the wound that solidified, then turned skin pink. Slowly, the stinging lessened to tingling pricks.

After a few seconds, Ethan could breathe without pain. He looked down at the stab wound. Other than a small scar, it appeared completely healed.

His stomach still sore, Ethan grimaced as he sat up. The unicorn lifted his head toward him, rose up on its hind legs, let out a triumphant neigh, and then sped off in a blur over the water.

With indescribable gratitude, Ethan looked into Lily's beaming smile, and even though he had not a drop of energy left, he pulled her into a tight hug. "Thank you."

She gave him a gentle squeeze. "It was a team effort."

Visibly shaken, and wiping tears, Lily moved back to let the others see that their one hope was still breathing.

Caitríona cupped Ethan's cheek with her hand. Swallowing hard, fresh tears streamed down her cheeks. Runyun kneeled on the other side of him, looking both apprehensive and relieved.

"Can you help me up?" Ethan asked him.

Runyun carefully set Ethan's arm over his shoulder and slowly lifted him to standing.

"Other than shaky legs, he's perfect," Runyun exclaimed.

Landover's soldiers cheered.

Runyun focused only on Caitríona. "He's going to be fine."

Caitríona pulled Ethan into a fierce embrace and he held on to her as tightly as she held him. It was finally over. Yet something in the hug felt different. He felt different.

"Where's Christian?" Lily asked, sounding concerned.

His temper flaring, Ethan let go of his mother. "Where's Christian? Dead, I hope."

"Ethan . . . ," Caitríona said softly, glancing at the stairs still filled with soldiers.

"Christian told them everything! Where we were hiding, that I had the gift! He's a traitor, and when I do find him, if he'd not already dead, he'll wish he was."

Stunned, everyone stood in an uncomfortable silence until General Niles ordered them upstairs.

"Where is he now?" Lily asked, seething.

"Escaped with Bean. The Ravens carried them off. How could I have been so stupid?"

"I should've seen it," Runyun said.

A minute later, Seamus arrived with Morgan.

Making her way to Lily's side, Morgan's warm smile fell on her niece. "Looks like I'm not needed after all." She tapped the side of Lily's head. "Smart girl."

"I'm glad to see you standing," Seamus said in a tone that made Ethan believe he really meant it. "The general would like to see you. With the potion on its way to the enemy, and Primland on our western border, we have preparations to make before leaving for the Council meeting."

Ethan opened his mouth to respond, but Caitríona beat him to it.

"Please inform General Niles he needs rest. He's going back to Weymiss; he can see—"

"Please tell him I'll be right up," Ethan interjected with a forced grin.

"Excuse me?" Caitríona folded her arms over her chest and pinned him with a stern frown.

Seamus tilted his head respectfully to Ethan, and started up the stairs with Morgan and Lily following.

"Ethan Makkai—" Caitríona started, but was interrupted by Runyun as he peeled open her hand, exposing the cut Bean had made. He held Lily's stained cloth over it. "For the wound." He squeezed the unicorn blood into it.

"Thank you." She cringed, but her face softened as she watched Runyun's hand circle hers. "You look tired."

"For sure. It wasn't easy to find you."

Caitríona smiled and Runyun returned her smile with a shy one of his own. Ethan had never seen Runyun shy with anyone in the last few days. If he didn't know any better, he could've sworn his father was blushing.

Since they were both otherwise occupied, it seemed like the perfect time to make his exit. "If you'll both excuse me, I'll be up with General Niles."

Caitríona grabbed his shoulder. "Ethan, you're pale, tired and in desperate need of rest. You're going to Weymiss. Now."

Ethan was tired and hungry and could sleep for a week, but that didn't change the fact that people were counting on him. "I'm fine."

"You can't lie to me, Ethan Makkai," Caitríona said in a tone of supreme annoyance.

Ethan bit his lip, trying to keep his tone in check, but failed miserably. "I can't lie to you? Did you really just say that to me? You lied to me about *everything*. You told me Runyun was dead. You told me we had no family, that they were all dead, *and* you told me that you came from Ireland—"

"That had some validity to it," Caitríona pointed out, trying to diffuse Ethan's temper, but it wasn't going to work.

"Semantics, Mom. Our ancient ancestors came from Ireland. It was a bold-faced lie. You kept everything about my life, about what my gift was, about Landover, and Tara, oh, and that small insignificant part about me having to become a king of a place I know nothing about, a secret. How could you do that to me?"

Wearing a deep scowl, Caitríona clutched her arms over her chest. "I couldn't tell you."

That was it? That was all he was going to get? "That's not good enough." Ethan started for the stairs, but Caitríona caught his wrist and pulled him around to face her again.

"I know this is hard to understand, but we had to stay hidden. It was too dangerous to stay in Tara."

"Too dangerous in Tara?" Runyun chimed in. "At least I could have protected you here. You lived as a Shadowwalker."

Caitríona raised her narrowed eyes to meet Runyun's. "Is that why you refused Tearlach when he asked you to go with me? You were afraid?" Her tone was thick with hurtful anger.

"What are you talking about? Your brother never asked me anything! He told me that the marriage was off and you never wanted to see me again."

"What?" Caitríona said, shocked.

Runyun ground his teeth together. "That arse purposely lied, to both of us."

Caitríona glanced at the sky then she took a step closer to Runyun. "Tell me the truth. If he had told you, what would you have said?"

Runyun, who stood a full foot taller than Caitríona, peered down at her, then at Ethan, finally returning his gaze to her. "At the time, I probably would've said it was too dangerous. That I could better protect you here."

"And Tearlach and I both knew that staying here was an impossibility. We watched our father die, betrayed by a loyal soldier in our own army, and I wasn't going to risk my son."

"Our son!" Runyun snapped.

"You're right," Caitríona huffed. "He's our son, and I'm sorry I left with him and you missed all those years, but honestly I didn't feel I had any other choice."

Runyun looked over at Ethan again and slowly nodded.

He has to be kidding me. "Don't you dare tell me you agree with her, Runyun?"

Caitríona threw up her hands in the air and then paced back and forth.

"Maybe I should have told you, Ethan, but I just wanted you to have a normal life. I wanted you to be free as long as you could. Not carrying around the burden of what your future held." Her Irish accent was in full swing.

"In what way was I free? I was a freak who talked to ghosts and had an insanely paranoid mother who followed me all the time. I had no life. No real friends!" Yeah. Okay. He was yelling, but not as loud as he could be.

"Ethan, you're being a little hard on her," Runyun said.

"You can't be serious?" Ethan had heard enough. He shook his head and started up the stairs.

"Ethan!"

He ground his teeth at Runyun's sharp tone and looked back at him. "Why are you yelling at me when you should be yelling at her?"

"Because she was right!" Runyun yelled back at him. "Moments ago, your mother and I stood here and watched as you almost died." Ethan's chest tightened at the pain in Runyun's eyes, but it didn't lessen his conviction.

Lily appeared at the top of the stairs. "Ethan? My da is asking for you. Runyun, he'd like to see you as well."

Runyun glanced at Caitríona, patted Ethan gently on the shoulder, and then ran up the steps.

Before Ethan could follow, his mother appeared in front of him. "Maybe I should've told you, but I did what I did because I love you." Her voice was filled with remorse.

With a heavy sigh, Ethan reached into his pocket, and lifted out her necklace and the crumpled sketch of the two of them. Carefully setting them in her hand, he met her wary gaze with one of his own. "I love you too, Mom."

R unyun, Ethan, and Lily entered a small tent where General Niles stood around a table with several other officers, staring down at a large map of Landover.

"Have the men at Dryden Lake set up a twenty-four-hour watch. I want to know if anything is even swimming in the waters between the Isle of Mord and Landover."

"Consider it done," one of the officers said.

The general glanced at Ethan, then dismissed the men. He picked up a cloak and swung it over Ethan's shoulders. "You'd do well to change your clothes."

Not only were they a shredded bloodstained mess but also a dead give-away that Ethan was not from Tara, something the general had mentioned his first day in Landover. "Got it."

Seamus walked in and stood beside his father, while Lily stayed close to Ethan.

"Lily, find Morgan. She'll need your help with the wounded," Niles ordered without taking his eyes off the map.

Disappointed, Lily nodded at her father and left.

Runyun moved around the table, examining the map. He paused next to Seamus and looked closely at a U-shaped town with the word COVEN-TRY scribbled above it. Square boxes indicated different buildings, and names of the businesses were written inside.

Niles touched a box called WENLOCK TAVERN. "This is where you will take the test tomorrow, Ethan. We'll bring you in through the back."

"Too obvious," Runyun dismissed. "Seamus, you, Adam, and twenty others will ride now for the tavern. Take five that are young, close to Ethan's age. Put them in the most decorative Landover cloaks you can find. Have them keep their hoods up to shield their faces. When you arrive, let five rooms. Make a lot of noise about how the heir needs his rooms right away, but make no gesture as to which is the rightful heir. When they're locked in their rooms, set two guards outside each door, and the others on patrol."

General Niles cleared his throat and stared crossly at Runyun, but that didn't stop him from continuing.

"Tomorrow, early, clear all the rooms but one. Keep the guards and the decoy in the one room until after all the other kings arrive. The rest of the guards should move into the great hall, where Ethan will take the test, and keep an eye out for anything suspicious."

"Since when do you give my men orders?" General Niles asked.

"Since we're talking about my son's safety. No one except a fair few knows what Ethan looks like. Most don't know he exists at all. You've done an incredible job of keeping his very existence a secret for fourteen years.

Now let's have a little fun with it. When Ethan arrives, rather than doing the obvious and going in the back, he'll walk right through town and no one will be the wiser."

"I don't think bringing Ethan in through town, even if no one knows who he is, is the safest idea. There are too many unknown variables. And Seamus will not be going ahead. He will travel with Ethan."

Ethan and Seamus exchanged an ominous look.

"Why?" Runyun asked. "You can trust him. He's your son."

"Exactly!" General Niles exclaimed. "Which is why I need him with me. The Ravens may have gotten to others of my men, as they did Christian. He and I will escort Ethan to Coventry."

"As will I," Runyun retorted.

General Niles shook his head. "You will take the lead on the cliff near Dryden Lake. You've had the most experience with Bean—"

"If you think Ethan is going to Coventry without me—"

"Ethan is my responsibility," General Niles insisted, his voice growing louder. "I will be escorting him. You cannot—"

"I cannot what? Go into Coventry without folks taking notice because Tearlach banished me?" Runyun snapped. "Trust me when I say that no one will see me."

General Niles set his fists on the edge of the table. "Therein lies the problem. I *don't* trust you."

"Enough!" Ethan slammed his fist on the table. "General, Runyun is coming with us whether you like it or not. Between him and you, I'm sure I'll be fine. Seamus and Adam should go ahead to Coventry."

Tossing a glare from Ethan to Runyun, Niles pursed his lips together. After a long, tense silence, he nodded to Seamus, who spun on his heel and left the tent. He crossed paths with Caitríona as she padded in, stopping behind Ethan.

"Ah, Caitríona, I was just going to send someone for you. I know I shouldn't ask you and Ethan to separate, but I would prefer if you took charge of the team remaining at Weymiss. You know the castle better than anyone and I worry Christian may try to enter with us gone."

"Very well, General." Caitríona cast a worried glance at Ethan.

"When do we leave?" Ethan asked.

Caitríona set her hands on his shoulders. "There is something you must do first."

Her tone sent a wave of fear through him. What could his mother possibly need him to do before he left? Judging from the look in her eyes, whatever it was, he wasn't going to be happy about it.

◙ THIRTY-FOUR ◙

General Niles wanted to leave in less than an hour, but according to Caitríona, Ethan needed to bathe and change.

Inside the castle walls, the remains of the battle with the Ravens and Bean had been cleared out. Landover soldiers filled the spaces formerly occupied by the vendors. Officers barked orders at men loading a series of catapults lining the wall, while archers took up positions in the towers. Battle preparations were under way. War was imminent.

With the moat destroyed, Ethan followed his mother around the back of the castle, entering through the kitchens. It felt so strange, seeing her so at ease. She knew exactly where she was going, like she'd been here a million times, because she had. This was her home, where she'd grown up, but it still felt so foreign to Ethan, much like everything else in Tara.

"Mom, what's the test going to be like?"

"I don't know. I wasn't there when your uncle took his," she said, her tone filled with regret.

"Why not?"

She set her hand on the handle of his door and looked at him sheepishly. "I missed it. I'd gone to Bramblewood to see Runyun. In retrospect, it wasn't a very nice thing to do to my brother."

Coming into his room, he sat down on the edge of the bed. "Can you tell me anything?"

"From what I've been told, the questions change every time. The ancients should appear when you summon them to aid in answering."

The word "should" hit Ethan like a sucker punch. He'd never summoned a ghost before. What if he couldn't? Or what if they refused to help him?

After bathing in the largest bathtub he had ever seen, Ethan wrapped a towel around his waist and went back into his room to find his clothes missing.

"They were disgusting. I threw them out." Caitríona walked into his room, carrying a red robe and a plate with a large hunk of bread and cheese. "Your wardrobes are full. I'm sure you can find something suitable to wear."

He had been wearing the same clothes for days, and he knew they made him stand out, but they were the last normal clothes he had. "Couldn't we wash them? Salvage them somehow?"

"They're gone, Ethan. Get over it." His mother passed him the robe, set the plate on the night table, and sat down on the side of the bed. "I spoke with Captain Bartlett. I thought you'd want to know he's going to be okay. He said that you've been very brave through all this."

Ethan slipped on the robe, padded over to the plate, and chowed down on the bread. "Did he tell you he said he was my grandfather?"

"That was a plan cooked up long ago, just in case," she explained.

"Yeah. It wasn't a good one. I didn't buy it." He popped a piece of the cheese into his mouth.

"I told him you wouldn't, but he's as stubborn as you are." She grinned at Ethan then looked around the room. "It's nice to be home. I'm glad I can finally share this with you. I wish I could've told you everything, but you were so young. And Runyun was right. I took a big risk taking you there. We couldn't take a chance on anyone finding out about Tara, or about you."

Ethan set the bread down and sat down next to her. It was his turn to apologize, and like Dratsuah, take responsibility for his actions. "Mom, I'm so sorry I left you." He swallowed the lump in his throat. "It's my fault the Ravens got to you. Captain Bartlett followed me."

"Perhaps. But I fear there were even too many for Captain Bartlett. You and he might've ended up hurt, or worse." Caitríona cupped Ethan's cheeks with her palms, and kissed his forehead. "We're a pair, aren't we? Both of us full of apologies, but we can't afford to spend any more time dwelling on what happened."

"We have to look to the future, not the past." Ethan repeated her constant refrain.

"Yes. And I can't believe I'm letting you go to Coventry without me." With apprehensive eyes, she pressed her hands together.

"General Niles is rightfully nervous about who he can trust and who he can't. He's not willing to leave the castle to Clothilde."

"I understand but part of me wants to shimmy down that rope and follow you." She pointed to the tied-together pile of sheets with the shredded, no-longer-white dress sitting next to the window.

"They told you about that, huh?" Ethan shrugged.

Caitríona walked over to the rope pile and lifted up the white dress. She dragged it along with the rest of the pile, until she stood beside him again. "This was to be my wedding dress."

"Oops."

She flicked him in the side of the head. "'Oops' is right."

Ethan felt horrible. "I'm sure Scully can get it fixed."

"Well, I doubt I'll have a need for it anymore anyway." She watched it fall to the floor with a look that made Ethan wonder if she still felt something for Runyun. She went to the wardrobe and pulled out a green cloak similar to the one General Niles wore and handed it to Ethan. "You must wear the coat of arms in the ceremony."

The patch of the three connected spirals was sewn onto the shoulder. He ran his finger over the intricate stitching, then folded it up and stowed it in a small leather bag Scully had brought for him to use.

Next, she handed him a shirt, a pair of green pants, and long black leather boots, then walked toward the door. "I'll be back in a few minutes to make sure they fit, so you better have them on." Caitríona closed the door behind her.

Letting out a disgusted sigh, Ethan tossed his robe on the bed and slipped on the pretentious attire. As he stepped to the mirror, the image looking back at him hit him over the head like a shovel. The reflection was of a person who belonged in Landover, in Tara, not in Los Angeles, and the irony wasn't lost on him. He was about to take a test that would commit him to Landover for the rest of his life. A commitment he wasn't so sure he was ready to make.

It was a full day's ride to Coventry by horseback. Fortunately, all the horses, including Devlin, had made it back safely to Weymiss. Seamus and Adam had gone ahead, following Runyun's instruction.

The plan was to get close to town, then stop overnight and enter Coventry in the morning, right before the ceremony was to begin.

General Niles protested when Lily asked to come, but Ethan stepped in and said he still wasn't feeling well, which sadly wasn't a complete lie. Although the unicorn blood had healed the wound, his side was still sore.

Niles acquiesced but made Ethan promise that Lily was coming as a healer and would leave if fighting broke out, which was fine with Ethan, so long as she was coming.

The road to Coventry was on flat land, cutting right through the heart of the farm country. With a sore side, Ethan couldn't ride Devlin at a gallop or even a canter, and trotting was painful even without a wound, so everyone was forced to travel at his slow pace.

In black pants and boots and a white shirt, Lily's outfit closely matched Ethan's. Her long braid bobbed as she trotted her horse to catch up to him. "I think I found something in Primland's scáthán. There was a banishing potion called bás dubh—black death. I started the brew, and Morgan is watching over it, but . . ." Lily paused and bit her bottom lip.

"But what?" Ethan pressed.

"According to the instructions, it will take three cycles of the moon before it's ready. Only then can I do the final incantation."

"But we don't have three days," Ethan reminded her.

"I know, but it was all I could find," she insisted.

With that comforting thought, they rode in silence for miles until Ethan's eyelids were so heavy he could barely see the road.

"Ethan, you look tired. We'll find a closer place to stop." General Niles had hoped to make it to the camp at Dryden Lake before stopping for the night. It was only a short ride from there to Coventry.

"No. I can make it." Ethan sat up taller in the saddle and took a deep breath, trying to wake up.

"Julius is right, Ethan. You need to get off that horse," Runyun replied.

"If we leave again at first light, we'll be there in plenty of time," General Niles added. "But where to camp?" He scanned the landscape. "There is so little cover here."

"What about the Gabhanns'? Their place isn't far," Lily commented.

"Good idea," Niles agreed.

"It's a great idea," Runyun bellowed. "Ethan, Bram Gabhann is the best bladesmith in Tara. With any luck he can fit you with a proper sword tonight, and I'll be able to give you a much-needed sparring lesson in the morning before we leave."

There was something in Runyun's "much needed" phrasing that grated on Ethan's last nerve. "Oh, joy. A morning sword fight. Just how I like to start the day."

Lily smiled at his comment. Ethan expected her to chime in with one of her sarcastic dingers, but she didn't. She'd been strangely quiet the entire trip.

After another hour of painful riding and awkward silence, they turned down a path that led to a simple two-story house made entirely of brown stones. The setting sun hung just above the roof, and plumes of smoke spewed out of the chimney.

After dismounting, Runyun led the horses into a fenced field next to an old barn. As the group approached the house, the wooden door flew open. Out stepped a girl about the same age as he and Lily, with long brown hair, wearing a simple blue dress.

"Lily, it's so good to see you." They exchanged a quick hug.

"Rosie, my father would like to speak with yours. Could you find him, please?"

"Of course. Hello, General Niles. Mr. Cooper. He's in the shop. I'll get him directly." Then her large brown eyes fell on Ethan. "Forgive me. Who are you?"

"That's Ethan," Lily said dismissively. "Please, your father?"

Rosie stood there, staring intensely and grinning oddly at him, making Ethan wonder if he should be ducking for cover. General Niles cleared his throat loudly, and Rosie's face turned bright red.

"Sorry. I'll get him. Please come inside and make yourself at home.

Mrs. Winston will get you some tea." She hurried toward the old barn behind the house about fifty feet away.

"Tea? It's nearly dark. I believe a well-deserved ale is in order," Runyun remarked. "Mrs. Winston?" He strolled into the home as if he owned the place. General Niles, Lily, and Ethan followed him into the kitchen, where a large fire burned inside a brick oven. A loaf of bread rested on a wooden board on the counter with a knife placed underneath it.

Without hesitation, Runyun grabbed the bread and cut himself a large piece. An older, heavyset woman with a short gray hair, wearing a pleated brown dress covered by a pale yellow apron, strode up behind him and whacked him on the back of the head.

"Where are your manners, Mr. Cooper?"

Still chewing, Runyun beamed at her and kissed her on the cheek. "Hello, lovely. Where's my hug then?"

"Oh, sit, you flatterer. General Niles, Lily, good to see you both. And who's this?" She stopped in front of Ethan, sizing him up.

Runyun swallowed then said, "My son, Ethan."

"What? Since when do you have a son?"

Runyun fingered the bread and arched a brow at Ethan. "It seems for about fourteen years now."

Scanning his face, she lifted Ethan's chin. "He's yours, all right. It's a pleasure to meet you, young man." She patted his cheek. "Sit. Let me feed you. If you're anything like your father, you're perpetually hungry."

Ethan leaned over to Lily. "Rosie's mother?"

Lily shook her head. "Her mother disappeared a long time ago. Mrs. Winston is their housekeeper," she whispered back.

"Disappeared?"

Lily nodded. "When Rosie was a baby."

They settled around the large rectangular kitchen table. Ethan was hoping to sit beside Lily, but she took the seat at the end of the table next to her father. Runyun sat next to him.

Mrs. Winston set the bread down in front of Ethan and passed out ceramic mugs filled with water and ale. The door swung open. Rosie came in, followed by a tall thin man with curly unkempt dark hair, dressed in a brown tunic and pants that were covered in dusty black soot. Bram Gabhann.

Bram greeted Niles and Runyun while Rosie sat down next to Lily, and whispered in her ear. Lily whispered back, then glowered into her glass. Ethan bit into a hunk of bread when he saw Rosie wave at him.

"Ethan, come sit here." Rosie patted the seat next to her. "Then Da can speak more easily to Mr. Cooper and General Niles."

Lily pursed her lips and kept her eyes on the table. It was painfully obvious she didn't want him sitting closer to her. Maybe she regretted kissing him. Maybe that was why she'd been so quiet. "Thanks, but I'm spending some quality time with my old man here." He patted Runyun on the shoulder.

"Old man?" Runyun elbowed Ethan's side. "Go and sit with them."

"Have you lost your mind?"

Runyun leaned toward him. "Do you know nothing about women?"

Runyun's love life didn't seem any better than his. "What I do know about them is enough to keep me at this end of the table."

Runyun smirked. "Playing hard to get. Good thinking." He took a long sip from his cup.

"It isn't intelligence. It's fear."

Runyun choked on a laugh and spit ale all over the table as Mrs. Winston delivered large steaming bowls of stew. "Mr. Cooper, if that's what happens on the first round, I'm cutting you off."

Runyun coughed and shook his head, amused. It was the first time Ethan had ever seen him smile.

Bram sat down next to Rosie, and everyone started eating.

"I fear going any farther in the darkness," General Niles explained to Bram. "Could we impose on you for a night?"

"Stay as long as you like. I know Rosie loves the company," he said softly. Rosie nodded in agreement.

"That's very kind, but we leave at first light for Coventry," Runyun said, then shoveled in a heaping spoonful of stew.

"Right. You're headed to the meeting of the Council of Kings," Bram surmised.

"We are," Runyun confirmed.

Bram dropped his fork and turned his weathered eyes on Ethan. "The rumors are true then."

General Niles's eyes grew wide. "What rumors?"

"You, you . . . ," Bram stuttered, pointing at Ethan, "You're Caitríona's son?"

"Bram, how do you know about Ethan?" Runyun asked, horrified.

"Everyone knows. The town's been full of gossip about it," Rosie added.

The general dropped his fork too. "No one in Landover knows he exists."

Ethan groaned and slammed his fist on the table. He felt so stupid. "It was Christian. He told the sprites in Bramblewood Forest."

"Why?" General Niles asked. "What would he hope to gain?"

Lily's eyes met Ethan's and he knew they were thinking the same thing. "He was trying to get the rumors to the Ravens, to let them know they had the wrong Makkai when they took my mother."

"What's this about Christian?" Bram asked.

"He's been conspiring with the Ravens and Fenit Traynor," General Niles explained solemnly.

"Tearlach's son is a traitor?" Bram glanced at Rosie, who seemed equally as stunned.

"Ethan, you couldn't have known," Lily said. "I've known him a lot longer than you and never saw this coming."

"You didn't see the way he looked at that Raven, Cyra, when she was dying. I even asked him if he knew her."

"What did he say?" Runyun asked.

Ethan ground his teeth together, fuming. "He never answered the question."

Runyun took a long swig of ale, then set his cup down loudly. "So the town will be filled with people who know you exist. That's not a worry. They don't know what you look like."

True. No one other than Suffie and a few other sprites in Landover had seen him.

With a nervous hesitation, Bram stood up, walked over to Ethan, and kneeled. "It's a pleasure to have you in our home, sire."

"Please, call me Ethan."

"Of course." Seeing the empty plate of bread, he called for Mrs. Winston. "More bread for our heir, please."

"Heir?" Mrs. Winston exclaimed as she reentered the kitchen. "Who? This boy?"

"Ethan is to be the king." Rosie gave Ethan a wry grin, which Lily noticed.

"Well, not yet," Lily added. "We have to get through not dying on our way to the Council meeting, and then there's still the matter of the test."

What was that about? Was she trying to make him nervous? "Thanks for reminding me."

"You're welcome." She tossed him a fake smile.

"Runyun Cooper, the world works in mysterious ways, doesn't it?" Mrs. Winston slapped him on the back. "Your son is going to be our king."

Runyun winked at her, took another long sip of ale, and set the finished mug on the table. Mrs. Winston promptly picked it up to refill it.

Realizing everyone had forgotten the bread, Ethan got up to get some from the kitchen when Rosie grabbed the plate from him. "I'll get your bread, sire."

Nodding thanks, Ethan sat back down and saw Lily glaring at him.

"What?" Ethan shrugged.

"Letting them fuss over you. It's ridiculous," she whispered harshly.

A second later Rosie came back with the plate and leaned over him to set it on the table. She paused an inch from his face. "May I get you anything else, sire?"

"No, thank you." Ethan gave her an awkward smile and she returned to her seat.

"Bram, I was hoping you might fashion Ethan a sword," Runyun said.

"Of course." Bram hopped out of his seat. "Master Ethan, please stand up."

He'd barely made it out of the chair before Bram lifted his hands to the side then took out a marked piece of string. Measuring Ethan's arms, he counted the black notches. "Have you worked with one before?"

Ethan felt the weight of Runyun's stare on him. "Not really."

Bram moved to Ethan's legs, then his back and shoulders. It was more like being fitted for a suit than a sword.

"Fine then. Good." Bram traced Ethan's hand on a piece of paper, then flipped it over and made additional markings on the back. Finally, he lifted him up.

"Whoa." Ethan wasn't used to having a strange man, or any man for that matter, pick him up.

"Sorry. Needed your weight." He turned to Rosie. "Bring my supper out to the barn." Without waiting for her reply, he left.

Rosie picked up his plate, smiled at Ethan, and walked outside.

"Speaking of the barn, Lily, please go tend to the horses," General Niles said. Lily didn't look very happy about being dismissed, but after another bite, she left.

That left Ethan alone with Runyun and Niles.

Runyun pushed his plate away from him and turned his chair so he faced Ethan. "Tomorrow, after the test, you must convince the other kings to stand with Landover."

"That's absurd. They have no reason to fight with us," Niles argued.

"He'll come up with a reason," Runyun said confidently.

"Oh sure. No problem." Ethan contemplated what he could possibly say to Maul or Fearghus to get them to stand with Landover against an unkillable enemy. Nothing particularly brilliant came to mind.

Rosie and Lily returned from feeding the horses, and Mrs. Winston shooed everyone out of the kitchen and into the living room. General Niles went to speak with Bram about supplies for the troops camped near Dryden Lake.

The living room had three comfy sofas positioned around a fireplace with a roaring fire that gave off inviting warmth. Bookshelves lined the walls and a small wooden desk covered with papers sat at the far end of the room where a few lit candelabras were perched.

Ethan sank into the sofa closest to the fire while Lily and Rosie sat across from him. Runyun threw off his boots and lay down with his feet up on the last couch. Mrs. Winston swept in and placed a tray of cookies and a glass of brown ale on the table in front of him.

"You are too good to me," Runyun said.

"It makes me happy to spoil you," Mrs. Winston replied. "Master Ethan, would you like anything else?"

"No, thank you. You've done too much already." Ethan tossed his boots off, put his feet up on the sofa, and set his head down on a pillow. With a full belly and the scent of eucalyptus coming off the fire, he enjoyed the first sense of peace he'd had in days. Within minutes, he crashed.

In the middle of the night, Ethan woke up to the sound of cannonballs crashing through the windows, but it turned out to be General Niles snoring. The general had taken the couch Lily and Rosie had been on when he'd passed out.

Ethan lay there for a long time, staring at the wood beams on the ceiling, trying to go back to sleep, but it was no use. Niles was too loud. Ethan thought about hitting him with a pillow but the man had no sense of humor and would probably kill him. Bare-handed.

He padded into the kitchen for some water, but there was no glass to be found. The countertop was bare. Everything had been put away.

"Couldn't sleep?"

Startled, Ethan's heart skipped five beats as he turned to find Lily standing in the doorway. "You scared the daylights out of me."

Grimacing, she pulled a small lantern from behind her and placed it on the table. "Sorry. Would you prefer if it were Rosie standing here?"

While Ethan was still in the same clothes, she wore a flannel shirt hanging past her knees that looked like it had been one of her brothers. It was the first time Ethan had seen her bare legs. She had really nice legs. Distracting. He realized he never answered her question.

"What? No. What's the matter with you?"

"What's the matter with you?" she snapped back.

"Nothing. I just wanted some water. Do you know where they keep the glasses?"

Lily picked up the lantern, walked to a wall of shelves, pulled down a tall glass, filled it with water from a pitcher on the counter, and held it out to Ethan. "Here."

"Thanks, but next time you can tell me where they are and I'll get it for myself." Taking it, he felt his fingers brush Lily's.

"Rosie can get things for you, but I can't?"

"You said I shouldn't have people wait on me." Ethan pulled out a chair and sat down, making sure to set his glass on the table with a loud clink.

Lily stood in the moonlight, staring at him with a conflicted expression. Her golden hair loose, hanging down to the middle of her back, she looked radiant.

Lily filled another glass and took the seat next to him. "I'm sorry. I shouldn't pick at you." She kept her eyes on the table and ran her fingers along a groove. "It's just . . . I kissed you."

"I remember." Ethan's stomach tightened, unnerved at where this conversation was going. Did she regret kissing him? That had to be it. It was a spur-of-the-moment thing and this was going to be her it-didn't-mean-anything speech.

"And . . ."

"And what?" Ethan shrugged, afraid to add anything else.

Lily wrapped her hands around her glass, unable to meet his gaze. "Never mind. Doesn't matter."

Ethan had lived with his mother long enough to know that when a woman said "never mind," she didn't want him to drop the conversation.

"It matters to me. Come on. Spill it. What's wrong?"

"Nothing is wrong. I thought by the way you were acting around Rosie, that you—"

"How was I acting around Rosie?" Ethan didn't think he'd been any different than his usual self.

Lily gave him a droll stare, then turned her gaze to the table and mumbled something unintelligible to herself. She sighed loudly. "Why is it so hard to talk with you about this? It was just a kiss." She rolled her eyes.

It was Ethan's turn to sigh. He'd been right all along. It had been the greatest moment of his life, and she regretted it. He sat back in his chair and decided to go with the truth. What could it hurt now? "It wasn't just a kiss to me."

The corners of Lily's mouth curled and her cheeks turned crimson. "Well, see, that's what I was trying to ask you." She set her hand on his.

For several long seconds, deafened by his pounding heartbeat, Ethan sat perfectly still, unable to take his eyes off their intertwined hands. Still bemused, he took her statement as a positive sign that she liked him; at least he thought that was what it meant. *Why are women so confusing?*

"Why can't you sleep?" she asked.

"I, um, was thinking about the test."

"That'll be easy."

He shook his head. "No. It won't. I've never been able to call a ghost and have one appear. They come to me." He fingered the glass and watched the light from the lantern reflect off the water onto the table. "What if I can't do it? I'll let everyone down."

"You'll do it." Lily turned in her seat to face him. "Do you know why I came with you when you left Weymiss?"

"I know what you told Christian."

"Part of that was true. I did want to prove something to my father. Women aren't allowed to fight for Landover."

Come to think of it, Ethan hadn't seen one woman among the soldiers at Weymiss. "Why not?"

"Too dangerous, at least that's what they say. I wanted, and still want, to prove them wrong, but . . ." She took a deep breath and let it out slowly. "I came with you because I was hoping you could help me talk to my mother. I've never actually heard the sound of her voice."

Ethan grimaced, knowing he couldn't do that. "You know I would if I could. All I've figured out so far is how to banish them."

Trying to hide her disappointment, Lily nodded then sat taller in her chair. "Let's think about this. What if it doesn't work like that? What if it's like the unicorns? Perhaps the ancients can come only when you *need* them to."

"I hope you're right. I'm going to really need them tomorrow." Ethan took another sip of water.

"You'll prove to the Council you're the rightful heir."

"The Council's all well and good, but it's the people of Landover that matter most. You heard Bram. Everyone has heard the rumors and will be in town, watching. What if I can't do it? Or worse, what if they don't want me? I'm not from here. They have no idea who I am."

Lily looked at him with parted lips that he desperately wanted to kiss, but her father was sleeping fifty feet away.

Then she put her warm hand on his arm, shattering his self-control. "Believe in yourself, Ethan, and they'll believe—"

He cut her words off with a passionate kiss. His heart sang and his entire body felt like it was on fire as her tongue gently brushed against his. He set his hand on her shoulder, wanting this moment to never end, when someone cleared his throat loudly.

Ethan wanted to kill whoever had interrupted them, but from the look on Lily's face, there was only one person who it could be.

THIRTY-FIVE

His hair standing straight up, his face flushed, clearly General Niles was contemplating exactly what form of torture to inflict on Ethan.

Runyun peered out from behind the general. "Did I miss an invitation to a meeting?"

Breathing deeply through his nostrils, Niles's glare moved from Lily to Ethan and back again. "Sleep. Now."

Flustered, Lily rushed from the room, stopping to give Ethan a worried glance, then disappearing. Without another word, General Niles turned on his heel, and headed back to the living room.

Runyun shook his head disapprovingly, then without saying a word, picked up Ethan's water glass from the table and drank from it.

"Weren't you the one who told me to go sit with them?"

Runyun arched a brow, then snatched up Lily's glass and set both in the sink. "Get to sleep before Niles decides killing you is more important than Landover having an heir."

Nearly dawn, Bram Gabhann slammed the barn door. Seconds later, Runyun shook Ethan's shoulder.

"He's done. Come. I can give you a few lessons before we leave."

Still groggy, Ethan could barely open his eyes. "Five more minutes . . ." He dropped his head, rolled over, and had just closed his eyes again when Runyun attacked.

"Hey!" One second he was happily horizontal, cozy under a blanket on the smooshy couch, and the next he was vertical and his feet were cold.

"I don't like to repeat myself. Get dressed." Runyun tossed Ethan his bag. "After last night, you need to understand how to defend yourself."

Ethan's eyes darted to Niles, who thankfully was still sleeping. He pulled his clothes out of the bag and slipped on a clean pair of black pants and a white shirt, while Runyun slid his dual-scabbard onto his back. As Ethan pulled on his boots, a salty-sweet aroma wafted into the room, making his stomach growl. Ms. Winston was cooking breakfast.

"How 'bout we pass by the kitchen first?"

"How about you get your arse outside?" Runyun replied.

"I can see you're a perky one in the morning." Ethan ran out the door before Runyun's backhand could make contact with his head.

Seconds later, they met Bram outside the house's front door. The cloud-filled sky was a hazy gray, and the air was cool and crisp. The grassy field next to the barn was covered in fallen yellow and red leaves. Good camouflage for the bloody damage Runyun was about to inflict on him.

Bram held out something wrapped in a gray cloth. Every inch of him was covered in soot; his hair looked like his fingers had run tracks through it all night.

Runyun nodded to Bram. "Good morrow."

"A good morrow to you. Master Ethan, your sword." He whisked the cloth away. Underneath was a perfectly polished steel sword that glistened, reflecting the soft white glow of the sun streams poking through the clouds. "As you can see, the length is proper for your height. The fuller only slightly deeper, lessening the weight, but the blade is still strong. Runyun prefers a longer cross-guard, as do I."

Ethan saw it was an inch longer on each end than his uncle's old one. "Why?"

"It serves a useful purpose. I'll let him explain." Bram gave a nod to Runyun then held the pommel to Ethan. As he reached for it, Bram pulled it back. "Forgot. The grip." He picked it up. "It's covered with a new leather strap I've been tinkering with. Let me know what you think."

Ethan took the sword. The first thing he noticed was that it was light but not too light, and there was only a small amount of wiggle room between the cross-guard and the pommel, giving his hand tight control, but still left room enough for him to comfortably add another hand. Ethan moved away from the house, and swung it a couple of times.

"The grip is sticky."

"Yes. And the sweatier you become in battle, the stickier it will become," Bram noted.

Runyun clapped Bram on the back. "Not bad, Bram! How about you wrap mine with that as well?"

Bram sighed, exhausted. "How about I give you some and you wrap it yourself?"

Both sides of the blade were etched with a design that ran from tip to cross-guard, and branded into the bottom was the familiar connected spirals. "Landover's mark."

"On the pommel. All soldiers of Landover carry our mark. It brings us luck in battle," Bram explained. "May it bring you victory over our enemies, sire. Almost forgot." He handed him a leather scabbard he'd been hiding under the cloth.

"I don't know how to thank you," Ethan said, taking it.

Bram set a hand on Ethan's shoulder. "Not necessary, lad. I'm your humble servant. Now, if you'll excuse me, I must get cleaned up."

Ethan watched as Bram walked into the house so tired that he stumbled through the door.

"He stayed up all night to make this for me. Why would he do that?" Ethan asked Runyun.

"Because you're his king, or will be soon enough." Runyun slid the new scabbard onto Ethan's belt. "The people of Landover have strong, passionate hearts. When they set about accomplishing something, they do it, and they'll support you, no matter what."

Ethan fisted the grip of his new blade. "You didn't support Tearlach."

"Of course I did. Fought by his bleedin' side more times than I can count. Doesn't mean I liked the pompous arse." Runyun lifted out a sword and moved into an open area.

Ethan followed. "I'm not sure how an hour of training is going to help when my enemies have been fighting their entire lives."

Runyun stopped and faced him. "Fighting comes naturally to us. We're Celts. It's in our blood. But you don't have a taste for it . . . yet."

"You think I'm afraid?"

"Not true. A healthy dose of fear would be a good thing for you. What you have is much worse." Runyun pressed his index finger to the left side of Ethan's chest. "No one can beat down an enemy with compassion."

Ethan winced. Runyun was right, and he hated him for it. With a deep breath, he tossed his sword from hand to hand.

"That's it. Get to know it. Your sword is a tool, a means to an end. Every inch of it can be used in battle, not just the blade. Thrust at me."

Ethan lunged the blade at Runyun's midsection. He blocked the stroke then stepped inside, running his blade up Ethan's until it hit his cross-guard. The swords seemingly locked, Runyun's face only inches from Ethan's. "Now it becomes a hammer." With a strong shove, Runyun's cross-guard headed straight for Ethan's eye.

Ethan ducked, and rolled wide to give himself some room.

"Good instinct. Don't be afraid of retreat. But next time, consider rolling the other way. Then come up behind your opponent. If you're quick enough, you'll be able to run him through the back before he turns around." Runyun came straight at Ethan.

Ethan lifted his sword, meeting Runyun's, stopping his blade, and locking them together again. This time, Ethan took a small step to the right, trying to roll off, but Runyun applied pressure, and Ethan lost his sword.

Runyun picked it up and handed it back to him. "The other way. Step inside on the diagonal. And remember, you're fighting the man, not the weapon. You'll know everything about him from his first attack, his strength, his tenacity, and his conviction in killing you. Size him up, and fight *him*. There are no rules. Punch. Kick. Do whatever it takes to win."

That gave Ethan pause. "You're saying to fight dirty."

"Fighting is always dirty."

Runyun swung again. Ethan met his blade, and then came toward him, moving slightly left, and shoved Runyun back.

Locking their swords again, Runyun said, "Good! But this time take the grip with both hands and twist while pressing down."

Ethan swiveled so his sword came over the top of Runyun's, and pushed with everything he had. Runyun was forced to drop his sword.

"Good. In a true fight, everything will move faster. You're small, but that will be an advantage. Don't try to defend from above. Force them to meet you at your level. They'll be hunched over, giving you more mobility. And you're fast. That I've seen." Runyun raised his sword. "Now, again."

They practiced for more than an hour, finally stopping when Lily came out of the house.

"May I?" she taunted, brandishing her sword.

"Please. I can use something to eat." Runyun slid his sword into his scabbard and jogged into the house.

Ethan desperately wanted something to eat too, but now that Lily was here, he was willing to argue with his growling stomach a bit longer.

Lily tossed her weapon from hand to hand. "Come on. Attack!"

"I don't want to hurt a girl," Ethan said, poker-faced, then swung down. Her blade easily met his, and she pushed him off. Then it was her turn.

Ethan tried Runyun's move, pushing her blade aside, but it didn't work. He tried another angle, but she spun out. Next thing he knew, the tip of her blade was on his stomach. The girl had some serious skills, and there was something incredibly hot about the angry scowl she wore when she attacked him.

"Lily, be careful! You'll hurt him!" Rosie barked, coming out of the house. In a red dress, her hair was pulled off her face, and twisted into an elaborate braid that draped over her shoulder.

"Don't worry. I meant to do that." Ethan had to save face somehow.

"Oh really!" Lily roared as she came at him. Ethan sidestepped and shot out his foot. She fell for it, tripped, and ate dirt.

"You okay?" Ethan offered her a hand.

"I'm the enemy! Don't check on me!" Lily leaped to standing and thrust. Ethan jumped back to avoid needing to summon another unicorn. He landed on a rock, twisted his ankle, and fell backward. Next thing he knew he was pinned to the ground with the bottom of Lily's boot pressing on his chest.

"Fine. I won't check on you anymore," he groaned. He grabbed her boot and twisted until she tumbled off.

Still on the ground, Ethan watched as Lily popped up and flashed him a wickedly charming smile, ready for more.

Rosie rushed over and stood between them. "Lily, your father called you."

"He did?" She looked back at the house.

Ethan shrugged. "I didn't hear anything."

"I'd best go check." Lily dashed to the house.

Rosie kneeled next to Ethan and touched his shoulder. "Are you all right? Lily shouldn't have gone at you so hard."

"I have a feeling an enemy wouldn't hold back, so it's probably for the best she didn't either." Ethan got up and dusted his pants off.

"I think it's because she has so many brothers. It's not a proper way for a girl to behave, though."

Rosie leaned toward him, her eyes falling on his mouth. "You're bleeding." She reached out and ran her thumb along Ethan's chin.

Lily walked out of the house and froze. Ethan turned, catching her angry scowl and took a big step away from Rosie. She pinned him with a heated glare, then stormed off toward the barn.

"Where are you going?" Ethan raced after her. He saw Alastair's head pop out from behind the barn.

By the time Ethan caught up to Lily, she had Alastair on the ground, her sword shoved against his gut.

"Where is Christian Makkai? Tell me!" she shouted at the Brownie.

Ethan pushed Lily off of Alastair, but the Brownie stayed on the ground, holding a hand protectively over his face.

"What do you think you're doing?" Lily snapped at Ethan.

"Let the guy speak." Ethan lifted Alastair up by his armpits. He was in worse shape than the last time Ethan had seen him. His clothes were shredded and bloodied, two deep gashes ran down each cheek, and his left eye was swollen shut. "Dilga did this to you, didn't she?"

"She did. But I left her with a few marks as well," he said, wiggling his eyebrows.

"Ethan, take him to my father!" Lily interrupted. When he didn't move, she added, "This Brownie works for the enemy. He works for Primland."

Ethan glanced back at her. "No. I don't think he does. Christian told him I was the heir before we left Weymiss, and he never told the Ravens." Ethan looked back at Alastair. "Why didn't you?"

"On the day my master was imprisoned on the Isle of Mord, he sent me to serve the Ravens. I would never tell them anything, ever," Alastair huffed.

"We can't trust him. He brought us the cursed ring. That's how the Ravens followed us," Lily exclaimed.

"True," Alastair acknowledged. "Long ago that ring was given to Bean by the Mistress Muriol. Somehow it ended up in the hands of Tearlach Makkai. I retrieved it from him and returned it to the Mistress. When Dilga ordered me to make sure you found it, I did. And yes, the Ravens followed because you possessed the ring. But—"

"But you knew that it could be used as leverage against Kiara, and that we might find out what Bean was planning," Ethan said.

Alastair nodded.

Ethan looked at Lily. "At Weymiss, when we returned from Algidare, he closed the door to the closet I was hiding in to keep Bean from finding me. Lily, he's not working for the enemy. He's helping us, not Primland."

"Primland is not the enemy," Alastair said in a soft voice. "Sawney Bean took my master and twisted his mind in hopes of securing Landover."

"Why? What does Bean want?" Lily asked.

"Don't know, but it doesn't matter anymore. He will take Landover. And soon after, the rest of Tara will fall."

Alastair stepped closer and his demeanor completely changed. He stared at Ethan with a twisted frown. "It was you"—he poked Ethan's chest—"who were to save us all, even Primland, but no more. *You* failed." He shook his head. "How could you let this happen? The deed is almost done. Sawney Bean is on the Isle of Mord at this very minute. When the sun goes down, they'll attack. The draugar, the undead, are coming."

Lily's eyes grew wide. "While we're in Coventry? I've got to tell my father." She sprinted toward the house.

"Alastair, I don't understand. Why do you believe I'm supposed to help Primland?"

Confused, Alastair tilted his head. "The unicorns, of course. Oh, but you don't know, do you? How could you? Not of Tara . . ." His voice trailed off as he leaned in closer. "As the gods and goddesses departed for the Otherworld, Bran the Blessed saw Tara's doomed future. His prophecy spoke of our clans again dividing, repeating mistakes of the past, leading to its fall into darkness once more. He said there would be no hope for survival, save one . . ." Alastair closed his eyes and held out his hand.

"Only one.
  He will possess the sacred gift, radharc.
  He will not be of Tara,
  But will come to understand the heart and soul of Tarisians
     like no other.

  And yet, an understanding alone will not be enough.
  For only if he can find an inner strength,
  Unattained by any mortal before,
  Can he can lead our sons and daughters out of the darkness."

Alastair opened his eyes and locked them on Ethan's.

  "For in darkness there is always light,
  And in the face of death a reason to fight."

Stunned, Ethan frowned. "And you think Bran the Blessed was speaking of me? Why? Because I wasn't born in Tara and I possess radharc? I don't know anything of the heart and soul of Tara or its people. And I know even less about how to fight." Ethan looked down at his new sword, which suddenly had become heavy in his hand.

"The Banshee Aibheill, whose bards carried the poem to us, was clear. She said the unicorns would return when the *one* has come to Tara." Alastair shook his head and moved even closer. "But you've failed, Ethan Makkai. Although it appears the unicorns have returned and saved you, you cannot save Landover, or Tara. There is no hope for any of us."

"There has to be hope," Ethan said as Alastair turned to leave. "Wait! Where are you going?"

Alastair stopped and looked back at him. "Sawney Bean has removed the charm, making it possible for my master to leave the Isle of Mord. A Brownie is born to serve, and a servant is tied to his master, no matter where that connection takes him. I must return to him."

"You can't! He'll kill you for betraying him. Come with us. Help us fight!"

"The girl was right. If I was forced to fight at this time, it would be against you, not with you."

"Ethan!" Runyun called.

Ethan turned his attention to the house. The horses had been saddled and Runyun waved, motioning him to return.

"I have to go." But when Ethan turned around, Alastair was already gone.

With a heavy heart, Ethan raced back to the house to get his cloak, but got only as far as the kitchen. Rosie stopped him, insisting he eat before leaving. She presented him with a huge plate of scrambled eggs. Not wanting to be rude, he sandwiched the eggs between two pieces of toast, scarfed it down, and chugged a glass of water.

General Niles came into the kitchen, carrying two plain brown cloaks. He swung one on and tossed the other to Ethan. "Wear this. The other one will draw too much attention. You can put it on when we get to Coventry."

Coventry. Ethan suddenly felt ill.

"Let me help with that." Rosie took the cloak out of Ethan's hands and wrapped it around his shoulders.

The cloak was surprisingly heavy, but it was nothing compared to the weight of the egg sandwich he'd just scarfed down. With his mind now firmly on the test, he felt as if he'd swallowed a twenty-pound bowling ball.

Rosie's hands were still on Ethan's cloak when Lily entered from the living room.

She took one look at both of them, and walked right out the door.

"Sorry. Gotta run. Thanks for everything." Ethan darted out after her.

When he got outside, he found Runyun, Lily, and General Niles standing together, waiting for him. General Niles lowered his eyes to meet Ethan's and set a hand on his shoulder.

"Remember, the bell on top of the tavern will chime seven times. When the people hear the first strike, they'll migrate into the great hall. We'll move inside with them. The heir must present himself before the last bell tolls. Once inside, I'll announce you. When I do, lower your hood. Show the people your face."

How could he forget? They'd gone over this a million times last night. It was burned into Ethan's brain. With a nod, he mounted Devlin.

Lily rode with General Niles. Ethan and Runyun brought up the rear.

"Nervous?" Runyun asked.

"Terrified," he answered. "What if I fail?"

"You won't," Runyun scoffed.

"But what if I do?" Ethan pressed.

Runyun's expression turned deadly serious. "Worry more about what you're going to say to the Council."

Runyun was certain Landover needed their support in the coming battle; that the realm would fall without it. Yet if he failed the test, no one was going to have any faith in him at all. Not the people of Landover, not the kings of Tara.

Landover's fate would be determined by whether or not Ethan could pass a test he was totally unprepared for. *We're so screwed.*

THIRTY-SIX

Ethan was going to die. The egg sandwich he'd eaten before they'd left still wasn't playing nicely with the extreme case of nerves in his stomach. He swallowed nonstop, hoping to stave off his growing need to throw up.

Still a mile out of Coventry, the wide dusty road became crowded. Both on foot and on horseback they traveled with a single purpose: to find out if an heir really existed.

General Niles led them off the main road and onto a narrow path, hoping it would be less crowded, but it wasn't. No one took notice of Ethan or the others until they came to a family traveling on foot.

"Good day," the mother said. "On our way to Coventry. You as well?" She looked up at Ethan, who pulled his hood down over his face.

"Yes," Lily replied, keeping her eyes forward.

"All we can do is pray the rumors are true," she said, sounding anxious. The baby she carried in a sling on her front began to cry. She patted its back and bounced up and down as she walked.

"They're rumors, love," the man with her said. He wrapped an arm around her shoulders. "Likely a last attempt by the Makkai family to save Landover." He glanced up at Ethan. "I've spoken to the Commis meself. They have no heir. *We* have no heir."

"Don't say that to the young ones," his wife scolded. She glanced up at Lily. "I'm told soldiers from Landover arrived yesterday, escorting the heir."

"And now you're filling their heads with lies. Don't give them hope when there's none to be had!" the man snapped. "We have no Ríegre, no king or queen, and soon we'll all be bowing down to Primland, our bodies and souls filled with the mist, leaving us mindless drones."

The baby cried louder.

"We need to get moving," Runyun said.

Ethan nodded, and as he prodded Devlin to pick up the pace, he looked back at the woman and winked. "Keep the faith."

The path twisted through a wooded area and past several small farms, their crop fields littered with post-harvest wilted plants. It wasn't until they reached a large rock with the word COVENTRY carved into it that Niles slowed the horses to a walk.

The dirt course joined a cobblestone road that ran up a hill and then leveled off into a large U-shaped courtyard lined with connected buildings made of various shades of gray and brown stones. Some buildings were tall with flat tops, others shorter with arched roofs. Compared to Quinsberry Gorge in Gransmore, Coventry was tiny and medieval.

As they reached the crowded courtyard, they dismounted and tied the horses to one of several short hitching poles that ran along the right side of the square. Runyun tossed a coin at a boy keeping watch over the horses.

Their hoods raised, they pushed their way through the masses. Ethan and Lily followed Niles closely and Runyun brought up the rear. Niles led them past several shops, including a bakery. The smell of baking bread filled the courtyard. Normally, it would have been comforting, but today it made Ethan's stomach lurch.

Lily reached into her pocket, pulled out a small amber-colored piece of candy, and passed it to Ethan. "Eat it. It's a dragée. A lump of sugar. This one is spiced with ginger. It'll settle your upset stomach."

"Thanks." Ethan popped it in his mouth. It tasted like a ginger ale–flavored jellybean. His throat burned, but at least it took his mind off his stomach. "Does this mean you're not pissed at me anymore?"

Lily grimaced over her shoulder at him. "Pissed? Upset? I'm not upset at you."

Ethan moved so he was walking beside her. "Could've fooled me."

Lily glanced sideways at him. "I know it isn't your fault that you're as gorgeous as your father and girls flirt with you. But that doesn't mean I like it."

Positive his ears were playing tricks on him, Ethan pulled her to a stop. "Can you please say that again?"

She gave him a hint of a smile. "You heard me." Then she hurried to catch up to her father again.

Even as he was walking into a mess like this, only Lily could make him feel like singing. A huge grin spread across his face until they reached the front of Wenlock Tavern and saw Seamus and Adam Niles staring ominously down at them from the porch.

Standing beside them, blocking the door to the tavern, was a man equal in height with dark hair slicked back into a ponytail. Lily tugged on Ethan's hand to get his attention and mouthed, "Lachlan Traynor."

General Niles lowered his hood.

"Julius Niles, why so glum? We all knew Landover had no heir," Primland's king announced loud enough for the mob to hear.

"What makes you believe that?" Julius asked.

People moved closer to hear the exchange. The sprites, including Suffie and Myrna, hovered above the crowd.

"Because he or she is not here," he said with certainty, and gestured to the crowd. "Fear not, good people of Landover. Primland would never allow our cousin's realm to fall."

"If the monarchs could please move back into the tavern, the heir will make himself known," Seamus announced.

Lachlan Traynor laughed in disbelief. "Sure he will." With a team of Primland guardsmen at his back, he walked down the steps of the tavern and into the courtyard, exuding outward confidence, smiling at Landover's people, as if he really cared, but he couldn't hide his true emotions from Ethan, his utter contempt. The people parted, forming a circle around him. "Forget ceremony. Forget tolling bells. The people of Landover deserve to hear the truth, do they not?" Lachlan Traynor bellowed.

"If our own general won't tell us the truth, then perhaps the king of Primland will!" a man behind Niles shouted.

Traynor glanced back at his men with a knowing smile, then turned to the masses, "The Makkais have no heir. The goddess Clíodhna has found none of their family worthy of Landover's great people. Tell the truth, General. Tell your people the truth."

"We want the truth!" a woman yelled.

Tempers flared. People started arguing among themselves, and Lachlan Traynor gave a caustic laugh at the chaos, eating it up.

"Get to the tavern," General Niles told Ethan. "I'll handle this."

But Ethan had a better idea. Across from the tavern sat a large flat rock. It was the perfect spot. He latched on to Lily's hand and pushed through the mob, hearing a frustrated Niles harshly whispering his name.

When Ethan and Lily reached it, he took a deep breath and was about to climb up when a hand seized his shoulder.

"Are you ready?" He recognized the voice instantly—Bartlett. Ethan turned and found the captain, his leg bandaged, but other than that he looked like his grumpy old self.

Ethan nodded.

"Then get up there and let everyone else know you're here before anarchy breaks out and I have to shoot my own people, not that some of these arses don't deserve to be lit up."

"Only you could make a joke right now." Ethan tossed Lily a nervous smile, and climbed onto the rock. He took a deep breath, scanning the angry mob, then lowered his hood.

"Ethan Makkai! I see him!" Suffie shrieked from above. She flew to where she hovered over him. "Look, you bloomin' eejits! The heir is right here! Now calm down."

Myrna joined Suffie in calling out Ethan's name. After a few loud grumbles, the town fell silent. Everyone circled the rock until Ethan was completely surrounded.

"I've never heard of a Makkai named Ethan!" a man yelled.

"That's because there isn't one! He's a fraud," another bellowed.

"Move. Please. Move please. I said move!" King Fearghus snapped. He, Bryg, Phalen, and two other Fomorians plowed their way through the crowd, causing the ground to shake. The king was dressed in a maroon tunic with Gransmore's mark branded into the chest. Unlike at Brimouth, he was armed with a sword on each hip.

Bryg pointed out Ethan and Lily to King Fearghus as they stopped next to Lachlan Traynor. Fearghus gave a knowing smile, and turned to Lachlan. "Why are we standing outside the tavern? The ale is inside."

Unfazed, Lachlan unfolded his arms from his chest and set a hand on the grip of his sword. "Because Landover has no heir."

"Really? Why would you think that?" Fearghus asked.

"Because—"

Fearghus held a hand up, silencing Lachlan. "That was rhetorical." The Fomorian king looked at Ethan. "Mr. Makkai, you're still breathing."

"For now anyway," Ethan responded.

Fearghus and a few in the crowd laughed.

Lachlan knitted his eyebrows together as he pushed past Fearghus, attempting to close the distance between them, but General Niles and Runyun cut him off.

"That's close enough," Runyun said.

Seamus and Adam took up positions on either side of the rock. Landover's soldiers shoved Primland's guards who were blocking the tavern door, forcing them to move. Then they made their way to the rock, displacing the crowd, pushing them back.

"Who are you?" Lachlan Traynor asked.

Ethan looked out over the people. "My name is Ethan Makkai. My mother is Caitríona, daughter of King Maximus, sister of King Tearlach."

Gasps echoed from every direction. Boisterous members of the crowd angrily argued: *Not possible. There is no such person! He's a liar!*

But the hopeful also made themselves known.

"The rumors were true!" a woman cried from the front of the bakery.

"Nitwits! All of you! He's not a Makkai," a man on Ethan's right barked.

The mother Ethan had met on the ride into town loudly asked, "Where did you come from?"

"He's been hidden, for his protection, and ours," General Niles said. "But he is the true heir."

More arguments broke out until Lachlan raised his arms, silencing them. "You possess radharc?" Lachlan asked Ethan.

A Buggane wearing a helmet of gold came next to Lachlan.

"Drakma Keeill. The leader of the Bugganes," Lily said.

Leader Maul stood on the tavern's porch, wearing a serious glower.

Ethan glanced at each of the realm's kings. The entire Council was present.

"Show us!" a woman cried.

"Prove it!" another yelled.

Ethan turned his gaze on Lachlan Traynor. "I'm ready whenever you are."

With a wave of Lachlan's hand, a heavyset man with short red hair and a full beard, wearing a Landover-green cloak, cleared his throat loudly, silencing everyone. He bowed and announced himself. "Duncan Flynn. Chieftain of the Commis."

Duncan gave an anxious nod to Captain Bartlett, who rolled his eye. "My new son-in-law seems a bit nervous."

"What do I need to do?" Ethan asked him.

"In order to prove you are the right and true heir, you must demonstrate radharc. You must answer a question from the scroll of the Banshee Aibheill, a question that can be answered only by the ancient monarchs of Landover."

Duncan gestured to another man dressed similarly who held a wooden box with the seal of Landover branded into the top. Duncan lifted off a chain from around his neck. Hanging on it was a large brass key.

As Duncan opened the box, Ethan glanced down at Lily, hoping to see a look of confidence on her face, one that might calm his extreme case of nerves, but she wasn't even looking at him. Her eyes were fixed on the box.

With the lid open, Duncan retrieved a foot-long scroll, but before he could unroll it, Lachlan ripped it out of his hands.

"An impartial reader," Lachlan said as he started to open the scroll. King Fearghus hurried toward him, sending the crowd rushing out of his way.

"Give me that!" He ripped the scroll from Traynor's hands. "I trust you don't mind."

Considering King Fearghus's size, the Primland king made a wise choice and took a big step backward. "Why would I mind?" His face filled with contempt.

Fearghus unraveled the scroll, and held the parchment up with two fingers. It looked like a Post-it in his enormous hands. He walked toward Ethan until they were both close enough to see it. It was blank, at first. But then three lines of black ink materialized.

Fearghus cleared his throat, and began: "'During the mighty reign of King Bronis Makkai, he journeyed with four Celts and three Faoladhs to the island of Talia to retrieve a magical object.'" King Fearghus paused and pointed his finger in the air. "By the way, it is not I who called King Bronis's reign 'mighty.'" The crowd laughed. "'What was the object they sought, and were they successful?'"

"That sounds like two questions," Lily called out.

"I didn't write it, Ms. Niles," King Fearghus responded.

Ethan nervously scanned the area for taibhsí. When he didn't see any, he closed his eyes, but nothing happened. There was no shiver, no tingling, nothing.

Please be there. . . . Ethan blinked open his eyes but all he saw were the angry and disappointed faces of Landover's people staring at him.

"Well," Lachlan said, drawing out the word.

"Fraud!" someone in the mob yelled.

"Quiet!" King Fearghus shouted. Then, in a softer voice, he said, "Go on, Ethan. Try again."

His confidence shaken, Ethan closed his eyes and felt something tickle the back of his neck. The wind abruptly picked up. He stepped a foot back for balance, and a melody began humming in his ears.

A woman's voice sang a sad tune, but he couldn't understand the words. The soulful song carried emotions on it, like Bartlett's map. Ethan gasped as he recognized them as coming from the crowd. They flowed through every cell in his body. Fear, anger, and confusion but also joy, happiness, faith, and love.

An icy blast slammed into his adbomen, launching him into the air. As he took flight he saw his body standing on the rock below in the middle of the crowd, and yet everything appeared out of focus. Horrified, he realized his soul had somehow separated from his body.

I'm dead. Why else would his soul leave his body? And yet, he could still sense a physical presence.

He wasn't dying. He was *seeing* through someone else's eyes.

Someone, somehow, had stolen his soul.

What the hell! Ethan fought against whatever was holding him, mentally kicking and screaming, but whatever had him refused to let go.

Ethan flew over the cliffs of Landover, into Brodik Bay, then to a tiny, island he'd never seen before. Scads of corpses lay side by side in a line, circling an old volcano. Ethan's sight traveled over the lifeless bodies. There were thousands of them and they appeared to be dead.

Ethan plummeted through a cave opening and into a pitch-black tunnel so fast he felt like he had vertigo. As he came to a halt inside a craggy cavern, a man in a tattered black cloak and the Raven, Dilga, watched Sawney Bean lift a spoonful of liquid from his cauldron and drip the potion on one of the dead Primland soldiers. His guts had been torn open, and his right hand blown off. The potion spread visibly through the corpse's veins, sealing his belly wound. As the man's hand grew back, his eyes fluttered open.

It was happening. Bean was raising the draugar army.

The sorcerer threw his head back and roared so loudly Ethan thought he'd felt his presence.

You have to hurry, Ethan.

Ethan gasped in relief at the sound of his Muincara. His soul flew back to Coventry and landed in his body. He shivered uncontrollably. When Ethan opened his eyes, he saw the same disappointed faces of the crowd staring up at him. Rattled, he scanned right and left, but there was not a ghost in sight.

Behind you.

Ethan spun around and found twelve auras floating, all wearing severe expressions. The men had sunken cheeks and deep circles under their eyes. Each in varying battle armaments with the unifying mark of Ethan's mother's home burned into their chest plates or, in a couple of cases, tattooed on their bare chests—the ancient monarchs of Landover.

There was only one queen.

With long blond hair and vibrant green eyes, she wore a long iridescent dark green dress. She stood behind the kings, yet hovered above them. Clíona. The daughter of the goddess Clíodhna and Padraig's wife. She was stunning.

One of the kings drifted forward. Built like a line backer with black hair and an oddly familiar stern frown, he bowed his head. *I am your Muincara, and your uncle, Tearlach Makkai.*

The hair. The frown. He looked exactly like Christian. Ethan couldn't breathe. He couldn't speak. His mouth went completely dry and it felt like he'd swallowed his tongue. He did the only thing he could think of, he returned the bow.

"He sees them!" someone cried.

"He does; he sees them!" Suffie exclaimed.

The question, Ethan, Tearlach pressed.

"King Fearghus, could you please repeat the question?" Ethan asked.

"Of course. 'During the—um—reign of King Bronis Makkai, he journeyed with four Celts and three Faoladhs to the island of Talia to retrieve a magical object. What was the object they sought, and were they successful?'"

It didn't go unnoticed that King Fearghus had left out the word "mighty" in the question this time. Ethan turned back to the twelve ghosts. The tallest stepped forward. His cheeks were covered in pockmarks. Not like acne scars, more like acid had eaten through his skin. His salt-and-pepper hair hung past his shoulders in two braids. His clothes were shredded like he'd been attacked by a wild animal, and a long scar stretched across his neck from one side to the other as if his throat had been slit.

Holding out his right hand, he used his index finger and drew in the air, leaving a trail of white marks. He made a circle, then a smaller circle in the center of it, and a line from one to the other, connecting them. A wheel. It was definitely a wheel of some kind. His eyes met Ethan's, and he very pointedly shook his head.

"Um, they went looking for a wheel," Ethan answered, "and no, they weren't successful."

The crowd held their breaths in hushed anticipation, including Ethan. Each passing second felt like an eternity.

Finally, King Fearghus nodded. "Correct!"

The crowd raised their arms and cheered.

"We have our king!" someone cried.

Ethan let go of the breath he'd been holding for way, way too long. He'd done it. Lily beamed at up at him. He caught sight of General Niles shaking Runyun's hand. They were actually smiling at each other.

"Glad to see I didn't waste fourteen years of my life trapped in Los Angeles for nothing," Captain Bartlett mused.

"Wait!" Lachlan Traynor interrupted. "Let me see that parchment."

King Fearghus hid it behind his back.

"What are you hiding, Fearghus?" Traynor held out his hand.

The Fomorian king's eyes slid to Ethan, then to the ground as he held out the parchment. Ethan's stomach dropped into his shoes. Something was wrong.

Traynor took it, and smirked. "The answer was not complete. There is nothing written on here but the questions."

"The answer appears when the heir has given the correct answer," Bartlett explained, sounding stunned. His long expression said it all. Ethan had failed.

"I don't understand. Did I answer incorrectly?"

Wearing a look of smug repugnance, Lachlan Traynor turned to Ethan. "They were looking for some kind of wheel, and they failed. King Fearghus, your General Niles, most of the Tarisian armies in fact know the answer you gave, Ethan Makkai. But what's the name of the magical wheel? What was the object? What were they looking for?" His voice grew louder and angrier at each question.

The crowd hushed.

King Fearghus couldn't meet Ethan's gaze. He was a gambler, like Runyun, and had been trying to help Ethan by cheating, but his poker face wasn't good enough to fool Traynor or the people of Landover.

And Ethan didn't want to trick these people. He had to prove he was the rightful heir or he didn't want the job. He didn't deserve to be the king.

Ethan looked out over the crowd and went with the truth. "King Bronis's throat was cut by something so powerful that even in death he can't speak."

Lachlan guffawed. "Convenient excuse, Ethan Makkai. This test is over."

THIRTY-SEVEN

Fighting broke out. Landover's soldiers tried to calm the situation, but it was no use. Ethan had failed the test and if he didn't do something, people were going to get hurt.

"Wait!" Ethan yelled. The crowd stopped and all eyes turned on him.

Ethan looked back at Tearlach. *Uncle, help me, please.*

I don't have the answer. Only Bronis knows.

Okay. Not the answer Ethan wanted, but it gave him an idea. He looked at King Bronis and thought, *Spell it.*

King Bronis nodded. He held his finger high again and sky-wrote, leaving a white trail of letters. The first was *R*, then *O*. He kept writing until he spelled something that Ethan didn't understand: *ROTH RÁMACH.*

"Here goes," Ethan muttered then look back at the crowd and said, "Roth raym-ach?"

"What was that?" Traynor flipped the parchment to show the questions still unanswered.

No answer was ever going to be good enough for this dickhead. "That's what King Bronis wrote."

"Ethan grew up outside of Tara. He would not know how to speak the ancient tongue or what it means," General Niles explained.

"Can I spell it?" Ethan asked.

This time everyone laughed. Ethan took that as a no.

Drakma Keeill grunted.

"The answer must appear on the scroll," Fearghus translated. "We

know, Keeill." Fearghus pursed his lips together. "Ethan, what did the magical object do?"

Ethan was going to fail. He stared at the ancient words. *ROTH
RÁMACH.* There was no way he could understand what King Bronis had
spelled out or pronounce it correctly. He thought about making something
up, but that would be even worse than saying nothing.

Ethan locked eyes with Lily. If only she could help him, but she couldn't.
She gave him a worried glance that reminded Ethan of her expression when
she had appeared on the dock and saved his life. When he'd been dying.

"That's it!" Ethan exclaimed.

"What's it?" Fearghus asked.

Ethan took a deep breath, closed his eyes, and called out the ancient
words he would never forget. "Beini liom!"

A gust of wind raced through the center of Coventry, toppling people
out of the way, leaving a trail of dust in its wake. It circled the rock, forcing
several of Landover's soldiers to roll back. A black steed with a shimmering silver horn settled next to Ethan and blew at the crowd.

"The unicorns have returned!" a woman cried.

"Impossible!" Traynor exclaimed.

King Fearghus's eyes widened with astonishment. Drakma Keeill and
the other Bugganes moved back to the tavern's porch and huddled by the
door.

Rising up on its hind legs, the unicorn neighed loudly, and when it
dropped back down, Ethan hopped on.

The crowd collectively gasped as the unicorn stepped in front of the
rock. Giving a protective high-pitch whine, the steed's eyes flashed from
brown to crimson, putting those watching on notice.

Ethan saw a small cut on its side. This was the one who had saved his
life on the dock. He softly touched the wound, and the unicorn shuddered.
"Thank you."

Let the comfort of your home give you power, Ethan, Tearlach instructed.
*Take stock in who you are and where you belong. Open your mind and
believe in your connections to this world and the Otherworld.*

Ethan locked eyes on those who had believed in him since his journey
had begun: Captain Bartlett, General Niles, his father, and finally Lily, and

looked into the hopeful faces in the crowd. He felt his power reach out, touching everyone around him. With their belief in him in the forefront of his mind, his hands warmed and he placed them on the unicorn's neck. A surge shot through Ethan's body. Shocked, he arched his back, and saw the world through dark red glasses until his eyes suddenly slammed shut.

In the darkness he saw King Bronis's written words, *ROTH RÁMACH,* heard the unicorn say them, and repeated, "Rah Ram-ah." He felt energy flow through him and his mind flooded with more information. "It's a magical flying device that belonged to Mug Ruith. It was stolen by the Raven queen centuries ago and it alone possesses the knowledge and power to get to the lost children."

Lachlan's eyes grew wide. "Páistí barllte." His words weighed heavy on the silent crowd.

"Interesting," he heard Maul say.

King Fearghus looked down at the parchment, and then triumphantly held it up for everyone to see. "You've done it."

The crowd erupted in cheers, bellowing Ethan's name. Lily beamed up at him. She looked proud and, for a brief second, Ethan let the happiness of the moment wash over him. But then it was gone. After what he witnessed on the Isle of Mord, passing the test was the least of Landover's worries.

Traynor ripped the scroll out of King Fearghus's hands to stare at it. Grimacing, he rolled it up, and then tossed it at Duncan Flynn.

With a sweeping pat on the unicorn's neck, Ethan climbed off, returning to the rock. As the steed sped off the way he'd come, Ethan waved his hands, signaling for the crowd to quiet. Shushing muffled the cheers, and everyone waited for him to speak. "At this very moment, Sawney Bean is raising the army of dead Primland soldiers left on the Isle of Mord."

"Sawney Bean is free?" a woman asked, her voice quavering.

"Yes," Ethan confirmed. "He escaped the cave and intends to attack Landover."

Panic filled the square. Everyone scattered, trampling one another, rushing to get out of town. Seamus, Adam, and the rest of Landover's finest tried to calm the crowd, but it was no use. Ethan groaned. His first proclamation as king was to start a riot.

With a furrowed brow, King Fearghus tossed an angry glare at Ethan. "I call the Council of Kings to order." Fearghus poked Ethan's chest with his finger. "You—inside—now."

As Coventry's courtyard emptied, Maul, Fearghus, and Lachlan Traynor hurried into the tavern. Bartlett stayed beside Ethan as he climbed off the rock, then he, Lily, and the captain met Adam, Seamus, General Niles, and Runyun outside the tavern door.

"Adam, Seamus, and I will keep watch," Bartlett said.

General Niles pushed open the door and looked at Ethan. "Shall we?"

Ethan walked into an enormous room in the back of the tavern, wishing Runyun had been wrong for once. The test was the easy part. He stared at the other kings, having no idea how to convince them to fight with Landover.

Sunlight shone through large windows that hung just below a carved wood ceiling depicting a huge battle in which Landover's soldiers on horseback fought beside Faoladhs with Fomorians nearby. Ravens and Primland guards attacked from the left while a large tiger stood on a rock, poised to strike. Ethan figured that must have been someone from Cantolin, Mysty's island. It was strange to see inhabitants of all the territories fighting together, but their enemy remained anonymous.

A large rectangular table in the center of the room was covered with a huge spread of roasted birds, bowls of potatoes, leafy vegetables, and a large pile of bread. King Fearghus sat at one end. Rhisiart stood behind his chair, and Bryg beside him, setting down new pints of ale as the King drained them.

There were four other chairs, two on the far side from where Ethan stood, occupied by Maul and Keeill. A Faoladh woman, wearing a cropped metallic top and flowing skirt, with pointy ears and a mane of blue hair, came beside Maul. Behind Keeill was a Buggane in a long brown cloak. Ethan assumed these were their sorcerers.

The only unoccupied seat was the one directly in front of him—next to Lachlan Traynor's.

Lily, General Niles, and Runyun remained by the door while Ethan walked with determination to the empty chair, pulled it out, and sat. "Your majesties, at this very second, Sawney Bean and Fenit Traynor are preparing to assault Landover."

"So you mentioned outside." Fearghus crushed his mug and slammed it on the table. "Ethan Makkai, new king of Landover, I believe you owe us an accounting of your past few days. I was told by my team"—he gestured to Bryg and Phalen—"that you and your party left Gransmore and returned to Landover."

"We did leave Gransmore." Ethan swallowed hard, knowing this next bit wasn't going to go over well. "But I borrowed your Conbata to get past your guard to get to the cave you told me not to go to, but when we got there, Bean was already out. The Ravens had released him."

"You took my Conbata? But how did you . . . Dratsuah!" He banged his fist on the table. "Where is it? Give it to me!" He got up from the table and started for him, but Bryg grabbed his arm, pulling him to a stop.

"It was safely returned."

Ethan held his hands up and nodded. "We left it with the guard and made him promise to get it back to you."

Fearghus calmed, slightly, and returned to his seat. "Go on."

"Then we followed Bean and the Ravens to Algidare, to Fiddler's Well," Ethan continued.

Drakma Keeill let out a vicious howl that Lachlan happily translated. "The boy, Niles, Cooper, and the girl there"—he pointed to Lily—"trespassed into Algidare and desecrated sacred ground, stepping into the tower, and left with stolen water from Fiddler's Well."

"That's not true, sires," Lily interjected. "Bean went in the tower. *He* desecrated it and stole the waters."

"And why would he do that?" Lachlan asked skeptically.

"For a potion to raise the dead," Lily answered. She came beside Ethan and set a hand on the back of his chair. "He needed three elements—the waters from Fiddler's Well, three leaves of the vivificus tree, and three drops of freshly spilled blood from the enemy, which is why they took Ethan's mother, Caitríona. The spell is in Primland's scáthán. It's called namhaid spiorad beo, 'enemy spirit alive.' Only, they had the wrong enemy." Lily pulled Ethan's arm and he stood up. She lifted his shirt, revealing the scar from the stab wound.

All of the kings eyed Bean's work.

"He has what he needs to raise the Draugar army," Ethan finished as Lily let go of his shirt.

Lachlan narrowed his eyes on Lily. "And how do you know so much about what is in Primland's scáthán?"

General Niles held up the book.

"Da!" Lily cried, trying to stop him.

But the general acted like he didn't hear her. "Because Ethan, Lily, and Runyun Cooper found this in Bean's cave."

"What!" King Fearghus slammed his fist on the table again, this time, shaking the whole room. Glasses spilled and food bounced in all directions. "That vile book of magic in my lands? Lachlan Traynor, explain yourself!"

Maul remained outwardly passive, eyeing the group, gauging their reactions, giving away nothing.

Lachlan stormed over to Niles. "Give me that!" He snatched the book and tucked it under his arm. "It is not I who must explain anything. That boy"—his arm shot out at Ethan—"stepped over the border and into Primland without prior consent or permission."

"Is that why your men now sit on the border outside of Bramblewood Forest? Because a *boy* stepped over a line?" Maul asked in a chiding tone. He glanced at the female behind him, and barked out an acerbic laugh.

"Yes. He didn't find our scáthán in Bean's cave; he stole it long before he arrived there. I demand that the Council take action."

Filled with rage, Ethan glared at the other kings. "You can't possibly believe him."

Precious seconds of uncomfortable glances and silence ticked by. *What the hell? Do they not understand that Landover is about to be invaded?*

"Look," Ethan said to Lachlan, "I didn't take your book. I found it, but you don't have to believe me because none of this matters anymore." He turned his focus on the others. "Don't you understand? Landover is going to be invaded and we need help." Ethan locked eyes with each of them, but only King Fearghus met his. "People are going to die! We can't defeat this kind of enemy alone!"

Keeill let out a series of grunts.

"Agreed," Maul responded, then turned to Ethan. "And why should any of our kinsmen help Landover?"

Runyun rushed the table. "Because this army won't stop with Landover. It will march over the border, just as Bean's mist in Primland has.

Once Landover is overrun, Gransmore and Kilkerry will be next, and finally Algidare. Bean will have what he's wanted all along—all of Tara."

"Rubbish. All of it," Lachlan snapped.

The room erupted, with each side of the table pointing fingers at the other.

Ethan, shut your eyes, Tearlach insisted.

As Ethan did, his vision blurred. When it came into focus, he saw smoke billowing off the Isle of Mord, creating a cover of black soot.

Tearlach took him straight into the dense fog. Underneath, the corpses that had littered the rocky surface of the isle now stood in formation with Bean high up on the volcano, bellowing orders.

"Ethan?" he heard Lily say gently.

"They're coming." Ethan shook his head and opened his eyes. "Thousands are coming. We've got to go." Ethan headed for the door.

"We've not called this meeting adjourned, heir of Landover," Leader Maul barked.

Ethan threw open the door. Runyun, Lily, and General Niles filed out.

"Allow me then. The meeting is over." He slammed the door behind them.

Ethan stormed out of the tavern after Runyun, General Niles, and Lily. Outside, the town was completely deserted, except for Adam and Seamus, who held the horses' reins.

"Captain Bartlett headed to his ships. He said he'd be waiting for your signal, General," Seamus told Niles.

With no time to spare, everyone mounted and headed out of Coventry. Minutes later, they were on the road to Dryden Lake. Ethan rode next to Lily. His insides twisting at the thought of her leaving, but he didn't have a choice. "Lily, you need to get that banishing brew."

"Why? It has only been one day. It won't work."

"Find a way to make it work. It's the only hope we have," Ethan insisted.

With a less-than-confident frown, Lily nodded. "Look for me on the hillside above the lake. There's an odd tree, one that has two trunks sprouting from the same root collar. I'll be there as soon as I can."

"Hillside next to a funny-looking tree, above the lake, got it. And, Lily—hurry."

She nodded again, and galloped off.

"Where is Lily going?" General Niles asked, sounding alarmed.

"I needed her help. She's been working—"

"You don't get to ask my sister for help," Adam warned.

"Adam—" General Niles interjected.

"Whoa. Excuse me?" Ethan was in no mood to be fighting with one of Lily's brothers. "Since when do you tell me what to do? I don't even know you."

"King or not, Lily is my sister. That gives me the right to tell you exactly what to do," Adam shot back.

"No. It doesn't." Ethan glared back at him.

Runyun rode next to Ethan, giving Adam a severe look. "Do we have a problem here?"

Niles motioned for everyone to slow down, but Ethan needed to put some space between himself and Adam Niles. He prodded Devlin to canter, and headed over a hill that led him to a small lake.

"Ethan!" Runyun shouted. "Look out!"

"Look out for what?"

A high-pitched whine escalated into a repeated pounding, like a jackhammer beating pavement. Three horrifying mutants crawled out of the lake and headed right for him. With the head of a shark and the body of a canine, they had long, sharp claws and jagged fangs.

"The Dobhar-chú!" Runyun yelled.

Shit! Devlin raced right, around the lake, but the Dobhar-chú followed, their jagged fangs coming extremely close to the horse's hindquarters.

Ethan barreled around a tree and one shot past but immediately circled back. Devlin dodged it with a sharp turn to the left, but the beast matched his moves.

Ethan turned Devlin so he'd pass under a low-growing tree. As Devlin went under, Ethan reached up and grabbed a branch, lifting off his horse, then dropped as the Dobhar-chú came underneath him. He landed on its back, slid out his knife, and stabbed right between its shoulder blades. They both went down. The creature flipped over and over, taking him with it, landing right on top of him.

Dizzy, Ethan tried to push it off, but the thing weighed a ton. Seconds later, the other two approached, frothing at the mouth, probably mad he'd just killed their buddy. Or worse. With Ethan's luck, he'd just killed their only sister.

The mutant in front of him pawed at the earth, leaving deep marks in the ground. Ethan tried scooting out, but his legs were trapped.

Runyun's arrows pierced the Dobhar-chús' backs, but seemed to have no effect. They crouched, preparing to pounce. Ethan braced for the worst when suddenly his not-so-sexy stalker, Glatisant, began singing again.

Gurrrr. Gurrr. Techt baeg amhin!

Ethan covered his ears as the familiar melody sang from behind him. The two Dobhar-chú froze. Their heads tilted, entranced by Glatisant's song as she slithered passed Ethan. The Questing Beast reeled back, unhinged her jaw, and sang again, but instead of aiming her song at Ethan, she looked directly at the Dobhar-chú in front of him.

Techt baeg amhin, Glatisant sang louder. The Dobhar-chú purred like a kitten, and willingly followed the Questing Beast as she shuffled off.

Ethan would've said congrats to the happy couple except he was still trapped underneath one of them, and the other was no longer in a trance.

A long sword swung down on the growling Dobhar-chú, silencing him. Frustrated, General Niles stared down at Ethan while Runyun and Seamus lifted the Dobhar-chú up enough for him to wiggle out.

"Some deadly moves back there, Ethan," Runyun commented.

"Don't encourage him," Niles said.

As he hurried back to Devlin, Ethan glanced back at the dead Dobhar-chú. "Lily will be so mad she missed this."

At the mention of Lily's name, General Niles's face flushed with anger. "You two have been spending too much time together. Something we're going to remedy when this is all over."

"What're you saying?" Ethan ground his teeth, trying to keep his temper in check, looking him dead in the eyes.

"You know exactly what I'm saying," Niles blurted out.

Seamus sighed and shook his head at his father. Adam tossed Ethan a smug grin.

Fuming, Ethan's hands clenched into tight fists. He was about to give the general an earful, but Runyun stepped between them. "You pick now to tell this to him? After everything they've been through together? And with what we're all walking into!" Runyun slowly shook his head. "I thought you were smarter than that, Julius." Runyun nudged Ethan toward Devlin. "Get on your horse. Your men need you."

Ethan got back on his horse, and tried to pretend Lily's father had never said anything about keeping her away from him. Not that it mattered. He probably wasn't going to survive the battle anyway. Thousands of zombified Primland soldiers were about to attack Landover.

And he had no way of stopping them.

THIRTY-EIGHT

The silence on the short ride over the hill to the camp was deafening. The sting of the argument still hung in the air and rattled in Ethan's brain, but he couldn't focus on it now. Too much was at stake.

The meadow was filled with soldiers, thousands of them, all wearing breastplates that carried the insignia of Landover. The impressive numbers were a comfort, but also a burden as Ethan wondered how many would be dead when this was over. *Think positive*, he told himself, but it wasn't working.

Apprehensive stares watched as they dismounted. A stout man with brown hair hurried over, holding a helmet under his arm.

"How many are we, Major Donah?" General Niles asked.

"Almost twenty-five hundred. Per your orders, Major Mullarchy led his troops to the border beyond Bramblewood."

Niles nodded. "Don't let us interrupt the preparations, Major."

With a quick glance at Ethan, Donah nodded, and left.

"General, who is at Weymiss with my mother?" Ethan asked.

"Five hundred men," Niles responded. Locking eyes with Ethan, he ran a hand along his chin. "Seamus, Adam, go back to Weymiss. Seamus, make sure they have secured every entry point, known or otherwise. Adam, you stay with Caitríona and Clothilde. Escort them into the southeast tower and seal it shut."

"You want us to leave?" Adam asked.

General Niles turned around to face him. "I want you to follow my orders without argument. Understood?"

Seamus nodded for Adam and then pushed him. "Move."

Once they were gone, Runyun left to check on armaments. Niles walked up the short incline that led to a cliff. Ethan followed.

"Mind the edge," Niles warned. The cliff dropped a hundred feet straight down into the water. "Let's see what's coming, shall we?"

In the distance, the Isle of Mord was plainly visible. Ethan recognized it from his visions at the Council meeting. Several ships were stationed between the island and the coast.

"Captain Bartlett's ships are in position," Niles said, then turned to Ethan. "The Deathly Straits are called that for a reason. The waters can turn vicious in an instant. Not a good place to battle the armies that are coming, but Bartlett's aligned the ships."

"The two rows. I get it. Create an easy pathway for them to travel," Ethan surmised.

"Exactly. We'll have the advantage of knowing where the enemy will come ashore," Niles answered, then his expression turned grim. "This is going to get messy. I'm not sure you should be here."

"Is that a question?" Ethan asked.

Niles stared down at him, and a small crease formed between his eyes. "No. It wasn't meant to be. You are the king. Perhaps it's best for you to take shelter at Weymiss."

Ethan didn't hesitate. "I need to be here."

General Niles pressed his lips together. "The trained man will always defeat the untrained."

"Perhaps, but I'm still not leaving."

Runyun laid a strong hand on Niles's back. "At it again?"

Niles rolled out of reach and faced him. "No. I was simply hoping Ethan would heed the advice of those with much more experience and take refuge rather than jumping headlong into a fight he can't win."

"That all depends on your definition of 'winning,'" Runyun countered.

With a frustrated sigh, Niles raised his hands in surrender, and stormed off in the throngs of soldiers.

Runyun stood next to Ethan with the same concerned look Niles had been wearing. Knowing what his father was about to say, Ethan decided to make a preemptive strike. "Look, I'm not leaving."

"Of course you're not." Runyun looked down at the sword hanging from Ethan's waist. "Remember what we went over at Bram's. Fight the man, not the weapon. Keep your eyes on your enemy's. They'll foretell their moves. They always do."

Ethan gave a nod and stared out at the bay again when he heard his Muincara's voice echo in his mind. *Trust in yourself and your powers, Ethan. You must not show fear.*

"Easy for you to say."

"Easy for me to say what?" Runyun asked.

"Sorry . . . not talking to you."

He shook his head. "I'm never going to get used to that."

Definitely not if he knew it was his uncle, the man responsible for separating Ethan's parents, someone Runyun seemed to hate with a passion, talking to him.

When this is over, your real training will begin—that is, if you survive.

"Not helping." Ethan looked back at the scores of men forming the front line. They were all depending on him. His uncle was right. He couldn't show fear. He had to put up a brave front to prove worthy of standing with them.

"Ethan," Niles called.

He walked tentatively back to General Niles, who was fastening his metal chest plate.

Expecting another earful, Ethan was surprised when Niles picked up a leather jerkin and chest plate from the ground and handed them to him. "These belonged to Seamus when he was your age. I brought them, hoping you wouldn't need them. . . ."

Ethan removed his cloak and slid the jerkin over his head. General Niles moved behind him to help him strap on the chest plate. When Niles was finished, he came to stand in front of him. "Looks good on you. May it bring you as much luck in battle as it did him." He looked at the ground and then at Ethan again with a contrite frown. A peace offering?

Ethan glanced out at the sea of Landover soldiers. "General, I'd like to address the men if that's all right with you."

"Of course." He waved at Major Donah. "Sound the carnyx for the king, please."

Donah lifted a long-necked war horn to his lips. It gave a short burst, and then all eyes fixed on Ethan. He walked over to a nearby tree, swung up on the closest branch, and then climbed until he was sure most could see him.

Staring at him were thousands of soldiers spread across several fields. In the frontlines were foot soldiers, standing on the cliff edge. Behind them were archers on horseback. Then came spear-wielders, also on horseback. And finally, more infantry, carrying swords, axes, and shields. It was an impressive sight.

Ethan glanced momentarily at the gray skies hanging overhead, hoping that something inspirational would come to mind. He took a slow, deep breath, and stared into the faces of the uniformed men surrounding him. Their expressions varied from apprehensive to severe, the inexperienced soldiers and the veterans, waiting for him to speak. His mouth dry, he cleared his throat.

"Most of you've never met me before. My name is Ethan Makkai. I only recently found out that my mother was from Landover, and that my uncle had died, and I was supposed to be the king. The truth is I'm not sure I know how to do that yet. . . ." His voice trailed off.

The men grumbled, tossing concerned glances back and forth.

"The king part, that's going to take time. Something we don't have right now. Today we fight so that we'll have tomorrow. I may not have been born in Landover, but it is my home." Ethan met the gaze of the men nearest him. "And a place I'm willing to die to defend." He looked back out over the scores. "Sawney Bean has raised Primland's soldiers on the Isle of Mord from the dead. At this moment, that Draugar army is preparing to descend on us."

Nervous chatter permeated.

Ethan's stomach tensed, and for a moment his voice failed him. He took a deep breath, and started again. "Although you may not have faith in me yet, I have faith in all of you. We'll fight together, side by side, until every last one is sent back to the grave."

"How, sire? How are we going to do that?" one of the men in the front shouted.

Ethan pulled his sword from his scabbard and raised it. "One piece at a time."

The men cheered and waved their blades in the air.

Ethan leaped out of the tree.

"Well done," Niles said.

It was a nice moment, one that didn't last long. With a series of ear-splitting booms, Bartlett's ships fired their cannons.

"Draugar!" the lookout on the cliff cried.

Ethan rushed to the edge and peered over the side as thousands of Primland soldiers crawled out of the water and onto the rocks below. The Isle of Mord was an island of stasis. The bodies hadn't decomposed, and there were so many, it looked like someone had stepped on an anthill. With no ropes, no climbing equipment at all, they scaled the wall at a fierce pace.

"Prepare to repel!" General Niles yelled.

He pushed Ethan back as soldiers came from all directions, forming a line on the edge of the cliff. One by one, they passed large rocks from the back to the front and cast them down, knocking scads of undead back into the water or crashing down on the rocks.

But as soon as one got knocked out, another appeared, and worse, the ones struck down weren't dying.

Carnyx rang out from all along the cliff's edge. General Niles, Runyun, and Ethan retreated with the foot soldiers while the archers stepped forward, giving them a clean shot of the hordes of Draugar coming over the edge, and onto the field, growling, calling for blood.

The archers released, sending hundreds of arrows into the onslaught. The sharp points struck their targets, but the undead didn't stop. They didn't even flinch. They yanked the arrows out of their own bodies and suddenly they were armed.

Runyun attacked, wielding two swords: in his left hand, the shorter blade with the curved cross-guard and brass-knuckles grip, and in his right, his long sword. Confronted by two Draugar, he kicked one back, and caught the other's arm midswing in the cross-guard, then sliced his hand clean off with his long sword.

Instead of blood a gelatinous black substance poured from its severed limb, which kept moving even after it was separated from its body.

The second Draugar returned with a vengeance, leaping at him. Runyun rolled and the undead fell into the first, both landing in a heap.

A Draugar came behind while General Niles was engaged with two others. With both hands clutching the hilt of his sword, Ethan swung, chopping its legs off at the knees. It fell, pushed up on its arms, and moved at Ethan.

Two more flanked the crawling Draugar. Ethan backed up against the tree, trying to remember the instructions Runyun had given him. *Fight the man not the weapon.* That was easy enough. None of them had weapons.

Ethan used the tree to shield him from their outstretched arms, but one of them got the jump on him and grabbed his left arm, twisting it. Ethan spun, relieving the stress in his shoulder, and swung his sword down, slicing the Draugar's arm off. When the undead lunged for him again, Ethan reached back with both hands on the grip, and swung, taking off its head.

Shuddering, Ethan expected another attack by the other two. Instead, he found Niles striking one through the middle, cutting its body in half. The other was in pieces on the ground.

"Thanks for the assist," Ethan said, winded.

Niles raised his sword in salute and returned to fighting.

The fields had completely erupted in battle. The lines were gone. The number of Landover's soldiers on the ground was uncountable. Although undead body parts littered the grass, the Draugar fought on and were now armed with swords from fallen Landover soldiers. They had to find a way to kill them, permanently, and for that they needed Lily.

As Ethan started for the lake, a loose hand grabbed his ankle and crawled up his leg at a furious rate to within less than an inch from his groin. Ethan winced as he slid his knife underneath, and flicked it off, then kicked it soccer style, sending it flying.

Ethan took off and had the lake in sight when a Draugar grabbed him by the waist and hoisted him in the air.

A blast pounded the undead in the back, sending both to the ground.

"Lad, this is no place for heroics." Bartlett dragged him out from under the floundering torso. Drenched in black ooze, Ethan started for the lake again, only to have Bartlett grab his arm.

"Let go!"

But Bartlett didn't. He dragged him to a horse that was tied to a tree next to the water's edge. "Get on and head for Weymiss."

Ethan ignored him. "Lily!" he yelled.

"Ethan Makkai, your protection is my responsibility!"

Ethan locked his eyes on Bartlett. "Not anymore it's not, but I could use your help. Lily was working on something to counteract Bean's potion. She said to look for her on the hillside, above the lake, next to the tree with two trunks from one root collar."

"There," Bartlett said, pointing to the other side of the lake. Ethan followed Bartlett's sight line and found the tree. It looked like a tuning fork.

"Do you see how many Draugar are between where we are now and that spot?" Bartlett added.

"Yes, yes, I do." They had absolutely no hope of getting there, but that wasn't going to stop Ethan from trying.

Bartlett took a deep breath. "I don't know how much power I got left, but follow me and I'll get you there!"

They hustled from tree to tree until they ran out of cover, then came out swinging. Working together, Ethan sliced as many Draugar as he could through the middle while the captain followed him, blasting whatever was left of them out of the way until they finally reached the other side.

Captain Bartlett immediately fell to the ground, dropping his left arm in the water. He lay panting, his one visible eye closed.

Behind them, more Draugar descended. They walked right into the lake, and soon all Ethan could see were the tops of their heads. Sadly, the Dobhar-chú seemed to have vacated.

"Ethan, hurry!" Lily called.

Relieved at the sound of her voice, Ethan flipped around to see her golden aura glowing next to the tree. At her feet was a large black pot, filled with something that looked like tar. She grabbed Ethan's sword and dipped it into the bubbling darkness, then handed it back to him. The potion left a greasy film over the blade.

"What is that?"

She plunged her sword in then removed it quickly. "Bás dubh—black death. It should send their souls back to the grave. Only, I'm not sure it's going to work. Besides the missing moon cycles, I had to finish it on instinct. My father gave Primland's scáthán back before I could—"

An arm grabbed her around the throat. Lily's sword dropped to the ground with a clink and Christian stepped out from the shadows of the tree, his eyes midnight black, saturated with mist.

Lily struggled against his grip, but he held tight.

Adrenaline coursed through Ethan and his heart pounded against his chest as he advanced. "Let her go!"

Christian set his blade against her neck.

"Lily has nothing to do with this!"

"She has everything to do with this. I know you've seen her aura. She would've been your sorceress, but Bean cannot allow that." Christian's arm pressed against Lily's jugular as he backed up to the water's edge. Ethan could hear her gasping for air. She beat Christian's arm with her fists, but he held on easily.

Scenes of the nightmare on the dock flooded Ethan's mind: Christian holding him down as Sawney Bean stabbed his knife into Ethan's stomach. Christian filled with jealous rage, wanting Ethan dead, while Caitríona had watched, her horrified, teary eyes on Ethan's.

Before Ethan knew anything about who he was, Christian had allowed their enemies to kidnap Ethan's mother. As he stared at his cousin holding Lily by the throat, whatever compassion he felt for him drained from his soul and refilled with fury.

Ethan wasn't the naïve innocent he had been in Los Angeles anymore. He knew exactly who he was, and felt his radharc powers surge inside of him, feeding his determination and strength. Christian was never going to take anything from him ever again.

"I'm going to kill you. Cut you to pieces and dance on your entrails."

"Really? Are you now?" Christian balked. "Say goodbye to your sorceress."

Before Christian could slice, Ethan closed the distance between them, and thrust, pushing his blade against Christian's, then shoved it off Lily's neck. Christian lost his balance and Lily ducked, escaping.

Once Lily was clear, Ethan attacked. He lunged and thrust, spun and struck again and again, beating Christian back until he was waist deep in the water and had to stop. Christian thrust his sword and Ethan parried. Their blades clanked. Both faded back momentarily, and Christian went on the offense. He beat his sword down on Ethan's over and over again, trying to knock Ethan's blade from his hand, but couldn't. Ethan countered, blocking every strike, Bram's sticky grip working like a charm.

Ethan sidestepped and caught Christian's hand with his blade, slicing into the muscle between his thumb and index finger. With a painful cry, Christian dropped his sword in the water.

Ethan charged, and Christian dived into the lake, trying to get away.

Before Ethan could catch him, Lily yelled his name. By the tuning-fork tree, a Draugar had her cornered while she tried to steady the cauldron, to keep it from spilling over.

Ethan raced back and confronted the undead soldier. When the Draugar spun to face him, Lily sliced him through the middle. The Primland soldier's body crashed to the ground and stopped moving. Its soul burst from its body, and into the sky, but unlike when Cyra died, its soul didn't leave. It hovered, watching the scene below.

"It worked!" Ethan yelled.

Lily called to the few nearby Landover soldiers and helped them dip their weapons into the pot. She filled several sacks with the black-death potion and asked them to do the same for the others. "Get it to everyone you can."

"Will that be enough?" Ethan asked.

"Aunt Morgan is on the other side of the battlefield with more. All we can do is hope."

From the right, Ethan heard Bartlett cough. A couple of Draugar stepping over him stopped when they saw him move. Ethan sprinted to Bartlett and reached him as one of them prepared to strike. Ethan deflected its sword, blocking the attack, but its pal lunged and suddenly he was fighting both.

Ethan dodged right, then left, pivoting until he got a good angle and kicked one. It fell into the other one. He slashed with his sword, striking both of them at once, and they dropped.

Bartlett coughed again, and his eye opened.

"You okay?" Ethan asked him.

"For sure. Using the eye takes the wind out of my sails. Just needed to recharge." Bartlett sat up. "How did you kill them?" He stood up and leaned on Ethan's shoulder for balance.

"That, Captain, was Lily's brew," he said. "It works!"

Battle cries and clanking metal flooded the grounds around the lake. One after another, Primland soldiers dropped. The potion was working and for a second, it seemed like Landover might survive. But then another troop of enemy soldiers came through the trees, heading straight for Ethan and Lily.

With a regal gait, dressed in a black jerkin and pants, a black hooded cloak draped over his shoulders, Sawney Bean stormed at Ethan, and he wasn't alone. Christian and Fenit Traynor were with him. Traynor looked a lot like his son, Lachlan, only his hair was longer, and his eyes matched Christian's, black as night. Alastair was right. Bean had gotten to him too.

Most of the men nearby had left to supply Lily's brew to those fighting near the cliff. Ethan, an exhausted Bartlett, Lily, and a couple of Landover's soldiers were going to have to take on Bean, Christian, Fenit Traynor, and about a dozen Draugar.

Odds of survival? Not good.

Within seconds, Ethan and Fenit Traynor were standing only a few feet apart.

"Hold!" Fenit Traynor ordered.

Primland's soldiers stopped. Christian came next to Bean on the right. Fenit stood to Bean's left, while the Draugar formed a protective semicircle behind them.

"Ethan, there's no need for any further bloodshed," Christian said.

"Maybe a little more bloodshed." With her sword leading the way, Lily charged him. Ethan threw out his arm, and held her back.

"Let me go!" Lily squirmed in his arms.

With his club of death in his hand, Sawney Bean snickered. "Smart lad. But please do let her go. It would make things so much easier if she were dead."

Knowing Lily would probably let him have it later, Ethan pushed her behind him. "I would stay away from her, if I were you," Ethan warned Bean. "Great-Uncle Fenit, why don't you call off your lapdog?"

With an ominous growl, Bean reeled his club back, prepared to strike, when Fenit Traynor stepped in front of him. Traynor's eyes shifted from Ethan to Bartlett.

"Ethan Makkai. Come here." Fenit took a step away from Bean toward

Ethan. When Ethan didn't move, he motioned with his arm. "Will you not meet me halfway?"

"No thanks. I'm quite comfortable over here."

"Very well. If you wish for your men and the girl to hear, that is up to you. You must see your lands are lost, my lad, but Christian is right. There is no need for more bloodshed. Primland will control Landover, but do not fear. I will rule from my homestead, and my great-nephew, your cousin, Christian, will remain at Weymiss as my trusted deputy."

The Draugar extended their semicircle, closing in behind them. With courage, the two Landover soldiers turned their backs on Ethan, and raised their swords to face them.

"How's your son gonna feel about that? You go back to Primland. Christian rules Landover. What's left for poor Lachlan?" Ethan asked.

Bean seemed mildly amused by the question.

Fenit clenched his jaw and through gritted teeth said, "He'll get used to it."

"Hard feelings, huh? Didn't like the way he locked you up on that island? It did look rather bleak."

Fenit's upper lip curled into a snarl.

Sawney Bean took a long step forward, wearing a smirk. "Don't fret, sire. Both this mouthy one and his father are going to die." Bean waved his arm, and two Draugar came from behind the trees, dragging Runyun.

Checkmate.

Bean pinned Ethan with an arrogant glare. "The only question is, who's first?"

◙ THIRTY-NINE ◙

Ethan's breath caught as he watched two Draugar heave his father between Traynor and Bean. Runyun's hands were tied behind his back. His right eye was swollen shut and his bottom lip was bleeding.

"You see." Bean wrenched the back of Runyun's hair. "This man must die or I will never be able to sleep at night, and you don't want to see me when I haven't had my beauty sleep. I can get very cranky!" Bean kicked Runyun in the back, sending him crashing to the ground.

Furious, Ethan took a step toward him, but Runyun shook his head, stopping him.

"Really? Your son shouldn't come to you?" Bean chided. "Oh, but I think he should. See, we cannot have an heir for the people to get behind."

"Sadly, he has a point," Fenit Traynor commented. "Christian?"

Christian raised his sword, and moved at Ethan until Bartlett's eye fired. Christian ducked but the blast grazed his shoulder, setting it ablaze. Screaming, Christian fell into the water, trying to put it out.

"Amusing, Captain, but your powers pale next to mine. I suggest you stand down or die with the young king," Bean said.

"My powers might pale next to yours, but as I recall this young lady stopped you cold at Fiddler's Well." Bartlett gave a nod to Lily.

Bean eyed her with an intense hatred that terrified Ethan. But as his radharc power spread over Bean, Ethan felt something else. Fear. Bartlett was right.

Meeting Bean's glare, Lily brandished her sword and stood waiting like a lioness ready to attack its next meal.

Bean grabbed Runyun by the throat and lifted him to standing. "Get over here now or your father dies."

"You'll kill him anyway and then you'll kill me. My cousin will get what he wants, Fenit Traynor will get what he wants, and you'll get what you want, but really, where will that leave me? Dead. Runyun? Dead. I don't think so."

Bean reached his club back. "Very well. Goodbye, Cooper."

Runyun head-butted Bean in the nose, breaking it. The crack was so loud it could probably be heard in Coventry. Stunned, Bean recoiled, giving Runyun the opening he needed.

A long, thin blade dropped from Runyun's sleeve into his waiting hands. He sliced the ropes binding his wrists and spun, thrusting the blade at Bean's heart.

"Caillan!" With a brilliant flash of light, Bean traded places with Fenit Traynor.

Runyun's dagger struck, piercing Traynor's chest. Primland's former king dropped to his knees, and then keeled over. Ethan watched for his soul, but it never left his body. His open eyes were still solidly black, then they slammed it shut.

A blood-curdling scream emanated from his body so loud, Ethan had to cover his ears. Blackened vapor escaped from his mouth. Like a bullet from a gun, it shot into Bean's chest; the mist was returning to its master, taking whatever was left of Traynor's soul with it.

With renewed vigor, Bean swung his club at Runyun.

Lily threw her hands out. Energy burst from her fingers, circling Runyun, putting a barrier between him and Bean before the club could make contact.

Bean growled and shot a blast at her, but Ethan knocked her out of the way, and it exploded on impact in the lake.

With a loud battle cry, hundreds of Primland undead came through the trees. They hurried behind Bean, who held up his hand, stopping them. Making little sound, the Draugar stood in a catatonic state, waiting for his signal to attack.

Runyun moved swiftly to Ethan's side. He exchanged a weary look with Bartlett, and yanked another short blade from his boot.

Christian, who'd vanished, came out from the wall of Draugar. He smirked at Ethan, and a slow smile grew over his face. With a raised his sword, he glanced at Bean, who nodded. "Kill them; kill them all!"

Christian charged Ethan, while the Draugar sprinted around the lake, heading for Bartlett, Runyun, Lily, and the few soldiers with them.

As Ethan moved to meet Christian, there was no fear, only rage-filled confidence. His cousin might have more training, but Ethan had already beaten him by the lake once, and they both knew it.

Christian struck first. Ethan met his sword with his own. He stared into his cousin's dark, empty gaze, and moved to retreat. But Christian pressed harder, sliding his blade against Ethan's until the swords were locked at the cross-guard. Christian threw all his weight on his sword. With both hands on the grip, Ethan spun left, rotating until he had the upper position, then kicked Christian in the gut at the same time he pressed on his blade.

Falling on his knees, Christian's sword dropped out of his hand. Ethan raised the edge of his blade under Christian's chin, sliding it against his neck. He wanted to do it. He wanted to kill him.

"What are you waiting for?" Bean hissed. He stepped out from behind a nearby tree only a few feet away. His club draped over his shoulder, as if he'd been watching Ethan and Christian's fight like it was on pay-per-view.

"Kill him. Do it!" Bean prodded.

Christian shook with fear, but the darkness in his eyes was unwavering.

Ethan's arms strained, his hands gripping his sword so forcefully blood soaked the handle. *No one can beat down an enemy with compassion.* Runyun was right. With a guttural roar, Ethan stabbed his blade into the dirt.

"Landover has a coward for a king." Bean sniggered, raised his club, and headed straight for Ethan. Turning to run, Ethan found his escape route cut off by Draugar. Bean closed in, his club in striking distance, when a red shot hit the back of his hand. With a painful gasp, Bean dropped his club.

Captain Bartlett was heading straight for him. Bean scooped up his club and grabbed Christian's arm, pulling him along while he shot some kind of energy blasts, trying to repel the captain. Bartlett dodged them all, still managing to fire back.

The Draugar rushed Ethan. With an exhausted sigh, Ethan tossed his sword from hand to hand, until an undead lunged, then he unleashed holy hell. With everything he had left, he fought, slicing the limbs off two, but it wasn't going to be enough. There were just too many.

Fierce battle cries rang out. Expecting more Draugar, Ethan was relieved when a huge mob of Coventry townspeople came roaring through the woods.

The ground shook violently as King Fearghus, Rhisiart, Bryg, Phalen, and at least fifty Fomorians pounded past the tuning-fork tree and joined the battle. Their weapons covered with Lily's potion, they sliced and diced the undead with ease, the bodies dropping and the number of Primland's hovering soldiers' souls mounting.

They moved collectively over Ethan, reaching out to him, begging for release. Their emotions weighed heavily on him, but he had to keep fighting.

The sprites flew overhead and rained arrows down at the Draugar as the horns sounded and more of Landover's soldiers came flying from two directions with Runyun and General Niles leading the way.

Moments later, Bean and Christian stood completely surrounded. Bean closed his eyes. Ethan sensed a huge surge of energy coming from him, but didn't move in time.

"Teiatcha," Bean hissed.

"No!" Ethan heard Lily cry, but it was too late. Ethan was yanked into Bean's waiting, outstretched arm. Primland's sorcerer pulled Ethan's back to his chest and set his club against it. "Stay back or he dies."

Ravens' cries echoed through the skies. Two swooped down and lifted Christian away.

"Don't worry, Cooper, I'll take good care of him." Bean tightened his hold on Ethan's chest as two more Ravens latched on to his arms, and swiftly lifted him.

Runyun ran toward him, trying to grab Ethan's feet, which were already ten feet off the ground, but missed. Ethan struggled, but Bean's grip was too strong.

Loud gasps were followed by a deafening roar. A heavy jolt knocked Bean and Ethan out of the Ravens' grasps, sending them crashing to the ground. Before Ethan could move, an enormous black panther latched on to Bean's arm. It was Mysty.

Bean cried out, and was forced to let go of Ethan as the ferocious panther attacked. Once Ethan was clear, Mysty backed away from Sawney Bean, growling.

"How dare you take sides?" he screamed at the giant cat. Bean's clothes were shredded, his arms bleeding. "You cannot interfere! Your life will be forfeit! Queen Donovia will hear of this!"

"Not from you. Your cave awaits, and this time, no one will ever be able to get you out," Runyun said.

Dilga landed next to Sawney Bean, and Alastair stepped out from behind her. The Brownie spread his long thin fingers over the ground. The earth responded with a major earthquake. The ground trembled so hard it was impossible to stand up without falling over.

Dilga gave a short whistle and several more Ravens dropped from the trees. The sprites tried to stop them, but the Ravens easily dodged their arrows. They lifted Bean and Alastair, and flew over the trees, toward the coast, vanishing from sight.

Triumphant cheers were quickly followed by somber moments. There were many casualties. Fortunately, Morgan had organized the Coventry townspeople, and as soon as the fight ended they were there to help the injured. But even as cleanup began, it was clear the repercussions of this battle would take a long time to overcome.

News traveled quickly from Weymiss. With Lily's brew arriving there first, Seamus and Adam killed the Draugar before they could get inside the castle walls. Caitríona was safe.

Lily went to help her aunt while Ethan remained lakeside. He walked the fields, talking with grieving families who'd come to claim their loved ones, but was interrupted when he saw the growing mass of Primland dead. Soldiers piled their bodies, one on top of the other, while the spirits hung like a cloud trapped, unable to move on to the Otherworld. For a few fragile moments, Ethan thought he was going to pass out from the cold.

Lesson two. Tearlach's voice echoed in his head. *Close your eyes. See with your mind's eye again.*

Following instructions, Ethan saw a small red spot behind his closed eyelids.

Feel the warmth radiate from the one spot and force it to spread.

Slowly, Ethan's head, abdomen, and finally his limbs thawed. His breathing returned to normal. He opened his eyes and smiled at his uncle's aura, which had appeared next to him. "Thanks."

Tearlach nodded. His expression soft, his uncle looked as though he wanted to say more, but kept silent.

King Fearghus stepped cautiously around the corpses until he stood next to Ethan. "I'm glad to see you're still alive, young man. And victorious in your first battle."

"*Our* first battle," Ethan corrected. "Thank you for your help."

"You're very welcome."

Maul watched the cleanup as he came to stand next to Ethan.

"Where were you?" Ethan asked, unable to hide his anger.

"Remaining neutral," he answered.

Ethan crossed his arms over his chest and glared at the Faoladh leader. "You do realize that Bean got away—escaped with the help of the Ravens. How long do you think neutrality will keep Kilkerry safe?"

Maul narrowed his eyes on Ethan's, then left without saying another word, stepping over to the untouched body of Fenit Traynor on his way out as Lachlan Traynor and several Primland guards approached.

When Lachlan reached his father's body, he stared down at him. His eyes were cold, his body stiff, trying to hide every visible emotion, but Ethan knew differently. Traynor's presence sent his powers into high alert, and he sensed relief. Lachlan was glad his father was dead.

Ethan's empathic ability picked up something very different as Lachlan moved to the mound of fallen Primland soldiers, and stared at them somberly. He was devastated.

"Understand, my father did this on his own. I've had no contact with him. I was never a part of his scheming."

"I've been informed that your men at the border of Bramblewood have now dispersed," General Niles said.

Lachlan looked back at Ethan and Niles. "Of course. As soon as I saw Bean and my father, I realized what the young man said was true. Although I still don't understand how Bean got hold of our scáthán. Rest assured, I'll find the guilty culprit who brought it to him, and they will be punished." His eyes returned to the fallen. "Now there is the matter of the deceased."

"They'll be returned to the Isle of Mord," General Niles ordered.

The taibhsí hovering above Ethan collectively gasped.

Damnú air! Is there no justice?

No rest either.

Why must we suffer eternally for the wrongdoings of a madman?

"No, General," Ethan said.

General Niles put his hand on Ethan's shoulder and spoke through clenched teeth. "Ethan, these men attacked Landover, twice now."

"I understand your anger, but look what happened when they were left unburied the last time." Ethan turned to Lachlan. "Take them home. Bury them so that their souls are released from serving Bean forever."

Lachlan nodded in appreciation. "Perhaps there is hope for peace between our two realms, and our families."

Ethan hadn't forgotten the story Christian had told him, about how Maximus Makkai had trusted Fenit Traynor to make peace. That hadn't ended so well for Maximus. "Perhaps."

Primland's guard and Landover's people worked together to load the dead into wagons. Ethan said his goodbyes to the kings and visitors from the other realms, and sat by the lake, watching the sunset beyond the trees to the west. The skies clear, the air cool and crisp as the day he came to Landover, yet the smell was no longer sweet. The stench of the battle still hung over the fields. Hopefully the winds would help carry it away, but as he watched another deceased soldier moved, Ethan knew the dead would never be forgotten.

Ethan picked up a rock and tossed it in the water. Lily walked over, took the spot next him, and let out a long tired sigh.

Even with her hair disheveled and her clothes battle stained, she still looked unbelievably beautiful. There was something about her proximity that brought him an unmistakable sense of comfort. He trusted her like no one else in his life.

Aside from liking her more than he'd ever liked a girl, he had no idea what Landover would be like if he didn't have her to talk to, to fight with, and to fight for. She challenged him and at the same time gave him the confidence to face those challenges head on.

But General Niles would never let them be together. As king and sorceress, or anything else. Ethan's stomach tensed, wondering if the general had already said something to her. Should he be the one to tell her? Maybe it was better to end it now. There was no hope for anything in the future.

"Next up for you . . . your coronation, sire."

Ethan laughed. "You called me sire."

"I believe you've earned that," she said, and then grew somber. "My father has ordered me home. My brothers are waiting."

Ethan noticed Adam and Seamus standing a few feet away. His heart ached at the thought of Lily leaving. "See you at Weymiss?"

She picked up a pebble, clutched it in her hand, and stared at the lake. "I'll try," she said, unable to look at him. "This is all very complicated."

"What is?"

Her conflicted gaze turned to General Niles, who had come to stand with Seamus and Adam. "Life. Choices. Family . . ."

That didn't sound promising. Niles had told her. She threw the pebble in the water. It skipped three times and dropped to the bottom of the late.

"You'll have to be there for the coronation at least, right?"

"I'm not sure," she said with her eyes still on her father.

Ethan wanted to grab her chin and force her to look at him so he could at least get some kind of read on what she was trying to say, but with the Niles clan hovering so close they might chop his hand off. He waited for her to give him a sign, a modicum of hope, a simple glance his way, but she refused to look at him. There was only one thing left to do.

Ethan leaned his elbows back against the bank. "Whatever."

Lily's face fell and she finally looked at him. "What does that mean? 'Whatever'?"

"It just means what it means. Whatever." There was a chill in Ethan's voice that sickened him.

"What's wrong with you?"

Ethan turned so he didn't have to look at her. "Nothing."

"Lily, time to go," Adam called.

Lily glanced back at her brothers but didn't get up. "Are you trying to pick a fight with me? Because if you are, you're doing a very good job."

Ethan lifted his eyes to meet hers. "I thought you said you were leaving."

"Fine." Without saying another word she stormed off with her brothers following.

Captain Bartlett came up behind Ethan. "What's wrong with Lily Niles? She seems a bit ticked off. What did you do?"

"What did *I* do?" Ethan shook his head as he repeated Runyun's exact words to him when he'd asked that question about his mother. "She had to go, that's all."

Unable to look away, Ethan watched Lily gracefully mount her horse, her golden aura glistening.

"Why are you looking at your girlfriend like that?" Captain Bartlett stared in the same direction Ethan was, at Lily.

"'She's . . . she's not my girlfriend." And never would be. "Lily glows, that's all."

"You see her aura?"

Ethan looked at Lily again. Her outline was barely visible against the darkening sky.

Ethan picked a blade of grass and tore it to shreds, then let it fall in pieces to the ground. "Since the first time she touched me." That was a moment he'd never forget. When the fight with Glatisant was over, after the unicorns saved them, Lily had touched his arm. It was the first time he'd felt his powers surge through him, and the first time he'd seen her aura.

General Niles stepped in front of them, his hands on hips, and glowered at Bartlett. "What're you up to? I told you—"

Bartlett raised a hand. "The king has found his sorceress, Julius. She is bound to him, just as your Riona was bound to Tearlach. One sorcerer, one monarch, and one scáthán. You know the order of things."

"My daughter will not be Landover's sorceress!"

Ethan glared at Niles. Unexpectedly, and without Ethan's consent, his powers reached out to the general. Niles's unmitigated worry sent shock waves through him. He sucked in a breath and let it out slowly, trying to shake off the general's anguish. The last thing Ethan wanted was to feel sorry for Niles. But he did.

Man. *Muincara, where's the radharc off switch?*

I'm afraid there isn't one. Tearlach sounded as unhappy about it as Ethan.

"The coronation must happen in seven days' time, and a king without a sorcerer, or in this case a sorceress, is a vulnerable king. Just ask Tearlach." Bartlett walked off, leaving Ethan in an awkward silence with the general.

Niles stared down, rubbing his hand along the back of his neck, then sat down next to him. "Ethan, what exactly do you see when you look at Lily?"

"I'm sorry, General Niles. I don't want to hurt you. But she glows. Not like a ghost but like the sun, and when she does magic, her whole being gets even brighter, like she has a star burning inside of her."

By the look on Niles's face, this wasn't what he wanted to hear. The general stared at the setting sun as Runyun came toward them, leading Devlin.

"Your mother is likely worried. I sent word you're safe, but better she sees you with her own eyes." Runyun handed Ethan Devlin's reins as he stood up.

Followed by a detail of Landover soldiers, and his father beside him, Ethan rode toward Weymiss, hoping for a few quiet hours of uninterrupted sleep.

◀ FORTY ▶

Reunion and relief. Reality and heartbreak. Palpable emotions Caitríona had felt too many times, and as glad as she was to be home, she rather missed the disconnected, noisy life she and Ethan had led in Los Angeles.

Early morning light cascading through the windows gave the dining room a warm glow. Their tiny, dim apartment in Los Angeles could fit in this room twice over, but for the first time in her life, Caitríona had little use for all this empty space.

She sat alone at the long wooden table, sipping hot coffee. Thank the gods Captain Bartlett had stocked his ship full of beans before the Ravens had struck. He'd even brought a French press and hand grinder. The man thought of everything.

Ethan had been sleeping for two days straight. Meanwhile, Weymiss tried to rebuild and prepare for his coronation. Her son. A king. And she with an array of mixed emotions. He would be forced to live under constant scrutiny from the Commis, the elected counsel, and Landover's people. Something she'd hated and run from her whole life.

What if Ethan was killed like her brother and father had been? Caitríona had to push that one out of her mind or she'd take him and go into hiding again.

Scully entered the room from the kitchen. His head bandaged, and in new clothes, he looked almost as good as new.

"More coffee?"

"No thank you, Scully."

He seemed relieved. "Good. I've asked them to ration the beans. I don't particularly want to have to pry them out of Captain Bartlett's hands again."

Caitríona gave a stilted laugh. "I understand. Has Ethan woken yet?"

"He's not. And I've given the room next to his to Mr. Cooper as you requested. However . . ." Scully paused.

"However, what?"

"He said he'd be leaving after the coronation. I thought you'd want to know."

Caitríona held her emotions in check, something she'd learn to do expertly during her years in Los Angeles. "And why would I want to know?"

Clothilde stepped inside the room from the hallway, padded over, and took the seat next to Caitríona's. Scully gave Clothilde a nod and vacated quickly, giving Caitríona the distinct impression she was going to be ambushed.

"Don't let him leave," Clothilde blurted out.

Surprised at her bluntness, Caitríona set her hand on Clothilde's arm. "I appreciate—"

"I don't think you do." Clothilde pressed her lips together and took a deep breath before continuing. "I knew Tearlach didn't approve of your marriage. And . . . I was there when he lied to Runyun Cooper, telling him you were already gone, and I was a willing participant." Clothilde nervously rubbed her hands together.

Caitríona sat back in her chair, stunned at her confession.

Clothilde raised her eyes to meet Caitríona's glare. "You had everything and wanted none of it. Always running away, even when your father was murdered, when Tearlach needed you the most. As much as it pains me to admit it, you were the only person he ever trusted. And you were too selfish to realize how much he needed you."

Caitríona swallowed hard at the truth. When her father had been killed, she'd run away to Bramblewood, to hide from grief and escape the gloom of the castle, and then she'd met Runyun.

"But having a child changes a person, for better and for worse." Clothilde paused, her face riddled with guilt. "And when Ethan returned, and I saw the young man, his tenacity, his grit, and his love for you, I realized that the Caitríona who left Weymiss wasn't the same one who had raised him."

"Thank you" were the only words Caitríona could choke out.

"I came to tell you two things: the first, I'm leaving Weymiss."

"Why?"

"Because I have no life here without my husband or my son. I have to figure out who I am"—she gestured around the room—"outside all of this. I've lost my way, as my son has, and I cannot stay."

"Where will you go?" Caitríona asked.

"My family's home on the White Islands."

Caitríona understood why. It was where she and Tearlach had met.

"The last thing I'll say is don't let Runyun Cooper leave, not without knowing how much you still love him."

Caitríona picked up and cradled her coffee mug. "Too much time has passed, Clothilde. As you pointed out, I'm not the same person I was when I left, and neither is he."

Clothilde smiled and set a hand on Caitríona's arm. "And because of that you and he might have a fighting chance. Second chances don't come around often in Tara," Clothilde added. "When they do, we should take them."

E than's mother pulled back the long curtains with a resounding thwack. The sun streamed in through the large windows, blasting Ethan in the eyes. "Come on, sleepyhead. You've got to get up. It's been two days."

After a long, much-needed stretch, Ethan forced himself to sit up. "I've been asleep for two days?"

"You have. I was going to send for Morgan McKenna, but your father was sure it was exhaustion." Caitríona sat down on the edge of the bed.

"Where is Runyun?"

"He's here. He's staying for the coronation."

And then he was leaving, Ethan inferred.

"Captain Bartlett needs to speak with you."

"Of course he does . . . ," Ethan said, annoyed, but then he'd been left in peace for two whole days, something he'd never take for granted.

Ethan set his feet on the floor and tried to stand. The muscles in his legs were still on vacation and buckled. He grabbed hold of the bedpost, hoping the blood would start flowing again.

After dressing, he followed his mother up several long flights. Out of breath, they finally reached the top, where a single door stood, made of plain wood with a big brass handle.

"It's usually locked, but it appears ajar. Just go through there. I'll bring you something to eat."

"Thanks," Ethan said as Caitríona headed back down the stairs.

With trepidation, he pushed the door. The square gloomy room was lit by candelabras positioned around the ceiling. There was only one small window in the far wall, covered by bars spaced so closely together not even a bird could fit through. To the right were three cushy red leather chairs, and filled bookshelves lined the walls. In the middle of the room was a wooden stand. Captain Bartlett stood over it, staring down at a closed book.

Without even a hello, he said, "Do you know what this is?"

Ethan glanced at the large leather-bound book. On the cover was the mark of Landover. "Landover's scáthán?"

Captain Bartlett met his gaze. "Very good. Do you know why it is called a scáthán?"

Ethan shook his head.

"The word 'scáthán' means 'mirror.' Each realm of Tara was given a similar book by the god of the sea, Manannán mac Lir. Trying to stop the bloodshed of our people, he thought to level the playing field. Each realm was granted a monarchy to rule their lands, and a sorcerer for their protection, the idea being that no one realm would be more powerful than any other. The inhabitants of each realm could fill their book with magic reflective of their values and morals. Once the book was filled, nothing more could be added or changed. The rules were set, the moral compass fixed in stone, so to speak." Bartlett paused. "Shall we sit?" He motioned to the three chairs.

Ethan scooted one of the chairs around so they could sit facing each other. Bartlett placed the book on Ethan's lap.

"Flip through it. Tell me what you see."

Ethan touched the old pages carefully, not wanting to tear any. Most of what was written he couldn't understand. It was in the ancient tongue. As he reached the end of the book, the words suddenly stopped.

"Empty pages," Ethan whispered.

"Smart lad. Landover's rules of magic are not yet finished. There are still pages to be filled in."

"With what?"

"That is for the king of Landover and his sorcerer or *sorceress* to decide. What kind of magic does Landover need to keep it true to itself?" Bartlett asked as he took the book from Ethan and closed it again.

"I don't know."

Bartlett gave a tight-lipped smile. "You'll be a wise king, Ethan."

"Because I don't know?"

"Because you understand what you don't know. Always remember that. Find wisdom in the ambiguity, for the answers will come when you need them."

"You're speaking in riddles."

"I can't give you the answers. I don't have the answers. If I did, then I would be king." Bartlett laughed at his own joke.

Ethan stared at the book. "I don't have a sorceress."

"You do. Ms. Niles."

"I fear that's a lost cause. Her father hates me."

"Bull. Julius's anger has nothing to do with you and everything to do with the fact that he lost his wife. He's worried he'll lose his daughter." Bartlett got a faraway look in his eyes. "But no father can keep his children from their destiny. Give it time."

"We don't have time. Bean got away. Alastair told me Bean wants more than just Landover. He wants all of Tara. And my guess is this is why Landover has to be first . . ." Ethan tapped the book.

"The empty pages," Bartlett said, his tone haunted. "Possible. If he claimed the land, the book would be his to fill. What else did the Brownie say?"

"That someone named Aibheill said that the one spoken of in some prophecy would bring the unicorns back. That's why he was helping me."

Bartlett sat back. "Bran the Blessed's prophecy. The Brownies are the only ones who would know Aibheill's whereabouts. She found shelter in their company centuries ago." Captain Bartlett lifted his eyebrows, shifting his patch.

"One other thing. The ghost in Bean's cave, Kiara, called Bean a demigod."

Bartlett's eye grew wide. "There are no demigods. Descendants of the gods, yes. Many. You descend from one, as do I."

"That thing you do with your eye. It wore you out during the battle, but when you touched the water, your energy was restored."

"Manannán mac Lir is my ancestor and where my powers come from. But a true demigod . . ." Bartlett rose. He took the book and placed it back in its box, then closed the lid. "If it's true, we're in for a long, arduous fight, one I'm not sure we can win."

◧ FORTY-ONE ◧

Morning came early on coronation day. It had been six very long days since Ethan had seen Lily. Between exhausting fighting lessons with Runyun and Niles, unsuccessful attempts by his Muincara, Tearlach, to help him release more of his radharc powers, and preparations for the big event, he'd been busy.

A long dark-skinned finger stroked Ethan's face, waking him. "Wakey, wakey," Mysty crooned. "I've got a present for you. It's black and has straps."

Ethan opened his eyes. "No way! My backpack! But how?"

"Took days to sniff it out. Apparently, some young woman picked it up. She had it in her apartment."

"Thank you."

"Don't thank me. It was all Bartlett. He said you needed those earplugs." Mysty pulled out his earbuds.

"Well, thank you for saving my life then." Ethan moved the backpack next to him, out of Mysty's reach in case she got pissed, morphed, and went panther on his ass for what he was about to ask her. "But why didn't Bean use magic on you?"

Mysty gifted him with a wry smile. "Cat Sidhe are impervious to *all* kinds of magic."

"That's why you're not supposed to interfere. Are you in trouble now, because of me?" Ethan hated the idea of that.

Mysty shrugged. "I tend to break rules like someone else I know." She pressed a finger to his nose, and stood up. "Enjoy the big day." Then she leaped out the window.

Ethan grabbed his iPod, slipped an earbud in his left ear, and hit the play button. To his relief, the battery was still charged. Just as Imagine Dragons' "Demons" blasted his ears, the doors swung open and Caitríona, along with two other ladies, entered the room.

"Is that . . . no way!" Caitríona ripped the iPod out of Ethan's hand, taking the earbud with it and what felt like a piece of Ethan's left ear. "Yes!" she sang. "And it works. Do you have my playlist in here? I'm in desperate need of some Ed Sheeran."

"Oh no. You're not wearing down what precious battery life I have with Ed Sheeran sap. Give me that back!"

Too late. She was already twirling around the room singing "Thinking Out Loud." " 'Maybe we found love right where we are. . . .' "

With a mischievous smile plastered across her face, Caitríona latched on to Ethan, forcing him to dance with her. He tried to escape, but she refused to let go. He shook his head in disgust. Did she have to torture him like this on his coronation day?

After a bath, Ethan slipped on a pressed white shirt and black pants Caitríona had left out for him. Since the event took place outside, and weather had turned cold, she made sure he had a new dark green cloak with Landover's insignia stitched into the fabric. He slipped it on and traced the mark with his finger. Brushing his hair off his face, he stood as tall as he could, but still the image staring back at him didn't look like a king. He didn't feel like one either.

Give it time . . . , Tearlach said.

Time . . . The word repeated in his head. Cringing, Ethan really hoped his uncle couldn't read his mind. With that last disturbing thought, he walked out the door.

Ethan followed Seamus Niles down three long hallways and several staircases that led outside. As they emerged from the castle and into the courtyard, the crowd erupted in cheers. The people of Landover lined the mazelike path set up to take Ethan the long way to the platform where the event was to take place.

People held out their hands to shake Ethan's. King Fearghus, Queen

Cethlenn, Rhisiart, Bryg, and Phalen towered above the crowd from the front row. They were the only realm to accept his invitation to the coronation.

As Ethan started up the final walk, he paused to say hello to Bram Gabhann and Rosie. His cheeks burned as she kissed his cheek and winked at him. Bartlett's daughter, Maggie, and her husband, Duncan Flynn, along with their herd of redheaded kids sat in the next row. He saw no sign of Lily. She really wasn't coming.

When he finally reached the stage, Caitríona came beside him. This was the first time he'd seen her wear a crown. It was a thick band of gold that rose to a point in the center. A small stone that looked like an emerald decorated the tip. In a long green dress, she looked so royal.

Ethan trailed after Caitríona as she climbed the steps of a twenty-foot-high wooden platform.

The tree sprites hovered overhead. Suffie waved, and Ethan tried to wave back, but Runyun nudged him from behind with a stern, "Hurry up."

Ethan almost didn't recognize him. There was not a speck of dirt on him. His hair was brushed and pulled back into a ponytail, and he was clean-shaven. He had on a crisp white shirt and pants similar to Ethan's but he also wore a brown leather tunic.

General Niles and Captain Bartlett were next to him in ascending order, and followed Ethan up, but Runyun stayed on the steps.

The crowd chanted Ethan's name. His heart pounding, he turned to find his mother and his breath caught.

Lily. His Lily. She was here. And she wasn't just glowing. Today, she shone. Her hair was loose except for a tiny braid pulled back on each side. She wore a blue dress with a stitched pattern on the front that formed little diamonds.

As he approached, her expression remained stoic. She kept her eyes on Morgan, who stood next to her. She wouldn't even look at him. So not his Lily anymore. His stomach clenched. *At least she's here.* That was something.

On the other side of Lily and Morgan were two wooden chairs with elaborate carvings on the back. General Niles and Captain Bartlett stood behind them. Caitríona moved in front of the farthest chair and motioned for Ethan to stop, which he did.

From the other side of the stage, two men and one woman, all wearing long green robes over their clothes, stepped on the stage. Embroidered into their robes, directly over their hearts, was Landover's mark set inside braided Celtic knots that formed an exterior triangle. The only one Ethan recognized was Maggie's husband. Next to him, the woman, who was at least six feet tall with a long braid of blond hair draping over her shoulder, smiled as she clasped her hands behind her back. The other man was bald, clean-shaven, and had thick black brows. He eyed Ethan with pursed lips.

Captain Bartlett came around them to face the crowd. He raised a hand and the mumbling ceased as all eyes settled on him. Clearing his throat, he gave a quick glance at Ethan, and looked out at the vast audience with a warm smile.

"I've asked the Commis"—Bartlett paused and nodded toward Duncan and the other two—"and Princess Caitríona, if I might speak first. Irregular, to be sure, but so is the young man who will take his vows today."

Irregular? Bartlett had called him all kinds of unflattering things over the past few weeks. Okay, Ethan had tossed out a few barbs at Bartlett too. But now? With all of Landover watching? Ethan suddenly felt nauseous. What exactly was Bartlett going to say? "Mo—"

Caitríona cut off Ethan's protest with a wave of her hand.

Bartlett held up Landover's scáthán. "As you can see, our scáthán has returned to Landover safe and sound. Caitríona Makkai now puts forth her son, Ethan Makkai, as the heir to the throne of Landover."

The crowd cheered.

But Bartlett continued, "He has proven to carry the gift, radharc, which was confirmed by the Council of Kings." Bartlett stepped closer to Ethan. "As many of you are aware, we're again at a time of great strife. Sawney Bean is free. In his first battle, Ethan rallied not only those in Landover, but aid from another realm to fight against Bean's onslaught." Bartlett nodded thanks to King Fearghus. "And then your heir fought bravely, securing our lands, and ensuring the safety of our people."

Bartlett took a deep breath before continuing. "And although battle skills are important, there is something else our people need even more. Tara again faces the divisiveness Bean brings between the realms. Landover will need a leader who will serve the people. One who thinks with not only his head but also his heart. One who understands loyalty, and who'll put the people of Landover ahead of his own needs. Ethan Makkai is all of those things."

Stunned at Bartlett's heartfelt words, Ethan's cheeks burned. The captain reached over and shook his arm the same way he did with General Niles the day they returned to Landover. There was pride in Bartlett's eye, something Ethan would never forget.

The crowd cheered even louder. "Long live the king!"

"Turn toward me," Caitríona said.

Ethan turned to face her.

"The oath, passed down for centuries, was crafted by the sea god, Manannán mac Lir, and first taken by Clíona Ratigan Makkai." Caitríona stared into Ethan's eyes. "With each who has spoken these words came an understanding that the gift passed down to them was a way for the past to communicate to the present. The ancients will speak to you, give you insight and wisdom only time and experience can bring, and you'll understand how and why Landover came to be as it is today. As they commit to you, you'll be committing to them. Are you prepared to take the oath?"

Ethan looked at the crowd. Everyone stared back at him, anxious. He glanced at Runyun, who shrugged; Bartlett, who mouthed, "Hurry up"; and finally at Lily, who gave him the reassuring nod he needed.

"Yes," Ethan choked out over the nervous knot lodged in his throat.

"Kneel," Caitríona said.

He did. His mother set a hand on his head, holding it down. "Having been chosen by the goddess Clíodhna, do ye, Ethan Makki, give ye body and soul to the people of Landover?"

Ethan had practiced his necessary response all week, but it never quite came out right. He took a deep breath and let it out slowly, trying to steady his nerves. "Mo chroí go hiomlán, a thabhairt liom. My whole heart, I do give."

No one laughed. Ethan took that as a good sign.

"Do ye promise to govern Landover and all who reside in it according to the laws of the land? Seeking counsel with the people's Commis and Landover's ancients on all matters of judgments?"

"I do."

Caitríona let go of Ethan's head. He looked up at the thick crown of gold his mother held. It was similar to hers, except where hers had a jewel, this one was plain. It was simple, and yet classy, like the people in Landover.

Caitríona placed the crown on Ethan's head. "Please rise." He stood up, and as he turned to face the crowd the crown rocked forward. It fell off his head, tumbling toward the seats below.

"Gníomhacha," Lily shouted.

The crown froze in midair. The audience collectively gasped and started mumbling. Lily didn't seem to notice. She reached out, picked up the crown, and placed it back on Ethan's head. "What would you do without me?"

"I have no idea." Ethan's heart melted. He looked out over the people, who stared intensely at Lily. "Uh-oh."

"It's all right, Ethan. I've made my decision." Lily looked at her father, and then at Ethan. "I hadn't planned on telling all of Landover yet but . . ."

Ethan stared into her fiery green eyes. Lily was smart, confident, determined, all things Landover needed in a sorceress if they were going to defeat Sawney Bean.

Ethan raised a hand and silenced the crowd. "For those who don't know her, this is Lily Niles, Landover's sorceress."

The people roared in excitement. Without a word, General Niles stormed down the steps. Lily made no move to go after him. She stayed by Ethan's side.

Not long after the ceremony ended, musicians played while the guests danced. People milled around, waiting for their turn to come up the steps to say hi to Ethan, Caitríona, and Lily.

General Niles and Adam had been standing at the bottom of the steps of the platform, glaring at Ethan, until Seamus organized Lily's other brothers and they insisted Niles and Adam leave their posts and come to eat with them.

R unyun vanished for most of the day. It wasn't until they'd all gone back inside the castle that he reappeared. Standing next to the large fireplace in the main hall, Runyun handed Ethan a package wrapped in dusty brown cloth.

Ethan folded the edges back and found a bow and wooden quiver, brimming with arrows. He picked up the long curved bow and marveled at the intricate designs carved into the smooth wood. "Thank you. I've never shot one before. Can we start with it rather than the sword tomorrow?"

"I'll mention it to Niles," Runyun said with a long face. He took the bow from Ethan and placed it back on the cloth.

Ethan fingered the feather of an arrow. "Not planning on sticking around." He couldn't hide the disappointment in his tone.

"You're not a child anymore, Ethan. You don't need a father, and since I never had one myself, I don't even know how to be one."

Leave it to Runyun to lay it all out. . . . He was the most honest person Ethan had ever met, and that meant everything to him. "Maybe not. But what I do need is a friend and an adviser and a teacher."

Unwilling to meet Ethan's weary eyes, Runyun looked at his gift and slid his finger along the bowstring. "You have Julius for that."

"No. You're the only person I trust in that role, Runyun."

Runyun scratched his head, pursed his lips together, and after several long seconds gave a slow nod.

"You'll stay?"

"For a little while."

Ethan grinned. "Good." He picked up the bow and pulled the string, thwacking his knuckle.

Runyun shook his head, trying but failing to hide his smile. "Don't break a finger."

As Ethan set the bow down, he noticed the door creak open, and glimpsed his mother's face. She'd been listening the whole time. "You know, Mom never dated anyone on the other side. I never thought she'd ever look at anyone the way she looked at you on the dock."

Runyun sighed. "Ethan, it's not that simple."

"No, it's not." With a deep breath for courage, Caitríona entered the room and closed the distance between her and Runyun, wringing her hands. Ethan had never seen his mother look so nervous. "Your son is right. There never has ever been anyone but you, Runyun Cooper."

Stunned by her revelation, Runyun lowered his head. "I'm sorry I wasn't there for you."

Caitríona reached up, grasped his chin, and tilted his head, forcing Runyun's eyes to meet hers. "We have to let go of the past, and look to the future."

Runyun's mouth fell open.

And Ethan had seen and heard enough. He cleared his throat. "I'm going to find Lily."

"Good idea," Runyun agreed, and pushed Ethan out the room, slamming the door behind him.

L ily wasn't in the dining room when Ethan came back. With his new security detail tailing him, he headed outside to track her down. The sun was setting as the coronation party officially ended, but that didn't keep King Fearghus and Queen Cethlenn and about a hundred other guests from continuing on with the festivities.

As he passed the dance area, Phalen and Bryg were on the dance floor. Bryg had some serious moves; Phalen, not so much.

King Fearghus waved and Ethan jogged over to his table. He was impressed they had chairs large enough for them. Apparently, this was the first time in more than fifty years that Fomorians had visited Weymiss.

"Thank you for coming, King Fearghus and Queen Cethlenn," Ethan said.

"Thank you for inviting us," Queen Cethlenn responded.

King Fearghus shifted in his seat so that he faced him. "I'm very proud of you, Ethan Makkai. You stood up to a bunch of old gasbags, and I believe the Council will be much better for it."

"I don't know. No one came to help us but you, King Fearghus."

"But I came, as did my guards." He nodded in Bryg's and Phalen's directions. Fearghus reached under his chair, lifted out a round shield, and showed it to him. "I noticed you didn't have one. This was Dratsuah's when she was small. It should fit you nicely. It's made from the strongest metal we mine in Gransmore, terrellium. Nothing can penetrate it." He handed it to Ethan.

Ethan traced the Gransmore mark that was painted on the front.

"Oh, hadn't thought of that. You can change it to Landover's if you wish," Fearghus added.

Ethan shook his head. "It would be an honor to fight with it exactly as it is."

Cethlenn gave Ethan an approving smile.

After a few more minutes, he continued his search for Lily and was about to give up when he finally found her, outside the castle wall, arguing with General Niles. Ethan waved to the two guards following him. They stopped but eyed him cautiously.

As Ethan approached the general and Lily, they fell silent. The general nodded at Ethan and then stormed away.

"Something I said?"

Lily's face contorted with rage. She pulled her sword from a scabbard she'd hidden under her dress and brought it down on Ethan's new shield, hard.

"Hey!" Ethan backed up. His guard details started for them, but realizing it was Lily, stopped. Ethan wasn't sure that was a good idea. She looked like she wanted to kill him.

"That was for being such an arse by the lake. Seamus told me what happened with my father and Adam. Why didn't you tell me?" She raised her sword again.

Ethan held firmly to the shield. "Because I didn't want you to have to choose between me and your family."

She rolled her eyes and thankfully lowered her sword. "As you were chosen to possess radharc, I was chosen to have magic. My powers weren't released until you came to Landover, but had you been here all along, Da would've known a long time ago. It's the shock, Ethan. He'll get used to it. And . . ."

Her expression pensive, Ethan kept his shield at the ready. "And what?"

"And I know where I belong."

Ethan lowered his shield so he could look into her softened eyes. He *sensed* her resolve, but also something more too. Her close proximity, her beautiful smile. It was more than he could take. After a quick glance to make sure none of her family was in view, he pulled her face to his, and kissed her.

And she kissed him back. His mind swam as their breath mixed. Ethan had never tasted anything as sweet. Her lavender scent surrounded him and her warmth consumed him, and when she wrapped her arms around him, it was all he could do not to blow the moment by smiling.

A few minutes later the Niles family headed home. When Ethan returned to the castle, his mom and Runyun were sitting on the big sofa in the living room in front of the fireplace, drinking from silver chalices and staring into the flames.

For a moment, he worried he was interrupting something, but there was only one way to get to the food. Famished, his stomach took priority over his parents' love life. He dropped his new shield on the floor, and started for the dining room for leftovers.

Caitríona sat up. "Ethan, that's not where that belongs. Put it away."

"Seriously? It's been a really long day, and this is a *castle*. It's not like there isn't plenty of room for a few things to land on the floor."

"We can't have articles lying around for people to trip over. And no one will be picking up after you, king or not," she added in a stern tone.

"Okay. Okay. Don't lose your mind," he groaned, picking it up.

Yeah, it was nice to be home.

◈ EPILOGUE ◈

FEBRUARY 1, ONE YEAR AND TWO MONTHS LATER . . .

Bartlett had woken Ethan up at sunrise, taken his key to the tower, and told Ethan to get dressed as fast as he could, and get up there. The only thing that could have Bartlett in such a state had to be Bean related. It had been more than a year since the battle at Dryden Lake, and there had been no word on Bean's whereabouts. But he was never far from Ethan's mind. Panicked, Ethan threw on his pants and a shirt and raced barefoot up the cold steps.

The door was closed, and locked. Ethan knocked.

"That you?" Bartlett asked sharply.

"Yeah. What's so top secret?"

Bartlett opened the door only wide enough for Ethan to slip through then slammed it shut behind him.

Nervous, Ethan peered around the stand holding the sacred scáthán. Nothing seemed out of the ordinary, but then he could have sworn he saw . . . "Holy mother of gods!" His mouth fell open. He couldn't believe what was seeing. Perched in the corner was a huge flat-screen television.

"Does it work?"

"It had better! Do you know what today is?"

Ethan folded his arms over his chest and shrugged. "Sunday?"

Bartlett whacked him on the back of the head. "Half right. It's Super Bowl Sunday." He held up the remote. "Pray I connected the thingy on the tower to the box right." Holding his breath, Bartlett pressed a button with his thumb.

A small circle in the lower left flashed green, and the television flickered on. A row of football commentators behind a desk chatted. A countdown clock in the upper left corner showed five seconds . . . four . . . three . . .

Overwhelmed by bro-hood, Ethan hugged the captain. "I think I love you."

"As you should." Bartlett shoved him off. "Do you know how long it took to coordinate this? Satellites, a receiver, wireless technology, and oh, the stupid generator that weighed more than your hairy arse."

"I thought you hated technology?"

"I do. This is strictly for research, and not allowed in Tara, so keep your big mouth shut."

Grinning from ear to ear, Ethan plopped in one of the cushy chairs. There were bowls of popcorn, pretzels, and even a small cooler with soda and beer cans. The Seattle Seahawks and New England Patriots ran onto the field for the coin flip. Bartlett sat in the chair next to him and opened a beer.

"How great is this?" Ethan popped open a can of Sprite and stuffed a handful of popcorn into his mouth, when there was a knock at the door.

"Ethan, are you up here?" Runyun called.

"Damnit." Bartlett muted the TV. "See if you can get rid of him."

Setting his can carefully next to Landover's scáthán, Ethan pulled the door open a few inches. "Hey."

"What're you doing? We were supposed to be on the range this morning." Runyun held up Ethan's bow. He was already dressed and ready for action with his bow and quiver draped over his shoulder.

"Oh, right. Can I take a rain check? Captain Bartlett needs me for a few hours."

"Needs you for what?" Runyun pushed on the door, but Ethan set his foot against it, holding it where it was. "Ethan, let me in."

"Um . . ." Ethan hesitated, and gaped at Bartlett.

"I'm not going to ask again," Runyun said, concerned.

"Fine. But only Cooper!" Bartlett said.

Ethan opened the door and Runyun slipped inside. When he saw the television, he leaned over Bartlett's chair and stared at it, wide-eyed. "What is that?"

"Football." Ethan grabbed his soda can and slid into the chair.

Runyun set the bow and quiver down and took a seat, while Bartlett opened another beer and passed it to him. He sniffed it, waggled his eyebrows, and took a long swig.

After a loud burp, Runyun held the can up. "Ale, in a metal container. Bleedin' brilliant. I don't even mind it cold. It's rather refreshing, especially at such an early hour in the morning." Runyun leaned over toward Ethan. "Let's not mention this to your mother."

Ethan nodded. "No problem." He grabbed another handful of popcorn.

Bartlett turned the sound back on, and proceeded to explain the rules of the game to Runyun.

A small, dainty hand reached inside the door. "Ethan, I need to ask you something." Lily popped her head in and her mouth fell open. "What is that?"

Ethan winced. "Forgot to close the door."

"Nitwit," Bartlett huffed at Ethan. "Lily Niles, your life depends on your silence"—and then as he turned back to Ethan—"shut and lock the door, sire!"

While Ethan moved to close it, Lily headed for the television without hesitation. She sat down cross-legged on the floor in front of the chairs. "Is this a sport? How does it get into the tiny box? And what're they doing? Why're they wearing all that padding?" She rattled off a million questions, but no one answered because the Patriots had run the kickoff all the way down to the one-yard line. With the next play, they got into the end zone.

The crowd roared and Bartlett leaped out of his seat. "Touchdown!"

Runyun and Lily laughed at him.

A picture of the Patriots quarterback popped up. The announcers went back and forth about how he'd just passed Brett Favre's stat for career passing touchdowns. Lily smiled at the screen. "He's a fine thing. Who's that?"

Ethan groaned. He sat down next to her and wrapped a possessive arm around her shoulders. She rewarded him with a quick kiss before turning her full attention back to the screen.

Thankfully, the television cut to commercials.

Ethan opened a soda for Lily. As she took a sip, she wrinkled her nose, and giggled. "The bubbles tickle. What's that?" She tried the popcorn, and grinned. "Light and fluffy. There's butter." She proceeded to put the bowl in her lap, and scarf down handfuls at a time.

Suddenly, the commercials were interrupted when they cut to local news in Los Angeles. The screen split in half with a dark-haired female anchor at a desk on one side, and a male field reporter on location on the other. The guy stood on a street that looked an awful lot like Ethan's old one.

A picture of Ethan and Caitríona popped up behind the anchor. ". . . Finally a break in the missing persons case of Caitríona and Ethan Makkai."

Ethan's stomach hit the floor. "Captain Bartlett? Are you seeing this?"

Bartlett stopped talking to Runyun and turned back to the screen.

"Yes, Bill. It has been fifteen months since Caitríona Makkai and her son, Ethan, vanished. Police have been completely dumbfounded. Their apartment was trashed, and yet there was not a single clue as to what happened to them. It was as if they disappeared from the face of the earth. But there was one person who never gave up hope. Their neighbor, and Ethan's friend, Skylar Petrakis. She canvassed the city with missing person's flyers when it happened, and has been running a blog, keeping the Makkais in the forefront of everyone's minds. And she's given the police their first real lead. Apparently, both mother and son have been seen, alive."

The camera panned to the left and there was Sky. Stunned, Ethan touched the screen. She looked the same, in her usual jeans and T-shirt, her black hair pulled into a ponytail, but also different. Older. And she looked nervous.

"Ethan, who is that?" Lily asked.

"Someone from home . . ." Ethan couldn't believe Sky would be trying to find him.

"Landover is your home," Lily said, sounding angry.

Then the camera widened out. Lily gasped. Ethan dropped his can, and made no move to stop it from spilling out all over the floor.

Standing behind Sky was none other than Sawney Bean. Clean-shaven, and wearing dark sunglasses, he was dressed in black jeans and a white button-down shirt.

"No!" Ethan's pulse rate shot so high it felt like he was having a heart attack.

"Yes. I saw them not long ago." Bean pivoted, and the camera moved in tighter on him. "They're both alive and healthy, and if they know what's important in life, which"—he lowered his sunglasses, and peered into the camera—"I know they do, they'll get in touch with this young lady very, very soon. . . ."

Glossary of Terms/Pronunciation Guide

A note about the Irish phrases and Celtic magical words used in Tara: Although there is a close connection to the various ancient Celtic languages spoken throughout Ireland, Scotland, and England, Tara's spoken language is not exactly like any one of them.

Why, you ask? The answer is obvious. Cultures evolve, as do their languages. So sit back, and just enjoy the ride through the terminology. Try not to think too hard how I stumbled upon them. I promise no linguists were massacred in the making up of these derivations.

Aire-echta (ADA ecda) In ancient times, the leader of the king's standing army.

ar ais (AIR jash) Back.

ar shiúl (AIR Hyool) Directly translated, it means "away."

ardaitheoir (ARD-AI-thor) Lift.

bás bán (BAHS BAWN) White death potion used to kill many in the Makkai clan.

bás deftoirt (BAHS def TORT) Instant death. This is Sawney Bean's favorite curse. Said while he's holding his father's club, it will kill.

bás dóibh siúd a pas a fháil (BAHS doyv shood uh PAHS a ayl) Directly translated, "death to those who pass." Etched into the stone archway over the path that leads to Sawney Bean's cave. A reminder to all who attempt ascension that death will come.

bás dubh (BAWS due) Black death. The potion Lily made to counteract Sawney Bean's *namhaid spiorad beo.*

beini liom (BIN-ni Lyom) Directly translated, it means "help me."

bolbasa (BOWL-bussa) An enchanted ball, filled with explosives. When thrown hard to the ground, it explodes, releasing an impenetrable shield wall that remains until the magic expires. Usually five minutes.

Brícath (BREE-gah) The very essence of life.

buail (Boul) Hit.

cas (CAHS) Turn.

Cat Sidhe (Cat shee) Shape-shifting panthers from the Isle of Cantolin.

caillan (CAI-lan). Those bound to Sawney Bean with *Náilanam* (NAHL-annum) are completely under his control. He can use this spell to trade places with them, something that comes in handy time and time again.

cailleadh anáil (CAL–agh uh-NAYL) Lose breath. A protection spell used to suffocate anyone attempting to ride up the path to Sawney Bean's cave.

caithfid an madra codlata tar eis (CALH-fid an MAD-ra CAWD-lawta tar EH-yes) Let sleeping dogs lie. A shield charm to keep Sawney Bean in his cave.

Caitríona (Ka-TREE-na) The proper pronunciation of Ethan's mother's name.

caod (Keej) Dark magic used to trap a living person in the darkness between life and death.

céim (Kim) Directly translated, it means "phase."

coiseaint (CO-saynt) Protection. Like POTUS is the president, Chosaint was Captain Bartlett's code name for Caitríona Makkai while in Los Angeles.

Conbata (CON-batah) The magical staff belonging to the king of Gransmore. If held, it will force anyone to bow to your will.

cosaht (KOSH-aht) Lily used this to release Leader Maul's hold on Ethan in Kilkerry.

damnú air (DAMNU-et) Damnit. A glorious curse word that should be used judiciously.

Dobhar-chú (DOOR-Hoo) The beasts that roam Dryden Lake. They have heads of a sharks, bodies like canines, with long sharp claws and jagged fangs.

dotheain (DO-hawn) Spell Sawney Bean uses to light the oil on fire.

dragain dóiteáin (DRAHG-ahn DOYCH-an). Dragon's fire. A spell that blasts flames from above, killing anything attempting to ride up the path to Bean's cave.

Draugar (DROW-gr) A body raised from the dead, similar to a zombie, but with full faculties of the person's living existence. They have inhuman strength and agility.

driom ar ais (DROM are AYSH) A spell to return an object to its original form. Lily uses this on the Conbata to shrink it to a manageable size.

dul amach (Doul ahmac) The words Ethan uses to force any ghost to re-treat to the world between worlds.

éin damnaigh! (EEN DAM-nayg) Damn birds!

Faoladh (FuEH-luh) Hybrid of human and wolf, hailing from Kilkerry, these inhabitants are ruthless and cunning.

fearg gheimhridh (FYER-ug GHAYM-righ) Winter's anger. A protection spell used to freeze to death anyone attempting to ride up the path to Sawney Bean's cave.

fuilgooladh (FULL-goo-lagh) Transformation spell uses by Sawney Bean to turn his blood into oil.

galgan (GAL-gun) The name for generals who serve Primland.

gníomhacha (GNEE-Vah-ha) Freeze. Lily's useful spell when Ethan dropped his crown.

goath (Gree) A Tarisian variation on the Celtic word "gaoth," meaning wind.

imeall scian (IMM-all SHKEE-un) Knife's edge. A hidden row of levered knives waiting to fire on anyone coming up the path to Sawney Bean's cave. These words keep the levers from releasing.

Lugh's Mirror (LOO's mirror) Lugh was the Celtic god of craft, known as the Shining One. With one look into his mirror, your soul can slip from your body, leaving it susceptible to being taken over by a *taibhsí*.

lúka (LOO-kah) The end of everything. A spell, when used in combination with Sawney Bean's club, has the power to wipe a soul from existence.

Manannán mac Lir (MAN-uh-nan mahc LEER) Irish god of the sea.

meidhreach (MEHJ-rahk) Directly translated, this means "happy." It is the home of the tree sprites, creatures who are not as friendly as the name of their enclave would suggest.

Milcai (Mil-Kī) Similar in form to a baboon, with a long thin snout, they patrol the borders of Gransmore, making sure no one slips across without the knowledge of the king.

mo carse (Moh Cahr-se) Literally, "my savages." Phalen's unique term of endearment for his Milcai.

mo chroí go hiomlán, a thabhairt liom (Mo-hree go-hamlown, ah hart lim) "My whole heart, I do give." Ethan's vow to Landover.

Muincara (MOON-caruh) A teacher or mentor assigned to those who have been passed the radharc powers.

náilanam (NAHL-annum) The ancient ritual Sawney Bean uses to touch the soul, drawing it into servitude, permanently.

namhaid spiorad beo (NAW-ayd SPIR-ad Bow) "Enemy spirit alive." The potion Sawney Bean crafted to raise the dead on the Isle of Mord.

nei bhogann (NAY Wah-gan) Directly translated, this means, "do not move." Sawney Bean uses this on Lily after she uses the wrong phrase in her attempt to stop Bean's movement.

páistí barllte (POSH-tee Bahr-lt) The mysterious words Lachlan Traynor utters upon hearing Ethan's response to the question for his test as heir to Landover.

pasáiste (PAH-sayeshtye) Directly translated, "passage." In Kilkerry, upon the passing of the leader, this is the name for the fight to the death for anyone wanting to claim the throne.

radharc (RYE-arc) The sacred power signifying the heir to Landover. Each heir is chosen by the goddess of beauty, and Banshee, Clíodhna.

Ríegre (REE-ghray) Heir to Landover.

Rónd Solais (ROND SO-lahs) The ring of light all heirs of Landover see when they have found their sorcerer.

roth rámach (Rah Ram-ah) A magical flying device belonging to Mug Ruith. It was stolen by the Raven queen centuries ago, and it alone possesses the knowledge and power to get to the island of lost children.

rúini na chroí (ROO-nee nuh CHREE) Secrets of the heart.

sada chra anosa (SAH-ja Kra Anaw-Sha) Spell used by Kiara in Bean's cave to put the gargoyles back together and move them to blockade the exit.

saoirse agus fírinne (SAYR-shuh ogus FEER-innuh) Freedom and truth. These are the passwords to release the spell holding the Conbata in its hidden location in the king's quarters.

scáthán (SCAH-hahn) Mirror, but in Tara, this also refers to the book of magic granted by Manannán Mac Lir to the main five of the realms.

sciath (SHKEE-ah) Directly translated, "shield."

scrios (SHCREE) Directly translated, it means "destruction." Lily uses this to remove the horses' tracks from the ground.

siorse (SIR-Sheh) Word to open the rock panel to the cove where Primland's scáthán is hidden.

soith (SOH) Bitch. Not a word to use around company, unless you need a good curse word.

solas (SO-lahs) Light.

sruthán (SROW-han) Technically means "stream." This spell from Bean inflicts unimaginable pain on the dead and the living.

taibhsí (TAIV-shee) Ghosts. Spirits.

taspeain dom an bealach (TASP-yan dom an byal-ak) Directly translated, "show me the way." The words spoken next to the snow-covered mountains in Algidare to reveal the way into Fiddler's Well.

te (Tay) Hot, as in temperature, not sexy. That would be *dathúil* (DAH-OO-l) in case you need that one.

techt baeg amhin (TECHT bagh ah-veen) The phrase the Glatisant sings to call to her prey.

techt lom (TECHT laum) The final song, and nail in the coffin for Glatisant's prey.

teiatcha (TEY-acka) A retrieval spell.

titallor (TEE-dallor) Release spell.